For Time and Eternity

For TIME & ETERNITY

ALLISON PITTMAN

Tyndale House Publishers, Inc., Carol Stream, Illinois

Visit Tyndale's exciting Web site at www.tyndale.com.

Visit Allison Pittman's Web site at www.allisonpittman.com.

For Time and Eternity

Designed by Jacqueline L. Nuñez

Edited by Kathryn S. Olson

Published in association with William K. Jensen Literary Agency, 119 Bampton Court, Eugene, Oregon 97404.

Scripture quotations are taken from the *Holy Bible*, King James Version.

Library of Congress Cataloging-in-Publication Data

Pittman, Allison.
For time and eternity / Allison Pittman.
p. cm. — (Sister-wife)
ISBN 978-1-4143-3596-4 (sc)
1. Married women—Fiction. 2. Mormons—Fiction. 3. Marital conflict—Fiction.
I. Title.
PS3616.I885F67 2010
813'.6—dc22 2010019711

Printed in the United States of America

16 15 14 13 12 11 10
7 6 5 4 3

FOR MY PARENTS, DEE AND DARLA HAPGOOD.

Thank you for keeping Jesus Christ
in the center of our home.

ACKNOWLEDGMENTS

What an amazing adventure this has been. Thank you, Bill Jensen, agent extraordinaire, for all of your support and encouragement. Wow, indeed. And thank you, Jan Stob, for even thinking about me for this project. And the rest of the Tyndale team—Karen, Kathy, and way too many others to name—thank you for trusting me to tell this story. I also must thank Mikey and my boys—Jack, Ryan, and Charlie—for your love and understanding during deadline time. Finally, as always, I praise my Savior, Jesus Christ. Throughout the process of this book I've learned to live in his grace, to write through his power, and to rest in his presence. Oh, how grateful I am to know him as Savior. How wonderful to love and be loved by an infinite, unchanging, life-giving God.

PROLOGUE

I never stop to ask myself if I should have done anything different. After all, how can you look at the assembled pages of your life and decide which should be ripped out and which should remain to press the treasures of your memories? Seems to me the greatest joy comes out of the pain that nurtures it, and you cannot keep one without the other. So I am forced, here at the end of it all, to fold every leaf together and say, as God did of his early people, that I did the best I knew how. I lived according to my conscience. He alone can forget the depth and breadth of my sin, and I claim the blood of his Son, Jesus, to all others who would judge me. I have lived now nearly forty years with my choices, and sometime hence I will die in his grace. That is the hope no man can steal from me.

Not again.

EXCERPT FROM "ESCAPE FROM ZION: THE SPIRITUAL JOURNEY OF CAMILLA FOX (NÉE DEARDON)," *Ladies' Home Journal*, July 1896.

CHAPTER 1

DEARDON DAIRY FARM, NORTH OF KANESVILLE, IOWA
June 1850

I could hear them singing in the darkness.

"There's more out there tonight."

"Come away from that window." Mama came up behind me, took the curtain out of my hand, and drew it across the glass. "Have you finished your reading?"

I hadn't even started, but Mama must have known that because the Bible was sitting on our table, closed. The strip of blue velvet still marked the chapter I read the night before.

"You'd best get to it before your father gets home." She

paced the length of the room and finally busied herself putting away the dishes drying on the sideboard.

I turned up the lamp, stretching Mama's shadow near up to the ceiling, and drew the Bible closer to me. Last night I finished the book of Ruth, so tonight would be the first chapter of 1 Samuel. I thumbed through the pages. Thirty-one chapters. One whole month. It would be the middle of summer before I made my way to Samuel's second book.

"'Now there was a certain man of Rama—Ramathaim—'" Eight words in, and I was ready to give up.

"Ramathaimzophim." Mother spoke over my shoulder.

"'. . .of mount Ephraim, and his name was Elkanah, the son of Jeroham, the son of . . .'" I looked up. "Honestly, Mama, I don't see why—"

"One chapter a night, Camilla. No matter what it says. Continue."

So I forged on, verse after verse, filling our kitchen with the rivalry between Hannah and Peninnah, Hannah's prayer, and the baby Samuel. None of it was new to me. I'd been reading a chapter of the Bible out loud every night since I turned seven. That was nearly nine years ago. This was the third time I'd read this story.

"What does this chapter teach you about being a better Christian?" Mama asked when I'd finished. She asked the same question every night. During my first year reading, she just asked if I understood what I read. I always said yes, even if I didn't. But by the second time around, I had to be prepared for this.

"It teaches us that God will answer our prayers if we ask him with a faithful, sincere heart."

"Mm-hmm." She was distracted now, back at the window. "And what does it teach you about being a better woman?"

This second question started with Genesis 1, where, after a little prompting from Mother, I learned that my purpose on earth was to bear children. I'll never forget the sadness in her voice when she shared this truth with me, her only child. It haunts me to this day.

"Camilla?" Her voice was more impatient now. Sharp. Still she stared into the night sky. "The lesson for being a better woman?"

"A good woman will pray to have children?"

She turned to me, letting the curtain fall again. "A woman realizes that her children are a gift from God. And just as he gives them to her, she must trust him with their care."

"Still," I said, trying to ease the tension in the room, "I'm glad you let me live here instead of dropping me off at the church. The pews aren't nearly as comfortable as my bed."

She rewarded me with a warm smile. "You should know. You've fallen asleep enough during the sermon. Now choose your verse and quickly. You've dawdled enough as it is."

I left the lamp on the table and ran upstairs to my room. No need for a light. There it was, right on top of my bureau. My journal. The binding was real leather with a red ribbon stitched to the cover. Back downstairs Mama had set out the ink and pen.

My eyes grazing across the page, I untied the ribbon and dipped the pen into the ink.

"And don't just choose the shortest one," Mama said as she did every night since we instituted this ritual last summer as a way to keep up my penmanship practice when school was not in session.

"I know." But I certainly wasn't going to choose the *longest*, no matter how appealing the truth. "I'm choosing the eighth verse."

I opened my journal to the next clean page and painstakingly copied the words:

Then said Elkanah her husband to her, Hannah, why weepest thou? and why eatest thou not? and why is thy heart grieved? am not I better to thee than ten sons?

I managed to have only three large blots of ink, and I wrote *Elkanah* in printed block letters instead of script to be sure I spelled it correctly. When I finished, I blew gently on the page to dry the ink and read the verse back to Mama before closing the book.

"And why did you choose that verse?"

"Because he loves her. Like Papa loves you even though I know he wishes he had boys instead of me."

"Nonsense, Camilla. You know your father loves you very much. You are his treasure."

"But I'm not much help on a dairy farm."

Before Mama could answer to that, our dog, Bonnie-Belle, jumped up from where she was curled up on the rag rug in front of the stove and stood at the door. Her tail made a *thump, thump* against the wall.

"There's your father now." She took one more look out the window, then moved quickly to the door and pulled back the big iron bolt at the top. With Bonnie-Belle right at her heels, she moved over to the stove and opened the oven, pulling out the plate of supper that had been warming. "You need to put those away now."

"I'll keep them out until he comes in," I said. "So he knows I finished my chapter and verse."

Normally I would have been chastised for my lack of obedience, but tonight she barely seemed to hear me. She lifted a wedge of corn bread left over in the pan and put it on Papa's plate along with a dish of butter and a jar of honey. She was just pouring a glass of water when Bonnie-Belle gave two happy barks, and my father walked through the door.

He was a big, barrel-chested man and bald as an egg. We had a neighbor once joke he looked more like a man who'd raise poultry than run a dairy. Papa laughed about it at the time, but it was a grim, polite laugh that made everyone standing around laugh, too, just hoping to make it funny. Truth is, most people were afraid of Papa to some measure, and for good reason. He might give his smooth scalp a good-natured rub and smile to everyone's face, but he turned away angry, vowing never to have a single chicken on his property. And indeed we never did.

"Ruth," he said before he crossed our threshold, "what did I tell you about keeping that door latched while I'm gone?"

"I didn't open it until I saw that it was you, Arlen." Her voice had a soothing quality, like fresh cream on a spring morning. "We've been safely tucked away all evening."

I was still at the table when he sat down, so when he bowed his head to bless his meal, I bowed mine, too.

"O Lord, for the bounty of this table we give thee thanks. Did you read your chapter?"

My eyes were still closed when I realized he was speaking to me. It wasn't like him to forget *amen*.

"Yes, Papa. I did. First Samuel, chapter 1. God answers Hannah's prayer by giving her a son, whom she dedicates to him by leaving the child at the house of the Lord."

He nodded, his mouth full of stew.

"I was just about to put these away," I said, gathering up the books. He nodded again, and I went into the parlor to put the Bible on the little table in front of our threadbare sofa. That's when I heard Mama ask about the meeting in town, and she was asking in that hushed tone that meant I wasn't supposed to hear, so I stayed in the dark room, holding very still so I wouldn't miss a word.

"Not much longer," Papa said. "They're heading out west. They don't want to stay here any more than we want 'em to."

"I can't imagine." I wasn't sure if Mama was surprised or frightened.

"I can't imagine any of it. Bunch of heretics."

"Arlen." Mama's voice dropped so low I had to strain to hear at all. "You don't think we're in any danger, do you?"

"They had ten of their men representing at the meeting tonight, and Mayor Scott made it very clear. We will pose no violent threat to them as long as they remain peaceful in their camp. They can trade with our businesses, but they may not assemble in town."

"My goodness, it sounds like a kind of wartime peace treaty."

"Mark my words," Papa said. I looked through the door into the kitchen and saw his shadow cast against the wall. He gestured and pointed with his fork. "This is nothing less than a spiritual battle, and if we as a town will comport ourselves as Christians, we will emerge victorious both here on earth and in eternity to follow."

Something in Papa always wanted to be a preacher, and this was one of those times he seemed to be working himself into a sermon. I could be trapped in our parlor for an hour before he exhausted this speech. So I crept out, hoping to make my way back to the stairs before he'd notice.

"Camilla?" Papa's voice stopped me in my tracks. "Did you hear what we were talking about?"

"Yes, Papa." I'd learned long ago it was best not to lie. "About those people camped by the river. The Mormons."

"That's right."

"Only I can't see that they'd start any trouble. I see them on my way to school every day, and they seem peaceful enough."

"And Lucifer was the most beautiful of all the angels." He spooned honey onto his corn bread and took a bite, not losing a single drop.

"I know." The verse was written in the journal I clutched close to me.

"See to it you remember."

With those words and a kiss from my mother, I was dismissed.

CHAPTER 2

I never did feel there was much to me to distinguish myself from the other young people in our town. Nobody would ever call me the prettiest girl in school—or the smartest. Far from either, as a matter of fact. Mama used to tell me I was so plain and quiet, I'd blend into a wall if I stood still long enough. On days when we had recitations, other girls would stand at the front of the class with ribbons in their hair and talk for five minutes, standing straight and tall. Those were the days I tried to get Mama to let me stay home. And most times she'd let me because I think she understood. She was a quiet girl too, and truth be known, I think she sometimes liked having someone else around the house to talk to. She might never have made me go to school if Papa and the county didn't insist.

We had three teachers and divided up grades. Our family helped contribute to their pay by giving them milk, butter, and cheese from our farm. About once a week I got to drive our cart and pony to school. Well, not exactly a pony. More like our old mule, Gracie, and the cart wasn't more than a hand wagon with a seat. But still, it made me feel important, and I enjoyed it especially on early summer mornings when a late night shower made the path into town a muddy mess.

The morning after that meeting in town was just such a morning. Chilly and damp, but with a promise of warmth later in the day. Papa had just loaded the final milk can when Mother came storming out from behind the springhouse.

"Arlen! Stop!"

He'd never been one to obey my mother, and this morning was no exception. He settled the can in place and lifted the latch at the back of the cart.

"Wait! She cannot take that milk in. It might be bad." By this time, Mama was at Papa's side, holding his arm.

"Might be?" He peered at Mama from under his hat brim.

She turned to me. "Camilla, do you remember when you brought the cows in from grazing yesterday?"

"Yes, ma'am?"

"Didn't you say some had wandered off?"

"Just Missy and Peggy, clear down to the southwest corner." And I had to beat them with a stick to get them in before dark.

"There must be a patch of wild onions sprouting there, is all I can figure," Mama said. "And it's flavored the milk. We won't be able to sell any of it for days."

I stood staring at the ground, the back of my neck burning despite the chilly morning. Somehow this would turn out to be my fault, no matter that I didn't know about the onions and

I'd been at school all the day they'd been grazing. Papa's lips narrowed and his jaw clenched; when he spoke, his voice had the haunting control that always made me nervous.

"How bad is it?" He spoke to Mama but looked right at me.

"Bad enough to ruin our reputation."

"Go get a dipper." This, clearly, was directed straight at me, and I turned on my heel and walked as slow as I could, muttering all sorts of horrible things just under my breath. Even though I was certain Father expected me to get the ladle out of the bucket that hung beside our well, I strolled right past it and waited for him to bark at me to hurry up. He didn't. I walked clear into the kitchen, where I pinched a corner off a cinnamon scone and grabbed the long-handled dipper from a hook on the wall. By the time I returned, Father had taken the milk can down from the cart and had it open.

"Taste." Only my father could compress an entire lecture into one word.

I dipped the ladle in the still, white liquid and brought it to my lips. I couldn't detect any odor, and the first tiny sip seemed fine.

"More," he said. "Take a big drink."

Bracing myself, I emptied the dipper with one big gulp, and while the initial taste was fine, soon after I swallowed, the inside of my mouth was coated with a bitterness I could not expel.

"I'm sorry," I said, determined not to make a sour face.

"Today, when you get home, I want you to show me exactly where you found those cows, and we'll dig up that patch."

"I can show you now. Take you right to it."

"After school. When you can help me dig."

"Yes, Father." I moved to climb up into my little cart's seat, but Papa blocked me.

"No need. You'll walk." He reached inside the cart, took out a bundle wrapped in rope, and formed the rope into a strap, which he dropped over my shoulder. It wasn't a staggering amount of weight, just uncomfortable, and I complained that I still had my lunch bucket and books to carry.

"Think about that next time you dally bringing in the cows," he said before leaving me alone in our yard with Mama.

"I'm sorry," she said, looking every bit as deflated as I felt. "I never imagined he would—"

"I'll be fine." Shifting my bundle, I reached into the cart for my schoolbooks, slate, and lunch bucket. Once the books were satisfactorily cradled in one arm, I stood very still while Mama kissed my cheek. Then I set off down the road.

We had a small rock wall, not quite three feet high, that flanked either side of our farm's wide driveway. It wasn't very sturdy, and it didn't extend far on either side. It dwindled into nothing more than a bunch of rocks within about twenty paces, but I know Papa envisioned it as some regal gateway. When he spared himself a day of farm labor on the Sabbath, he filled his time hauling stones from the riverbed, stacking each one, extending first one side, then the other. He had us all believing in a great, victorious day when the two sides would meet at the back of our property.

I'd barely made it past the wall when the rope bearing the weight of the bundled cheese and butter dug painfully into my shoulder. The ache in my collarbone was already so severe, I thought the pain would cut my head clean off before I reached the bend in the road to school. No amount of shifting helped, at least not for long. Soon I felt the strain of this burden down my entire back, and my step slowed to a precarious shuffle.

I liked to think that Papa didn't realize how heavy it was. That he was so strong himself, he couldn't have imagined I wouldn't be able to just sling it across my back and be on my way. I thought about the Bible verse telling us to lay our burdens at the feet of Jesus, and since home was a lot closer than school, I was about to turn around, walk back, and drop this burden at the feet of my father. Whatever punishment might follow would be well worth the relief.

It was the thought of that punishment that made me hesitate, and it was during that moment of hesitation that I first saw him. He stood at the top of our road, at a place where, if I turned right, I'd head into town; if I turned left, I'd be heading for the river, to the place they camped. The Mormons. That's the road he'd been walking.

My head filled with all the bits of conversation I'd heard in town, at church, and around my own kitchen table. Added to the pain of the rope across my shoulders was the unique pain that comes with fear. As if my breath wasn't strained enough, now it seemed to stop dead in my throat, and my feet stopped in my path.

I must have looked every bit as frightened as I felt, because he held up his hands like an offer of peaceful surrender. Still, I might have summoned the strength to actually turn and run had he not taken off his hat, smiled, and said, "Would you let me help you this morning?"

Those were his first words to me, and his voice was like honey. He had a smile wide and perfect. I'd never seen a smile like it before. Mama had a phrase she'd say about people who smile too much. Something about butter never melting in their mouth. I never liked that because it made me think of a person being cold—like they had a root cellar for a heart. This boy's smile was warm, like he carried the sun itself between his lips. I worried for the butter in my bundle, that it might turn straight to liquid and pour out of the canvas. Still, I couldn't hold back. I found myself moving again, straight toward him, not stopping until I had a clear look at his eyes—the palest brown I'd ever seen—and the faded green-checkered pattern of his shirt.

"That looks heavy," he said. "I'm heading into town. May I carry it for you?"

For the life of me, I couldn't imagine what he was talking about, and we stood there, just staring at each other until he put his hat back on, stepped forward, and took first my lunch bucket, then my books. These he stacked and balanced on his forearm and reached again, saying, "Here. Give that to me."

The next thing I knew I was shrugging myself free, and the relief of it felt like a hundred birds taking flight from my body. He took the bundle and looped the rope around one shoulder, not even a flinch at its weight.

"After you?" He nodded in the direction of town.

"I'll take my books."

He extended his arm and I took my little bucket, then my books. His sleeves were rolled up to the elbow, and I tried not to touch him as I lifted them away.

As it turned out, the road was perfect for walking—not muddy as I had feared. There'd been just enough rain to pack down the earth, no mud squelching, no dust rising. Somehow our steps fell in perfectly with each other.

"So," he said once we'd established our pace, "do you mind telling me what I'm carrying?"

"Cheese," I said, keeping my eyes trained on the road in front of me.

"You must plan on being really hungry."

I looked at him, but he was looking ahead, smiling, and I laughed, straight out loud. Mama always told me a lady politely covers her mouth when she laughs, but my hands were full.

And even if they weren't, there didn't seem to be any way to stop it.

That was the last sound either of us made until we reached the schoolyard at the edge of town. Other girls I knew were practiced in the art of chatting with boys, but anything I could think to say lodged in my throat. He wasn't a boy to chat with. I don't think he was a boy at all. More like a man in size and stature. Every now and then I took a sidelong glance only to see him striding so purposefully beside me. Even in profile his face was pleasant—smooth and round. He kept his head high and seemed to be just as familiar with this road as I was, even though he was a stranger.

I was walking with a stranger.

It wouldn't matter if I held my silence now, or even if I never spoke to him again. When word got out that Arlen Deardon's daughter walked to school with a stranger—let alone one of them, the Mormons—there'd be no telling what punishment I would face.

Oh, Lord, I prayed. *Don't let them see me.*

"What's the matter?"

That's when I noticed I'd stopped walking, and he was touching me. Not touching, really, but his hand hovered over the cuff of my blouse, and I clutched my books closer to me.

"I shouldn't be walking with you." I don't know if I was telling him, or myself. But that was the truth of it.

"Oh." He drew the word out, nodding like we had both come up with a grand idea. "Because a young woman is so much safer walking alone?"

"No." He'd called me a woman.

"Because I'm some kind of monster?"

That brought out my laughter again, but this time it died as it settled back on my lips. "I don't know what you are."

Coming from any other girl, this might have been coquettish. But not from me. I didn't know how to flirt.

"My name is Nathan Fox. I'm from Springfield, Missouri."

"I'm—"

"Camilla Deardon."

"You know my name?"

"We're neighbors, aren't we?"

"Hardly that."

"What do you mean, 'hardly'?" He shifted the weight of the bundle and took a step away. "Your property line runs right along the edge of our camp. From what I hear, that makes us neighbors."

"We don't speak to each other."

"We are now."

"We don't know each other."

"We could."

Off in the distance I heard a familiar sound being carried on the morning air. It was Mr. Teague, the upper-grades teacher, my teacher, whistling the same tune he did every morning. The tune announced his presence more than any clanging bell ever could. In a matter of seconds he would round the corner, twirling his ring of keys on one long, extended finger, and unlock the front doors to each of the three buildings that made up our school. Being the only man, he alone was trusted with such a chore.

"You have to go," I said, shifting my books to my other arm so I could take the bundle Nathan carried.

"Oh no." He turned his shoulder out of my reach. "This hasn't gotten any lighter, and you haven't gotten any stronger. Where shall I take it?"

"No." I glanced around, nearly frantic. "You can't be seen here."

"I come into town all the time." His smile was back. He was teasing, and I felt the warmth that came through him touch my face.

"Not with me. Not to my school."

The tune was getting louder. Discernible now: "Yankee Doodle."

"Then you just go on." He made a scooting sign with his free hand and reinforced his grip on the bundle's rope with the other. More than that, he took one, then another slow, deliberate step backward down the path, until his dismissive gesture turned into a wave.

"What do you think you're doing?" Although he was moving farther away, I dropped my voice to a whisper. More like a hiss, because the whistling stopped, and I heard Mr. Teague calling out "Good morning!" to someone else about to round the corner and find me out.

"Follow me!" Nathan Fox made no attempt to lower his voice, and it fascinated me to see he walked with just as much purpose when he walked backward.

I spun on my heel to see Mr. Teague behind me, engaged in conversation with Miss Powers, the pretty lady from Philadelphia who taught the primary grades. Safe, for now.

"You're stealing!"

He gave a wide shrug. "Shouldn't those with plenty feed the hungry?"

I thought of the wheels of cheese, the pounds of butter in that pack. And his original joke. "You cannot be that hungry!"

His countenance changed then. Not to anything dour, but a new softness came through, and it seemed more of an effort to keep his smile intact.

"But my people are, Camilla. And you have done the work of Heavenly Father in feeding us. He will bless you for that."

He lifted his hat and held it over his heart, keeping pace even as he offered me a deep bow, then turned around. I forced my feet to remain planted in the path.

"Miss Deardon?" Mr. Teague's voice called from behind. I inched myself around, hating the fact that I wouldn't be able to see Nathan Fox disappear.

"Y-yes, sir?"

He stood, alone now, at the top of the schoolhouse steps. "Would you like to explain what just happened?" He craned his neck, looking well over me at the bundle of charity making its way down the path.

"The cows got into an onion patch," I said, trudging my way across the yard. "None of it's any good."

"What a shame." He looked down his long, beaked nose. "You'll have to be more careful next time."

I squinted into the morning sun and thought of Nathan Fox.

"I know."

CHAPTER 3

I looked for him at noon as I sat beneath the shade tree eating my buttered bread before waiting my turn with the other students in line at the little spring well behind my school. I can't remember a word of what my friends talked about, let alone what Mr. Teague tried to teach throughout the morning. When Mr. Teague finally released us from that endless day, I bade a quick farewell and ran through the school yard. I slowed my steps when I hit the main road, and even more when I got to the turnoff to the path that led to our farm. For a time, I even walked backward, trying to produce that same blind, confident stride he'd had when he backed away from me. But my steps were too unsure, and after one stumble I figured I'd better turn myself around lest he come out from the trees and find me flat on my bottom in the dirt.

When I came to Papa's rambling rock wall, I set my books and lunch bucket down and climbed up on it. Their camp butted up against the western edge of our property, and though the light of their fires could sometimes be seen through the darkness, I couldn't see anything from here in the daytime. We'd hear their songs coming on a breeze, and they sounded just like the very songs we sang in our own church. Often the pounding of carpentry and a blacksmith's hammer reverberated through the stillness of the afternoon. I remembered seeing the men in town, driving away with a wagonload of lumber purchased while the clerk behind them laughed about the price it had fetched. Until this morning, this was all I knew of the Mormons. Never did it occur to me that they could be so handsome. So charming. And hungry.

"Camilla!" Papa's voice carried from the barn. He held a hoe balanced across his shoulder and a shovel in one hand. "Get out after that onion patch."

"Yes, Papa." I picked up my books and lunch bucket and headed for the house. Mama was stirring something in a pot. It didn't smell delicious yet, but the day was young. I dropped my things on the table and reached for a corn muffin on a plate under a towel.

"Better take some gloves," Mama said without turning around. "Don't want to get yourself blistered up."

We had a little wooden trunk just inside our back door with sundry work clothes. The lid creaked as it opened, and I was faced with a jumbled mess of hats and boots and gloves. All the while I looked for a matching pair, Papa was yelling my name out in the yard, and it seemed a fine thing to risk getting a few blisters compared to what might be waiting for me once his patience wore out. I slammed the trunk shut and ran out the door, pausing just long enough to grab my old calico bonnet. The sun was still up high and strong, and while a girl could hide the roughness of her hands, there'd be no disguising a sunburned face.

Papa was waiting for me in the yard, just where I left him, and he said, "Show me," when he handed me the shovel. I wondered what kind of man it was who couldn't find an onion patch, especially when he'd been told real clear that it was on the south side of the property, but I said nothing.

The shovel's handle set heavy on my shoulder and I set my face toward the south pasture and started walking. I fought my skirt to keep my strides long, knowing Papa was probably frustrated with the shorter steps he had to take to walk behind me. We weren't even halfway out before I was flat exhausted. The arm holding up the shovel was numb shoulder to elbow, and there was already sweat running down my back. By the time we were out of sight of the house, I could hear Papa getting impatient behind me. He still wasn't talking, but he had a kind of scuffling to his step, and I felt him coming up on me, then backing off again.

"Should be just over there." I picked up my step and shifted west. I knew we were close to the spot where I'd found the cows yesterday. There was a trio of stumps from trees Papa had cut but hadn't dug up yet, and it was just past them where I'd seen the pretty violet-colored blossoms. I should have told Mama and Papa last night what the cows had been into—should have warned them that the milk would be bad, but I honestly didn't know how much they'd eaten. Or if they'd just nibbled the leaves or dug up the bulbs. Truth be told, I didn't care, even if it meant I'd spend the rest of this day digging up my mistake.

"Well?" The impatience had left my father's feet and was full in his voice.

"It was right here, I swear."

"You what?"

"Sorry." Stupid to swear. "But they were right over—"

A few more steps and we walked right up on a story. Or a mystery, rather. The earth was littered with the same violet-colored blossoms I'd seen waving in the sunset breeze the day before. But that was the only evidence there'd been any wild onions growing in the southwest corner of our pasture. Instead there was a patch of dug-up earth, about six feet square. Freshly overturned, big, moist clumps of it.

"What's this?" I turned to my father and lowered my shovel, dropping it down by my side. "Why'd you drag me out here if you already dug it up?"

But I could tell from his face that he didn't have any more answers than I did. He looked past me, his eyes scanning all across that dug-up field. Seemed right then a cloud crossed over his face, and one might as well have passed over the sun, too, because my body took on a chill that connected with the sweat running down my back and made me shiver.

"It's them people." Papa's voice might have been calm, but he swung that hoe down from his shoulder and shattered a clod of dirt into nothing but crumbs.

Months ago—maybe even yesterday—I might have asked, "What people?" But since that time, I'd seen a smile full of sunshine and mischief, and I knew.

Nathan Fox appeared there the next morning, at that same little crook where the drive to our family's dairy farm meets the main road into town.

"Good morning, Camilla." He touched his hat without tipping it, and I forced a steadying to my stomach.

"I shouldn't talk to you." I didn't even slow my step.

"Then don't." Yet his stride matched perfectly to mine.

"I shouldn't listen to you either."

"If you don't listen, how will you ever know just how grateful my people are for your generous donation yesterday?"

"My father would beat me if he knew about that 'donation.'"

"Why would a good man be angry about feeding the hungry?"

"Because that food was supposed to feed my hungry teachers; that's why."

"I've seen your teachers. They don't look hungry."

I somehow managed to stifle my laugh.

"In fact," he continued, "I'll bet it's been a long time since your teachers wept at the sight of butter. For some of us, it's been months since we've had such luxury. And do you know there were children there—little children—who had their first ever taste of cheese? There they were, thinking it was going to be just another supper of grits and salt pork. Their little faces glowing in the supper circle. But it wasn't the firelight bringing that glow. No, it was a little white wedge of cheese. A brand-new treasure on their plate. Ah, their faces. I wish you could have been there, Camilla."

His words brought the warmth of the fire to me. Our paces still matched, but we walked slower now, our feet strolling through his story.

"It was just cheese," I said, tasting its sweet bitterness.

"But to a hungry people, it's life."

"And there wasn't much. Just one wheel."

"Our brother once fed many more with far less."

My mind turned for a moment. "You mean Jesus? with the loaves and the fishes?"

"You know the story!" He spoke with the fun, false enthusiasm a teacher has for a child who has just come upon the most obvious conclusion. I knew that voice, and I hated it. It was the voice that followed utterance after utterance of veiled impatience. I'd heard it all my life.

"Don't talk to me like that. I'm not stupid. He is our Lord."

"And our brother."

His response turned my mind once again. *God is my Father in heaven. Jesus is his Son.* I'd never thought of Jesus as a brother before, only as a Savior. But I'd always wanted a brother—someone to share the chores with—and the thought of having a brother like Jesus made me smile.

That's when I noticed we'd stopped walking. Without the sound of our feet scuffing against the occasional pebble, the world turned silent. It was another damp morning, and I could feel my nose about to run. Faced with the two unladylike options of a sniff or a swipe with my sleeve, I chose the sniff, turning my head away and being as mousy quiet as I could.

"Here." He held out a folded white square when I turned back around. "Take it. Don't worry; it's clean."

I wondered for just a minute what Mama would have me do. Didn't seem right, somehow, to have such an intimacy with a boy I barely knew, but I couldn't very well stand there with a runny nose. Truth be told, Mama hadn't told me much about boys at all. Papa, either. Until yesterday none had ever even talked to me, save for Michael Bostwick. And all he ever cared about was borrowing my history book because his parents were too poor to buy him his own. So I took that handkerchief and brought it up to my nose. It was warm from his pocket and smelled like strong, clean soap. To that, at least, Mama could not object.

"Thank you."

"You're getting a cold. Should you go back home?"

"No," I said, my voice muffled against the white cloth. "It's just a sniffle." I finished wiping and refolded the square, uncertain.

"Keep it. In case you sniffle again."

Nodding, I slid it into my own pocket and took the first new step toward school. His step joined mine, and we walked for just a little while in silence before I found my courage. "I have a question to ask you."

"Are you sure you should? I thought you weren't supposed to talk to me."

"Did you dig up the onion patch?"

"I wondered when you were going to get around to that."

"My father was furious."

"That seems an odd reaction to an act of kindness."

"I think he sees it more as trespassing. How did you even know?"

The warm smile was back. "We're neighbors, remember?"

I could tell he believed that answered my question, so I believed it too.

"My father wanted to go into your camp, you know. To find out who was responsible . . ." I didn't allow myself to speak all the accusations he had.

"Why didn't he?"

"Mama stopped him. She said that we weren't going to do anything with those onions except chop them up for mulch. Said you'd done us a good turn by digging them up for us." Again, I left so much unsaid. How she called Nathan's people a tribe of thieving, godless savages. And I knew at the heart of my parents' anger was fear. If only they could join me on this path, stand right here with me in the damp cool of the morning, hear this gentle voice surrounded by the calls of the morning birds, what would they possibly have to fear? "So I guess, in a way, she was glad to be rid of them."

"Like the town will be glad to be rid of us?"

"I suppose." Such an honest question deserved an honest answer.

"What about you?"

I shrugged. "I never much thought about it." Which was true. I hadn't. All winter and spring they'd been encamped next to us, my life was just one chore after another. School and home. Until yesterday. "I guess I never really understood what everyone's so upset about."

"God's people have always been persecuted. Surely you know that. The Israelites were enslaved. Early Christians sacrificed to the savages of Rome. Shouldn't be any surprise that the followers of a new prophet would face the same trials. But we can only follow Heavenly Father's plan."

"And what is this plan?" Something stirred within me, even then. I don't know if it was the anticipation of having inside information, something I could share with Papa at the dinner table, where I usually sat in obedient silence, or the first stirring of revelation, or the simple beauty of this beautiful golden boy beside me.

"Zion." One word, and it felt like I was hearing it for the first time. His voice lifted it out of the pages of the Psalms. I looked up, and his face was poised in a crescent smile, his eyes fixed above him, envisioning this place. A place he knew was real. "When we get word from those who went before us that the journey is safe, we'll pull up stakes and join our brothers and sisters."

"And where, exactly, are you going?"

"Utah."

Zion.

"Imagine it, Camilla. Building a new city on a new hill. Or in our case, a valley. I've heard them speak of it. Majestic mountains and fields ready for harvest. Like a piece of creation Heavenly Father reserved specially for us. And we'll be able to worship freely. Raise our children . . ." He stopped, and to my amazement, he blushed. Bright red splotches on his cheeks, and while he had been speaking to the treetops, he looked now right at me. "That is, of course, if we are lucky enough to have children."

The call of the mourning dove tempered the silence that followed, and though he did not touch me, something reached inside and nearly scooped my heart right out of me. My feet continued to propel me on the familiar path to school, and I suppose the rest of me followed, though I don't know how. Sure as on the day I was born when I could only lay helpless in my mother's arms, that moment a few steps back when Nathan Fox looked into my very soul marked the first breath of a new life, and I wanted to linger in it. His eyes held the very image of Zion, and his step matched to mine seemed a promise to take me there. I didn't hear another word he said that morning, and if I replied, those words are lost to me too. I know he brought me to the edge of the empty school yard, and I know he touched me. Just one trace of a finger along my cheek before turning away. I remember watching him. The breadth of his shoulders in the already-familiar shirt. The hand that had just touched me tucked into his pocket. The steadiness of his pace now that we were no longer walking together. How quickly he moved. How soon he was out of my sight. The few breaths it took for him to round a corner in the path and disappear. And how I never, ever wanted to step foot inside Mr. Teague's schoolroom again. How could I, being so newly born?

Later that morning I knew Nathan Fox had been right about one thing. I was catching a cold. By the time Mr. Teague rang the first bell calling us into class, I had a tiny tickle at the top of my throat, and when the younger children were dismissed for their first recess, it had grown to a licking flame. I could not concentrate on the letters of Thomas Jefferson, and while Michael Bostwick stood at the front of the classroom giving his impassioned recitation, I could do little more than rest my fevered brow on my hands and quietly wish to die.

At noon, I begged Mr. Teague to dismiss me to go home. He touched his own fat hand to my face and, satisfied with its temperature, released me with instructions to read the next twenty pages in our history text. I didn't even bring the book home. Instead, I launched myself down the path, my lunch pail dangling from listless fingers. Befuddled as my mind was, I couldn't help but hear Nathan's words with every step. *This is where he talked about children. This is where he spoke of persecution. And of a prophet. A new prophet.*

Seemed we had new preachers in our church all the time. Men in the midst of a journey, stopping for a week or so to thunder out the promise of a fiery eternity in hell for the condemned. But there was no such fire in Nathan's voice. Only warmth. Nothing called down from heaven, but some kind of inner ember. I touched my cheek where he'd touched me, fascinated by the heat there. But of course, that was due to my cold. At least partly.

Soon I was at the place where he met me. I lingered there, wondering if, by some chance, he might return. Might be waiting for me, even. But of course he wasn't. I staggered onto our property and braced myself against the stones of my father's wall as a wave of dizziness caught me. For a moment, everything was lost. Twirled around and ripped away. I could only hear my mother's voice coming closer, shaking with the impact of her running footfalls. Then she was here, one arm wrapped around my waist. Her cool palm on my forehead.

"Oh, Mama. I'm sick."

And safely home, I closed my eyes.

CHAPTER 4

I slept the rest of that day and through the night, my dreams peppered with images of Nathan Fox, my body trembling with unrelenting chills. The next morning I made a halfhearted attempt to rouse myself for school, but Mama would have none of it.

"You're still burning with fever." Her soft voice seemed to come from far away as she touched a cool rag to my face.

My throat felt too swollen and sore to reply. The simple nodding of my head proved painful. Nestling deep into the mattress, I pulled the blanket up to my nose and closed my eyes. No doubt Mama thought I was sleeping. She said a few soothing words before going downstairs to make me a cup of tea.

Listless and lethargic as I felt, though, sleep would not come. My wakefulness allowed me to craft new dreams of Nathan. When I slept, he was always just out of reach. I'd see him on the path, but every step I took drove him one more step away. But in these waking hours, I could control him—make him stop and wait. Turn to me and reach out. I could intertwine my fingers in his, have him pull me close. My visions were clear, if fevered, but incomplete. I didn't know what a boy would do once a girl was in his arms. And Nathan was more than a boy. He was a man. I knew even less of that.

It was quite early in the morning. My father's voice still rumbled in the kitchen. If I were going to school, it would be at least an hour before that appointed time. I heard the kettle rattle on the stove and imagined Nathan sitting next to a nearby fire. My own stomach growled for lack of food, and I wondered if he had eaten yet. My mind etched his face, down to the crease at the corner of his mouth when he smiled, and I burned to see it again in flesh before me. Would he be waiting again at the path? Would he worry when I didn't arrive? The thought of it made me want to swing my feet over the side of the bed. Put on my dress and shoes and somehow find the strength to leave this house. But my body groaned at the slightest stirring, and my mother's appearance at the door bearing a tray of steaming grits and weak tea stifled the very notion.

I awoke later to a broken fever and a high noon sun. Like someone washed up by some sort of tide, I was soaked clear through, as was my blanket. Determined now, I climbed out of bed and shivered at the coolness of the wet nightclothes against my skin. My mother hummed from somewhere downstairs, but my cocked ear caught no sign of anyone else.

"Mama?" My dry throat cracked with the weak effort, but there was no pain in speaking. I licked my lips and called again.

The humming stopped and steady steps brought her into my room, wiping her hands on her apron.

"My fever broke."

"So I see." It occurred to me that I must not have been nearly as sick as I imagined, because there was no hint of blessed relief in her voice. I had clear snatches in waking memory of her sitting at my bedside, clutching my hand, whispering prayers. But she now seemed so removed from a woman given to vigil that I felt a little silly for having called her.

"My, um, gown is wet?"

"Let's get you into another." She went to her knees by the trunk at the foot of my bed and opened it. After some rummaging around, she came up with a fresh, if wrinkled, gown and another sheet and blanket. I changed while she stripped the bed.

"Why don't you go down to the kitchen," Mama said. "Do you some good to get out of this room. Let the mattress air out."

"Is Papa downstairs?" I didn't want him to see me in my gown.

"He's out with the cows. Takin' them down by the meadow."

"Fine." I crossed over to my bureau, but froze as a movement outside the window caught my eye. Not believing, I leaned closer, resting my head against the glass. There he was, Nathan Fox, leaning against my father's makeshift stone wall, twirling his hat in his hands. Just then he looked up. Toward the house, but not at me. Not yet.

"That's a good idea," Mama said, busy with the ticking. "Why don't you open the window a bit. Let in some of that fresh breeze."

"All right."

He didn't notice me until I'd slid the window up nearly halfway. And when he did, he slammed his hat on his head and took two running steps toward the house.

"No!" It was out of my mouth before I could think. Certainly not loud enough for him to hear me clear across the yard, yet somehow he knew to stop. But he didn't back away. He just stood there, staring. An expression on his face I couldn't read.

"What was that?" Mama stretched her small frame across the bed, attempting to fit the clean muslin sheet over the far corner of the mattress. I left the window and went to help her, smoothing the cool material at the opposite corner and tucking it under the foot of the ticking.

"I—I was just surprised to see how much of the day has passed. I can't believe I slept so late into the afternoon."

"It's the best medicine." She stood back to admire her work before unfurling a fresh, clean quilt over the sheet. "But let's see if we can keep you up for a while. You didn't get a chance to read your Scripture last night. How about we do that now? Your father will be so pleased to see you keep up. Even in times of illness. Scripture can be such a comfort."

"My head hurts, Mama." Which it did. "I don't think I could concentrate on reading right now." Inching steps took me back to the window. He was gone, and it felt like I was taking the first clear breath since seeing him.

"Oh." She smoothed one hand over and over a corner, and I felt a new weakness, an overwhelming need of her. My head and heart had been spinning for days, and I longed to pour both out to her. I couldn't, of course. Not everything. Nothing about Nathan Fox and our walks to school and the way he touched my face and the hope I had when I saw him standing at the wall. But she was, after all, a woman. And so, apparently, was I.

"But maybe you could read it to me?" I offered. "We could sit together, in the parlor."

"Well, I don't know 'bout that." Mama stooped and gathered the soiled linens into one big armful. "There's so much to be done yet. I haven't even started supper."

"Just one chapter." Still unused to talking, I had to cough before I could continue. "We could have tea and biscuits in the parlor. Like a regular social."

"I suppose there's time before your father gets back," she said, standing. "I'll drop these on the back porch and get the water on."

Alone again, I went to the window and leaned clear out, craning my neck to see if I could get even a glimpse. Nothing. But even his absence held a hint of promise.

"Well, aren't we a couple of fine ladies in the middle of the afternoon?" Mama sipped her tea, eyebrows arched high over the steam.

"I suppose we are." My own tea was cooler, tempered with milk.

"Now," Mama said, setting her cup on the small table beside her and lifting our Bible into her lap, "do you remember where you were?"

I nodded. "First Samuel. Chapter 3."

Mama turned to the page and started to read, but I had to stop her after the first verse.

"What does he mean by 'there was no open vision'?"

She thought for a moment before answering. "It says the word of the Lord was 'precious,' so I suppose it means that not everybody could understand it. Or hear it. God was only speaking to a certain few."

Satisfied, I sipped my drink as she continued to read. After the first verse, it became a familiar story, that of young Samuel being called from his bed by the Lord. Only Samuel didn't know it was the Lord at first and thought it was the old priest Eli. Mama read it like it was a story, not the Bible, and I wished for a minute that I could do all of my Bible readings this way. Or even just sit and let her tell me the stories without reading at all. Surely she knew them all by heart. Since I didn't have the page in front of me, I couldn't count down to the end of the chapter, and I was somewhat startled when her voice silenced.

"That's it?"

"One chapter at a time, Camilla."

I knew it was time for me to answer the question of what this chapter teaches about being a better Christian. But I wasn't ready to think about that just yet. Instead, I wondered about what Nathan said about following a new prophet. Samuel was a prophet because the Lord spoke right to him.

"How come in the Bible God is always talking to people, but now he never does?"

Mama thought for a minute, her eyes turned up to the ceiling, her hand running softly over the open page. "It was an older time, I guess. Closer to Creation. Maybe he was nearer. Maybe people needed to hear him because they didn't have the Bible to read."

"Has he ever spoken like that to you, Mama? right out loud?"

"No, darling. Not like that. Not right out loud."

"But he could if he wanted to?"

"Of course. He can do anything."

"Then why doesn't he? Wouldn't it be easier if he did? Then we could just listen to him and know what to do."

Mama laughed. A treasure so rare I wanted to keep it forever. "Your father and I tell you what to do every day, and sometimes you still find ways to be disobedient. That's why we have the Scriptures. No matter what our parents—or anybody else—tells us, we'll always hear God's voice in these pages. This is where he tells us what we should and shouldn't do."

"But the world has changed a lot since those times."

"Not so much," Mama said. "Not in ways that matter. People still seek him, and he still loves us. Remember that, Camilla, all your days. If nothing else, know that he loves you. And because you love him, you must obey his teachings."

I don't remember ever feeling as close to my mother as I did that afternoon. Like the whole world just stopped for a moment to let us talk to each other. Sometimes I think of how things might have turned out so different if we'd had a chance to do that more. If I could have known every day of my life that we could slip into our parlor and talk about God's love and the world's frustrations over a cup of tea, I might not have taken the path I did.

Still, I tucked my feet up tighter beneath me, not brave enough to ask what was really on my heart. I knew she and Papa would disapprove of my morning walks with Nathan. Partly because he was an older boy and a stranger to our town. But mostly because he was one of the Mormons. And I knew they didn't approve of the Mormons, but I didn't know why, exactly. So far, in all of my Bible readings, I couldn't remember anything that would make Nathan a bad person. Mama had just said that God could still speak to people, just as he had to Samuel, and it seemed Nathan believed the same. She was looking at me now with such an open face, it seemed she was more a sister than a mother, and all the loneliness I carried around with being the only child in this house dropped away.

"Do you think they believe his teachings?"

"Who?" She looked confused, since I forgot I hadn't said all of my thoughts out loud.

"Those people by the river. The Mormons."

Just like that, her eyes narrowed and her whole face pinched up. "No, Camilla. They don't."

"But they have a prophet who heard God's voice."

"He's a false prophet."

"But how do you know?"

"Because their teachings are wrong."

"How? What do they—"

"Enough about this."

"How can you be sure that—"

"I said enough." There she was, my mother again. Small and tight, her tea untouched beside her. "Now, what verse do you want to record in your journal?"

"I don't know." Already the story of Samuel was lost. I leaned forward and put my cup on the little table in front of the sofa. "My head hurts too much to remember." Which was mostly true. "Can you read it again?"

"Don't be silly. There's not enough time. I'll choose one for you." She ran her finger down the columns of words and made an impatient clicking sound with her tongue against her teeth. "Here, verse 19. 'And Samuel grew, and the Lord was with him, and did let none of his words fall to the ground.'"

The brief respite of health began to fade, and I could barely muster the strength to pick up my journal, let alone open and write in it. True, a good portion of my weakness was nothing more than disinterest—disappointment, really. Still, I managed to sound pitiful when I told Mama I couldn't bring myself to note down the words.

"Can you write it for me?"

She glanced over her shoulder into the kitchen before answering. "Very well; hand me the pen."

I complied, then sat back to watch her write, fearing for the paper as she bore down on it. Although Mama could read with a practiced air, writing seemed much more difficult for her. In fact, I could recall only a handful of occasions when I'd seen her do so. Her eyes darted constantly from the Bible's printed page to the empty page on the journal, and her brow took on such a look of concentration I feared the furrows would be etched there like stone. The only sound in the room was that of the scratching pen. Watching Mama write was as laborious as writing myself, and I looked away, choosing instead to stare at my own hands listless in my lap.

"There," she said when the scratching stopped. "Now, how can this verse help you be a better Christian?"

"Can you read it again?" I'd already forgotten what it said.

There was none of her earlier gentleness left as she forced the words through her ever-narrowing lips. "'And Samuel grew, and the Lord was with him, and did let none of his words fall to the ground.'"

"Oh," I said, trying not to smile at the irony. "I suppose it means that I need to know exactly what the Bible says."

Mama accepted this answer and posed the next question, about how this verse could help me be a better woman, but for that, I had no ready answer. I simply shrugged and said I figured it meant the same thing, being a woman or not.

"No." She closed the Bible and my journal, tying the ribbon to hold the pages closed. I can still hear the silk snagging against the roughness of her hands. "It's different for women because you will someday be the mother of children. And it will be your job to know the Word of the Lord so you can teach it to them."

I felt myself blushing again. For the second time in as many days, somebody was talking about children.

"What about fathers? Don't they have just as much responsibility?"

"Yes. And a good man will. Like your father."

"He doesn't really talk to me."

A bit of compassion hinted at the corner of Mama's eyes. "He does the best he can, Camilla. He's not an expressive man."

I thought about Nathan, the broadness of his smile, the warmth of his words. "Was he ever?"

"Maybe," she said. "A little. Hard work takes its toll. Sometimes the person you marry isn't the same person you end up being married to."

We both chuckled and, by an unspoken agreement, picked up our tea and sipped.

"Did you love him instantly?" The details of my parents' courtship had never been a topic of conversation.

She nodded. "Almost. He was so handsome. And godly. That was important to me. He would lead the church in prayer, and I felt like he was lifting all of us up."

My tea was cool, but I still took small sips. "And did he love you?"

Something like a shadow passed across her face as she

stared into her cup. "It's harder for men, you know. To express their feelings. It takes time. Why all these questions all of a sudden?"

"No reason." I fidgeted in my seat, untucking my feet. They were beginning to tingle, and I worried they might not carry me back upstairs. The shadow was back on Mama's face, only now it seemed there to stay as she hardened right before my eyes.

"Are you seeing a boy?"

"No, Mama. Of course not."

"Because you know your papa and I wouldn't approve—"

"Trust me, Mama. None of the boys in this town want anything to do with me."

"They better not, nor you with them. You're only fifteen—"

"How old were you when you met Papa?"

I knew the answer to this, but it was worth it to see her have to take a deep breath before answering me.

"Sixteen. But things were different then."

I wanted to say that it couldn't be so different. After all, she just said that the world was much the same as it had been since Samuel was a boy. What could have changed so much in her short life? But I didn't, because I knew. I knew I'd lied and that there was a boy and I liked him very much. Right now, though, he was a treasure to ponder in my own heart. I knew the minute I opened up and showed him off, he'd tarnish in the light.

Later that night I found myself in bed, tossing and turning after a day spent dozing. I listened to my afternoon conversation with Mama over and over in my head. Sometimes, I imagined it ended differently. I heard myself telling her that, yes, I met the most handsome boy in the world and he touched my face. She'd set down her tea and say, with actual tears in her eyes, that she knew his heart must be pure if he loved a girl like me. But of course, none of that was said at all. It ended when Papa stomped into the kitchen hollering for the whetstone so he could sharpen a tool in the barn. Mama jumped up to find it and didn't seem to think of me again until she brought up my tray for supper.

The house at night was dark and silent and seemed especially so from my room. Mama and Papa slept downstairs, in the house's original bedroom. I'd been sleeping in what used to be an attic storeroom ever since I grew too big for the trundle under my parent's bed. Papa had built a wall straight down the middle, and there was a little door in my room leading straight across to what was still used for storage. The ceiling was high at that end, but sloped down to almost nothing on the other. When I was little, I used to pretend I was a giant, barely able to fit beneath the roof.

When the attic became my room, Papa had to build a staircase to it too. There was no hallway or landing up here—just a ladder straight up from the kitchen through my floor. Before that, you got into the attic by climbing a set of stairs outside, built straight against the outer wall of the house and leading up to a door. Papa had framed out that door and made it into a window, and tonight I was especially glad because the moon was full and my room filled with light.

Then I saw the shadow. Thankfully, I was too terrified to scream.

"Camilla?" His voice was muffled by the glass, but still unmistakable. I didn't know what time it was, but surely it was late, and I prayed that my parents were lost to sound sleep below. He rapped lightly on the glass, and I swung my legs out of bed. Mindless of the fact that I wore nothing more than a white cotton gown, I ran the two steps to the window and, after a quick glance to be sure my father's head wasn't about to emerge through the floor, placed my finger to my lips, imploring him to be quiet.

"Open the window." He spoke as much with his hands as with words, and with the threat that he might make even more noise if I failed to obey, I opened the latch and slid the pane up.

"Are you trying to get me killed?"

"I was worried when I didn't see you this morning. Thank God you're all right."

"I'm not all right." I summoned a cough. "I'm sick."

"See?" He leaned against the window frame, making himself at home. "I said you were catching a cold."

I suppressed a smile. "What do you want?"

"I want you to tell me I was right about you being sick."

"You were right." It seemed best to agree.

"I really did worry that you'd gotten into some trouble with your father. I'd feel terrible if he'd been in any way violent with you."

"My father—" I lowered my voice—"is not violent."

"Harsh, then. I didn't want you punished for something I did."

"I haven't been. Unless being sick is punishment."

He smiled, and it rivaled the moonlight. I was so happy he'd chosen tonight to visit. Last night I would have slept right through, no matter how he called my name. Seeing him there, though, brought to mind what Mama'd said about the Mormons, and it put a touch of fear in me. The same wrestling fear I had when I first saw him. Excitement all tangled up with terror and doubt, fighting to see which one would win the match. Right now Nathan and I were just standing up there together, him on my top step, and me inside. Nothing but moonlight between us.

"Can I see you tomorrow, Camilla?"

Terror won. "No. My parents would never let me. I don't think I should see you at all."

"Well, don't worry. Pretty soon you won't have to. We'll be gone in the next few days, but we're having a sort of celebration tomorrow, and I thought you'd like to come."

My mind lingered on one word. *Gone*. "Why would you want me there?"

"We've been slaughtering chickens all day. . . ."

"What?"

His smile returned. "I thought that would get your attention. We can't travel with them, so we've spent the day plucking and stewing, and what do you think we used for flavoring? The wild onions from your very field. The least you should do is come have a taste."

"I can't." Although my own giggle threatened to betray my resolve. "My parents would never let me."

"Don't tell them." His eyebrows did a dance that brought my laughter to the surface. Like it would be just that simple. "You're sick. Tell them you're coming upstairs to rest. Then straight out this window and down the stairs. Your room was designed for escape."

"Like you're going to do right now." I reached for the sill, fully intending to close the window, but he reached his hands through, grabbing just the tiniest pinch of my gown. Nowhere near my body, but still a pinpoint of my flesh burned.

"I'll be waiting for you. Where the path turns."

"I can't."

"Listen." He strengthened his grip, holding a handful of the cotton fabric. I lowered my hands and he let go of my gown, gripping my wrist instead. Not hard. I could break away if I wanted to. But I listened. "You don't know how lucky you are. Growing up with a home and a family. I never had that. I lived in an orphanage until I was turned out onto the street. And these people—yes, they're my family. They love me and I love them and we take care of each other. But I don't have anybody of my own. I don't have anybody who belongs to me."

"I don't belong to you." Somehow, I found the breath to say it.

"Really? Because I feel, very strongly, that you might. I've known it since the minute I saw you, and Heavenly Father confirmed it after the first time we spoke."

"When you stole from me?"

"I'm sorry. That was wrong. But I felt, even then, that what was yours, was mine."

"But that was my father's."

"Stop it!" His grip tightened, then released. "I would love to have just one conversation with you where you didn't mention your father. Or your mother. Or the fact that you can't meet me tomorrow."

"Shh!" I went and stood by the square-cut hole in my bedroom floor and listened. No stirring. When I returned to the window, he was once again leaning comfortably on his elbows, his head on my side of the glass. Even given this proximity, I kept my voice below a whisper. "You have to go."

He cupped a hand to his ear and mouthed, "What?"

I took a step closer, pointing. "Get out. Now."

The next thing I knew his hand captured mine, and if the touch of our flesh wasn't enough, he brought it to his lips, grazing my knuckles across them, then turned my hand and opened it, pressing my palm against his mouth. And then my wrist. I knew my pulse pounded; I could hear my heart in my ears. Without any effort on his part, I'd been drawn to the window, stooped down until mere inches separated our faces. When I was that close, he said, "Come to me tomorrow."

I felt his words rather than heard them, and my own reply wasn't much more than a whimper.

"I'll be waiting where the path turns," he said, releasing me at last. "I'll be there at dawn. I'll stay there all day."

And then he left. I kept the window open, feeling the night breeze cooling my body through the folds of my gown. Then I closed it and watched, my face against the glass, as he made his way through the yard, escorted to the rock wall by our faithful Bonnie-Belle. I remember thinking how odd it was that she didn't bark. Not a peep. And she's usually so vigilant about strangers. Apparently she loved Nathan Fox too.

CHAPTER 5

I slept very little during the remaining hours of the night, but the sleep I had was deep. The kind Mama called the sleep of the dead. And when I did wake up, I felt like my life had turned over on itself during my absence. I spent the first few minutes of wakefulness staring at my ceiling, trying to sort out what was real and what had been a dream. Never had I woken to such exciting reality.

My fingers fumbled with buttons and ties as I dressed myself. The trembling was something new. I stopped and squeezed my eyes tight, saying, "Don't think of him. Don't think of him," right out loud into the empty room, but it didn't help. I couldn't bring myself to brush and braid my hair, so

I left it long and loose, figuring I'd throw myself on Mama's mercy and get her to do it for me after breakfast. That is, if I could will myself to eat.

Turned out for all my worrying, I'd slept too late to get breakfast at all, and Mama in all her mercy hadn't tried to rouse me. I came downstairs to a single plate covered with a blue-checked towel sitting in the middle of the table. Underneath it was a cold biscuit.

"I'm sorry, sweetheart." Mama ran a damp cloth around the inside of the wash bin after dumping the dishwater out the back door. "I figured it was best to let you rest, and now there's no time to cook you anything else."

"I'm fine," I said, feeling a little hungry after all.

Papa appeared in our doorway, wearing his second-best shirt, his hat gripped in his hand. "Ruth? I've got the team hitched up."

"Just one minute, Arlen." Mama set the washbasin on its shelf and reached behind to untie her apron. "Let me run a comb through my hair."

"Is she going?" He gestured toward me with his hat.

"Oh, I don't think so." Mama turned to me, adjusting the sleeves that had been rolled to her elbow. "You still don't look well, dear. Do you feel up to going to the market?"

I'd forgotten that today was market day—a convention our town observed the first Saturday of every month. It wasn't an officially sanctioned event, more like a tradition struck among the local farmers and craftsmen. A day they all gathered to trade goods and services with each other, occasionally accompanied by a community picnic lunch during fair-weather seasons. I usually enjoyed the day, even if I spent most of it at my parents' side or running from one wagon to another trading cheese for a dozen jars of pickled carrots or gathering bids on one of Papa's spring calves. But on this morning I could think only of my late-night visit and Nathan's invitation. When Mama asked if my health would allow me to spend an afternoon outside of the house, only one answer came out of my mouth.

"No," I said, conjuring up my weakest voice. "Not today."

"You do look pale." Mama stopped on her way to her bedroom and laid the back of her fingers against my brow. "No fever, though."

"She looks well enough to me," Papa said gruffly.

"Sometimes a girl likes to have a day of leisure," Mama said. "To recover."

She left me alone with Papa, and while I felt the hint of a cough at the top of my throat, I suppressed it, for fear it would sound too affected.

"Better get yourself upstairs, then," Papa said. "Don't want to hear about you being too sick to go to church tomorrow."

"Yes, sir. Let me just say good-bye to Mama first."

I went into their room and there she was, standing in front of the oval mirror hanging on one wall. She'd tidied her hair with a damp comb and was tying a pretty blue ribbon at her throat.

"Now, you just relax today," she said, giving the loop a decisive tug. "If you feel like it, you can catch up on your studies. But if not, there's always next week."

The lie was so big in my throat I couldn't speak.

"And Miss Joanna says she'll have about a dozen straw bonnets. Plain, of course, but we can trim them up at home. Would you like one?"

I nodded and managed to say that a new bonnet would be nice this summer before Papa's voice called from the yard.

Mama grasped my shoulders and, in a gesture usually

reserved for very special occasions, kissed my cheek. Then, even more uncharacteristically, her lips moved to my forehead and lingered.

"No, no fever." She held me at arm's length, anchoring me not with her grip, but with the intensity of her pale blue eyes. "Camilla, is there something you want to tell me?"

I gave a brief shake of my head, but when she seemed still unsatisfied, I told her I was feeling a little weak. "Perhaps I should eat something?"

"Well, there's not much in the kitchen, but I could—"

"Ruth!" Papa's voice now boomed, and I suspect every woman named Ruth in the county took a step away from her stove and went to the door to see what beast summoned her.

"I'll be fine, Mama." I stepped into her embrace, wrapping my arms around her thickening waist and laying my head against her bosom. She smelled of butter and flour and barnyard and hay. She must have been up early that morning, helping Papa with the milking, doing my chores as I slept. I squeezed her tight until Papa bellowed once again. Then I let her go.

The minute the wagon disappeared from the yard, all thoughts of venturing out to meet Nathan vanished as my guilty conscience took over my planning for the day. I reached under the blue-checked towel and grabbed the cold biscuit, nibbling on it as I made my way into the parlor. I was still a day behind on my readings (a point Papa had taken pains to make the night before at dinner), so I curled up on the sofa with our Bible and opened to the fourth chapter of Samuel. I struggled through the verses. Wars and great shouts. "Woe unto us . . ." and "Fear not; for thou hast . . ." How different it was to read the Scriptures alone, without my mother at my side to answer questions. So many names—Philistines and Egyptians, Ebenezer, Hophni, and Phinehas. The words swam around meaninglessly, and I had no illness on which to blame my confusion. I considered abandoning my journal, but that would only mean having to read the chapter again under my father's watchful eye, so I took another bite of biscuit and doubled over the page as the crumbs dissolved, salty, on my tongue. Finally, in frustration, I settled on the last verse of the chapter because it was the shortest. Mama would have scolded me, but she wasn't there, and by the time she knew, it would be too late to change it.

When I opened my journal to record the verse, I saw for the first time my mother's labored penmanship from the day before. Her letters had an odd squareness to them, nothing like the fluid script Mr. Teague insisted his students produce. In fact, if you didn't know, you might be confused as to which verses were written by the mother and which by the child.

I turned over the page so as not to be distracted and wrote:

> *And she said, The glory is departed from Israel: for the ark of God is taken. 1 Samuel 4:22.*

I knew I would face the two questions, so I prepared my answers, speaking them aloud into the empty parlor.

"This makes me a better Christian because it reminds me that I must remain close to God. It makes me a better woman because I should give my children meaningful names."

With no one to tell me differently, I deemed my answers perfectly adequate and closed my journal and put the Bible back on its little table. Then, perhaps feeling guilty about my careless study, I clutched my journal close to me and bowed my head.

"Heavenly Father . . . ," I began, but no other words would come. So I just sat, very quiet and very still, waiting.

Lord, I prayed, the words coming from within, *forgive me if I seem disrespectful of your Word. It's difficult sometimes for me to understand just what you're trying to say. I get lost in the stories, and sometimes they all sound alike. And the names are strange. And it just seems so . . .*

I opened my eyes and stopped myself from calling the Word of the Lord *dull*.

"Thank you for letting me feel better. For my healing." And then again, silence. Because I hardly knew how to pray about what was most pressing on my heart. Should I ask God to keep Nathan away? Should I pray for Nathan to come to my door so I could tell him to go away? In the end it seemed best not to pray about Nathan at all. I asked the Lord to give Mama and Papa a good day at the market before saying amen and taking my journal upstairs.

I spent the next half hour doing anything I could to keep myself occupied. I brushed and brushed and brushed my hair until it crackled in the air; then I plaited it into two thick braids, which I wrapped around my head and secured with pins pilfered from Mama's little glass jar. A much more grown-up style than I usually wore, but one easily taken down the minute Papa's wagon turned in to our yard. I pulled off my shoes and opened my mother's armoire, where I found her treasured pair of silk brocade slippers. I truly believed they were princess shoes, and Mama agreed, as long as I understood the princess who wore them was just a farmer's daughter at a city hall Christmas dance. Slipping them on, I wriggled my toes in the luxury of them, then took a turn around the room with a graceful, gliding step. I hadn't done this since I was a very small child—and it had been just as long since I'd seen Mama herself wear them. Impractical, she said, living on a farm. And I had to agree, although it did give me the slightest thrill to see how well they fit my feet.

I prowled through the kitchen looking for something to eat. True to Mama's prediction, however, there was little. Nothing, really, save a few strips of dried beef and a few soft potatoes at the bottom of the bin. Hopefully Mama and Papa were negotiating with some farmers right now for some of the fruits of their gardens. Certainly something good could be harvested this time of year. Something that didn't come from a cow or a pickling jar or even one of those new tin cans.

The little round clock ticked on its shelf, and I'd been home alone for nearly an hour. It felt like an eternity. I never remembered a day in my life so full of emptiness. And that was the very thought tumbling through my head as I climbed the stairs to my room that morning. Empty, empty as my feet moved silently across the floor. To the window. Of course I couldn't see clear to the place where the path turned, but I could see as far as my father's wall.

And there he was.

I wanted to believe I wasn't hoping he'd be there, but that was long before I'd learned to lie to myself. In an instant he'd seen me, and even from this distance his smile filled all the corners of that empty house. I could have leaped through the window—even without the outer stairs to carry me down. His eyes would hold me, reaching across the yard and safely guarding me until my feet touched the ground. But though I was wearing my mother's princess slippers, this, after all, was no fairy tale. In an instant I jumped through the hole in my floor, ran to my parents' room, and found my own shoes where I'd left them carelessly by the bed. With steadier fingers than I'd had just a short time ago, I laced my own brown, sensible leather boots and tucked Mama's slippers safely away.

Any moment, I thought I'd hear a knock at the door, but none came. I paused briefly at the mirror and considered my reflection. I couldn't tell if I looked more or less like a little girl with my braids pinned up. Surely my eyes looked bigger and wider—like my face was being pulled—and my neck seemed long and elegant. I thought about taking the style down, lest Nathan think I pinned my hair up just for him, but even as my fingers hovered over a pin, I stopped.

"This isn't me," I said to the glass, and the image inside confirmed it.

Forcing myself to breathe, I took slow, measured steps to the front door and waited. Wanting him to knock. Hoping to be called on—like a beautiful girl with an eager beau. Finally, though, I simply opened it, only to find our porch empty. And our yard empty. Nothing but his voice in the distance, calling from the uncertain pile of stones.

"Come on! Let's go meet my family!"

And I ran.

He held my hand the entire way, chattering the whole time about the wonders I was about to see. The friendliness of the people, the richness of the fellowship, the commitment everybody had to creating this new city.

"Because that's what we're doing, you know." Breathless, he carted me along. Sometimes beside him, until my feet couldn't keep up with his pace. Then I'd be dragged behind. He said nothing about my hair, asked nothing about my health, and cared nothing that I was with him under deceptive circumstances. "There's nothing here—nothing in your life that can compare to it. These people saved me, Camilla. I can't tell you how empty my life was before I met them."

I wanted to tell him I didn't need my life changed, that I was just going along to taste the chicken stew, but as I tripped along that narrow path, I couldn't help feeling I was on some sort of an adventure, too.

My father's property bordered a brushy forest, nearly half a mile's worth, separating us from the river. Nathan pulled me right through it, taking me along what barely constituted a path. At one step I was swallowed in green, and the next I walked into a wide clearing, like something out of a story. Fire pits dotted the cleared land, with fallen logs stationed around them as makeshift parlor furniture. Small, neat tents made a semicircle on either side, and if we kept walking straight, we'd come to a place where trees had been cut down to make a wide opening out to the river.

For weeks I'd been listening to the sounds coming from these people at night, their songs rising on the night air. Perhaps it was the thin quality of darkness that carried the music. The thickness of the midmorning muted everything. I held my breath as I watched them—so ordinary-looking. Just men and women and children. They milled about the clearing with a unique sense of purpose. Every sound they made blended to a single pleasant hum. No outbursts of laughter or anger. No harshness at all. Just a peaceful dignity. Oh, how very full their lives looked, even in that first moment.

Perhaps I can't be trusted to give a faithful account from this point. It could be that all of my remembrances of the time before I left are seen through a justifying lens. Maybe my father wasn't as harsh and boorish as I render him, nor my mother as weak. My own loneliness and longing certainly exaggerates the instant admiration of the Mormon families in the clearing.

Only my portrayal of Nathan Fox can be trusted. As we stood together, hand in hand, our feet still planted in the forest, we gazed on the scene before us with a single heart. I don't know if he loved me yet, but I loved him, and I knew he wasn't just showing me his family; he wanted to give it to me as well. He'd sought me out, somehow. And my only answer was that the Lord himself had brought him to me. Answered my prayer the way he answered Hannah's. Not with a son, but with a companion, somebody to walk along the road with. So much more than that, as I discovered the night before.

Now as we stood at the edge of the clearing, he squeezed my fingers and turned me to face him. He took my other hand and brought them both up to his lips and pressed them there—not exactly a kiss, but a claim. There was none of the breathless thrill like had come with the moonlight. Our eyes met over our joined hands, and that simple gaze carried a promise. I would step into that clearing with him. And somehow, I would stay.

The shouts of children interrupted our reverie.

"Nate! It's Nate!" Suddenly we were surrounded, hemmed in with boys and girls on every side, all surprisingly neat and clean given their living conditions. They peppered him with excited questions: Did he know they finished building the last wagon? Did he see the new team of oxen? Did he hear about the new letter from the prophet? A steady chorus of "Who is she? Who is she? Who is she?" underscored everything.

Nathan had dropped my hand at their arrival, and he crouched down now, taking each question in turn and answering with such loving patience, he could have been each one's own father. No waving hand was ignored, no question repeated too frequently to warrant a harsh, impatient response. As to the question of who I was, that was left to the very end when he once again took my hand and said, "Children, this is my very good friend Camilla Deardon." Then, to me, he introduced each child by name, no small feat given that there were nearly fourteen coming from ten different families. He also managed to mention the infant siblings too young to attend this little gathering.

I greeted each one with a smile, knowing full well I'd never remember any of their names. I shook one little hand after another, saying "Thank you" to the girls who thought my hair looked pretty.

"This is the young lady who gave us the cheese and butter," Nathan said, and this revelation started a new round of excited chatter. How humbling to see all those little faces alight with sincere joy and gratitude, and in the midst of it, their names came clear: Josiah, Rebecca, Daniel, Sarah. Whatever grudge I might have held at Nathan's theft disappeared as I graciously accepted credit for the act of charity.

We walked together into the camp, though he'd long since dropped my hand, and the children hovered behind and around us making me feel like I was leading a sort of swarm. Soon, more interesting pursuits presented themselves, and the children peeled away to recommence their games of tag and chase. Or they were summoned to finish whatever chore they'd abandoned. I tried not to bristle at the unabashed suspicion in the women's eyes as they drew their children close to them. Not entirely unfriendly, but definitely guarded, although their mouths greeted me with broad smiles and words of welcome.

"So, this is the one, is she?"

The voice came from behind, and its slicing honey sweetness chilled my spine. I stayed still and would have remained so if Nathan hadn't put his hand on my shoulder and physically urged me to turn around.

"Hey there, Rachel. Yes, this is Camilla."

She was, without a doubt, the most beautiful girl I had ever seen. Easily as tall as Nathan, her thick blonde hair was pulled away from her face, but without giving that pinched, taut look that plagued so many women. Instead, her hair seemed to have floated back of its own accord, leaving soft, wavy furrows in its wake. My first thought was to reach out and touch it, to see whether it was real or some molded plaster of perfection. I squelched this impulse, of course, but I did hold out my hand.

"Nice to meet you." I was the first to extend the greeting. She said nothing, but gave me such a perusal I felt I'd been turned inside out on the spot. Her pretty mouth twisted into a quirky smile, and when she finished her inspection with the second appraisal of my pinned-up braids, she looked not at me but at Nathan.

"She's nothing like what I expected, Nate."

"Few things in life ever are, Rache." His smile matched hers.

I looked from one to the other. There couldn't have been a stronger bond between them if they'd been chained together at the neck. "This must be your sister."

He left my side then and wrapped a protective arm around her shoulders. "It is indeed. The lovely Mrs. . . . What's the name again?"

She made a face. "Crane."

"Ah, yes. How could I forget. Married to Tillman Crane, Esquire."

"You could forget because you're just too hateful to remember, even if you did practically bribe the man to marry me."

Their tone was easy, teasing, and playful. She seemed far too young to be anybody's wife. Caught up in the spirit of banter, I said so out loud.

"Nonsense," Rachel said, her expression not quite drawing

me into their game. "I'm nineteen. Some would say I'm nearly an old maid."

"I'd never say that, Sis."

"Brother, you'd shout it from the mountaintop." She leaned closer to me and cupped her hand around her mouth, prepared to convey a secret. "Wouldn't want me to miss out on my chance at eternity, now would he?"

But there was no whispering to her words. Behind her, Nathan swallowed, and his eyes took on a serious glint.

"It's because I love you, Rachel. I want you to have a better future than what we came from. And I want you to have that forever."

Rachel dropped her hand and turned, giving Nathan a hug and a kiss on his cheek. "I know, Nate. And I love you, too. Now, let's go break Evangeline's heart."

As she led me away, I glanced back to see Nathan putting up a weak protest before turning his back and walking in the opposite direction.

"Where's he going?"

"We're leaving in three days. Lots of work to do." I had no choice but to allow this to suffice as an answer. She walked me across the clearing to a cook fire being tended by a girl who, from the back at least, appeared to be about my age. Few people can claim to have a striking feature from the back, but this girl defied any sort of anonymity. Straight down her back, barely submitted into one thick braid, was the brightest, reddest hair I'd ever seen. Red, in fact, might not be the best color to name it, as further inspection revealed it to be almost orange. Where Rachel's hair lay thick and smooth around her head, this hair sprung out in curling wires in every direction, dancing in the breeze like coppery unattached spiderwebbing.

"Evangeline!" Rachel sang the name, and as a result the

girl turned, her face initially one of hopeful curiosity. But one glance at me and her countenance fell.

"Who's this?" she asked, attempting congeniality.

"You know very well who this is," Rachel said with gentle chastisement. "This is Camilla of the cheese and butter. And, Camilla, this is Evangeline. Madly in love with my brother, and therefore not likely to be anything more than terrible to you."

I had no idea how to react to such an introduction, but Evangeline's sincere, raspy laughter gave me license to do the same.

"Don't listen to a word she says." Evangeline popped up from her seat, reaching out to grab my hands. "I haven't been in love with Nathan since, oh, about an hour ago. No hard feelings?"

"None at all," I said, echoing her humor. In an instant I'd learned there would be no way to harbor any harsh feelings toward Evangeline Moss. She had thin, green, catlike eyes that nearly disappeared when she smiled. Which was often. Her easy smile revealed small, even teeth, but it was her face that gave her a most distinct appearance. Her eyelids, her earlobes, from her hairline to her sharp little jaw—all were covered with masses of freckles. More freckle than face, as Mama would say. I truly didn't mean to stare, but I've never been able to disguise my reactions. My amusement at her appearance must have been obvious to Evangeline, because she batted her pale eyelashes and brought her face even closer.

"Go ahead. Pick a favorite. Mine's this one." She rested her finger on her cheek. "Or maybe this one." She moved it to the middle of her forehead. "Or maybe—bother! There's just so many to choose. Rachel? Which one's yours?"

Her voice had the same quality mine had the day before

when it hurt too much to speak, and I wondered if she were suffering from a cold. The sound of it combined with the ridiculousness of the conversation made me laugh even harder, and in an instant I felt we'd been friends forever.

"Oh, my," Rachel said, taking a deep breath. "You know I could never choose a favorite. I love them all so dearly."

"Well, then, it falls to Camilla. Come on, girl. You can't really be a part of us until you pick a favorite freckle."

I wanted to tell her that I *wasn't* a part of them—and had no idea if I wanted to be. But friendship had never been so easily and openly offered. I found my hand shaking a bit as I lifted it, pointing squarely at Evangeline's ear.

"That one," I said. "I've never seen a freckle on an ear before."

Evangeline clapped her hands together, her face beaming with mock pride. "Wonderful choice, Camilla. Really. I like a girl who knows her freckles."

"My mother says they are angels' kisses."

"Then our little Evangeline must be downright divine," Rachel said, offering a one-armed hug to her friend.

"And if that doesn't make me good enough to marry the prophet, I don't know what will."

I didn't join in on the next bit of laughter, having no idea what the joke could possibly be, and at the passing of one sharp-eyed woman, both Rachel and Evangeline hushed themselves, looking straight at the ground until their smirks abated.

"Are you hungry?" Rachel asked when all were composed.

"A little. Nathan said something about a chicken stew?"

"Flavored with—*the onions*." Both girls chimed in on the last two words and looked to the sky. "Honestly," Rachel continued alone, "you would think those old wild onions were precious cargo from the Far East."

"Between the butter and the cheese and the onions, you're our own personal grocer," Evangeline said.

"But, like a miracle grocer."

"A manna grocer!"

And the two girls collapsed into each other's arms, laughing again. The brief window of camaraderie appeared to have closed, and I began to take one step back.

"Oh, now—" Rachel reached out for me—"don't look so frightened. If you could just hear how my brother speaks of you—"

"Like you're some kind of vision—"

"This apparition of hope in his lonely world—"

"Wait a minute!" I surprised myself with my own volume. "How could his world possibly be lonely?"

At this Evangeline and Rachel hunkered together, assuming a conspiratorial pose. Holding their arms akimbo, they spoke in unison again, their words fitting the rhythm of a familiar children's rhyme: "'For want of a woman a kingdom was lost!'"

And there they were, giggling again, only this spell was short-lived and snuffed out with Rachel's apology.

"Poor Camilla. You have no idea what we're talking about." Then she turned to Evangeline. "If the stew's done, why don't you go see if you can scare us up some bowls and spoons."

"But it isn't quite lunchtime."

Rachel gave her a nudge. "Give us a minute."

Evangeline acquiesced with a little bow and backed away, leaving Rachel and me relatively alone.

"Let's sit." She moved around to sit on a fallen log and patted the seat beside her. I joined her, shifting my weight until I found the perfect level of comfort. I also used this shifting time to look over my shoulder, wondering just where Nathan had gone to.

"Relax," Rachel said, scooting companionably closer. "He actually wanted me to talk to you."

"Really?" I shifted again. "Why?"

"Because he really likes you. I'd go so far as to say he's smitten."

"What did you mean a minute ago when you said 'For want of a woman—'"

"'—A kingdom was lost'? It's just a silly little—"

"But what does it mean?"

Now it was Rachel's turn to shift in her seat, and for the first time a hint of vulnerability crossed her face.

"Look, Camilla, I'll tell you, but I want you to promise not to let it frighten you."

"All right," I said, fully frightened anyway.

"Nathan and I, we never had any real family growing up. And now, with us getting ready to make this journey—well, it's scary. He's a man, of course, and would never admit to being afraid of anything. But I think deep down he knows that plenty have died on this trail, and he doesn't want to be one of them."

Her response did nothing to either ease my fears or answer my question. I still saw no connection between what she just told me and myself, and I told her.

"He wants to have a family," she explained.

"He has you, doesn't he?" I gestured widely. "And all of these people."

"He doesn't have a family of his own. No wife. No children. You don't understand the way these people—the way *we*—believe. Our marriages continue on after we die. He doesn't want an eternity alone."

I tried to scoot away, but my skirt snagged on the rough bark. "You mean he wants to *marry* me?"

"Relax." She reached out to grasp my arm, and I wasn't sure if the gesture was meant to soothe or control. "I don't know if *he* knows exactly what he wants. I only know that he likes you. He spent weeks talking about the quiet, pretty girl who always seemed to be alone. Like she was set apart just for him. If you could have seen him working up the courage to talk to you the first time . . ."

"He's never struck me as being shy."

"He's not, exactly. He simply hates to fail."

That, I could understand. "Your brother—Nathan—is very handsome." I hated how I stammered over the words. "I think he could have any girl he wanted. He doesn't need me."

"True, but in our little party there aren't many to choose from."

"There's Evangeline."

"Who would bore him silly. One look and she'd be attached to his hip. You, on the other hand, make him work a little harder."

I didn't dare tell her how easily I'd been convinced to join him today, and I wouldn't have to because just then his very voice rang out, saying, "Soup's on!"

I turned my head to see him and Evangeline coming toward us. She with a square of flatbread, and he with a stack of four perfectly balanced bowls.

"Don't believe a word she's been saying." He pointed toward his sister with a handful of spoons. "Unless it's good. Then, trust me, it's gospel."

If I thought we were going to have a cozy lunch with just the four of us, I was mistaken; soon the fire pit was surrounded by men, women, and children. About two dozen in all, and as I craned my neck to look around, I saw a similar scene taking place at the cook fires throughout the clearing. Everybody came to a simultaneous hush when an older man rose up, standing on a stump in the middle of the camp.

"Brothers and sisters," he said, holding his hat over his heart. In one motion, all of the men and boys followed suit. "Heavenly Father has blessed us with this meal we are about to eat. Let us thank him."

"That's Brother Thomas," Rachel whispered in my ear. "He's in charge of our group."

All around me heads bowed, and I did likewise.

"Our God," Brother Thomas intoned, "we thank thee for this food. We ask a blessing on those who prepared it. As the time of our journey draws nigh, we petition thee for the strength we require to follow your plan. May this nourishment grant us the health and vigor we need. And may you bring us all safely to Zion. In the name of Jesus Christ we pray."

And there was a chorus of amens. I added my voice to it as well, and I opened my eyes to see Nathan staring at me with such intensity, I clasped the hand of Rachel beside me for support.

In the brief silence surrounding the end of the prayer and the commencement of the meal, Nathan pushed past the two of us, handing the bowls and spoons off to Evangeline, and leaped up on the log behind me.

"Excuse me! Attention everybody!" What little murmuring there had been stopped, and all eyes turned to Nathan. Brother Thomas had been about to step down, but he, too, turned his attention to Nathan, watching with an expression of curiosity that soon became one of approval. "I would like to introduce my guest," Nathan continued. "This is our neighbor Camilla Deardon, who is joining us for our meal today. Her family's generosity has fed us in the past, and it is truly a blessing to be able to share with her. I hope you will make her feel welcome."

By the time he finished speaking, I could feel my face burning, and I could not bring myself to lift my gaze beyond by own boot tops.

"Don't worry," Rachel said, putting a protective arm around my shoulders. "We don't bite."

I sat down again right next to where Nathan was standing, and just like that he hopped down and settled beside me. Evangeline put a bowl in my hands, another in his, and another woman—possibly Evangeline's mother, given her coloring—ladled hot, steaming soup into the bowl. I lifted it to my nose and inhaled deeply.

"It smells good." My stomach agreed and nearly flipped out of my body in anticipation. Somebody put a hunk of flatbread in my hand, and I watched as Nathan took his and dunked it into the soup, bringing it up dripping and soft. He slurped the excess broth, then bit off the rest, somehow managing to chew and smile with the same mouth.

"Try it," he said, adding the act of speech.

"I'm letting it cool," I replied, giving it another blow for good measure.

"Soup's best when it's hot." He dunked his bread again. "I think the flavor's in the steam."

"That's the silliest thing I've ever heard." Still, I dunked my bread too, an act that Mama would never have allowed at our own table. Careful not to drip onto my chin, I took a bite, pleased with the gooey, warm, flavorful mass. "It *is* delicious," I said once I'd swallowed.

"It's the wild onions, I tell you." He tipped his bowl and took a great swallow. "And to think, your pa would have thrown them right onto the compost pile."

Indeed. I balanced my bread on my knee and fished around in my bowl with my spoon until I found a bite of chicken.

Lifting it out of the broth, I blew until the steam no longer rose and plopped it into my mouth, chewed, and swallowed. And the rest of our meal was just like that. Warm and silent.

CHAPTER 6

It seemed for the rest of the afternoon I was handed off from one person to another. I told my family's story at least a dozen times—that we had a small dairy, that I would be sixteen in September, that I met Nathan on my way to school, that the butter and cheese were my mother's specialty. In return, I learned very little. True, I asked fewer questions, but those I did all seemed to garner the same curious answer: they were all given over to the will of Heavenly Father. And given the peaceful smiles on their faces, they were happy to be so.

Slowly, I began to make sense of the family groups—who was the husband of which woman. What children belonged to which family. From what I could tell, there seemed to be a dozen families in all, plus Nathan and Rachel. Maybe fifty people. Brother Thomas was the oldest, and his wife, the fragile Sister Ellen, told me their children and grandchildren waited for them in Utah. That seemed to be the story for many of the people here. They had parents, children, brothers, and uncles who had gone on ahead to build the great city in the new Zion, marking the trail for the Saints to follow, so they said. Listening to them, I felt none of the fear I thought I should, given my father's suspicions. For the most part, I could have been at a picnic with my very own church family, I felt so much a part of their fold.

Still, I took great comfort when Nathan's now-familiar hand came to rest on my arm, and I turned to look into his welcome eyes.

"Walk with me?"

"Of course," I said, suddenly eager to get away from the crowd.

He led me to where the clearing opened out to the river's edge. It was a secluded spot, probably a mile south of the tiny dock our town had set up for its crossing. Here along the shore were six wagons, all lined up. Alongside them were barrels and open trunks, waiting to be filled and packed away, I assumed.

"We have quite a few people at your town's market today," Nathan said, anticipating my question. "If they trade well, they'll come back with flour and cornmeal. We've already cured some beef and pork."

"So you leave in three days?"

"Fewer, actually." He spoke with his jaw clenched. "I spoke with Brother Thomas a few minutes ago. He's received word that the rest of our party is waiting for us in Lincoln. We'll pack tonight, and since tomorrow's the Sabbath, we'll spend it in prayer and preparation."

"And leave Monday?"

He nodded. "We used the lumber we cleared to build a ferry—"

"But we have a ferry! Mr. Moore's—"

"We want our own. It isn't much, just enough to take two wagons at a time. But our people have told stories—some ferrymen charging outlandish fees to transport wagons. Or torching them midcrossing."

"Mr. Moore would never—"

"We've seen too much of what good people would *never* do. Homes burned. Children killed. Innocent men tarred and run out of town. Somewhere—" he looked out across the river—"there's a place where our people can live in peace and worship God with the same freedom allowed to your people. I just wish—"

He stopped as more voices came from the clearing. Men carrying small wooden chests and women with arms full of folded quilts. Even children carried the odd tool or utensil.

"Come here." He took my hand and led me back into the trees. The bustling activity at the river's edge disappeared, leaving nothing but forest shadows. I'd never spent time exploring the woods so near our home. Mama had been clear in her warnings about how easily a girl could get lost. No sun, no direction, no wind to carry your voice. She, of course, had in mind the dangers of being in the forest alone, yet she would take little comfort at the thought of me being so isolated with a boy. Any boy. As the leaves and branches closed in around us, I felt my own sense of fear. Inexperienced as I was with both forests and boys, I knew he'd brought me here to kiss me. And there, with the heels of my boots backed up against the mossy base of a cottonwood tree, he did.

To say that I had never been kissed before is a statement so obvious, it barely warrants words. I shied away from his first attempt, holding my hand up between us and saying, "Please, Nathan. Don't." Had I walked away, found my path back to the river's edge, left him in the darkness of the forest, I know he would not have followed. This is but one of the moments I remember, one of the final crossroads where I stood, blind to the obvious path of escape. And I will not say that Nathan forced his kiss upon me, lest God cut me down for lying. It came down to this: Neither of us took a step away from the other. Nor one closer. My hand remained suspended between us, and I remember looking up and seeing nothing but his eyes. Hearing nothing but his breath. Feeling nothing but the beating of my own heart. And then, imperceptibly, my finger moved. It must have, because the tip of it brushed the rough cotton of his shirt. He could not have felt my touch—I barely felt it myself, and it was my own flesh.

Then he spoke. Just one word. My name. When he did, everything he'd ever made me feel, all those whispering tendrils of fear and hope, joy and anticipation found each other, twisting themselves into one strong cord, and anchored someplace deep within, pulled me to him.

It was, at first, nothing more than a sweet, simple kiss. Nathan's lips did little more than graze across mine before he pulled away, smiling that half-moon smile.

"I love you, Camilla Deardon. Do you believe me?"

I nodded, my heart too full to let him know that I loved him, too. But he soon would because no girl would give herself over to the embrace that followed if she did not truly love. This time, when he bent his mouth to mine, he lingered, cradling my face in his hands to draw me closer. I offered no resistance. In fact, as our kiss grew more ardent, our breath ragged, our bodies entwined, it was he who pulled himself away, leaving me flushed and bewildered. Unsteady on my own feet.

"I'm sorry." He turned away from me, running both hands through his hair. His voice had the hoarse, haggard quality of a man emerging from some great battle. "I should not have done that."

"It's all right," I said, my hand against my swollen lips. "I—I wanted you to."

Three steps away, he stopped and turned. "Why?"

I dropped my hand and looked at him, terrified of the answer.

The sound of dried twigs underscored his journey back to me. He grabbed my shoulders and stooped down, his eyes level with mine. "Tell me, Camilla."

"I suppose I love you."

His face became a burst of sunshine in the middle of the shadowed forest, and the loud whoop he cried sent some small creature scuttling off in the distance. I felt the ground beneath me disappear as he picked me up, and it swirled beneath me as he danced us around.

"I'll never forget this day," I said when the earth was once again firm beneath me.

"You don't have to. Come with me, Camilla, and every day can be just like this."

The very thought of it was dizzying, and I could hardly believe he was serious. I laughed and told him so. "I'm only fifteen years old. My parents would never allow—"

"Fifteen? *Only* fifteen? How old was David when he slew Goliath? How old was Jesus when he instructed the rabbis in the Temple?" Nathan had dropped his grip on my arms and now strode about the forest floor, his tone an unsettling mixture of imploring and force. "Who's to say you can't begin your life the moment it changes? Do you know how old Joseph Smith was when he had his first visit from Heavenly Father?"

I shook my head, backing away.

"Fourteen. All alone in the woods, asking God, 'Which church should I join?' And God could have said, 'You're fourteen years old. Go to the church of your parents.' But no. He told Joseph to begin his own church. He put new prophecy into the mouth of a fourteen-year-old boy. Do you know why?"

I didn't, of course, but suddenly I longed to. I'd been sitting on one wooden bench every Sunday of my life, had read the entire Bible through, and had never until this moment felt such a stirring at the mention of the voice of God. Nathan must have sensed my need because he drew near to me again, his face mere inches away.

"God understands the power of youth. He didn't allow his own Son to grow old. And the church? Look at it—nothing but dry, dusty old men who have forgotten the passion of doing the Lord's work. Come to think of it, I was just fourteen myself . . ." Nathan's voice trailed off for a moment and he stepped away, looking about him as if accessing a long-ago scene. "Fourteen years old and out on the street—*living* on the street. Because the orphanage—run by the *church*—put me there when I turned twelve. And I heard him speak."

"The Lord?" I asked. I couldn't imagine any other voice could bring about the rapturous expression on Nathan's face. The entire forest around us had disappeared, leaving him back on that street corner.

"No—well, yes. Both in the same. I'll never forget. The prophet was standing on a crate, right in the middle of the street." To demonstrate, Nathan leaped onto a stone, towering above me, and struck a dramatic pose, turning the trees into a crowd. "And the way he spoke—it was like nothing I'd ever heard before. There must have been a hundred people gathered in that street, and you know what he did? He looked right through that crowd and found me." Nathan crouched down on the rock and reached his hand out. "And he said, 'You, young man. How will you answer the call of Heavenly Father?' And it was like he cared. No one had ever cared about me before. I followed him then, and I've never looked back. I brought my sister with me, and we were brought into a family. I want you to be a part of it too. Now, my love, is the time to change your life."

I took his outstretched hand and attempted my best coquettish smile. "My goodness, Mr. Fox. I don't know if you're trying to seduce me or convert me."

He smiled and in one smooth motion brought my fingers to his lips and leaped off the rock. "Yes, if I win your soul, I'll have an eternal reward. And if you're my wife, you'll share that eternity with me. Can you imagine—" he drew me closer—"this moment, over and over, through endless time?"

He kissed me again, and time did stop. Or maybe it stretched, wrapping itself around us. I couldn't think in any manner close to clearly, and every time I tried to pull myself away—just enough to gather my thoughts—Nathan pulled me closer, his embrace more eager with each renewal, and I felt myself on the brink of surrender. Had he taken his mouth from mine and asked me to follow his faith, his family, his future, I would have joined myself to him. Unquestioning. So part of me prayed he wouldn't, and I welcomed his kiss and his touch, finding safety in the timelessness.

When we did separate, it was only for the briefest of moments—just long enough for him to look into my eyes before wrapping his strong arms around me. The homespun cotton of his shirt scratched against my cheek, and his lips moved against my hair as he said, "I don't ever want to leave you."

"Then don't." I hugged him tighter, my words muffled. "Stay here. Maybe you can work for my father."

One step, and there was an inch between us. Then two. He tucked his thumb under my chin and raised my face to look at him. "That's impossible."

"Why? There's more than enough work to be done. Papa might even—"

"Could the Israelites remain in Egypt?"

"What?"

"I'm not just some pioneer looking for a homestead or a fool rushing for the last of California gold. I want to be able to worship God in the way he's revealed himself to me. I can't do that here or anywhere but the Zion that Brother Brigham has found for us in Utah. The Gentiles have made that very clear."

Gentiles. "That's what I am, though, isn't it? That's what Evangeline called me."

His smile was back, softer now. "A Gentile is someone who has closed his heart and his mind to the new teachings of Jesus Christ. But you . . . I can tell. You have a seeking spirit. Tell me, sometimes when you read your Bible, don't you find yourself wondering what it all means?"

I swallowed hard, nodding.

"Gentiles don't wonder. They know. Or they *think* they know. And rather than look any deeper, they take up their guns and their torches—"

"Not all. You've been welcome here."

"We've been *tolerated* here. Because we made it very clear we weren't staying."

"Perhaps if I'd met you sooner . . ."

I didn't finish the thought, having no idea what difference such a change in circumstance would make. Apparently neither did he, as he touched a finger to my lips to stop any such musing. "We shouldn't question the Lord's timing. Everything he orchestrates is perfect. I never gave any thought to marrying until we came here. He held that very idea away from me until I saw you."

I smiled beneath his touch and tried to believe him.

"Come with me, Camilla, and I promise you, if you're not happy, I'll bring you home. I mean it. I'll get the fastest horse I can find—I'll even steal an Indian pony—and I'll fly us on its back."

The image was so beautiful, so romantic, it would be worth the risk of an unhappy day to attain it. No matter what I might try to tell myself later, I was poised at that moment to say yes. My lips were parted, my throat full of agreement, but the only sound was the long, lingering sound of my name as it was shouted by my father just beyond the trees.

CHAPTER 7

Everything dissolved around me. In those first seconds, I stood frozen, no recollection of where I was or how I came to be there. All of Nathan's words—his promises and declarations—were wiped clean away with the relentless shouts of my father.

Nathan still held my hand, and though his pulsed with warmth, mine had turned to ice within his grip.

"What do we do?"

"Stay here," he said, attempting to draw me close again. But I knew Papa, and he would pace and shout until he found me.

"I have to go." I wrenched myself from Nathan's grip. "You stay here. Papa'd kill you if he thought—"

"No, Camilla. You don't need to face him alone."

"I'll be fine." Still my father's voice raged beyond the trees, and I hesitated, steeling myself for the encounter.

"Stay with me." Nathan's words were little more than breath behind my ear.

"I can't." Yet my feet seemed rooted to the forest floor.

"Then go with me."

Now he was just being cruel, because even if I had allowed myself to indulge in the fantasy of a lifetime in his arms, the reality of my world encroached upon us, gaining in volume and clarity. I would return to my father's home, pick up my life much as I had left it—chores before dawn, long dull days. After tomorrow, our family evenings would return to their oppressive silence when the faint singing of the Mormon people disappeared with their wagons.

"You know I can't."

"I'll talk to your father."

"No!" I wish I hadn't turned around because the sight of him standing, looking so slack and hurt, threatened to break my resolve to leave. "My father wouldn't understand," I said, reaching out.

"What wouldn't he understand? That we love each other, or that God has a new plan for his church?"

"None of it."

I stood helpless as Nathan placed one final, soft kiss on my lips.

"We're spending tomorrow in prayer for a safe journey, and I'll be pleading with Heavenly Father to bring you to me. And if he doesn't, I'll come to you. At midnight, the night before we leave, I'll be there. Right where we've always met. I'll sleep there if I have to. I'll be the last to cross the river with my brothers and sisters. Tell me you'll be the answer to my prayer, Camilla."

"*Camillaaaaaaa!*" So close it rustled the leaves.

I squeezed my eyes shut. "Good-bye, Nathan."

The shouts of my father led my steps toward the clearing, and soon I emerged from the protective cover of trees to see him. His back faced the trees, giving me enough time to gather a deep breath.

"Here I am, Papa."

He turned, and I was instantly comforted by the look of relief on his face. The reassurance didn't last long, though, as his face reddened, and the hands that had been cupped around his mouth, ready to shout my name again, dropped to his side and hung there, clenching into fists. "Where is he?"

I trembled at the control in his voice. "I don't know who you—"

"Do not lie to me, Camilla Deardon. I've not brought you up to be a liar, and you've done nothing but lie to me and your mother for days."

"But I haven't! I've been sick—"

"Struck down is what you've been. For lying and dishonoring your parents. Now where is he?"

"Papa, there's nothing—"

"Enough!" He hadn't raised his hand to me since I was a very little child, but there it was, suspended against the clear blue sky. Instinctively I cried out, crouching down and covering my face to avoid the blow.

"Stop there!" It was Nathan's voice—I'd know it anywhere. Still cowering, I turned to look behind me, and there he was, a blanket of forest behind him. He stared past me, looking at my father, and just the sight of him gave me courage to stand and face Papa myself.

From a few yards away where men were still toiling to

load the wagons, someone called out, "Do you need any help, brother?"

"I'm fine!" Nathan replied, never taking his eyes off Papa.

"You," Papa said, his hand now a meaty fist pointing one accusatory finger. "You're the one I've heard about."

"I believe you have me at a disadvantage," Nathan said, turning this confrontation into something more like two men meeting on the church lawn. Completely undeterred by my father's aggressive posturing, he walked forward, his hand inexplicably stretched out in friendship. "I'm Nathan Fox. And you must be Mr. Deardon, Camilla's father."

"What is this?" Papa grabbed my arm and yanked, pulling me away from my position between them. "How dare you after what you've done? I know everything." He turned to me, tightening his grip on my arm. "I spoke with Mr. Teague today. He asked me about the young man who's been squiring my daughter to school every morning."

"So it's a crime now to share a road with someone?" Nathan's hand, once offered in friendship, now nestled in his pocket.

Papa didn't even look away. "Every morning this week—"

"Actually, just two."

I craned my neck to look over Papa's shoulder, imploring Nathan to please, just be quiet. At this, Papa let go his grip, pushing me aside none too gently, and strode toward Nathan, who remained smiling, unblinking, rooted in place.

"You stole from my family. You trespassed on my property. You've wormed your way into my daughter's life, and God alone knows what treacherous, blasphemous lies you've filled her head with." Each accusation brought him closer, his voice rising in volume and anger with each step. "How dare you? I know about your people. Their filthy, whoring—"

"Papa!"

"Hush!" He threw the word over his shoulder. By now the men whose help Nathan earlier refused dropped their wares and headed toward us, striding purposefully along the river's edge. Still, never once taking his eyes off Papa, he halted them just a few steps away with the simple raising of his hand.

"Mr. Deardon," he said without the slightest trace of fear, "I must insist that you not use such crude language around a young lady." He broke his gaze long enough to send me the quickest of winks. "And as you and everybody in your town can attest, our people, as you would say, have caused no problems. We've kept peacefully to ourselves. Let's not sully our last days with anger."

"Oh no. You'll not soothe me with your honeyed words. I'm not some wide-eyed, aimless twit you can rope into your lies. Nothing but a batch of false prophets and con men, the lot of you. What? Have you sunk so low as to seduce your converts now?"

"Mr. Deardon, you really shouldn't say such things in front of your daughter."

"That's right! She is *my* daughter. And she may not be bright enough to recognize the wolf behind such romantic wool, but I am. No true Christian boy would sneak a girl off for such an afternoon. And—" he turned to me then—"no God-fearing girl would let herself be so taken. Look at you. It's written on your face."

But I didn't know how he could claim to see anything written there, as my face was buried deep in my hands. I felt my flesh burning against my palms, too riddled with shame to face either man so embroiled in an argument about me.

"Don't listen to him, Camilla."

I parted my fingers enough to see Nathan's face, and I knew

the hurt I saw there was for the ugliness of all Papa said to me. I wanted to run to him, fling my arms around him, and protect him. Instead, my arm was yanked away, nearly crushed in my father's grip.

"I'm taking you home."

Silently I followed, not having much of a choice. By now a crowd had gathered, and they all stared at me with sad, wistful eyes. Many bowed their heads in prayer as I passed. Rachel, clutching a bundle of clean linen, reached her hand out and grasped mine, our fingers pressed together until Papa's gait tore us apart.

An odd thought occurred to me then. Even as I was being marched away like some prisoner, I had a new, odd sense of power following me. Papa was one man, but here was a band of people standing in my silent defense. No doubt if I decided to rebel—to truly fight my way from his grip and run back to their fold—they would envelop me. Alleviate my fears with warm soup and soft words. I entertained the thought for a moment, just until the point where we reached the road that would lead back to our property. I turned my head and saw nothing but a bend in the river and distant figures. Papa finally stood still and took me in a strong, awkward embrace.

"Your mother was half-sick with worry." His voice held an unfamiliar hoarseness.

"I'm sorry," I said, wriggling away.

"We'll go home. And you'll tell her everything."

I nodded and fell into silent step beside him.

Of course I didn't tell Mama everything. Yes, Nathan took the cheese and butter, but only because his people were hungry, and I only let him because I thought it might be spoiled. And yes, he and some others dug up the wild onions on our property, but only, again, because of their need. Forgotten were his visit to my window in the dead of night and his calling here to escort me to their camp. Instead, I had been resting in my bed when two girls—Rachel and Evangeline—came to the house to invite me to try their soup.

"And your hair?" Mama had been sitting at the table across from me, silently snapping beans as I spun my tale.

"Th-they pinned it. The girls did."

"It's a mess. Flying all around your face." To prove her point, she reached across and smoothed a strand. "Your father said you were in the woods with that boy. Is that why?"

"Mama, please."

"Girls have to be careful." She returned to her beans. "Boys will take liberties."

"He didn't take any liberties, Mama."

"Would you know if he did?"

"He's very kind, Mama. And sweet. And good."

"Which is why you might be more inclined to allow him to do things. Take things." She leaned closer, hiding our conversation from Papa, even though he'd gone out to the barn after depositing me at the front door.

"He kissed me." I took a bean from the bowl and nibbled its sweetness.

"Did he? More than once?"

"He said he loves me."

"Before or after he kissed you?"

I didn't know how to answer that because the afternoon was such a blur. A lifetime had passed since then. The way she continued with her industrious snapping led me to believe that she didn't want an answer at all, her jaw set firm, her brow furrowed. In some ways it seemed Nathan told me he loved me the first time we spoke, when he knew my name. But Mama wasn't one to be given to such romantic notions, so I gave her a response full of practicality.

"Before. He told me he loved me, then asked if he could kiss me."

"You can't trust him."

"You don't know him."

"Neither do you, my dear." She scooped up her work and dropped it in a pot. "Boys will tell you what they think you want to hear."

"He's not just a boy, Mama."

"I know." She left me alone at the table, busying herself at the stove and speaking at the window. "Your father says those people are leaving tomorrow."

"Day after tomorrow."

She wheeled around. "Not a day too soon. You're not to leave this house, do you understand me? Not one step through the door until they're gone."

"Yes, Mama."

She came back to me then and smoothed my hair again, her hand damp and cool against my skin. "I'm sure you believe you love him, too."

"I do."

"It will pass. There'll be other boys. Better ones."

"Better?"

She knelt beside me. "God has a plan for your life. He has a man chosen for you. A good, strong Christian man."

"Nathan is a Christian."

"No, Camilla, he's not." Her words weren't exactly stern, but they were serious, and from her position on the floor she had to look up at me to say them. Seeing Mama from this angle made her seem softer, somehow, the lines of worry that so often creased her face smoothed away. She grasped both my hands in hers. "Listen to me very carefully. I admit I don't know everything those people teach. I've only heard rumors. But I know it's wrong. I know they've been run out of town because of the danger they pose to the society around them."

"You've never met them, Mama. They're kind, wonderful people. They love the Lord just as much as we do."

"They've written their own Bible."

"Nathan knows the Bible just as well as I do."

"What has he done to you?"

"Nothing. I'm the same girl I was this morning."

The fear in Mama's face made it clear she meant something far deeper than any physical liberties, and her eyes searched mine, trying to retrieve something long lost.

CHAPTER 8

After sitting in front of a warmed-over supper without touching a bite, I was banished from the table. Papa declared that the mere sight of me made him angy and ordered me to leave. Not only was I to remain in the house, I wasn't even to leave my room.

"Arlen, be a little softer with her," Mama chastised. "There's nothing here that warrants such a harsh tone."

In truth, though, I was glad to escape. I felt safer the moment my head poked up through my little square door. I'd brought a lantern with me, and I relished the cozy glow of its light, ready to be alone to relive this day.

If I thought my escape from our kitchen table would spare

me the severity of a lecture from my father, I was mistaken. His accusations seeped through my floor, though I couldn't catch every word.

"Stupid, stupid girl—"

"Now, Arlen—"

"When I think of what could have happened. Those people—"

—were kind and generous. They welcomed me in without question. I tried to imagine Nathan calling me a stupid girl. But I'd only ever heard him tell me I was beautiful. An answer to prayer. But really, I was nothing more than a girl banished to her room for being disobedient. If Nathan could see me now, he'd be embarrassed that he'd ever considered me anything more than some silly schoolgirl he met on a path.

Whatever romantic ideas I had about running away with him—no matter how briefly I'd entertained them—vanished. Silly fantasies, both on my part and on his. In fact, he was probably sitting next to a dying fire right this very minute, wishing he could take all of his declarations back.

And I would help him do that.

I tiptoed across the floor to my bureau and fetched my journal and a pencil to my bed. Turning to the back, I found a blank page. After a few thoughtful licks on the tip of my pencil, I pressed it firmly to the page and wrote.

Dear Nathan,

"Godless! Blasphemous, whoring parasites . . ."

Then, again, something gentle from my mother, but Papa would not be soothed. I'd seen him angry before—I'd provoked such anger before—but this was the voice of a man I didn't recognize.

"I'll hunt her down if she steps another foot out of this house."

"She won't."

"Not until we see the last of them—"

"Soon, darling. You said so yourself."

I could not bring myself to write the words I needed to say with such hateful interruptions. Willing to incur further wrath, I gathered my journal and pencil and crossed over to the window.

"This room was made for escape," Nathan had said, and though I had no intentions of running away, I did welcome the chance for a respite from the rousing argument below.

I closed the lamp for my run across the yard, lest one of my parents choose this moment to glance out the window. I myself did not look back because their shouts reassured me I had done nothing to garner their attention. I ran until I reached the rock wall at the edge of our property. Crouching down on the other side, I opened the lamp as much as I deemed safe and turned again to my letter.

Dear Nathan,

You will never understand how much you changed my life.

I looked up to the stars in disgust. My handwriting was laborious; the words, childish and dismissive. He would be nothing more than a sweet memory someday. The boy against whom all future boys would be measured. I poised my pencil, wondering if I wanted him to have that much power over me—now or ever.

Before I could continue on, I heard an explosive shout coming from the house. Quickly closing the lantern, I ventured a peek over the wall, only to see my father burst through the front door, leaving a triangle of light and my pleading mother in his wake.

"Tonight, I tell you!"

"Arlen, it's the middle of the night."

"We've let it go on too long already. They've got the whole town fooled. Well, I'm going to make sure our people know just how vile and predatory they are!"

He stormed into our barn and emerged minutes later astride our riding horse. My heart caught in my throat when I realized he reined the horse with one hand and carried his rifle high in the other.

"You're going to get yourself killed!"

Whatever Papa replied was lost in the thundering of hooves as he drove the horse across our front yard and through the gate. I tucked myself in, not wanting to know how close I came to being kicked to death. I stayed still and small until I knew he'd reached the place where the path to our property crossed the path into town. Mother had gone back inside, and I knew it was just a matter of seconds before she would discover I had disappeared. And given my father's temper, not much longer before he would be storming into the Mormon camp.

I had to choose: save myself, or save Nathan. No choice at all, really. I faced the possibility of my parents' wrath, but he might well be the victim of my father's murderous intent. I remembered how Jesus said in the Bible that thinking about a sin is the same as doing it in your heart. Papa hated Nathan. He hated the Mormons. It was only a matter of time.

I opened the lantern the tiniest wedge, just enough to give me a sliver of light until I reached the trees bordering our property. This was where he'd taken my hand to lead me through the forest. Feeling safe, I allowed myself the fullest measure of light, and I ran, trusting my feet to remember the path, because my mind had no recollection. The darkness meant nothing; the noises called up no fear. One step after another, my boots pounding the needles and leaves underneath, the light bouncing furiously through the trees, I ran. *Lord, guide me. Lord, guide me.* My silent prayer in rhythm with my steps, I ran. Finally I burst upon the clearing.

And they were gone.

How could it be that, where only hours ago an entire community bustled with life here, now there was nothing but an expanse of hard-packed earth? If it weren't for the fire pits, now cold and dark, I might have thought my sense of direction was worse than I imagined. But no. There was the log where I sat and sipped soup, giggling with Rachel and Evangeline. There was the stump upon which the old man had led us in prayer. In my mind's eye, I saw every bit of it. Everything but Nathan.

"Camilla?"

I'd first heard him say my name only days before, but I would recognize his voice in my grave. It came to me now from the darkness, and I lifted my lantern high.

He walked into its glow—light coming into light. Fear and fatigue took its toll, and I felt my legs disappearing beneath me.

"Nathan?" It was a call for help, and I was in his arms just as I came to the point of collapse.

"You came. I can't believe it. Thank you, Heavenly Father—she came." He spoke into my hair, peppering me with kisses between words. My lantern had fallen to the ground, but still I clutched my journal, crushing it between our bodies as he held me.

Finally, once he became still, I stepped back and asked, "Where is everybody?"

"I went to Elder Thomas and told him about my conversation with your father, and he got a little uneasy. We gathered some men to pray and seek God's direction, and we decided it was no coincidence we were already so prepared to leave."

"So you—"

"Loaded up and crossed the river."

"Everybody? Everything?"

"Heavenly Father gave us long light and still water."

And he was here. My heart soared, like it does when God answers a prayer you hadn't thought to pray. "You stayed?"

He set his hands on my shoulders—clearly a gesture to curtail my joy. "Not for long. I said I'd wait for the last ferry out. I've been helping load and helping cross, coming back after every time to see if you were here. I hadn't dared hope. They're waiting for me right now, but I begged—let me check one more time. And when I saw you, saw your light . . ."

The more he spoke, the more my heart sank. He might be here now, but he wasn't staying. And when I thought about my father's anger, I figured that might be the best thing.

"I—I just came to warn you. All of you."

"I think I can handle your father, Camilla."

"But it's not just him. He was so angry, like I've never seen him before. And he rode off—to get some of the other men from town, I think. He had a gun, Nathan."

His hands still rested on my shoulders, his eyes lifted to heaven. "Heavenly Father, when will your kingdom come?"

"You need to go. Now. Before they get here."

"Come with me."

"You know I can't."

"I know you can do whatever your heart leads you to do. Otherwise you wouldn't be here."

"There's a difference between running through the woods and running away."

"Listen to your heart, Camilla. Desire and faith—they're all in that first step."

"Stop," I said, stepping away from his touch completely. "Stop asking me. It's not fair."

"I'm sorry." He looked hurt, which surprised me because I'd never hurt another person before. "I forget sometimes that not everybody feels things as strongly or deeply as I do."

"I feel—"

"You are the answer to my prayer, Camilla, whether you want to be or not. The Holy Spirit has said that to me so clearly. I have to obey what it tells me, and it told me to wait for you. To come back to you. I have to obey God; you have to obey your father."

The way he said it made my protest seem so trivial, but he hadn't witnessed the fullness of Papa's fury.

He bent down to pick up my lantern; when he stood, he took my hand. "Will you at least walk with me to the river? let me have as many minutes with you as I can?"

I could not refuse. I needed to see him take his final step away, to know that I'd never again stumble across a clearing in the woods and find him standing there. Without another word, we walked together to the water's edge. There was the ferry—a simple, flat structure. Hard to believe it had the ability to carry wagons and people and stock, but the faint flickering light on the other side of the river testified to its strength. It butted up against a makeshift dock, and four or five shadowed figures gathered there. A few shouted greetings to Nathan, lighthearted banter about Romeo's return.

"You have no idea the ribbing I'm going to get if you don't come with me. You're all I've been talking about for weeks now."

"Sometimes a sad story is more entertaining than a happy one, you know."

"I've had a lifetime of sad stories," he said. "I don't want another one."

The men had stepped off the ferry now; Nathan and I stood at the edge of the dock.

"I'm sorry," I said.

"Come with me."

"I can't."

And he kissed me, right there in front of everybody. In one ear I heard the men's stifled, self-conscious laughter. In the other, something quite different. Nathan heard it too. He pulled away, and we both looked upriver. Horses and riders—at least a dozen—guided by the light of burning torches.

I pushed Nathan's chest. "Go."

He shook his head. "I can't believe you would choose this."

"Those men have nothing to do with me."

"One of them is your *father*."

"Which is why you're in danger. Go, before they see me." I looked over my shoulder. "Or see you. Just go!"

"Listen to her," one of the men on the ferry said. They'd untied the line and stood, poles ready to begin their journey to the other shore. By now the riders were well in sight, so close that I could clearly make out my father as he rode at the front of the pack. When I heard him shout my name, I knew he could see me, too. Then a terrifying sound—the discharge of a gun. I screamed and started to fall, but Nathan caught me.

"It's all right," he said. "They're not close enough to hit us. Yet."

"I can't believe my father would shoot anybody."

"Hate is strong, Camilla. Promise me you won't let it take over your heart."

"I could never hate you, Nathan."

"I want to believe that."

I didn't realize it at the time, but we'd been inching our way down the dock throughout our conversation, and somehow we'd come to the place where a thin ribbon of river ran between us, as Nathan stood on the ferry.

"Camilla!"

My father's voice was closer now, but I dared not turn around. He shouted it over and over, joined by the angry shouts of his fellow townsmen. Another discharge of a gun, and again I jumped.

"I promise you," Nathan said, "your first unhappy day, I'll bring you back. But choose now."

It was one step—though it seemed so much greater. Like I was walking across his words as much as walking across water. I almost lost my balance, but once again he caught me, and I thought at that moment that I'd take any risk if it meant ending up in his arms.

"Praise the Lord," he said, drawing me close. Those piloting our ferry echoed his sentiment.

I turned around then and saw the riders had come to a halt yards away from the river's edge. I could have jumped off and waded to shore; Papa could have ridden his horse out to fetch me. Both of us stared at each other, waiting for repentance and rescue. Instead there was only the soft lapping water and the snorting of horses.

Nathan stood behind me, whispering into my ear, "I promise. Say the word, and I'll find the swiftest horse and bring you home."

Slowly, my father got smaller and smaller. I believed Nathan's promise, but God himself hadn't created a horse fast enough to bring me home. The home I knew had disappeared, lost behind my father's shouts, the moment my foot left the shore.

CHAPTER 9

Immediately upon landing on the other side of the Missouri River, I was taken in by the Moss family, and Evangeline instantly became my dearest friend and confidante.

"You don't mind, then, that Nathan loves me?" I asked her one night as we lay next to a dying campfire.

"Of course not," she said. I can still see the way the moonlight cast soft shadows on her face. "Who knows? Maybe someday he'll be married to both of us."

The first time she said it, I laughed loud enough to earn a chastising word from her mother, who slept in the wagon with the younger children.

"That's impossible." Though it was a warm night, I felt a chill run through my whole body.

"Not at all." Her voice was calm. "Lots of our men do. I think Joseph Smith had at least a dozen. But we're not supposed to talk about it."

"Then stop." I turned my face toward the fire and closed my eyes against the stinging smoke.

We never spoke of it again for the rest of our journey. Indeed, nobody did. Instead, there was so much for me to learn about my newfound family. I sat with the children for the evening catechism and learned the stories of the heroes from the *Book of Mormon*. Sometimes when Nathan was in camp, he would act them out, much to everyone's delight. In the shadows cast by the dancing flames, he transformed into a man called Abinadi, prophesying about the coming Christ and later dying in a fiery furnace. Or he would sweep us up in an imaginary battle as one of the two thousand sons of Helaman's army.

Later, when we would have a chance to walk alone under the stars, I'd ask him why I had never heard any of these stories.

"They've been hidden away," Nathan said. "They were written on golden plates and buried, waiting for the right time, the right man—the right prophet to bring them to the world."

"Joseph Smith?" I thought back to what Evangeline had told me about the man. "But how do you know it's all true?"

"It's faith, Camilla. Nothing more, nothing less."

He spoke with such a comforting authority. Not stern and austere like Papa, but with a commitment that seemed to well up from within. With it came an enthusiasm I'd never felt during the hours spent in our church pew or at home with our family Bible. Nathan brought the stories to life—even those more familiar to me, like Moses and Joseph. Soon they began to meld together for me, and I was hard-pressed to say which hero came from which text. All were equal gospel for these people, and they became so for me.

Nathan would be gone for days at a time during our journey west as he would ride ahead with some of the other men and scout the trail. Our company was one of the lucky ones, unmolested by Indians and only lightly touched by death. There were three babies born during the months of travel, though only one would survive to grow up in Zion. One little boy suffered a broken neck when he tumbled headfirst from a wagon. I stood next to the open grave of the young woman who succumbed to fever, and I joined in singing "Amazing Grace" for the elderly man whose heart stopped in the middle of the night. Through it all I remembered what Rachel had told me about Nathan being afraid to die alone on the trail and to enter eternity without a spouse to share it with, yet for weeks he did little more than court me, and I truly began to fear that I had been stolen away from my home by a lie.

"Don't be silly," Rachel said one evening when I aired my fears to her. "He cannot marry you until you've been baptized."

"But I've been baptized." Though the evidence of such—my certificate and lacy white gown—were tucked away in Mama's keepsake trunk at home.

"That doesn't count. You have to be baptized into their church. Our church."

And so I was baptized in the Platte River. Wearing a white homespun covering, I stood in the waters with Elder Thomas, also dressed in white, where I pledged to follow the teachings of Christ. Afterward I sat on a smooth, flat stone while several of the men stood round me, laying their hands on my head and declaring me a member of the church. I was supposed to keep my head bowed, but I did look up to catch a glimpse of Nathan, standing outside the circle, looking on with what can only be described as hunger. Whether it was hunger for me or for those privileged enough to declare me a Saint I couldn't tell.

Our party agreed to tarry in camp one extra day, and I awoke to find Rachel and Evangeline on either side of me, each holding a hand and saying, "Get up! For today you shall be a bride!"

My hair had been left free to dry after yesterday's baptism, and it had dried into soft waves. Secreted away in the Mosses' wagon, Rachel ran a brush through it, and rather than giving me my usual childish pigtails, she pulled it softly away from my face, securing it with a length of blue silk ribbon at the crown while allowing the rest to remain long and loose down the middle of my back. She held a mirror up so I could see the resulting image.

"What do you think?"

Despite the protection of a borrowed bonnet, my skin had grown quite tan after so many days walking beneath the sun. Still, the face looking at me from the glass was cleaner than it had been in weeks. It was thinner, too, bringing new height to my cheekbones and a sharpness to my chin.

"I wish I were prettier."

"Nathan thinks you're beautiful."

"What do you think?"

Her face appeared over my shoulder within the mirror's frame, and any aspirations I had of beauty disappeared.

"I think you aren't nearly as lovely as you're going to be someday."

"Yoo-hoo!" Evangeline's distinctive voice preceded the poking of her head through the wagon's canvas. She gave me an approving smile and looked to Rachel. "Have you shown her yet?"

"I thought I'd let you have the honor."

At Evangeline's command we scooted closer to the front of the wagon and let her in. She lifted the lid of the wooden trunk that had been serving as my seat as Rachel fixed my hair. After some rummaging, she brought forth a blue calico dress covered with a lawn of bright purple poppies.

"It's borrowed."

"And the ribbon is blue," Rachel added.

"And this is from Sister Ellen." Evangeline handed me a small blue case, like a miniature steamer trunk, with a tiny brass latch at the top. I opened the latch and discovered that, rather than a little box, it was a Bible, its pages locked within the clasp. "It's old."

"It's beautiful," I said, running my finger along its velvet top.

"Something new will be a little more difficult," Rachel said.

"She's newly baptized," Evangeline said with triumph.

Rachel looked at me and cocked her head. "So be it."

Before my own, I'd been to only three weddings in my life. All of them took place in the home of the bride, where tables laden with the bridal feast held much more appeal for me than any spoken vows. They'd been stuffy, curious affairs—too many people packed into too small a room. The women cried, the men shifted from foot to foot, and the children stayed restless until the time came to cut the cake.

I remember, after the wedding of my cousin Ila, riding home with my parents, and the only thing Mama said for the entire drive was "Oh, that poor, poor boy."

Whatever sadness I felt at the idea of my parents' not being with me on my wedding day disappeared the moment I stepped down from the Mosses' wagon. To my surprise, the entirety of our company stood, making an aisle. It was like walking a winding path through a forest of family—a blur of smiling faces and hands reaching out to bless me as I walked by. They whispered, over and over, "God bless you, Sister Camilla," and "May God bless your family." Finally I came to Nathan, standing on the riverbank, right where I'd been baptized the day before. Morning still blew cool across the water; sunlight touched his hair. More than any other ceremony I'd ever attended, God seemed an invited guest to the union of two lives. He stood as a witness in the clouds; his creation, our altar.

Once I took my place next to Nathan, the assembly redistributed themselves, sealing off the path I'd taken to form a looser gathering around us. Later that night, Nathan and I would find a more secluded spot along the river's edge where I would become his wife in every sense of the word. I would lay my head on his shoulder and tease him for tricking me.

"What choice did I have?" I said. "It was either burst through that mob or swim across the river."

He would hold me close, thrilling me with the feeling of laughter rumbling through his chest.

"God works as he will, my love. There's no escaping his plan."

CHAPTER 10

Cottonwood Canyon, Utah Territory
Fall 1856

The oxen were yoked eight to a team. Their hooves plodded along the dusty road.

"Can I touch it, Mama? Can I touch the stone?"

"We both will," I said. "And say a prayer."

Abandoning our wash basket beside the creek, we took each other's hands and made our way through the tall October grass to the roadside, where we stood an arm's length from the great lumbering beasts. So slowly did they move, we could easily reach out to touch the enormous limestone slab tied to the oxen's cart and stroll along beside.

"Heavenly Father," my daughter prayed with the sweet sincerity of her five years, "please keep the oxen safe as they bring the stone to build thy temple. And all the workers, too. And bring Papa home. Amen."

I echoed her prayer silently, and we took hands again to watch the entire train of beast and stone.

"Do you think they'll finish the temple by the time I'm grown-up?"

"I don't know, Melissa. Brigham Young has such a plan, I don't know that it'll be finished by the time *I'm* grown-up."

She rewarded me with her bubbling laughter. "Silly, Mama. You're already old. You're twenty-one! And you're going to have another baby."

I sighed. "I suppose you're right." Bending down as much as my expanding belly would allow, I touched the rim of my bonnet to hers, creating something of a dark tunnel between our faces. "Am I wrinkly yet?"

"Just a little, but I think you're pretty."

I hugged her to me and pushed the bonnet off, dropping a kiss on top of her warm blonde head. "I think you're pretty too. You look just like your father."

She looked up, squinting in the sunlight. "Papa's not pretty!"

"I think he is."

The last of the laborious turning wheels passed, and I looked up to see a familiar figure high on the road where the teams disappeared at the top of a gently cresting hill.

"It's Papa!" Melissa tore out of my arms and began to run toward him.

"Wait," I called her back. "Take the wash basket to the house. We'll be there shortly."

"But—"

"No arguments. Go."

She pouted, but she obeyed, and when she was safely on her way home, I took my first steps. Walking at first, then running, though it was a heavy, clumsy, waddling run, making me feel every bit as lithe as the oxen hauling the stone.

He jumped down from the wagon's seat and, abandoning the rig, came toward me. Long before he was visible in detail, my heart leaped just as it had the first time I saw him. And as he got closer, the worn blue shirt, the patched buckskin jacket, the familiar smile shining beneath the shadow of his hat's brim, I felt every bit the young girl again. I counted the steps until I was in his arms, and though we were a good distance from our cozy little cabin, I felt at home the minute he wrapped them around me.

Neither of us spoke. Instead, he reached under my chin and untied my bonnet, tossing it to the ground before swooping me closer for a deep, warm, welcoming kiss.

"You're home a day early," I said once I could bring myself to release him.

"Had I known I'd get such a warm welcome, I'd have been here yesterday." He gave me another quick peck and turned his attention to my rounding belly. "And how's our boy?"

"Growing, as am I. If we're not careful, they're going to mistake me for an ox and yoke me up to one of those wagons."

"Well," he said, looking deadly serious, "we all must do our part in the service of Heavenly Father. It seems only fair that if I cut the stones, you should haul them."

"I didn't marry a stonecutter. I married an artist."

"Carpenter, not artist."

"And what did they say this time?"

I knew it wasn't good news, as he smiled straight ahead. "I don't think they were nearly as impressed with my artistry as you are."

"Oh, darling." I resisted the urge to peek back into the wagon, but I knew what was there. For the past two years, since Brigham Young's call for the Saints to bring their offerings to the temple, Nathan had set about on a quest for longevity in worship.

"This temple will be built by the hands of the Saints who worship the Christ of the latter days," the prophet had said during a rousing assembly at our little chapel. "You will tithe your time and your talent, blessing Heavenly Father with both."

We'd sat awestruck as he related his vision, and on that day Nathan dedicated himself to designing the very chairs for the most exalted of the worshipers—the elders, bishops, and apostles.

"But I'll try again," he said with his particular jovial resilience. "I want to leave a legacy."

"You do that with every stone."

"So does every other man. I may have limited talent, but I have limitless time."

"And I have a new chair for the table?"

"I don't know about that. If it's not good enough for an apostle of the church, what makes you think it's good enough for you?"

I tried to think of a clever reply, but I was never as quick as Nathan was, so I gave him a playful slap on his arm, followed by a quick kiss where I'd landed the blow.

He feigned injury and rubbed his arm. "Just for that I'm not giving you a ride home."

"I'd rather walk anyway. It's getting harder and harder to

climb up in that seat, and all that bouncing can't be good for the baby."

"Might make him come a little sooner."

"Sooner's never better with babies."

The horses stood silently beside him and, at the slightest click of his tongue, fell in step behind us.

"So how are things in town?" I asked, ever hungry to hear news.

"Busy, as usual. You wouldn't believe. Another new mercantile. And two restaurants. Plus one little shop set up just for buying cookware."

"I'll be in a little better shape for traveling next time."

"And we'll have a new baby boy to bring in for a blessing."

"You're so sure it's a boy?"

He brought our joined hands to his lips. "God has given me everything else I've ever asked for. What's left?"

"And did you go to the post office? Was there mail?"

Nathan stopped, and I did too. Silently, he reached into the worn leather satchel strapped across his shoulder and brought out a small bundle of envelopes.

"Three."

As always, I allowed myself the briefest moment of hope when I took the letters—each addressed to me in my mother's careful hand. With shaking fingers, I drew out the string to untie the knot that held them together.

"Camilla, don't. Wait until we get home."

But I would not be stopped. When the knot proved unyielding, I simply wrenched the letters free. Heedless of the date of posting, I tore open the first to find within it only another envelope, addressed by me, sent to Mr. and Mrs. Arlen Deardon, Kanesville, Iowa.

"Not even opened."

"Darling, I'm so sorry."

"This one," I said, holding up the first, "has locks of the girls' hair in it. I was trying to explain how their hair—Melissa's, especially—is the color of spring butter. And this one—" I held up another—"Lottie wrote her own name at the bottom. More of a scribble, but she was so proud. And I posted this one after I knew we were going to have another. . . ."

I broke into tears, and Nathan's strong arm caught me at my elbow, holding me up against him.

"I don't know why you put yourself through this time after time."

"They're never going to forgive me."

"You've done nothing for them to forgive. You followed God's prompting. And look how he's blessed you. A home, two beautiful daughters. A loving husband and a son on the way."

Once again he'd managed to reverse my tears, and as he named all the details of my life, I had to realize that my days of joy had rarely been tempered with moments of regret. Even the grief of this moment dissolved into something more akin to disappointment.

"I just wish they knew all of that. I think they—at least Mama—would want to know about our life. My life, at least."

"If nothing else, they know that you're alive and well. Otherwise, you wouldn't be sending letters at all. I'm sure your mother takes comfort in that."

"We have been blessed, haven't we?"

"More and more each day." He swept a stray hair behind my ear and kissed me once more before putting his arm around my shoulders and guiding me home. For the rest of our walk he filled me in on the rest of the news from town. The temple, he said, would someday be the miracle of the western frontier, no less because of the dedication of the men who built it. "Can you imagine what the world would be if every man gave one in ten days' labor to the Lord?"

"You give more than that. Between the quarry and the workshop. What if God called you to choose?"

He thought for a moment. "As much as I like following in the steps of Jesus in my workshop, there's nothing I like better than being in that quarry. Chipping that granite out of God's creation, knowing it will be a new creation built unto him."

"But you'll stay home for a few days now? You have some creations of your own that need you."

"How soon, do you think?" He looked down at the swelling of our child.

"Oh, a few weeks yet. But I was referring to a fence that needs mending and a filthy chicken coop."

"And the garden?"

"We'll have more than enough to put up for the winter. Oh! Did you get a chance to see Rachel and Tillman? How are the boys?"

There was just enough hesitancy in his step to catch my attention, and though we did not stop walking altogether, he brought a slowness to our pace that had me nearly dragging my feet.

"Is everything all right?" I looked up to see his face set stoically forward.

"Yep," he said, jaw clenched tight.

"What's wrong?"

"Nothing." He wouldn't look at me.

"Nathan." I clutched his sleeve and brought him to a halt. "Tell me."

"Tillman's taken another wife."

The news hit me like a stone to the small of my back, and I held tighter to the worn blue cotton of my husband's shirt.

"Another? That's—"

"Four. I know."

"What does Rachel think about this?"

"Exactly what any saintly wife would think. That we are all to follow the will of Heavenly Father as he reveals it to the prophet."

Of course this wasn't the first time I'd heard of such things. Two of the families who'd traveled with us from Iowa were made up of one husband with two wives and sets of children. And I'll never forget meeting Rachel's Tillman the day we arrived dirty, weak, and exhausted, only to be introduced to the woman who would become Rachel's sister wife.

"Poor Rachel," I muttered, not realizing I'd spoken out loud.

"Don't pity her." His voice held the taint of envy that came whenever he spoke of a highly regarded Saint. "She's the first wife of a prominent family. Tillman owns half of the Eighteenth Ward. She'll never want for anything on this earth, and just think of the glory she'll have in eternity."

"But she'll never have what I do."

"What's that?"

"A simple life. Long nights with her husband. Long talks. Secrets."

"She has all that." He sounded unconvinced.

"But she has to share. And I don't think I ever could."

He remained silent one breath too long.

"Could you, Nathan?"

"The Lord led me to you, Camilla. I obeyed his will. That I will always do."

He began walking again, leaving me no choice but to follow. We were silent now, our steps in sync, but I feared our private thoughts were miles apart. The moment our little home came into view, we both quickened our pace. Nathan cupped his hands around his mouth and hollered, "Helloooooo!"

Our distant front door opened and our daughters poured out of it. Long hair flying loose about their faces, they tore through the gate of our fenced-in yard and ran, their little arms and legs pumping, until they were close enough to leave the ground altogether and leap into their father's embrace.

"What is heaven doing without its two prettiest angels?" He swung them in a wide arc before setting them, giggling, on four wobbly feet.

"Presents! Presents!" Lottie had been able to speak of nothing else since he left.

"Now, Lottie," I said, gently chastising, "your papa's safe return is present enough."

Her lip pouted out the way only a three-year-old's can, and she stomped her little foot.

"Maybe," Nathan said, "just maybe after I've had a chance to sit down and eat some supper, I can go through some of these boxes and see if I don't have a few presents for each of you."

"For Mama, too?" Lottie asked.

"For Mama and Melissa—" he touched the older girl's nose—"and even for our new baby brother."

"Or sister," Melissa chimed in.

"Or sister," he conceded with a gentleness unlike anything I'd ever heard from my own father.

When Nathan peeled off to settle the team in the barn, the girls and I went into the house to see what we could scare up for an unexpected supper. Inside, Kimana was already busy at the stove, laying slices of bacon to fry. She turned around long enough to grace me with one of her rare smiles.

"Mr. Fox home?"

Kimana had been a member of our family since her own

had been largely destroyed in a cattle dispute before Lottie was born. Severely wounded by a gunshot in her thigh, she'd been too weak to travel with her people and too proud to be a burden to them. It was Nathan who had found her, still as death in the middle of a scorched field. And it was he who brought her to our home, himself covered with her blood, determined to make restitution for the violence done to her people.

"Yes, he's home. A little earlier than we expected. What a nice surprise. Of course, I wish I'd known. We could have put on a stew with some of the lovely things we pulled from the garden. But bacon's fine. And maybe eggs?"

I prattled on, nervous, wishing I'd had a chance to get the house in order. The kitchen was still cluttered with pickling jars, and I hadn't bothered to sweep the floor since Nathan left.

"Mrs. Fox." Kimana's calm voice interrupted my monologue. Her smooth brown face ever placid, she shook her head and clicked her tongue. "Be happy he has come home. And make him happy too."

"Of course; that's what matters."

Still, I enlisted the girls' help, giving Melissa full charge of the broom while Lottie straightened the jars into neat rows along the back of the long kitchen shelf. Leaving Kimana to fix a light supper, I went into the yard behind the house to hang up the afternoon's washing.

After a time, I heard the sound of water being pumped in the front yard and, having hung the last of the girls' stockings to dry, poked my head around the corner to see Nathan standing at the bucket. He'd stripped off his worn blue shirt and plunged it now in the water, using it as a washcloth to cleanse himself of the dust from the road. I watched, marveling at the beauty of him much as I did that first night on the shores of the Platte River, even though the child now moving within me bore testament to the maturity of our love. The teaching of the prophet rang in my ear, telling me I should be ashamed, seeing my husband bare-chested, without the covering of his sacred undershirt. But I squelched it, choosing instead to revel in the beauty of this man God had given me.

True to his word, once we cleared and washed the supper dishes, Nathan gathered us around the table to dispense the gifts brought from this latest visit into Salt Lake City.

"Really, my dear husband, you're going to spoil us if you insist on bringing back gifts with each visit."

"And what could be the harm in a little spoiling?"

I admit, I was sometimes as foolish as the girls, my mind racing with the possibility of what might be hiding inside the boxes and bundles he'd brought down from the wagon. Nathan always had the ability to make me feel like a woman and a little girl at once—loved and desired and indulged.

As we settled into our seats, Kimana wished us good night and was headed out to her one-room cabin behind our house.

"Just wait one minute," Nathan said, lifting a package wrapped in plain brown paper. "I have something for you, too."

Kimana's eyes shone like jet beads, and she stood before Nathan, her hands softly clasped in front of her.

"Open it."

She took the package and carefully, unused to such an activity, unfolded the paper. Lottie jumped up and down at her elbow, urging, "Faster! Faster!"

Finally my little girl snatched the loosened paper from the old Indian woman's hands. The puzzled look on Kimana's face captured all of our attention, and I stood to look over her shoulder and see what she'd been given.

It was a small oval frame, not much bigger than the palm of my hand, and inside it, a very familiar image.

"It's Joseph Smith," Nathan said proudly. "He is our leader. Our founder. Our 'chief,' if you will. And I thought you might like to have a picture of him to hang in your room."

Kimana stood, unblinking, her eyes transfixed on the small portrait. Melissa and Lottie were highly disappointed and returned to their seats to kick impatiently at the chair legs. Nathan beamed, but I felt my own face burning with the uncertainty of how such a gift would be received.

Finally Kimana said, "Thank you, Mr. Fox." Her words often lacked inflection, and I couldn't tell now if she was truly grateful for such a token or if her reaction fell somewhere between amusement and offense. She held it carefully away from her as if it might bite or break and, wishing us good night, walked out into the quiet darkness.

"Did you get us something better, Papa?" Lottie asked. Her hair glowed gold in the lamplight, and her eyes shone wide, fearing a portrait of the prophet might be in her future too.

"Mama's next," Nathan said, handing me a long, canvas-wrapped bundle. "And be careful with that. It's fragile."

I set the bundle on the table and carefully unrolled its wrapping.

"Oh, Nathan," I said when the contents were revealed. It was a lamp, the base of which was frosted blue. Young girls danced all around it, connected by a flowing white ribbon. "It's beautiful."

Melissa held out a cautious finger to touch.

"Your aunt Rachel made that," Nathan said. "She painted the design, anyway."

I could picture her, sitting at the little table by the window in her new ladies' parlor, the room she'd begged Tillman to add to the house last summer.

"I'll have to write a note to thank her." I looked around

our sparse room. There was the table at which we sat and two other chairs by the fireplace. We had a cookstove and a wide kitchen shelf. "I don't know where I'll display such a fine piece. The mantel is really too narrow." Then, worried Nathan might think I lacked contentment, I said, "Perhaps in our room. On the little table next to the bed. Wouldn't that be perfect?"

"Who would have thought we'd someday have trouble finding a place for our possessions. After all—"

"When she hopped on the ferry, she had nothing more than an old notebook and a piece of silk ribbon." Melissa's voice held none of the warm nostalgia usually given that story. "Now us, please?"

"Oh, I don't know." Nathan let out an enormous yawn, stretching so that the shadows of his arms reached from one wall to the next. "I'm pretty worn-out from the ride home. Maybe yours can wait until tomorrow?"

"Don't be cruel," I said, raising my voice above the understandable protest.

He made quite a show of digging into his knapsack and brought out two oblong boxes, each tied with a bright pink ribbon. He held one to his ear, seeming to listen, before declaring it belonged to Melissa, and the other to Lottie. On a count of three, both girls tore into the packages—with me helping Lottie untie the bow.

"Oh, Papa!" Their twin exclamations filled the room as each little girl lifted a brand-new doll from its newspaper nest. The dolls had sweet, painted porcelain faces and hands, with rich, curling hair cascading to their calico shoulders.

"Mine has yellow hair, like me!" Lottie cried.

"Mine looks like Mama," Melissa said thoughtfully.

"I thought it only fair that you girls should get your own new baby, since Mama is getting hers," Nathan said.

Within minutes the dolls were given names after the girls' favorite flowers—Lilly for Lottie's, Rose for Melissa's. After a quick face-washing and prayer, my daughters were snuggled in, clutching their babies and drifting off to sleep before I even snuffed the candle. In our room, Nathan was already underneath the covers, arms behind his head, dozing. I took off my apron and sat on the edge of our bed, ready to begin the struggle of taking off my shoes. My gyrations shook the frame, bringing a sleepy comment from my husband.

"I think I'll just need to stay barefoot until the baby comes," I whispered. He responded with a sleepy nod.

By the time I had my hair down and brushed and braided and my warm cotton gown stretched over me, he was snoring outright. When I climbed in beside him, one arm instinctively curled around me, and I settled my head against his heart, soothed by its rhythm. This was the time of night the baby always sprang to life, and I felt him—or her—roiling within me. Nathan must have felt it too because he cuddled me a little closer and brought his hand to rest on my shifting stomach.

It was one of those moments when I felt perfectly content and safe. I imagined God looking down on our little family, and I hoped we pleased him with our love and devotion. Surely he could ask no more of a man than to love his wife and care for his children. I chased away thoughts of Rachel, alone in her own bed somewhere, her husband in another room, with another woman.

My breath in sync with Nathan's, just as our steps had been as we walked home, I placed my hand on his, and together we touched the child within. Soon I drifted off, praying, my heart full of so much gratitude, it had no room for fear.

CHAPTER 11

The birth pains started the first morning I awoke to a hard frost on the ground. I stayed in bed almost until sunrise, waiting for one and another pain to pass. I had a vague recollection of Nathan kissing my cheek before going out to milk the two cows and draw up the wash water—both chores that fell to me whenever he left our little farm to cut temple stone out of the quarry. I must have gotten a full extra hour's sleep, and by the tightening pain I felt across my back, I would need it. With God's will and protection, our newest child would be born before nightfall.

Kimana gave me a knowing look the moment I walked into the kitchen, attempting to tie my apron strings.

"It comes today?"

I nodded.

"I take the children to Mrs. Ellen."

Brother Thomas and Sister Ellen, besides taking us under their wings as we journeyed here, were our nearest neighbors. Our little town was one sprung up from necessity, serving to meet the needs of those who worked in the temple quarry. Therefore, it lacked the precise, gridlike organization of other settlements. Each day I had only the distant puffs of chimney smoke to bear witness that I had neighbors at all. And yet, in times of need, they seemed only steps away.

"After breakfast," I said, scooping flour for biscuits. "We don't want to be an imposition, and there's hours yet before the baby comes. I'll have Nathan drop them off on his way to get Sister Maude."

Kimana made a dismissive sound and gently nudged me away from the mixing bowl.

"If it were up to me, I would have you as my midwife, but Nathan is very particular about these things. The church is, I mean. You understand?"

"I understand. I thought things might change now that I have a picture of your leader."

So rare was it for Kimana to make a joke that I had to stop and consider if she had made one now. If the flatness of her delivery gave no clue, the twinkle in her eye did, and I knew I'd been forgiven.

"Maybe," I said, breathing deep, "instead of taking the girls to Sister Ellen's, they could just spend the day with you. You could help them make some new clothes for their dolls."

Her smile rewarded my idea, as did the delighted agreement of Lottie and Melissa.

I spent the morning moving about the house, sitting for a

spell, then standing in the open doorway, taking great gulps of crisp fall air. The sky had that special lavender hue I'd never seen anywhere but here in the Utah Territory, and I looked to God beyond the distant mountains.

"Keep me safe, O Lord," I prayed, "and deliver this child."

By noon I'd taken myself to bed, sitting up to take sips of the fragrant tea Kimana brought in a steaming mug.

"He's doing well," she said, her brown hand rough against the quilt stretched over me.

"He?" I handed the mug back in preparation for an oncoming pain.

"I am certain."

Just then the front door opened, and soon after, Nathan ushered in Sister Maude. The woman had served as midwife for both of the girls, and I felt as comfortable with her in the room as I would have with my own mother. Maybe more. Over the years, her hair had so melded together blonde with gray, I could scarcely tell which was which, and it always seemed like she had pinned it up on her way out the door. Now she bustled into the room, rolling up her sleeves, barely giving Kimana a brief, dismissive look.

"And how are we feeling?" Her voice was like honey.

"Tired," I said truthfully.

"Time for that later, missy." Sister Maude sat in the chair at the bedside and took my hand between her soft ones. "Be sure you have plenty of water on to boil and clean towels ready." I assumed she was speaking with Kimana, though she never turned her head. Kimana came to the same conclusion, as she silently backed out of the door. "Now, Brother Nathan, come lead us in a prayer."

The three of us joined hands, but whatever words Nathan prayed aloud were lost to me as my body was seized with another birthing pang. I tightened my grip to the point where the slickness of the sweat from my hands threatened to disjoin us all, while I waited for it to either pass or be lessened in the wake of my husband's words. Neither happened. Instead, his voice grew stronger and louder, gaining power through my pain.

I remember thinking, *Will he never say amen? Can he not reach out to his God without holding on to me?*

In the end it was Sister Maude who, at the next hesitancy of phrasing, offered up a conclusion and released herself from my grasp.

"Now, Brother Nathan, if you'll busy yourself elsewhere, I'll send for you when the babe is arrived."

He knelt beside me for just a moment, and the pain subsided. By the time he kissed my brow and told me he loved me, I was quite at rest again, strengthened by his goodness and faith.

It was, after that, an easy birth. Some women will tell you there's no such thing, and maybe that's because we like to claim those hours as our particular brand of heroism, but I recall very little pain after that shared moment. I like to think that God knew how precious little time I would have with the life being born through me and didn't want me to spend any part of it engaged in battle. His ways and reasons are lost to me. All I know is that shortly after nightfall I was holding a precious, perfect baby boy in my arms.

By that time the room was lit with the lamp Rachel had painted for me, and I counted it responsible for the distinctive blue tinge to my son's tiny, wrinkled body. But the lamp's light could not account for his shallow, catching breath, and by the time Nathan was at my side again, I'd dedicated my life to memorizing his tiny, startled face.

"Send Kimana for Elder Justus," I said, stroking the baby's warm, soft head. "I think we'll need the blessing soon."

For two days Kimana and the girls worked tirelessly, preparing our home as they would for a celebration. Every inch from floor to ceiling was scrubbed clean; the aroma of baking breads and pastries filled the spaces in between. Word was sent to all of our neighbors, with someone sent into town to fetch Rachel and her family. I, in the meantime, was restricted to equal time resting in bed or sitting in the rocking chair Nathan had made in the months before Melissa was born, holding the tiny, struggling form of our son and praying, "Lord, give him strength for one more breath." Moment by moment my prayers were answered, and I thought I could spend the rest of our lives just like this, holding him until he was a man full grown.

To spare him the effort of crying, I held him to my breast every hour, through the day and night, praying my milk would fill in whatever it was his body lacked, and during those moments, his bright, button-blue eyes looked up into mine with a gratitude that fueled me.

Nathan was by my side when he could be, holding the baby when I permitted myself scattered minutes of sleep. I heard him in the darkness, whispering, just as he had to our daughters during their first days of life. "When you were still a spirit up in heaven, I was a little boy . . ." And he went on to tell all that he could remember of his childhood. Nothing about his parents, as his earliest memories were those of living in the St. Benedict Home for Abandoned Children, but about his very life in that orphanage. Boys he played with, hours spent learning the craft of carpentry, his fierce protection of his sister.

In the past, I'd often pretend to be asleep so he could tell his stories without the usual guard he put up whenever he had occasion to share a memory with me, but this time I found myself startled into wakefulness.

When you were still a spirit up in heaven . . .

The first time I'd heard Elder Thomas speak about a preterrestrial life—the idea that all humans live as spirit children born to Heavenly Father before being reborn into this earthly life—I found it to be a rather sweet, comforting idea. Imagine, all the while I was preparing to be this child's mother, all those years living as a child myself, this little baby was a mature, healthy spiritual being.

Oh, I'd heard Nathan tell the story over and over. But I listened to it now with new ears, and only half of it rang true. Yes, Nathan had lived before now—he'd been a little boy, a young man, my husband. But he and I made this child, through the miracle of God's design. I listened, waiting to hear some word about the role I played in the child's creation, wanting to share some part of the spiritual lore, but heard nothing. Instead, I heard empty words whispered by a father about to lose the very son he'd longed for, words that held more wonder at the life the child had already lived than sadness at the one he never would.

As that tiny spirit fought for every living breath, something inside of me began a slow, sour churning. I closed my eyes and listened to my husband's secrets and my son's struggle, but both were eventually drowned out by a smaller voice within me repeating a single refrain.

It isn't true.

It was the first time since my foot stepped onto the ferry that any part of me questioned the teachings of Joseph Smith. Perhaps my blinding love for Nathan or yearning to be a part of this exciting, fervent spiritual family had kept me from ever questioning what I'd been told. I'd faced famine and locusts and storms and drought and death with these people, supposing their unshakable faith to be a testament to their doctrine. Not until now did I see a chink in the armor of Joseph Smith's revelations.

Of course I knew that God himself had chosen to take on human flesh when he came to earth as a helpless baby. But that was a miracle. That was Jesus, God's one Son, his only Son. And he came for a purpose—to grow and live and die. But what "spirit child," what glorified spirit being, would come to be born in the frail, ever-weakening shell that was my son? Who, outside of a Savior, would choose to be born, only to die? Because I knew, from the first minutes of his life, that my son was going to die. Not in the same vein that we all will—someday, in the full timing of God—but *that* day or the next. I knew his life would be measured in days, in hours. And only a creature made from the equally frail coupling of two human vessels could come to be so mortally doomed.

How strange to think about such things in those shadows where I counted each shallow breath, measured each spoken word. It was, for me, my comfort. Every woman who loses a child wonders at the wisdom of God. The purpose for ever touching such unbearable pain. But for just a moment, I no longer despised my own heartbeat, and the wonder of God's grace shone clear. The entire purpose for my son's existence—within the womb and without—was to bring me to this tiny moment of doubt.

He would be known in the church record as Arlen Nathan Fox, named for my father. No promises were made to dedicate him to the teachings of Jesus Christ; no requests were made for a life of good health, no prayers for his future wife and children. Just our little family gathered by the warmth of the stove, and Elder Justus, a towering, bearded presence, holding the bundled form of our baby as Nathan's hand trembled on his shoulder.

"Heavenly Father," the elder's voice boomed, "we give this child over to you." Soon after, he placed little Arlen in my arms, and as our front room filled with whispered prayers, my son fought for his final breath before passing into his first peaceful sleep.

I must have cried out, though I don't remember making any noise, and I clearly remember not wanting any intrusion on this final moment. I simply sat, trusting the chair to hold me upright as I knew my own body never could, until little Lottie was standing at my elbow, reaching one soft, chubby finger to move the blanket aside from her baby brother's face.

"Has he gone back to heaven, Mama?"

I couldn't answer. *Father God, forgive me for the lies I've taught this child.* I felt the eyes of Elder Justus boring into me, and I knew if I didn't say something, he would. Clutching the still form of little Arlen to me, I simply said, "Yes, Lottie. He is in heaven now. With Jesus."

It was truth as I knew it, sufficient for now. Lottie nodded sagely and withdrew her hand.

By noon a funeral wreath hung on our front door, and all those people whom we'd invited to the blessing of our child came instead to minister to us in our grief. Our little table, laden with food, fed them through the day, but I ate none of it. I tried to be gracious at first, accepting the warm embraces of my sister Saints and the brothers' attempts at spiritual comfort, but each word of condolence only tightened the wrench of my grief. I could never, ever explain that the solid rock of pain and confusion occupying my head had very little to do with the death of little Arlen, for I knew he was resting in the arms of Jesus. No, my trepidation grew as I listened to them speak, constant murmurings punctuated with words of Heavenly Father, of the prophets and Brother Joseph. All of it tainted with a falsehood I'd never heard before. I felt I'd been reborn with the birth of my son—my ears and eyes as new as his own. When I finally claimed the right of a grieving mother and slipped away, back to the room where I'd borne my child, I curled up on my bed and wept. My tears fell freely for the loss of my son, but the words I spoke aloud repented what I'd lost with my Lord.

"Father God," I spoke into my pillow lest anyone hear me, "forgive me. I abandoned you, tossed away your truths. I see now what my father warned me about, and I ask your forgiveness for my disobedience. Lord, help me—"

The knock at the door was soft but insistent, and I found myself powerless to rise up against it.

"Camilla?"

That unmistakable voice pulled me from my depths, and I sat straight up.

"Evangeline!"

Seconds later my dear friend was in my arms, or I was in hers. Her hair was loose around her shoulders and I buried my face in that scratchy sea of red curls and sobbed as I hadn't yet.

"There, there, sister . . ." When she whispered, the normally hard edge of her words softened, and she rocked me like she would a child weeping against her. "Rachel came too. She's talking with Nathan now, but she'll be here in a minute. It'll be just like old times."

I pulled myself away and looked deep into the face of my friend. The intervening years had not been particularly kind.

The freckles remained, numerous as ever, but they sat on a canvas of sallow skin. The girl who had been petite and quick and lithe was now merely small and gaunt, her arms like sticks within her sleeves. All in all, she had the effect of a woman not so much growing up, but drying up. I feared she might crackle when she moved.

"How—how is your father?"

A shadow flickered behind her green eyes. "He passed. Finally."

A new wave of sadness hit me, one we shared. "Oh, sister. I'm so sorry. When?"

"A week ago." She looked up, calculating. "No, nearly two weeks now. Two weeks on Tuesday."

"You should have sent word. We would have come."

"I knew you were near your time. I didn't want to be a bother."

"But Nathan? He would have—"

"There really wasn't much of a funeral." She patted me, reassuring. "Only our closest neighbors even knew he was still alive. When we posted the notice in the paper, most people either had no idea who he was or thought he'd died years ago. To think I've been living all these years with a ghost." The corner of her mouth had its same quirky turn, almost bringing her back to the girl she'd been. "Now it seems I'm to become one myself."

"Evangeline Moss!" The doorway filled with the silhouette of Rachel, her figure perfectly displayed in black silk. "Now is not the time to burden poor Camilla with our problems."

"No, really, I don't mind," I said. And I didn't. "Sometimes the best way to lighten the burdens of your own heart is to carry the weight of somebody else's." I patted the space next to me on the bed, inviting Rachel to join us.

"That's beautiful," Evangeline said. "What book is that in?"

"My own."

"Still, my problems seem so insignificant compared to . . ." Her words trailed off as her eyes turned toward the empty cradle in the corner. "It must be the worst pain ever."

"It's the worst so far," I agreed. "For me, anyway. But you, dear friend, your loss is no less significant. You've now lost both of your parents."

Evangeline gave a sad, tight-lipped smile.

Rachel reached across me to grab Evangeline's hand. "Now you can finally get on with your life."

"Taking care of Father was my life."

"And now he's gone."

I both marveled and trembled at the strength and finality of Rachel's tone.

"I received a visit from Brigham Young the other day," Evangeline said.

"Himself?" I could only imagine such a thing.

"No, that might have made the news easier to take."

"What news?" Rachel's brow furrowed, creating the only lines in her otherwise-smooth face.

"They—the church, I guess—have been allowing us to live in that house without any sort of contribution. On their charity, you might say. Our home and all our needs. Because of Father's incapacity to work and my mother gone and the brothers so young."

"But they worked in the mill, didn't they?" I remembered a visit years ago; though twelve and thirteen, they looked like such little boys heading off in the early morning hours.

"Yes, but now they're on mission in England. From there, who knows? And I can't just keep the house."

"Who says you can't?"

"Brigham Young, of course." Rachel made the name sound like a conviction.

"And he's right to do so." Evangeline was quick to the prophet's defense. "I can't expect to have food and shelter for the rest of my life at the Saints' expense. I have to do something. Go somewhere. They'll give me the winter, but after that . . ."

"Well, it's terrible timing on your father's part," Rachel said, smoothing her silk. "A few months ago and I could've had Tillman marry you and bring you into our little household. But he's not due for another wife for at least two years. That's how long it takes for the novelty to wear off."

Her words couldn't have shocked me more if she'd shouted them through a blare horn. Evangeline recoiled from an unseen physical blow. "Sister Rachel! You mustn't be so flippant about something as sacred as the celestial bond of marriage."

"I'll take it seriously when my husband does. Let's see . . ." She ticked off the numbers with her fingers. "I was eighteen when Tillman married me. He was thirty. Wife number two, Joanna, was twenty—a bit old for his taste, but I'll admit there wasn't much choice in the early days. Then three years later, Marion, seventeen. And now sweet Tabatha, just sixteen. On second thought, if this one can keep her looks, he might be occupied for quite a while."

"That's blasphemous." Evangeline hissed the word. "You're taking a holy sacrament and turning it into something vile."

Rachel's reply was equally venomous. "What else do you call a man's continuous rotation of women in his bed?"

"It's the desire of Heavenly Father. The divine revelation of our prophet. The very basis for the Celestial Kingdom. Just last month the prophet stood behind the pulpit and urged us to recognize our duty to build large, strong families in this world to bring blessings to Heavenly Father in the next."

"And my Tillman proudly obliged him by bringing home Miss Tabatha the very next week. Come to think of it, our Nathan was in that service too."

I'd been sitting between the two, my head bouncing back and forth with the debate. Rachel's question couldn't have been clearer if she'd asked it, but it was one I was not prepared to answer, so I asked my own. "Do you think Tillman loves his other wives as much as he loves you?"

She threw her head back and let out a mirthless laugh. "That's one question I never bother to ask him or myself. Remember, even though he married me first, I came into his life second. We'd only spent a few weeks together before he came out here and married Joanna. He had a whole year with her before I arrived. I never had a choice but to accept it."

"Nor should you," Evangeline snapped. "You don't have any choice but to accept the teachings of the church. Baptism. Tithing. Why should marriage be any different?"

"Nathan and I love each other so much. I can't imagine any other life."

"And you don't have to." Rachel put her arms around me from behind and nestled her head on my shoulder. I could smell her perfumed lotion. Roses. "My brother is content. More than that. You make him happier than I ever thought he could be."

"But he'll never reach—"

"You hush with all of that!" Rachel squeezed me closer even as she scolded Evangeline.

"He so wanted a son," I said, my eyes burning anew.

"Yes," Rachel comforted, "and he'll have one. You'll give him one."

Evangeline opened her mouth to speak; instead she

crumpled under Rachel's glare. But her words, though unspoken, were as present in the room as the three of us and the empty cradle.

Or another wife would.

CHAPTER 12

What can I say about the months that followed? In some ways they were much like any other winter. Kimana and the girls and I spent evenings sitting by the fire, carding wool. We didn't have sheep of our own, but a few of our neighbors did, and sometimes we'd gather two or three families in a home to pass the time telling stories and singing, all underscored by the rhythmic combing. Snowflakes tumbled through the dark winter sky as our baskets filled with soft tufts of white wool. I never have developed a deft hand for spinning, so when the women gathered for those afternoons, I busied myself frying doughnuts and pouring cider. Anything to keep busy. Both of the girls had been born in the spring, so I never had the joy of a newborn in the winter. I'd been looking forward to long, dark, cold nights sitting by the fire. The muffled winter air made our house seem all the more quiet. Try as we might, we could not fill the void left by the life that ended all too soon.

For the first time in our marriage, Nathan was lost to me. He left our bed in the wee hours of the morning to tend to the livestock—chores that had been mine until the final days of my pregnancy. When I protested and offered to at least join him in the work, he'd touch me lightly on my cheek and say, "No, love. It's cold outside. Stay here and sleep a little longer."

But it haunted me, that room. It seemed the cold of winter seeped through the very walls. The moment Nathan and I stepped through the door, we ceased to speak, and the bed that had once been an island of warm refuge now gave all the comfort of a hard frost. We hadn't been together as man and wife since before the baby was born, when we laughed at the awkward intrusion of my pregnant belly. A month after Arlen's birth, when I knew my body had fully healed, I turned to him in the night, but he turned away. And the next night. And the next.

I found myself daily carrying the helplessness I'd felt when I held little Arlen in my arms. The love Nathan and I shared was dying every day, and I was powerless to breathe new life into it.

Whatever brightness and love we had in our home during those early winter months came from Melissa and Lottie, who simply refused to succumb to the sadness that gripped their father. Oh, Melissa, always the more solemn of the two, crept about the house for a while, burdened with the strain of trying not to be a bother to anyone, but little Lottie simply refused to be sad.

"Baby Arlen's in heaven with Jesus," she'd say whenever

the thought of him crossed her mind. She made such assertions without a hint of mourning—just a matter-of-factness that I envied.

Once, when she left her new doll in the baby's cradle, I gave her a solid scolding. I gripped her arms and yanked her clear off the floor, screaming, "That bed is for the baby!"

Calmly, her big green eyes looking straight into mine, she said, "The baby's sleeping in the arms of Jesus. He doesn't need the bed."

That very night Nathan took the cradle out to the barn, and I packed away the stack of tiny shirts and socks and blankets I'd made in the months of preparation. And for the life of me, I don't remember ever talking about baby Arlen again.

One evening in early February, Nathan came to the table with the usual layer of sweet-smelling sawdust on his shirtsleeves.

"Elder Justus is coming to dinner tomorrow night."

"Oh?" I ignored the shiver at the base of my neck and spooned boiled potatoes onto Melissa's plate. "That'll be fine. Kimana trapped a rabbit this morning. We'll make stew."

"He wants to talk to you, Camilla."

"Really? I was just in their home last week cutting quilt blocks with Sister June. Surely he could have talked with me then."

"Now, stop it." I can recall very few times before this when Nathan had ever spoken to me in any kind of a harsh tone, and never had he done so in front of the children. When he said this, the words barely escaping his lips through his clenched jaw, I was startled to the point that I nearly dropped the bowl to the table, and my cheeks burned so that I was certain they were steaming along with the food. "You know very well why he's coming. You haven't been to a church meeting since—"

"That's not true." And it wasn't. Right after the funeral I went to Sabbath services, where I'd had to endure all those long, pitying looks from women whose children trailed like ducklings behind them. "I couldn't bear the sound of all those babies. . . ."

Melissa was staring at her plate, listlessly moving her food around its surface.

"How do you think it makes me look," Nathan said, his voice eerily calm, "not to have my wife and children at my side for the church service?"

"We attended all through Advent," I offered, "and the New Year."

"I won't stand for this."

"Then Lottie had a sore throat, remember? And I . . ."

"You what?"

What could I say? This wasn't the time to air my misgivings. I'd been thinking that perhaps my doubts were somehow wrapped up with my grief, and I'd allowed myself to remain mired in mourning, leaving all thoughts beyond my own heavy heart largely unnoticed.

"I'll go tomorrow," I said finally. "We all will. Kimana can cook while we're gone."

He smiled, revealing a hint of the boy who had met me on the road all those years ago, and reached for my hand.

"You need the healing of Heavenly Father. We all do."

That evening Kimana and I bathed the girls, washing their hair and combing out the tangles by the warmth of the firelight. The wind blew cold outside, bringing in a frigid rush when Nathan came in from tending the stock.

On nights like this, Kimana would spend the evening

sitting with us until it was time for her to go to bed in her own small cabin behind our house. She busied herself braiding rags into what would someday be a thick, warm rug just like the one the girls sat on now. As I sat knitting in the rocking chair in the corner, they clutched their dolls and listened with rapt attention while Nathan told the story of the angel Moroni appearing to Joseph Smith. It was not a new story to the girls; they piped up with details every time Nathan paused for breath.

"And a light filled the room!"

"And he was as tall as the ceiling!"

"Yes," Nathan said, restoring solemnity, "and his robe was exceedingly white, and his whole person glorious beyond description."

"And his countenance truly like lightning," Melissa said, quoting the text she'd heard so many times.

"That's right," Nathan said, leaning forward in his chair and holding our older daughter's face in his hands. "Like lightning. And Moroni told Joseph that God had work for him to do. That his name would be had for both good and evil in all the nations."

"Who would think he was evil?" By this time Lottie was in her father's lap.

"Many people," Nathan said. I could feel his eyes upon me, but I continued to focus on the reflection of the firelight on my knitting needles, knowing we were both envisioning the same thing—a group of riders illuminated by torches on the bank of the Missouri River. "You know the stories of our people. Not everybody is ready to believe the truth, especially if it's different from what they've been taught all their lives."

"But Joseph Smith believed the angel," Lottie prompted.

"About the golden plates," Melissa added.

"Indeed." Nathan picked up the story. "Moroni said there

was a book, written on gold plates, and that book told the truth of the everlasting gospel of the savior."

"Jesus!" Lottie bounced on her father's knee.

"How he came to America," Melissa said with the authority of an older girl who had the experience of going to Sunday school. "And he began to quote the Bible, from the book of Malachi."

"Although not exactly," I said, not as quietly as I intended.

"What was that, darling?"

I looked up to see Nathan holding a contented Lottie against his broad, strong chest, Melissa sitting at his feet. A quick glance at Kimana showed the woman bent lower over her work, her face its usual placid mask.

"That's part of the story." I returned to my knitting. The clicking of the needles echoed in the room, competing with the crackling of the fire.

"She's right," Melissa said. "He said the angel changed some of the words. We learned it in Sunday school. Do you want to hear?"

"Of course," Nathan said, and I paused midstitch.

Melissa stood up and handed her doll to her little sister before assuming a very poised posture, hands clasped before her. "'And he shall plant in the hearts of the children the promises made to the fathers, and the hearts of the children shall turn to their fathers. If it were not so, the whole earth would be utterly wasted at his coming.'"

"Marvelous!" Nathan reached around Lottie to clap his hands.

"And did you ever study the true Scripture?"

As much as I hated how my question crushed her triumphant spirit, I feared the increasingly familiar tugging on my spirit that caused me to ask it.

"That *is* the truth, Mama. That's what the angel said."

"But that's not what the Bible says," I insisted. "I was just wondering if you were taught both."

"What are you saying, Camilla?" For the second time that evening, there it was—that tone of chastisement and distrust. "Do you know the *true* version? You grew up reading your Bible. Every day, you told me. Can you quote those verses from the fourth chapter of Malachi?"

The three of them stared at me, waiting, and it broke my heart to see Melissa now looking smaller than her younger sister.

"No," I said. "I can't." I looked straight at Melissa. "I suppose I wasn't taught as well as you have been."

That brought back my girl's smile—or at least a shadow of it. She took her doll back into her arms and sat again at her father's feet. Moving noiselessly, Kimana rose from her seat and, wrapping a length of towel around the handle, lifted the bed warmer from the hearth and disappeared into the girls' room to run it along their blankets.

"And the golden plates?" Lottie demanded, tugging on Nathan's sleeve. But the magic of the tale had disappeared. He gathered her close and kissed her good night, promising to finish the story the next evening. I set my work aside and held out my arms, gathering each little girl to me, breathing in the scent of soap and damp hair. Lottie crumbled warm against me, but I couldn't ignore Melissa's stick-straight posture, identical to the one she held as she recited from Smith's story.

"I love you, Missy." Perhaps the familiar name would warm her.

As an answer, she kissed my cheek—a quick, dry peck—before waiting patiently for me to drop my embrace.

"I'm afraid I hurt her feelings," I said once Kimana ushered the girls to their room.

"You need to be careful, Camilla." Undeniable warning in his voice. "Your salvation rests in your belief. In your faith."

"I know."

"And your eternity rests with me."

That's when I realized I'd been pressing the knitting needle into my palm. I concentrated on the pain there, pushing it harder against the flesh.

He rose from his chair and came to kneel beside me. "I can understand your grief. But don't let that turn into doubt."

"I love you, Nathan." It was all I could think to say.

"And I love you. And I thank God that he's given you to me."

"Lately . . ." I couldn't finish, but I didn't have to.

"I know," he said, pushing my work aside and burying his head in my lap. "I know."

I ran my fingers through his hair. Short and coarse it was, still bearing the dust of his workshop. We didn't speak, and I realized he was weeping. These were the first tears he'd shed since the day he held his son, and I sat perfectly still, allowing them to seep into my skirt. When his body finally became still, I reached down, prompting him to look at me. His tear-streaked face took on a particular shine in the firelight, and I thought of the words of Joseph Smith describing the angel. A countenance like lightning. There was no lightning here, just a soft, warm glow, and in his eyes everything I loved in this world.

"Do you still love me, Nathan? as much as you did when I was just an ignorant, Gentile girl?"

He stood and, in that motion, lifted me out of the chair. From the corner of my eye I saw the figure of Kimana, wrapping her bright wool shawl around her shoulders. There was a tiny shock of cold air as the door opened and closed behind her, but by the time I heard the click of the latch, my husband had carried me into our bedroom. Soon the frigid cold disappeared, powerless against the warmth of rekindled love. Later, in the dark, I folded myself against him, my ear to his heart, forcing myself to think of nothing else.

At least not until the morning.

"*A mighty fortress is our* God,
A tower of strength ne'er failing.
A helper mighty is our God,
O'er ills of life prevailing.
He overcometh all.
He saveth from the Fall.
His might and pow'r are great.
He all things did create.
And he shall reign for evermore."

My voice mingled with the others, each of us sending little puffs of steam into the room. I never tired of hearing the richness of Nathan's voice. Truthfully, neither did the congregation, as he was often called upon to lead the singing. But this morning he stood close beside me—too close for complete propriety, had we not six years of marriage between us. We were flanked on either side by our daughters, who sang just as robustly as any other Saint.

By the time we all settled in our benches after the time of singing and prayer had ended, the little stoves at the front and back of the building were glowing, and some semblance of warmth was working its way through the room. With my body pressed hard against Nathan's side and Lottie in my lap, I was actually quite comfortable—enough that I could take off my gloves and place them beside me.

Elder Justus made his way to the front and took his place behind the satin-smooth pulpit that was Nathan's pride and joy—the result of months of work ending in seamless perfection.

"Brothers and sisters," he intoned. It was the voice that pronounced the blessing over my son, and the memory of it numbed me. "We gather here in the dead of winter, a month into the new year. The tenth since our people first entered into Zion."

A little rumble of approval ran through our congregation, few of whom had been in the first company.

"We journeyed from persecution to prosperity. We tore free from the murderous grip of the Gentiles who would see us burned to the ground and instead have established a new kingdom of God. To think of the miracle of an inland ocean—the Great Salt Lake, our own Dead Sea. It is no mistake that Heavenly Father led us here, as we are the descendants and brothers of his chosen people."

Indeed, we journeyed often to the lake in the spring and summer, and in the middle of this winter afternoon I found myself harking back to our last visit. The frothing of the water at the shore, the constant chatter of the playful shorebirds. Nathan delighted in wading with the girls, letting them float on the salty water's surface while I unpacked a basket of lunch to eat on a blanket stretched over the sand. I could almost feel the warmth of the sun on my face, so much so that I actually closed my eyes for just a moment before Lottie shifted her weight and brought me back to Elder Justus's sermon.

"Our city thrives, surpassing some of those cities that have been in existence for centuries in our country. It is a testament to the work of the Lord, our obedience to his will as revealed to the prophets."

Agreement spread through the benches, for each of us took pride in the miracle of Salt Lake City. It was the jeweled reward at the end of our pilgrimage, a welcome final step to all who walked across the country. Even when we first arrived, all those years ago, I remember marveling at the perfectly aligned streets—all of it laid out in precise squares. The girls and I eagerly awaited any time we would get a chance to visit.

"And why do those folk in our city enjoy such prosperity? Are they harder workers than you?" An unvoiced yet understood *no* swept through the benches. "Are they more likely to tithe their money or their time?"

We were bolder with our protests now, at least those around me were. I clutched Lottie closer to me and turned an ear, feeling chilled after all.

"Ah, brothers and sisters, I urge you to look deeper into your hearts before you commit yourselves to the sin of religious pride. Perhaps you see yourselves as being out of the reach of the hand of the prophet, but no man can hide in the darkness of disobedience, not even if he makes his home in the shadows of the temple. For we are blessed to live so near God's temple—oh, not the magnificent structure formed by the hands of men, but within reach of the very stones themselves. Such proximity should bring us to a deeper sense of obedience, but I fear the opposite has happened."

There was an uncomfortable restlessness in the benches now as we simultaneously dared Elder Justus to tell us where we had fallen short and feared that he would do so. I glanced at Nathan, who stared straight ahead, his face set like flint.

"For we have had our share of disobedience, and I count myself the first among sinners. Not long ago, Brother Brigham requested that all families contribute to the production of silk, and I have yet to compel my wives to do so."

Nervous laughter then, as no one that I knew had taken on the responsibility of nurturing silkworms in their kitchen.

"And what have we to show for our disobedience?" He pointed a finger that seemed to part us all like waters. "Brother Farley, how many sheep did you find dead in their grazing pasture last summer?"

We all knew the answer to that. Nearly a dozen, and we'd spent the better part of July in a frenzy of paranoid accusations.

"And, Sister Maelyn, have you found any relief from your ailment?"

I heard a chorus of rustling as my fellow Saints turned to look at Sister Maelyn, but I kept my eyes straight ahead. I didn't need to see the woman to picture her gray pallor and wasted body. A few sympathetic clucks popped through the congregation before people returned their attention to the man behind the pulpit.

"And Brother Nathan Fox."

No.

"The birth of a long-awaited son."

No, no, no.

"As fine a boy as I've ever seen. A Saint sent from heaven, and he couldn't bear to be here. Couldn't will himself to live among us."

I clutched the fullness of my daughter closer to me. Only the warmth of her body keeping me from turning to ice. And shattering. Looking to Nathan, I pleaded, silently, *Make him stop! Stand up and tell him he's wrong!* But where Nathan would not look at me, every other eye in the congregation sought me out, and I equally froze and burned under the weight of their scrutiny.

Somewhere through the fog, Elder Justus's words came coiling around me. "We are not free to pick and choose which spiritual laws of the prophets we will obey. Heavenly Father has called us to total obedience and has said that he will spew the lukewarm from his mouth. Our leaders have long taught the divine necessity of plural marriage. For how else are we to build Zion and fill it with the voices of children—the very spirits waiting to be born? Men, how can you hope to reach the highest reward in the next life if you do not build that which is pleasing to God in this one?"

What can I say? It was like a floodgate of fear opened within me. Like a blister perched upon my heart burst open. I felt the change in Nathan beside me. Felt him sit up a little straighter, the hard defiance in him dissolve.

I knew what these people believed. Nathan was convinced—as were they all—that marrying and having children was the path to celestial rewards. The more wives and children on earth, the more glorious his family in heaven. What better eternity could there be for a man who had spent his childhood unloved and alone?

"Listen," Elder Justus said. "Listen to what your spirit is telling you right now. Feel that stirring in your bosom, leading you to confess your sin. Where are you lacking faith? Where do you see fault in your brother? your sister? We have been called to something higher. To be the new church of Jesus Christ. We are the Saints of a new day. Our ways are not the ways of the world. Our truth is not the truth of the Gentiles."

By now the souls around me were stirring. Women weeping, men standing in their places, waving their hats in the air. I wanted to disappear, and in truth I don't know that anybody would have seen me, so caught up were they in the elder's stirring oration. In fact, I went so far as to tighten my grip on

Lottie and edge slightly closer to the front of the bench, when I felt Nathan's hand on my elbow.

"Stay there." His grip punctuated his words.

"Make no mistake." Elder Justus now had to nearly shout above the crowd. "We will come under fire for our faith. The Gentile-driven government will come down hard upon us. For they know not the truth of the prophets. Their hearts have not been stirred by the revelations of Jesus Christ. But did not each prophet in his time face persecution? Were not the first Christians stoned in the streets? And what if they had abandoned the teachings of their Lord?"

Just the thought of it brought an uproar. Elder Justus stepped away from the pulpit, coming out in front of it, and paced the narrow width of the room, his fist stirring the air.

"Come to me now and confess! There, in your seat, turn to your fellow Saint and confess! Fall to your knees and confess! You who are lacking in faith! You whose works are not worthy of heaven! You who have wronged your neighbor! You who have neglected worship! You who cling to your selfish desires like a blight in the eye of God!"

By now Lottie was terrified. She'd turned in my lap and wrapped her arms around my neck, her cold nose pressed up to my ear.

"What is he yelling about, Mama?"

"Nothing, darling," I whispered.

Any semblance of decorum was gone. What there were of aisles filled with weeping women and pacing men. They fell in and out of embraces, their shouts fueled equally by accusation and rousing affection.

Somewhere in the midst of all this, Nathan let loose my arm, and when I felt him stir, I held out hope that he would lead us out. Instead, he stood beside me, his eyes and hands and arms lifted high.

"Heavenly Father!" His words sounded clear amid the din of the crowd. "Forgive me!" Then his hand was on me again. Through the layers of coat and clothing I felt each of his fingers digging into the flesh on my upper arm as he tugged, forcing me to stand beside him. "And forgive the sins of my wife."

Shifting Lottie to my hip, I attempted to wrench myself from his grip. My actions called his attention away from heaven, and he looked down at me with a glare stoked with the fire of celestial authority.

"I told you to stay."

"You will not confess my sins for me."

"I don't trust that you'll confess them for yourself."

"And how do you know I have anything to repent?"

The way that he looked at me answered my question. There in the chaos of this babbling crowd, everything stripped away.

A stirring beside him caught my attention, and I looked down to see Melissa clinging to him, her face buried in his sleeve. She was trembling.

"I'm leaving."

"No, you're not. Stay."

One hard tug, though, and I was free. "The girls are going with me."

I began to shoulder my way through the crowd, violently shrugging off the well-meaning hands that tried to detain me. The wall of noise surrounding me sounded no more like the utterances of worship than did the voices raised at the tower of Babel. In my heart I knew God did not look down on this with favor, and even then I knew much more would be required of me than simply walking away from this meeting. But it was a step, and at the moment, it was all I knew to do.

Once outside the stifling confines of our little church, tears spilled freely, making stinging, hard rivulets on my cheeks. I still clung to the girls, one small hand clutched in each of mine.

"Are we going to go back inside?" Melissa asked.

"No," I said. "Not today."

I lingered long enough for Nathan to come after us, but he didn't. The volume within the walls increased, leaving doubt that any other Saint would dare to wander from the fold. So, with the promise of rabbit stew and dumplings awaiting us in the warm house, my daughters and I made our way down the frosty road to home.

CHAPTER 13

For two weeks after that Sunday, the chill of winter blew just as fierce within our home as it did outside. We did not speak, Nathan and I. He continued to tend to the morning chores, though now there was no pretense that he did so out of consideration for my feelings. I woke up each day to an empty bed, spent the day moving in wide circles around him when we found ourselves in the same room, and nearly ruined my eyes stitching by lamplight waiting for him to come in from his workshop in the evenings.

It didn't take long for me to learn that he would not come in until I'd extinguished my lamp, so on especially cold evenings I blew it out early and climbed into bed, counting the minutes until I felt his weight beside me.

This silence, thankfully, did not extend to the girls. During those moments he was with them, he was as jovial as ever, engaging them in story and song like a self-appointed jester. I knew, of course, exactly what he was doing. He told stories of the Mormon heroes, sang hymns I'd never heard before coming here.

And I steeled my heart.

Somehow, the revelations of Joseph Smith took on a maliciousness I could never have recognized the first time I heard them. After all, these were not the warm summer days of our new love. This was a bitter, dark winter, one child in a grave.

One day as Kimana and I washed up the breakfast dishes, the sound of bells danced on the midmorning air. I looked out to see a beautiful cutter, shining black with blood-red runners, drawn by a team of four matching horses. I didn't have to wait until the driver came into view for me to know who held the reins. I'd wrapped my shawl around my shoulders and was outside calling, "Rachel!" before she brought the team to a jangling stop.

She was dressed in fur from the top of her stylish hat to the trim on the skirt peeping out. Hopping out of the cutter, she hugged me close in a grip every bit as strong as the bear that once wore the coat she did now, then abruptly let me go when the girls flew out of the house and threw themselves against her.

"Where is that worthless brother of mine?" she said once the squeals had died down. "Someone needs to tend to the horses."

After dispatching Melissa to fetch her father from his workshop, I linked my arm through Rachel's and led her into the house. Kimana offered a quiet glimpse of a greeting before taking Rachel's hat and coat to hang on a hook behind the door.

"I've come to take you away," Rachel said, settling down at our kitchen table.

"Oh, have you?" I paused at the window to watch Nathan emerge from his workshop. As always, his cheeks took on bright red blotches in the cold, yet he wore only shirtsleeves. He did, however, put on his gloves before taking the horses' reins and leading them into the barn. Melissa and Lottie skipped in circles around him, and he eventually stopped and gave a deep, princely bow before helping them clamber into the sleigh for a quick ride into the barn.

"Camilla?"

I didn't turn around until I heard my name called again, this time accompanied by Kimana's gentle tug on my arm.

"Goodness, sister," Rachel said. "Your eyes are at the window, but it seems your mind is on the moon."

"It's a beautiful team," I said, taking a seat next to her. "And how lovely to have such a nice surprise visit."

"It's not exactly a visit." Rachel tugged her gloves off finger by finger and dropped them on the table. They were made from beautiful fur-lined calfskin with dainty pearl buttons. Without thinking, I reached out to touch them, wincing at the roughness of my own chapped skin. "I've come to steal you away for a while."

"Oh, really?" The second glove landed on the table, and I ran my finger across its palm.

"It's been so bleak and dreary, I thought I'd come whisk you away to spend a few days with me in town. Keep me company."

"I hardly picture you lacking company. In fact, I imagine your household is fairly crowded."

"True, but I thought you might come and stay a spell with Evangeline. Poor girl. Even if her father couldn't speak, he was at least someone to talk *to*. I dropped in the other day, and she hadn't even combed her hair. Imagine that. Ten o'clock in the morning, and barely dressed."

"I don't think I'm the person to cheer her up," I said, thinking I knew well how it felt to spend hours in a house with no one to talk to.

"Nonsense. It'll be just like the old days back on the trail. Just us girls."

"What about Lottie and Melissa?"

"Bring them. They can stay at my house and play with their cousins. All of them," she added, wrinkling her nose.

"I'll have to ask Nathan, of course."

"Of course."

Kimana set a cup of water in front of Rachel, who lifted it daintily, sipped, and set it down again, never taking her eyes off me.

"Well?" she asked expectantly. "Are you going to talk to him?"

"Now?" I stammered, trying to cover my hesitance. "I thought you and I might chat a little first."

"We'll have plenty of time to chat on the drive." She made a shooing motion. "Now, go."

I attempted to match her playfulness as I rose from my seat. Before going outside, I asked Kimana to pack a bag for the girls, including one nice dress for each and their warmest nightgowns, and to lay out a few things for me as well. Then, shawl wrapped tightly about me, I opened the door to brace myself against the cold.

I could hear the rhythmic jangling of the sleigh bells accompanying the girls singing some silly tune. Nathan chimed in with an echoing baritone, and it pained me to think of how abruptly the music would stop the minute I stepped through the barn's door. That thought alone kept me standing on the other side, listening, until a resounding, quasi-harmonious final note signaled the end of the song.

"Mama! Sing with us!" Lottie had herself ready to launch into another tune, but I held up my hand.

"Girls, go inside."

"Did Aunt Rachel bring us something from town?" Melissa asked, wide-eyed.

"Yes," I said, tugging her braid. "She brought herself. Now, go visit with her."

Lottie and Melissa resumed their song, singing it all the way from the barn to the house. Nathan and I remained in our now customary silence. He had unhitched Rachel's team, and now each horse stood, covered with a blanket, nibbling at the hay in the manger.

"They're beautiful horses," I said, laying one tentative hand on a chestnut flank.

Nathan said nothing as he hung the harness over a hook on the wall.

"She's not planning to stay long." My words lingered as steam in the silence. "In fact, probably just an hour's rest for the horses. She aims to go back today." He settled the pitchfork in its place. "And she wants me to go back with her for a visit."

That captured his attention. His back was to me, but I saw the stiffness in his posture, the twitch of his shoulder blades as he squared himself to face me.

"You should go."

They were the first words he had spoken directly to me since he fought to keep me beside him. And now he was sending me away.

"Are you sure?"

"Might do you good."

He walked past me, back outside, where he began to inspect the sleigh from all angles, running his gloved hand along the runners. I was on his heels.

"What is that supposed to mean?"

"Just that maybe some time spent with Rachel will teach you a little bit about how to be a proper wife."

Back into the barn he went, and again I followed. Perhaps I imagined the curiosity in the horses' glances. On the far side of the barn was the door to Nathan's workshop, and when he got there, he spun around and leaned against it, arms folded across his broad chest, creating a second barrier.

"I don't want you to go in there."

"I don't care about your workshop." And at the moment, I didn't. "How can you say I'm not a proper wife?"

"You haven't been, since the baby—"

"Don't you dare."

"You've shown no respect for me as the leader of this home."

"How—?"

He rose up huge before me and pointed in my face. "You've abandoned any spiritual instruction for the girls. You haven't been back to church. And you're keeping me from being the man Heavenly Father wants me to be."

"Nathan." I reached out, touching him for the first time since I'd wrenched myself from his grip. "Don't—"

He brushed my touch away; then, taking a deep breath, he gripped my arms, fingers digging into my flesh.

"All my life—" my neck snapped as he shook me, emphasizing each word—"*all my life*, I thought of nothing but the day I would have a family. A home. A wife. Children."

"You have all that."

"It's not enough to have it here. I want this forever. And you're taking that away."

"I'm not—"

"We can never build a family in heaven if we can't build one here."

He loosened his grip then but did not let me go. I could have stepped away, but I stood, part of me grateful to hear his voice—no matter how ugly the words—and the rest of me longing to comfort him, despite his accusations. Slowly the brick wall of a man started to crumble; his grip grew to an embrace, and he pulled me to him. He whispered my name, and I had the distinct feeling that he was not merely holding me but clinging to me. I wrapped my arms around him and braced myself for strength.

"We have a fine family, Nathan." I breathed deeply the scent of sawdust and winter. "And who knows? In time . . ."

"What? More children?"

"Maybe." I rose up on my toes and kissed the warm hollow of his neck. "But if that's what you want—"

Oh, how little it took to thaw the ice that had built up between us. His mouth was on mine, and I fell hard against him as I melted under his kiss. I felt like I was fifteen years old again, experiencing for the first time what it meant to be loved by a man.

"My wife, my wife . . ." He repeated the phrase as he dragged his mouth along my jaw to my ear, my neck.

"Yes," I whispered, fully given over to his touch.

He took my hand and led me to the back corner of our barn, where fresh, clean hay formed a sweet-smelling hill that climbed halfway up the wall. From a shelf nearby he produced a thick wool blanket, and with one swift snap, it settled, crackling.

"Oh, Nathan. We can't—your *sister* is in the house."

"She can wait." He pulled me close once again and, ignoring my protests—weak as they were—drew both of us down. "Long time since we've had a straw ticking."

"And now I know why." I fidgeted against the poking straw, longing momentarily for the thick feather mattress of our bedroom. But soon I could feel nothing but the touch and breath of my husband.

"And I love you, Camilla."

"I know."

"Have since the moment I saw you."

I responded with a girlish giggle, still in awe that he chose me to love.

"Remember that."

"I will."

"No matter what happens."

A tiny, dancing chill knotted itself around my spine. I opened my eyes wide and braced my hands against his chest, pushing him away. "What could happen?"

"I told you. I mean to have a family."

"You *have* a family." The hay rustled beneath me as I scooted away. "You have a wife and two daughters. And a son in heaven. And more, Nathan." I reached out and touched his face, forcing him to look at me. "All the more that you want. All that I can give you."

"That's not enough, and you know it."

"It's what God has given us."

"You and I alone can never fulfill the wishes of Heavenly Father, Camilla. How can one man and one woman ever do enough to build his church?"

We were both sitting up by now, side by side. I twisted a strand of golden straw around my finger, watched the fingertip turn violet, then let the straw go slack. Three times I did this in the silence that followed, all the while pondering—*one man, one woman*—all the while feeling the heated passion of the last few minutes dissipate, until I was nothing but a cold shell.

"How can you ask me to share what we have?"

"You already share me, darling. I belong to God first, then to you."

"God began with just one man and one woman," I said. "And we seem to have grown just fine."

"But I don't answer only to God," he said, picking up a handful of hay and wrapping it into a cord. "I must uphold the teachings of the prophet as they were given by God. And he commands—"

"He has no right to command." My outburst was loud enough, harsh enough to warrant a corresponding reaction from one of Rachel's horses, who stamped her hoof in response. Instinctively I lowered my voice. "Joseph Smith was only a man. And Brigham, too. They cannot compel you to betray your very heart."

He looked at me, his eyes steady. "And what makes you think they have?"

The tiny chill niggling at my spine exploded, filling me with a kind of cold that takes the breath away. Indeed, it had, as I fought for words. "B-because you love me. You said you love me. And if you do, how could you ever love—"

"I am the man God created. Could Jesus Christ love only one person?"

"But you're not Jesus Christ!"

"No!" He stood up, and this time the horses did startle, lifting their forefeet off the floor and snorting in concert. "According to the Gentiles in this world, I'm nothing more than a worthless orphan. Tossed on the street, left to grow up with the rest of the trash. But Heavenly Father tells me I can be more. I'm made of the same stuff as our savior. And can be what he is. If you love me, how can you not want me to fulfill what my God wants me to do?"

Not caring about the bits of straw that clung to my skirt and back and hair, I stood up slowly, reaching one tentative hand out to touch him, my fingers barely resting on his fist-clenched arm.

"Have you ever thought," I said, my voice barely above a whisper, "that they might be wrong? The prophets. About marriage."

He recoiled, burned from my touch, and lifted his hand as if to strike me. I didn't flinch because at the time, the thought that Nathan would hit me was such a foreign idea, my body would suffer no such reaction. I merely held my gaze steady and matched my breath to his until, slowly, he lowered his arm, leaving it dangling harmlessly at his side. "They cannot be wrong."

"They are not God."

"Listen to me." A look came over his face then—one I'd never seen before. His eyes narrowed to mere slits, his mouth somehow managing its full range of motion despite the clenching of his jaw. "Do you know what it means if they're wrong? It means I have nothing."

"You have me! You have the girls!"

"For now. And that makes me like every other Gentile out there slaving away through this life, living just to get through to death. But I've placed my *soul* in their hands."

"But that's impossible. . . ." That's when I realized he was speaking to me not out of anger, but out of fear. It was one of those moments when I could well imagine him as a little boy, equally full of hope and hurt.

"You made a vow to me, Camilla. To be my wife for all of time and all of eternity."

"Of course I did."

"Then go now, with Rachel. And see how Heavenly Father intends for us to live. The power he's given us in our Zion."

In light of all that had happened since I walked into the barn, though, the thought of leaving him alone posed a bigger danger than anything we could do to each other if I stayed. My fears must have somehow registered on my face, because to my surprise, he burst into a smile like I hadn't seen since before the birth of our son, threw his head back, and laughed.

"Don't worry." He dragged me into a hug that could only be described as jovial. "You'll come back to the same household you left. Just me and Kimana and the girls."

"Actually," I said, my face smashed against his shirt, "I was going to take the girls with me."

"Even better." He held me at arm's length and kissed the top of my head. "They're the next generation, growing up in a world that knows the truth. It'll be good for them to see what we are building."

CHAPTER 14

At the time, the four-hour trip zipping across the snow-packed land basin seemed as long as our four-month journey from Iowa. True, we had sleigh bells and songs. Rachel did her utmost to keep the girls excited and entertained as we snuggled close under the pile of bear and buffalo blankets. I could barely bring myself to join in. She had given me a good-enough teasing when I came in from the barn picking straw out of my hair, and made hooded comments about Nathan and me engaging in a proper good-bye. If my protests weren't enough to convince her she was mistaken, Nathan's restrained conversation when he came in later certainly painted a more accurate picture of our state of affection. When it was time for us to load up, he embraced each of the girls with a giant, warm hug before lifting them into their seat and tucking the blankets warmly about them. I, on the other hand, was given a kiss every bit as chaste as the one given to his sister, although he did take a moment to hold me close and tell me that he loved me.

Try as I might to hold on to those final words, they paled in the shadow cast by all the others he said. His zealous desire to build our family, even if it meant marriage with another woman. His fear for his very salvation. And somehow, amid the soft clomp of hooves and jingling bells and sweet voices raised in song, I took in that fear too.

"Faster, Aunt Rachel!" Lottie's sweet voice, muffled by the thick woolen scarf wrapped up to her nose, piped up during the next lull in song.

"Just for a little bit," Rachel said, laughing. She gave a capable snap of the reins and off we went—flying. The girls squealed in delight, and I even laughed as I wiped away a soft clump of snow sent flying up from one of the horses' hooves.

"See?" Rachel leaned over the girls' heads to talk closer to my ear. "This is what you all needed. To get away."

I tried to ignore the churning in my stomach and nodded.

"What's the matter?" Rachel asked. "Too fast?"

I breathed deep the biting cold air. "Just promise to bring me back safe."

The sky was tinged with purple when we came to a stop in front of the house Rachel shared with Tillman and her sister wives. It was an impressive structure by any measure, but when I thought about our modest home, it loomed even grander.

Three stories tall with gables spiraling even higher, its focal point was a double front door with a set of stained-glass windows boasting an intricate beehive design. Warm light glowed from within, and before we could even climb out of the sleigh, the doors flew open and three little boys came tumbling out.

"Aaron! Caleb! Toby!"

Rachel's chastisement of the boys for running out in just their shirtsleeves blended with my girls' shouts of joy at seeing their cousins, and soon the front porch was a tangle of little arms and legs that somehow got herded through the front door and into a cozy, warm entryway.

"There you are!" Tillman's voice boomed from the parlor, and soon there he was among us, holding a newspaper under one arm as he wrapped the other around Rachel, giving her an affectionate kiss on her cheek. He was a man of impressive stature, broad and strong as an ox, with a square, handsome face framed with a perfectly trimmed beard. "I was worried you wouldn't make it home before dark."

"We very nearly didn't," Rachel said, peeling off her gloves.

"And Nathan didn't put up a fight to keep you?"

I smiled to match the harmless, jovial tone with which the question had been asked and said, "Just a little."

"Wouldn't be anything at all if he had another wife back at the house to take care of him."

"Tillman." Rachel laid a quieting hand on his arm. "You need to take the boys out and put away the team."

"Yes, dear," he said, though he kept his eyes on me. For the first time I had a feeling there might be more to this impromptu visit than an opportunity for me to come into town. Still, Tillman said nothing, gathering the boys and taking them outside. Meanwhile, Melissa and Lottie and I followed Rachel into the parlor, where we stood by the roaring fire peeling off layers of coats and scarves and hats.

"I'll take those for you."

I looked over to see a young woman with raven black hair falling in ringlets down her back. Without a word, Rachel piled our things onto the girl's outstretched arms. When she'd gone, I whispered, "That's the new wife?"

"Yes," Rachel said with a bright, tight smile. Then, after a moment's thought, she called out, "Sister Tabatha!" bringing the girl back to pop her head around the doorway.

"Yes, Sister Rachel?"

"The little girls will be staying in your room with you for the next few nights."

"Oh?" Her lips were full and pink and made the most perfect O. "Does Tillman know?"

"I'll tell him when he comes in." She turned back to the fire, effectively dismissing young Tabatha, and rubbed her hands vigorously in the fire's warmth. "That will be more fun for everybody. Perhaps the girls will let Tabatha play with their dolls."

I stifled a laugh and tried to ignore Melissa's curious glance. Moments later, when Rachel declared us warm, we followed her into the kitchen, where her two other sister wives were busily clearing away supper dishes. Joanna, Aaron and Caleb's mother, tried to maneuver from table to sink with a tenacious three-year-old daughter clinging to her skirts, while Marion managed to do twice the work with one baby balanced on her hip. Both women stopped the moment we walked in, though, and came over to greet the girls with warm hugs offered all around.

"I'm sorry we missed supper," Rachel said, holding her arms out to Marion's baby. The child held out two chubby arms and gurgled with joy at being handed over.

"It's venison stew," Marion said. Now freed from the baby, she smoothed her apron and came over to offer me a tentative embrace. "Joanna's specialty. It's delicious."

I took my arms from around Marion's girth, thinking that her figure bore testament to the deliciousness of Joanna's cooking. Indeed, the kitchen smelled wonderful, and I realized that neither I nor the girls had eaten since breakfast.

Joanna staggered back to the stove, clingy toddler in tow. She wore her hair in one thick braid down her back, though at the moment it seemed there was just as much out as in. She stirred the contents of the large iron pot, saying, "There's bread in the keeper and molasses cookies for after," before ladling great, steaming portions into white porcelain bowls and carrying them to the enormous butcher-block table.

"Now, Joanna," Rachel said sweetly, running her hand over the baby's fine, soft hair, "we have guests. Don't you think it would be more fitting to serve us in the dining room?"

I detected the slightest slumping of Joanna's shoulders as she reached the ladle again into the pot.

"I'll set the table," Marion said quickly, gathering up the bowl and heading through a second door. "And perhaps you'll have your cookies later in the parlor?"

"That would be perfect," Rachel said, practically cooing to the baby. "It's been a rather difficult day."

Later that evening, Rachel and I sat on the edge of her bed while I ran a brush through her hair. It was still as lush as it had been the day I met her, and I could tell that it would curl into little tufts just like Nathan's if cut short enough to be given the chance. A fire glowed behind an ornate grate, and long-handled bed warmers waited on the hearth. Across the hall, my daughters were nestled in with young Tabatha, who'd seemed eager to pull the covers up to their chins and tell stories into the night. Every now and then, the sound of a giggle seeped under the door, punctuating the rhythm of the boar bristles against my palm.

"They sound like they're having fun," I said, dividing Rachel's hair into three sections to plait.

"Tabatha's a sweet girl." Rachel held a small mirror up to her face, and our eyes connected in the glass.

"You treat them like servants, you know."

"I have a position in the household. The first wife. If I'm not careful, they'll run right over me. Run me out of my own house."

"I can't believe that."

"It happens all the time. So be careful."

I took the piece of ribbon Rachel handed over her shoulder and tied it around the end of the braid. Then we both stood, wrapped towels around the handles, and took the bed warmers from the hearth to run them along the length and breadth of the feather mattress before climbing inside.

There was a light rapping on the door and Tillman's voice came through.

"Good night, Rachel, dear."

"Good night, darling."

No such salutation was granted to me, but I did hear him say the same to Tabatha across the way, and then, moments later, down the hall, I heard the sound of a closing door. In the light of the dying fire I lay among the feathers, mentally counting the number of bedrooms in the house. Rachel must have read my mind because she interrupted my calculations and said, "He'll sleep with Joanna tonight."

"Oh."

"For a while he had his own room, and we each shared a room with our children when we weren't . . . But when Marion came along, we just gave one room over to the boys and, well, it's easier."

"I don't mean to pry."

"It's the way of things."

"I don't see how you can bear it. The thought of Nathan in another woman's bed . . ."

"There are worse hardships, you know."

"I can't imagine."

"Watch yourself, and you won't have to imagine."

I propped myself up on one elbow and turned to look at her. "What do you mean?"

"You won't be able to stop him, Camilla. If his spirit is telling him to take another wife, that's exactly what he's going to do."

"How do you even know—?"

"When he was here last fall—before the baby—he talked to Tillman."

I doubt I would have felt much more betrayed if he'd actually come home with a second wife in tow. Words failed me as I clutched the sheet in my hand. Rachel must have taken my gesture as a precursor to a violent blow, because she sat up and scooted away.

"Now, wait just a minute." She held up her own hand in defense. "He only talked to Tillman *after* he'd talked with Brigham."

"Brigham Young?" How strange to hear the revered name of the prophet dropped so casually in conversation.

"Yes. When Nathan met with him about the—"

"The chairs."

"Right. The chairs. Apparently Brigham asked him about his family."

"He didn't tell me any of this. Why would he not tell me?"

"He's a man," she said, finally relaxing against the headboard. I followed her lead. "What man wants to admit failure?"

My thoughts went back to that afternoon, the tightness in Nathan's face and the fight for control in his voice. "*He didn't like the design for the temple chairs*" he'd said, and I thought he'd carried the burden of rejection.

"Are you saying our family is a failure?"

Rachel reached out a reassuring hand and patted my arm. "Of course I don't believe that. And neither does Nathan. But he doesn't have the luxury of seeing life through his own eyes. He's measuring himself by the words of the prophets."

We remained silent for a while as the room grew darker and darker. As the final shadows disappeared, I whispered, "Rachel?"

"Yes."

"Why did you bring me here?"

"To show you."

"Show me what?"

"That really, darling, it's not so bad."

The next morning I awoke to an empty bed and a full agenda. Downstairs, the kitchen was a bustle of breakfast making with all four women deftly dodging the antics of six rambunctious children.

"Boys! If you're late for school again, your father will have you cutting a switch when you get home."

It was Joanna who issued the warning, and the three boys

took it to heart, shoveling last bites of biscuit into their mouths before tearing out. To my surprise, Rachel wore a plain day dress covered by a blue apron and stood at the stove, stirring a large skillet of sausage gravy.

"You slept late, Mama!" Melissa and Lottie ran and hugged my legs. I bent to give each a kiss on top of their heads.

"Why didn't you wake me?" I spoke to Rachel, who was lifting a plate down from the cupboard. "I could have helped."

"Consider yourself on holiday," she said, her smile as bright as the morning sun streaming through the window. "We're certainly able to put breakfast together."

Sitting at the kitchen table with a heaping plate of eggs, biscuits, and gravy before me, I saw neither the haughtiness nor the subservience of the previous evening. The four women jostled each other good-naturedly, handing both chores and children off to each other with equal ease. Their low laughter added to the warmth from the cookstove, and I wrapped myself in it, pushing away thoughts of long, quiet evenings with only Kimana's dark-eyed silence for conversation.

While Marion and Tabatha finished the dishes, Joanna took the baby and ushered my girls and the toddler upstairs to wash up and get ready for a day at the market. Rachel, meanwhile, took a large, square basket from a hook on the wall and began to pack it with loaves of bread wrapped in clean tea towels, jars of jam, and a ball of butter.

"We'll take this to Evangeline," she said. "And some of those cookies from last night." She continued rummaging through the cupboards, taking out all kinds of jars and packages and sacks cinched with ribbon, moving with a sense of purpose that defied the watchful eyes of her sister wives.

When all was tucked in and covered with a cheerful square of bright red flannel, she took my plate—scraped clean—over to the washbasin and summoned me to follow her into the front parlor, where she had "just a few things to tend to."

The full light of day showcased the parlor in all its splendor. Lush red upholstery on the sofa and high-backed chairs, raised red velvet on the wallpaper, intricate floral design on the carpet. I stood at the window and looked out to the well-groomed, busy street. Each of the homes probably had a parlor just like this one. Households just like this one, and I thought, *This is what Nathan wants*.

Rachel sat behind me at a small mahogany writing desk, her pen filling the room with a scratching noise as she composed a note on a piece of thick, cream-colored stationery.

"Do you have anything to post?" she asked. "The mail's running next week."

I'd composed a letter to my parents, telling them of both the impending birth of our third child and the sad news of losing him so soon. Perhaps if they knew about my unhappiness—if they could picture their daughter so far away and lost and hurting—their own hearts might soften toward me.

"It's upstairs," I said, letting the lace curtain drop against the glass.

Walking along the sidewalks of Salt Lake City with Rachel felt like being an attendant to a queen. She held her head high and regal, dipping it to say good morning to every third person we passed. I was right beside her, and occasionally the return greetings were extended to me, but for the most part I was more like a rumpled shadow, half a step behind, carrying the regal basket packed for the poor.

I never ceased to be amazed at the changes in the city

each time I visited. More streets, more stores, more people. On that day I noticed women shopping in pairs—or even threes or fours—with passels of children in tow. *Sister wives*, I thought, and I scrutinized each one, looking to see if I could recognize any spark of friendship or affection. Most wore an eerily identical serene expression, like a polite mask they'd wear to church instead of to a dry goods store.

By the time we arrived at Evangeline's home, my nose felt as frozen as the smile on my face, though we'd probably walked less than a mile. The houses on this street were markedly different from those where Rachel lived. No picket fences or wide walkways here. These were simple, unadorned one- or two-story buildings, constructed with an unsettling uniformity. Of course I'd visited Evangeline before, when her father was alive, but those visits had been in the spring and summer, when window boxes planted with bright flowers lent a cheerful air to these modest structures. Now, in the end-of-winter bleakness, they appeared uninviting. When we reached number seventy-one, I noticed Rachel's deep breath and squared shoulders before she raised her leather-gloved hand to rap smartly on the door.

Even given reports of Evangeline's dire circumstances, nothing prepared me for the girl who opened the door to us. I say girl because that's how Evangeline always remained in my mind, even though we were the same age. Perhaps it was because she'd been so devoted to caring for her father and younger brothers that she'd forgone the responsibilities of marriage and children. Or maybe her looks—bright red hair and freckles—gave her an aura of perpetual youth. Whatever the case, Evangeline had always been some form of the cheerful, exuberant girl I'd met in the clearing by the river all those years ago.

Until today.

Every last drop of that girl was gone, soaked up by something within, drying her up until only this shell with a shock of unruly red foam remained. Her face was drawn to a point, her lips cracked at the corners of her mouth. Her eyes darted between the two of us in momentary feral fear before she stretched her face into a thin, tight smile and opened her door wide.

"What a lovely surprise! Come in, girls; come in."

Rachel paused over the threshold to bend and receive a welcoming kiss, and when my turn came, I followed suit. Her lips were dry and rough against my cheek, and I couldn't ignore a distinctive sourness about her as I bent closer.

We walked into a modest front room, curtains drawn against the winter sunlight. A threadbare sofa and two wooden chairs anchored a worn rug. A small porcelain dog sat on the mantel above a small, dark fireplace.

"Goodness, Eve," Rachel said, "it's as cold in here as it is outside."

"I lit a fire this morning. It's just burned out."

"Well, would you light the stove?" She headed into the kitchen. I automatically followed. "I'd like to put some water on."

"No, Rachel." Evangeline sounded like a woman on the brink of losing control in her own home. "I need to be frugal—"

"I'll send Tillman over tomorrow with some wood," Rachel said over her shoulder. Without missing a step, she strolled into the kitchen and instructed me to set the basket on the table. This room had a little more cheer, with a bright rag rug and a collection of blue glass bottles lining the windowsill. Making herself at home, Rachel began to put away the contents of the basket, placing the loaves of bread on the shelves of the empty pie safe and stacking the jars of pickles and preserves on the shelf above it.

"Thank you so much," Evangeline said, giving tiny

adjustments to each item after Rachel put it away. "I wasn't sure I'd be up to baking this week."

I looked around the meager kitchen and wondered if she had the ingredients to make even a single loaf of bread. The hunger in her eyes and the gauntness of her cheeks fueled my doubt, but I said, "How nice, now, that you won't have to."

"Oh, Camilla," Evangeline said, newly noticing that I'd walked into the room. "I haven't seen you since the baby. How are you?"

She held out open, thin arms to me, and what could I do but walk into her fragile embrace. Her hair scratched at my neck, and her voice rasped words of comfort. As I looked over her shoulder, I saw Rachel rummaging through the basket once more, which puzzled me, because we'd already put away everything we'd packed. Then I saw that she wasn't going through the basket itself but was reaching under the large square of linen that lined the bottom. From there she pulled a small, flat box I didn't remember packing.

"What is that?" I asked once I'd been released from Evangeline's clumsy embrace.

"Evangeline doesn't approve," Rachel said, squinching her nose. "And for that matter, neither does my husband or the sister wives or just about anybody in this entire place."

"Not to mention the prophet," Evangeline said. "Or Heavenly Father."

"And I say *bother* to all of them," Rachel replied. She lifted a bundle of linen out of the basket and unwrapped it to reveal a small copper kettle, and then I knew what was in the mysterious flat box.

"Tea!"

"Shhh." Rachel and Evangeline both held their fingers to their lips, though for Rachel, at least, the warning was in jest.

"You know it's forbidden." Evangeline crossed her spindly arms.

"Forbidden, *pshaw*. It's discouraged, if anything. Looks like somebody needs to go back and read her Word of Wisdom."

"You know very well I've studied the *Doctrine and Covenants* as much as anybody. I know exactly what it says: 'Hot drinks are not for the body or belly.'"

"Oh, spare us the sermon, Evangeline."

Throughout the conversation, Rachel continued her preparations—lighting the stove, pouring water from the pewter jug into the copper pot—a scene both achingly familiar and strange. I hadn't touched tea or coffee since leaving home. At first I thought it was merely a case of rationing on the trail, but when we arrived, when we had our home and the means to stock a pantry and kitchen, Nathan wouldn't have it in the house. Now Rachel reached up to the top shelf in the cupboard and took down a single cup. After a brief hesitation, she reached down a second, dangling it by its handle and looking at me questioningly. Without thinking, I nodded, already anticipating the comfort of feeling the warm cup in my hand.

"Disgraceful," Evangeline said, pulling out a chair and dropping herself into it.

"I brought sugar." Rachel produced a small paper packet. "But no milk. Can you spare us a little milk, Sister Evangeline?"

"I notice you're not brazen enough to do this in your own house. You come sneaking into mine."

"Tillman wouldn't have it. And those others—"

"Oh! I get so tired of listening to you complain about your life, Rachel. Why, if I had—"

"Stop it, both of you." The stove was just beginning to warm up the room, and I couldn't bear the coldness of their snapping. "Can't we just enjoy an afternoon together? with friends? Don't you see what a luxury that is?"

Evangeline looked down, pouting, and Rachel continued spooning tea.

I sat in the chair opposite Evangeline and reached across the table to touch her hand. My fingers could have encircled both of her wrists at once. "I remember once, not long before I met both of you, spending an afternoon with my mother, drinking tea and reading the Bible. I remember feeling so grown-up. So much like a lady, I . . ." Words lodged in my throat as I forced down the memory. It seemed cruel to force such an image on Rachel, who had never known a mother, and Evangeline, who had never tasted such a ritual. But most of all, it seemed cruel to me, to think about how I'd walked away from that life and wandered into this one that was beginning to twist my soul.

"When I was in the orphanage," Rachel said, joining us, "once the girls turned twelve, we would get to have tea with one of our teachers every other Saturday afternoon. My poor brother was already out living on the streets, working where he could, and there I was, sipping hot tea in a parlor. I told him about it once when he came to visit. I cried and cried, feeling so guilty. But do you know what he told me?"

"What?" I asked, curious. By now there was little I didn't know of Nathan's childhood.

"He told me that when I grew up, I'd have a china tea set and a parlor and I'd have tea with my lady friends every day."

"And think how empty that life would be," Evangeline said.

"Don't say that." The lump in my throat dislodged, allowing me to jump to Rachel's defense.

"I just meant—" she turned to Rachel—"that was before. If you had achieved that, you wouldn't know the revelations of the prophet. You might have some temporal comfort, but what about your eternity?"

"I refuse to see the connection," Rachel said, and her tone ended the argument.

By then the water was boiling, and she busied herself getting the tea to steep, working with her back squarely to us. While the little kitchen grew warmer with the heat from the stove, it grew colder with silence. The next sound was that of tea being poured into a cup. And then another. Evangeline remained stony, her thin lips and brow equally furrowed. Rachel picked up her cup and formed her lips into a pretty O to cool the surface. I merely stared at mine for what seemed an eternity, watching the steam rise and dance above the rim. But a longing to taste it consumed me. I wrapped my hands around the cup, comforted by the heat, and bowed my head.

Surely, Lord, my soul means more to you than this.

Finally I lifted the cup to my lips and took a sip. It was hot—wonderfully so—and I did not let it linger on my tongue. Instead, I swallowed quickly, relishing that moment it balanced at the top of my throat before winding its way down, leaving a heated trail of bitterness tinged with sweet.

I must have sighed or made some sound of contentment, because Rachel sent me an indulgent smile and said, "Good, isn't it?"

"You two make me sick," Evangeline said, but I could tell her anger had softened.

"Do you know what would be nice?" I asked, overwhelmed with the memory of the last time I'd had tea with my mother. "Let's read a little Scripture together."

Rachel rolled her eyes, but Evangeline declared it a fine idea and started to jump up from the table. I grabbed her hand, refreshed by how cool her skin felt against my palm. "Bring a Bible."

"All right." But she didn't sound happy about it.

Once she'd left the room, I leaned close to Rachel and whispered, "Is this why you brought me here? To sneak a cup of tea?"

"Don't be silly." She took another dainty sip. "But it is delicious, isn't it?"

It was, and I responded by taking another satisfying gulp. "Why *are* we here?"

"Are you happy with Nathan?"

"Of course I am." But the question shocked me so, I sloshed my tea and had to set my cup down to slurp what I'd spilled on my hand.

"I want you to think about your home—your cozy little house with Nathan and the girls. Now look around you here."

I didn't have to. It struck me today just as it had every time I'd come to visit Evangeline. Her home always seemed so silent and bleak and gray. Bad enough back when her father had lain in the bedroom upstairs, incoherent after his stroke. How much more now that she lived here alone, squirreling away her fuel and waiting for the next charity basket to stock her pantry.

"What are you asking?"

"At least it would be somebody you know. Somebody you already love as a sister."

The impact of what Rachel was suggesting burned more bitter than the tea. "I—I couldn't."

"Nobody's ever going to marry her." She spoke quickly, furtively, her eyes darting to the kitchen door.

"Why not? She's young—"

Rachel snorted.

"What? She's my age," I said, though as I thought about having had three children—even with one of them buried—I felt anything but young. "And she's such a Saint." With that, I hoisted my cup of tea, making a toast.

"Too much, really. I think most men would consider her a threat to their spiritual authority. Face it—" she scooted closer—"she's going to live alone, die alone, and then get married by proxy to some old coot trying to increase his eternal family."

"I don't believe that."

"Don't believe what?" My back was to the kitchen door, so I hadn't seen or heard Evangeline's approach.

"Same old argument," Rachel said, surprising me with the ease of her lie. "To tea or not to tea."

I giggled despite myself and was relieved to see that Evangeline smiled too. She slipped back into her chair and slid a worn leather-covered Bible across the table. "Here, you read, Camilla."

I tried to block out Rachel's insinuation, stalling for time as I took one more sip of my drink before setting my cup down and running my fingers across the delicate tooling on the cover. "It's beautiful."

"It was my father's. From before he joined the church."

I had no idea what to read, where to turn. We read from *The Book of Mormon* every night in our home—always Nathan, his voice filling our little sitting room, wrapping us up in sacred words. In truth, I must confess, there were nights I wasn't sure which text he was reading from. Joseph Smith's words seemed to be so carefully crafted to match those of Paul or Moses or David. But today, I would know.

"This is the Word of God," I said, more to myself than to the others. "What do you want me to read?"

Rachel merely shrugged, but Evangeline drummed her fingers on the table, deep in thought.

"Shall I just flip open to a page?" I suggested.

"Something from the Psalms," Evangeline said. "That's all Papa ever wanted to hear when he was sick, and it would be nice to hear somebody else reading them for a change."

"No," Rachel said, pulling the Bible to her. "I'll read." She began immediately to thumb through the pages, backward and forward, until finally seeming satisfied. "'Now it came to pass,'" she read, "'in the days when the judges ruled, that there was a famine in the land.'"

At first what she read was little more than a list of unfamiliar names—the very passages that so frustrated me as a child. But then, one came along that I recognized: Ruth.

And she continued on, about the death of Naomi's husband and sons and these three women left alone. How Orpah returned to her people, but Ruth . . .

"'. . . whither thou goest, I will go; and where thou lodgest, I will lodge: thy people shall be my people, and thy God my God. . . .'"

The very same words Nathan had said to me one long-ago afternoon; rather, the words he had enticed me to say. At the time they'd seemed so romantic, so full of the promise of a life built together. Hearing them now, though, the romance was stripped away. These were the words spoken from one woman to another. Words of survival. A chill raced across me, and I looked to the nearly empty wood box next to Evangeline's stove. Then I looked at Evangeline herself, her narrow, catlike eyes now wide as she took in the story of this woman given the chance at a new life with a man willing to take her into his home.

At points during the story, Rachel lifted one perfectly arched brow and looked at me over the book. By the time she came to the final verse, my tea had grown cold, half of it untouched in the cup.

"Such a beautiful story," Evangeline said.

"Isn't it?" Rachel closed the Bible carefully and slid it across the table. "What do you think, Camilla?"

I knew what she wanted me to say. Nathan had been her Naomi, arranging her marriage and securing her future. Now she wanted him to play the role of Boaz, giving shelter and a home to our own redheaded Ruth. But I steeled myself against such an appeal.

"Beautiful, indeed." I gulped the rest of my now-cold tea and wiped a sleeve across my mouth in a most unladylike manner. "I should get back to the girls."

If Evangeline wanted to have company for the rest of the afternoon, she made no show of it. Within minutes Rachel and I were escorted to her narrow front door, where we repeated the same ritual of hugs and quick, dry kisses with which we had greeted each other. This time, though, Evangeline held me a little tighter, and I, her.

"I'm going to be all right, Camilla," she whispered in my ear. "There is a plan. We are all in the hands of Heavenly Father."

"I know," I said, but I knew then that her plan would never be my plan. In fact, I was beginning to wonder if her God was my God.

CHAPTER 15

My visit to Salt Lake City lasted three more days, most of which I spent in various charitable pursuits. Several of the families in Rachel's ward were well-off and mindful of their responsibility to less-fortunate Saints. They put together housewarming kits to be presented to those families who would be arriving at the end of summer; many of their afternoons were spent piecing together quilts, cutting and hemming sheets and towels, or knitting socks and scarves. So many women in so many parlors, sometimes twenty of us in one room. Most of them were sister wives—some literally so, as they were sisters married to the same man. Children climbed in and around us. Daughters as young as twelve years old joined in both the task and the conversation. It occurred to me each day that I felt full and safe. Cushioned on all sides from loneliness and melancholy. Hours would fly by and I wouldn't give a single thought to anything beyond the next amusing story or bit of gossip.

Rachel didn't say another word about Evangeline becoming a second wife to Nathan, and neither did I. The matter sat between us like an uneasy, unspoken truce. It occurred to me after spending so much time in Rachel's world that the subject of one man having multiple wives was hardly a topic worthy of any discussion. It was such common practice, we'd just as well discuss whether or not dogs should bark or birds should fly.

On the last night of my visit, after Tillman leaned through the door to give Rachel a swift peck on the cheek, I asked her if she still loved him.

"As much as I ever did."

And then another question—one that had been nagging at me since my arrival. "Does it bother you, then? to think of him sharing a bed with another woman?"

"Is that why you're so reluctant to agree to Nathan taking a second wife? because of what will happen in bed? Tell me, Camilla, is the marriage bed the all-consuming center of your marriage?"

"Of course not." I was glad of the dark room to hide my blush.

"A marriage is work. Building a home and building a family."

"But if you knew—right from the start—that Tillman would take several different wives, would you still have married him?"

"I didn't have a choice."

"But if you *did*."

"When my brother arranged this marriage for me, he was

doing the best he knew to do. He found the strongest man of faith—"

"But if you knew what that faith meant, Rachel—what it would ask of you—would you . . . ?" I couldn't go on because we both knew that I wasn't asking about her marriage to Tillman anymore.

"Are you asking whether or not I would join the church?" Her voice dropped to a whisper so low, the sounds barely registered.

I nodded slowly, feeling my own fear spread within me. "I need to know—because lately . . . How do I explain?"

"Like an unsettling in your spirit." She took my hands and together we knelt before the fire. "Like everything that Joseph Smith said is just—"

"Wrong."

We finished the sentence together, but Rachel's voice lilted up, asking a question, while I gave an emphatic statement. If I'd been hoping for a sympathetic ear—and the impromptu tea party the other day surely gave me such hope—I was sorely mistaken. I watched her beautiful face turn to steel before my eyes, her changing nature reminding me of Nathan, in no comforting way.

"No. Do you hear me?"

"But—"

"Do not speak blasphemy against this church, Camilla."

"Blasphemy?"

"The word of the prophet is a direct word from Heavenly Father. You know that. And if he commands us to build our families, if he urges our men to take several wives, if he—"

"Tells us not to drink hot beverages?"

The challenge hung in the air, unanswered, while Rachel took a moment to compose a response.

"That was wrong of me," she said finally. "To be such a poor example. When I was supposed to . . . help."

"But don't you see? How can we grant one man the power to make decisions over the most trivial matters as well as those that govern how we live our very lives? If you can disregard one doctrine, why not another?"

"Some doctrines are more important than others."

"But none of this is from God!" There, I'd said it, and far too loudly for the circumstances because the look of utter horror on Rachel's face caused me to clamp my hand—too late—over my mouth and glance over my shoulder to the door I fully expected to be replaced with Tillman's looming figure.

"Watch what you say." The edge of warning was impossible to mistake.

"I'm sorry. I didn't mean—"

"Listen, I don't much care one way or another." She'd been looking past my shoulder at the door behind me too but stared deep into my eyes once she was satisfied that her husband wasn't about to batter it down. "I simply want peace in my home. Now—" she cocked her head and smiled—"let's get in bed and get to sleep before the fire burns out. Shall I say an evening prayer for us?"

"If you like."

We joined hands and bowed our heads. My eyes shut tight, so tight that I could see shadows of the fire dancing within my darkness.

"Heavenly Father, thank you for my husband and the life we have built together. I lift my sister Camilla up to you, that she will have peace in her heart . . ."

Whatever else Rachel may have prayed is lost to me, as my mind filled with words of my own petition. *Spare me from this life. Give me strength. Help me, Lord, to make a home that is pleasing to you.*

Later, I lay on my back, hands behind my head, listening to the last cracklings of the fire. We'd nothing left to say to each other, but the silence between us was not uncomfortable. Then, a small sound. At first I attributed it to the sound of a house full of people moving into sleep. But it became clearer, familiar. Unwelcome. Tillman had built an impressive home for his family, but there was no disputing the thinness of his walls. Apparently he'd chosen to exercise his rights as a husband, regardless of the fact that he had a guest under his roof.

It was my intention to ignore the noise coming from down the hall—feign sleep, if need be. But Rachel chose to distract me with conversation instead.

"Do you love Nathan?"

"Of course."

"Would you die for him?"

I'd never considered such a thing before, but I knew the answer. "Yes."

"Then you're ready. See, that's what you have to do. A little of me died the first time Tillman brought home another woman. And a little bit of me dies every time—"

"I can't do it."

"You have to. You're his salvation. Joseph Smith was his savior in life, giving him direction. Your job is to save him in the next one. Without you, he doesn't have the promise of an eternal family."

"He has me."

"It's not enough. One woman, one wife. Marriage to you alone will never get him to the highest level of heaven."

"Somewhere, deep down, you know as well as I do that

no person can determine another's salvation. I have no say in where Nathan will spend eternity."

"Then you just love him in this life. Give him what he wants now. Let him have the hope that he'll have you to love in the next one."

The next day, as we were clearing away the lunch dishes, Lottie's voice carried clear through the house.

"It's Papa! Papa! He's come to take us home!"

I heard Melissa's echoing squeal and felt my own heart flutter. I clutched the serving platter I was drying to my chest, just to keep me still. It wasn't a matter of fear, though I surely wasn't the same woman who had arrived here three days ago. It was, in fact, anticipation. The same little thrill I got every time I was about to see Nathan when we'd spent days apart. After putting away the dish, I wiped my hands on my apron and walked out of the kitchen, shouting an admonition to the girls not to run through Aunt Rachel's pretty house. I was summarily ignored as four eager feet stomped through the front hall and the front door flew open. Melissa and Lottie ran outside without their coats, a fact that seemed insignificant when I emerged onto the front porch. The afternoon sun bore down, and the air sat breezeless and dry. If I'd stood still long enough, I might have been tricked into thinking it was springtime. But I didn't stand still. Not for long. Nathan had climbed down from the wagon and stood beside it, holding Lottie in the crook of one arm while Melissa stood with her arms wrapped around his waist.

He looked up from kissing the top of Melissa's head, and his eyes found mine. He wore his butter-colored buckskin jacket and the wide-brimmed hat decorated with a band of woven straw. He took the hat off when he saw me and slowly lowered Lottie to the ground. At that moment, only one thought rang in my head.

He is mine.

There was something precious about that moment—something as weak and temporary as the snow that was in danger of disappearing all around me. That day, when I walked into his arms, when he lowered his head and kissed me, when he held me tight and whispered in my hair how very much he loved me, how very much he missed me, I knew. My heart was full to bursting with love as much as it ever had been. And as much as it ever would be.

"Take me home," I said, breathing in the smell of him.

"That's my favorite thing to do." I looked up and he was smiling that devilish grin. "How soon will you be ready?"

"We packed this morning."

Before we would start the drive home, however, Nathan had business to attend to.

"I've brought six to present," he said, slapping the side of the wagon filled with half a dozen canvas-draped structures. By then Rachel and Tillman had joined us outside, and Rachel draped a welcome shawl across my shoulders before greeting her brother with a bear-size hug. Tillman shook his hand and peered into the wagon's bed.

"Trying again, Nate?"

"Look at this." Nathan climbed into the wagon and, with theatrical flair, untied the twine holding the canvas and lifted it, revealing the secret underneath. Anybody passing by might think we were all giving far too much attention to an ordinary wooden chair, but I knew that, for Nathan, what one person would deem a simple chair was actually a work of art—a carefully crafted piece, the result of countless hours in his workshop at the back of our barn. And this one was particularly beautiful. It was, at first glance, a simple, armless wooden chair with three wide slats across the back. Closer inspection, though, showed that each of the three slats had a slight slope rising from the top and creating the effect of a beehive shape. The beehive design was repeated on top of the spires on either side of the chair's back, and at the top of each leg. All of this was stained to a rich honey color.

"Oh, Nate," Rachel said, reaching one hand out to touch it. "If Brigham doesn't want this . . ."

"It's beautiful work," Tillman said, rocking back on his heels.

"Go ahead." Nathan handed the chair over to him. "Have a seat in it."

Obliging, Tillman set the chair on the ground and made quite a show of settling his weight on the seat. "Very nice," he said, shifting his position this way and that.

"Not as intricate as the last," Nathan said. "None of the scrolling. Solid wood seat—much sturdier than the woven leather."

"It's beautiful, darling," I said, my heart filled with the same pride I saw in his eyes.

"The others are a variation on the same design. I have an appointment to meet with him at one o'clock—"

"With Brigham?" Tillman stood and handed the chair up to Nathan.

"More likely with one of his associates."

I could tell he envied Tillman's easy use of the prophet's name.

"Well, if your meeting is at one o'clock," Rachel said, consulting the little watch pinned to her bodice, "you'd better hurry. I suppose we can keep Camilla and the girls entertained for another hour."

"I think they should go with me," Nathan said. "I'd like to show them the temple."

Melissa and Lottie obviously agreed, as they jumped up and down in place, clapping their hands in delight.

"Not much more than a pile of stones right now," Tillman said.

"Maybe so." Nathan finished securing the canvas around the chair once again before swinging himself over the side of the wagon and landing with a slight bounce beside me. "But I want my girls to see it. So when they're grown women and they come to worship, they'll remember."

He put his arm around my shoulder, drawing me companionably close. I resisted the urge to freeze in his embrace. I didn't want to see the temple, and I certainly didn't want to see Brigham Young, no matter how remote the possibility. But I knew what this meant to my husband. Those bundles of canvas in the back of the wagon represented his life's work, and he wanted to share that with me. So I tucked myself under his arm and lifted my cheek to his kiss, saying, "Of course, darling."

Rachel called into the house for Marion to fetch down our bags.

It took some stern talking to convince the girls that no, they could not sit in Papa's chairs during the drive to Temple Square. My argument, that at the first jostle they could fall over—and possibly out—met with pouting protest. It wasn't until Nathan turned in his seat and reminded them that those chairs had been crafted for the elders and apostles of the church, to sit in the frontmost rows of Heavenly Father's sacred temple, that they uttered a halfhearted, "Yes, sir," and sat on their bottoms.

We hadn't had any new snow for days, and the afternoons had been warm enough to melt much of what had been on the ground, leaving overturned lumps mixed with mud. A mess to be sure, but an early harbinger of spring, a hint of warmer days to come. I couldn't wait to get back home, where I could close my eyes and breathe deep the sweetness of moist, cool air—that which came before the world surged green with new life. Perhaps Nathan and I could have a new life started of our own. I scooted closer and slid my arm through his.

"I missed you, Millie," he said. "But did you have a nice visit?"

"Mm-hm. But busy."

"Did you visit Sister Evangeline?"

"Just for one afternoon."

"And how is she?"

"Hard to say for sure. You know how she's always joking."

"Aunt Rachel says Auntie Evangeline needs to get married or she's going to end up a charity case until the day she dies."

"Melissa!" I twisted in my seat to look into her mischievous blue eyes.

Nathan laughed. "That sister of mine has always had a way with words."

"A talent I hope our daughter doesn't inherit."

By then we had arrived at the hub of activity in the heart of the new Zion. Blinding white stone, its brightness the envy of the snow, hewn and fit perfectly together. As close as we were, it was impossible to take in the whole building in one glance. The entire structure was intersected with scaffolding, and the music of men's voices raised in song rang through the sound of hammers and saws and pulleys.

"Look, girls," Nathan said, bringing the team to a halt. "Those walls? That's what comes from the quarry. Imagine, just a few months ago, that wall was just part of a big rock until we dug it out and brought it here to smooth and square it off."

"Can we go inside?" Lottie was stretched so far over the wagon bed's wall that Nathan reached back to grab her.

"There is no inside right now," he said, lifting her up and over into his lap. "And I'll be an old, old man before there is."

"We're lucky," I said. "We get to enjoy these very stones in their real temple."

"What do you mean, 'their *real* temple'?"

"Back home. In the quarry. Where they're part of God's creation. There's more of God in the side of any mountain than in any temple built by man. The Bible says our very body is a temple. All of this—" I gestured to the construction in front of us—"is simply—"

"Our way of showing our devotion to Heavenly Father."

I could sense Nathan's disapproval and opted to say nothing more, but I couldn't quell the distaste I felt for the scene. So much work; so much sacrifice. Building this temple, the same way men like Tillman were building their families, and what did they have on the inside? Or Evangeline, with her heart so devoted and her life so empty.

"I just meant that we're lucky. To have so much."

Seeming satisfied with my response, he settled Lottie on the seat between us and climbed down from the wagon. Once he was on the ground, he took off his jacket, revealing his nicest green wool shirt and leather suspenders. He also lifted his hat and quickly ran his fingers through his hair before replacing it.

"You look very handsome," I said, sounding more like a proud parent than a supportive wife. My little attempt at humor did nothing to lighten the moment, however, and he simply rubbed his hands together and looked around, seeming lost. That's when a man dressed in an impeccable black wool suit came upon us. He was a stranger to me, but he looked like any other powerful Mormon in the basin—white hair, thick jowls covered with wiry whiskers, narrowed blue eyes encased in soft folds. He and Nathan were obviously well acquainted because he took Nathan's hand, offering a friendly greeting.

"What have you got for us this time?" He looked up into the wagon. "Besides your lovely family, I assume."

"My wife, Camilla," Nathan said. "And my daughters, Melissa and Lottie. This is Bishop Johansson."

I nodded. "Good afternoon."

Bishop Johansson did little more than acknowledge my presence before turning his attention back to Nathan. "Show me."

"Show him the beehive one, Papa!"

For the second time that afternoon I found myself turned around, hushing Melissa. Nathan barely gave her a glance. Still, he lowered the wagon's tailgate and lifted out the same chair he'd shown us earlier. Somehow, here in sight of this massive structure, the chair seemed significantly diminished.

"You know," Bishop Johansson said, slowly circling the chair, "we are getting so many new European converts. One man who just arrived last summer from Brussels is a fifth-generation craftsman. A true artist."

I could not have felt the sting of his words more strongly if he'd slapped my face with them. I didn't turn to look at Nathan, but I knew him well enough to know the expression on his face. His eyes would be bright, his jaw set, his lips such that the top would seem to be swallowed by the bottom.

"Our papa's an artist. He makes furniture for everybody."

This time I did not hush Melissa's outburst but silently reached my hand back to find her shoulder and give it a quieting pat.

"Of course he is," Bishop Johansson said. "But we are dealing with matters of great importance here."

"I understand completely," Nathan said, and I knew he'd taken a deep breath and put on a big smile. "Perhaps I'll leave these with you for you to consider—"

"I'll make a sketch." The older man reached into his breast pocket and produced a small notebook and pencil. "I'll share it with Brother Brigham at the next opportunity, and we'll send word to you of his opinion."

"Fair enough." Nathan held his arms up and summoned Lottie to climb down into them. "In the meantime, I'll take my girls—all three of them—for a little stroll."

Without questioning, I gathered my skirt and allowed Nathan to hand me down from the wagon's seat.

I waited until we were out of earshot before asking what he thought of the bishop's reaction.

"He thinks I'm a fool. I could design the throne of heaven and he wouldn't care."

We walked the expanse of the temple's foundation; we could fit the whole of what we claimed as our property within its midst. If I thought the tour would soften the blow of the bishop's opinion, I was mistaken. By the time we returned to the wagon, the man was gone, having abandoned the wagon full of Nathan's handiwork to the street. His judgment could not have been more pronounced.

"That's it," Nathan said. "Let's go home."

Another long ride. Our conversation slogged every bit as much as our wagon's wheels. Not even the girls' enthusiastic recap of the week's events could elicit much more than a preoccupied grunt from their father.

"This is pretty slow going. You must have left home in the middle of the night to have arrived so early."

"I woke up in the middle of the night missing you." No light hint of romance in his reply.

"I missed you, too."

"Nonsense. There are a dozen people living in that house."

I hazarded a quick kiss on his shoulder. "But none of them are you."

Silence for at least another mile.

"Would you like to stay with her for the summer?"

"No," I said, uneasy with his question. He never asked questions unless he had an idea of the answer he wanted to hear. "Why would you ask such a thing?"

"Because I don't know if I want you and the girls to be alone."

My uneasiness dug deeper. "Where would you be?"

"I had a chance to talk with Tillman today—just for a moment when you were getting the girls ready. There's a company coming in from England, due to land in New Orleans. They want to hire men who can give them a swift, safe passage."

"There's no such thing."

"There is if you have money for new wagons—and you're not one of a hundred of them."

"They're not part of the Emigration Fund?"

"Nope. Private party."

"Why would you do this?"

"Money," he said without much thought. "Enough to cover whatever work I'll miss while I'm gone. To give us an easy winter when I get back."

"All right," I said, unconvinced. He'd never been one to care about money before.

He slouched in his seat, letting the reins go slack in his hands. His head drooped, and I knew he was searching for the words that would be least hurtful. I waited. Silence was not a new thing to us. Finally, after taking a deep breath, he spoke, still keeping his gaze focused on the ground that passed beneath our wagon.

"I've lost my way, Camilla."

For the briefest moment, I almost brought myself to a different conclusion. I hoped to hear that my absence had convinced him that he needed me—and only me—in his life. That moment was the brightest of the entire drive. Maybe, if I'd never asked, "In what way?"

"I'm nothing here."

"You're everything to us."

"I'm nothing in the eyes of the church."

"Would you rather the opinions be reversed?"

I don't know that he even heard me, for which, looking back, I am grateful. His answer may have been unspoken, as most obvious answers are.

"I can't contribute my art to the temple. I don't have the approval to go on a mission. The last time I felt a true burning in my spirit was when I was on the trail here. I figure if I can't bring people into the church, I can bring the church into Zion."

"Are you quite certain the burning in your spirit didn't have something to do with me?"

He tilted his head and offered me a crescent smile. "Of course that played a part."

Living so near the quarry, I'd heard the iron chisels being pounded into granite, and that contact creates a sound that you feel in the very back of your teeth. Such is precisely what I felt at that moment.

"I don't suppose," I said, speaking through the sharpness of the pain, "the same will play a role again?"

"I can promise you, that isn't my design. But I have to contribute something. I have to *do* something."

"Does it matter what I say?"

"I'd love to have your blessing."

"But you don't need it."

"No."

"When do you leave?"

"First of May. Tillman is giving me the pick of his horses."

"A swift pony?" I made no attempt to disguise my bitterness.

"Hardly. Beautiful Thoroughbred. Two-year-old bay named Honey."

"I was talking about the promise you made to me. How you'd take me home if I ever lived an unhappy day."

"I didn't understand back then how God works. We can't run away from unhappiness, Camilla. It'll just chase us down."

"And you can't chase happiness, Nathan. It'll just run away."

"I'm not chasing happiness, love. Trust me, the horse that will take me east will run just as fast bringing me home."

CHAPTER 16

I mourned Nathan's absence as would a widow, and at first I was treated as one by our neighbors. Not a day went by without having someone show up at my door with a gift: loaves of bread, rinds of cheese, and jars of anything that came out of their spring gardens. And every gift came with the same conversation:

"We miss seeing you and your lovely daughters at church."

"You can return the platter when you come to the Sabbath meeting."

"The recipe? Of course! I'll bring it to church on Sunday."

But I didn't go. Not once. And the only tug on my conscience came from the fact that I'd promised Nathan we would.

Every Sunday morning I felt I was living a lie to him. Still, I reasoned, it paled in comparison to the promise he'd broken.

It wasn't long before our community abandoned me as surely as he had. The first week of June marked a week since I'd entertained any sort of social call or, for that matter, any friendly return of a greeting when I made my way to our trading post. Normally, on trading day, all of the children would play outside while parents conducted their business inside. Today I'd brought five balls of good butter and two dozen eggs, which Brother Nelson grudgingly took from me, giving me a sparse handful of coins in return. At first I thought there had been a mistake, that he'd miscounted or confused the value of our newly minted money. But when I asked if that were the case, he merely shook his head and turned his back, tending another customer with contrasting grace.

As I was turning to leave, Melissa appeared at my elbow, complaining that none of the children would play with them.

"They called you a heretic, Mama." She looked just like her father then, her face set in the same mask of hurt and defiance I'd seen on his so many times before. "What do they mean?"

Lottie was clinging to my skirts, her thumb in her mouth.

"Who said that?" I dropped my voice to a whisper.

"Mary Justus. She said Papa was weak-willed and that you were a heretic. And she sounded so mean."

"What did you say?"

"Nothing, because I didn't know what the word meant. What is it, Mama?"

"Never you mind." I dropped the money in my pocket and gathered the girls to me as I walked out of the store, fully aware of every eye following.

The walk back was brisk and silent. Whenever one of

the girls asked a question, I simply picked up the pace, rendering all of us too breathless for conversation. When we finally arrived at our house, Kimana was pulling a pan of biscuits out of the oven. A nagging at the base of my skull compelled me to latch the door once we'd gone inside, an action not lost to Kimana's watchful eyes.

"Problem?" she asked, poking her finger through the top of one biscuit to check that it was baked through.

"Not at all." I made no attempt at cheerfulness.

"Good trade?"

I offered a wan smile. "We've had better."

"Sit," Kimana said as both an invitation and a command. "I'll get you a drink of water."

I eased myself into the rocking chair, still breathless from the walk. My throat felt parched, the word *heretic* lodged at the top of it. I tried to gulp my fear down with the water from the cup Kimana brought to me, but it only grew with each swallow. At last, when I wiped my sleeve across my mouth, Melissa took the cup from me and set it on the table.

"Can you tell me now, Mama? Is it something awful?"

"No," I said, drawing her into my lap, big girl that she was. Lottie was engaged with Kimana, rolling and cutting another batch of biscuits, oblivious to our conversation, though I knew Kimana wasn't missing a single word. "It's not necessarily awful. Not in my case."

"What does it mean?"

"A heretic is somebody who believes things are different from the way you believe."

"What kinds of things?"

I thought carefully, choosing my words. "Religious things, mostly. A heretic has different ideas about who God is or about what happens after we die."

"But how could anybody believe anything different? Everybody knows there's only one God."

"Yes, but they see him differently. For example, what do you know about Jesus Christ?"

"He is the first baby born to God in heaven."

"And, you see," I stalled, knowing my place in this family would never be the same after this conversation, "I don't believe that to be true. I believe Jesus was born to Mary, in Bethlehem, just like we celebrate at Christmas."

"Well, of course he was," Melissa said. If she'd been standing, she'd have had one hand on her hip. "But he was born in heaven first. Like we all were."

"I don't believe that, either."

Melissa pulled away from me. "Mama! It's true!"

"Oh, darling." I pulled her close to me again and let the chair rock. I looked over the top of her head to see Lottie, happily eating a lump of biscuit dough half the size of her fist. Kimana locked her eyes with mine, and in them I saw something I'd never seen before. Understanding. This was more than those times when she empathized with my pain or shared my frustration. This was a moment where our souls seemed to be reaching out to each other, and something stirred within me.

She knows. Somehow, she knows what I'm trying to say.

And then another message, unspoken but clear.

Be careful.

"So," Melissa said, listlessly twisting a lock of her hair, "is a Gentile and a heretic the same thing?"

"I don't want to talk about this right now."

She ignored me. "Papa says the Gentiles hate us. And that they used to burn our houses and hurt our people. Is that true?"

"Some did." I remembered the last time I saw my father. "They were afraid, I think."

"Afraid of what?"

I didn't know how to explain. At the time I had wondered the same thing. What was to be feared from good, kind, God-loving people who simply went to a different church? I couldn't have known then just how much there was to fear. How everything I knew to be true about my Lord would be stripped away. How my children would be brought up not knowing the truth of who Jesus was. And how they would raise children under the same lie.

Melissa craned her neck and looked at me, demanding an answer.

"It's difficult to explain." All I could offer.

"You were a Gentile before you met Papa, weren't you?"

"Yes."

"Were you afraid?"

"No. But I loved your papa first. . . ." If I hadn't, I wouldn't have been holding this little girl in my arms. I squeezed her and kissed her nose. "And I'm so glad I did."

"Our neighbors act like they're afraid of us." Had I blinked, I would have missed the quiver in her chin; if I looked too closely, we would both be in tears.

"They're not." My own lump of fear grew again.

"Is that why we don't go to church anymore? Because you don't believe in Jesus?"

"Don't say that." I spoke more harshly than I intended, startling Melissa and even calling Lottie's attention away from her overworked dough.

"You must listen to your mother." Kimana came over with a warm biscuit for Melissa. "She knows Jesus. In her heart. She'll teach you."

"Papa used to teach us," Melissa said. She dabbed her tongue on the biscuit. "I miss that."

"I miss Papa too," Lottie said, nibbling her dough.

"Me too." I held out my arm and beckoned Lottie to me. She squirmed into my lap, and the chair creaked under our combined weight. "But there's no reason I can't teach you lessons."

"But you told me you don't believe—"

"I'll teach you the lessons I learned when I was a little girl. Would you like that?"

"I suppose," Melissa said, sounding unconvinced.

"I would like to learn your lessons too, Mrs. Fox." Kimana kept her eyes on her flour-dusted hands.

"That would be fine." I jostled the girls out of my lap and stood. "We'll have our first lesson this evening right after supper. For now, girls, go play outside."

When they were gone, I stood facing Kimana, neither of us speaking. Her face was its usual placid mask—mouth turned down slightly at the corners, eyes a sparkling deep brown. Then, in a gesture of unprecedented affection, she held her arms open wide to me, and the little ball of fear that had been wedged in my throat burst open, bringing with it tears that I shed on her soft shoulder while I wept in her arms. She made soft clucking sounds in my ear, which I eventually recognized as quiet words spoken in her native tongue. Nathan forbade any such utterances, claiming they were the heathen sounds of a godless people. But I found it profoundly soothing, as I instinctively knew that she was whispering prayer.

"Oh, Kimana," I said even as she held me. "What have I done?"

"You have spoken your heart." She ran her soft hands in circles across my back, and I felt myself relaxing against her. My own mother could not have given more comfort.

"I don't think you fully understand."

"I know more than you think." She held me out at arm's length. "You do not share the same God as these other people. Not here." Kimana placed her hand over her heart, leaving a dusting of flour on her dress. I smiled, thinking of the similar trail she must have left on my back.

Still, looking at that mark, I knew. Never had I let the teachings of Joseph Smith worm their way into my heart. I indulged Nathan by listening, but suddenly I felt like I'd been a polite party guest all these years. Like I'd built up a wall around me made of false prayers and forced enthusiasm. But like that wall my father worked so hard to construct around our property, this one was incomplete. I guess I'd never fully closed the gap around what I knew to be the truth—that Jesus Christ needed no new revelation, that his church had not failed, that those who said otherwise were dangerous. My father knew of the danger, as had my mother, but I didn't listen to them. And now I couldn't go back. There'd be no swift horse for me.

"You know," I said, backing away from Kimana's reach, "I'm suddenly quite tired. Would you keep an eye on the girls while I lie down for a quick rest?"

"Of course." She wiped her hands on her apron, her normal air of reservation restored. "I'll take them to see if we can find some wildflowers after I take the last batch out of the oven."

"That would be lovely. Thank you." Before leaving the room, I grabbed her by her wide, soft shoulders and gave her another hug. She gave no reaction but was smiling when we separated and humming one of her native tunes when I shut the bedroom door.

I truly was exhausted, but I had a need far greater than any amount of sleep would provide. I immediately fell to my knees at our bedside, my face flush against the quilt. I did not weep because in that moment, I had no use for tears. All the cleansing I needed would come from within, from my holy, heavenly Father, from my Savior, Jesus Christ, and from the Holy Spirit—so long neglected—who had been dwelling within me since I was a child.

Oh, Father God. I spread my hands out flat on top of the bed. *Forgive me. I've given my ear to false teachings, and I've abandoned your truth. Restore me, Jesus. I know you are my salvation. You alone. Only Jesus.* I repeated this over and over into the silence: "Only Jesus. Only Jesus. Only Jesus." Not Joseph Smith. Not Brigham Young. No golden plates; no angel Moroni. Only Jesus and his death and his resurrection. My sin—this very sin of denying that power—forgiven with that sacrifice.

I don't know how long I stayed on my knees. Indeed, I slept for a time, waking up feeling stronger and better rested than I had in recent memory. Renewed in mind and body. Restored. And though I didn't fully know it at the time, ready to fight a battle beyond my strength. I would not fail my children the way I'd failed my parents. Above all, I would not fail myself.

That evening, after a quick, light supper, the girls and Kimana and I gathered around our table. The blue lamp with the dancing ladies glowed warm in the center, next to a bowl full of cheerful mountain bluebells. I ran my fingers along the cover of our only Bible. It was the small, velvet-covered book I'd been given as "something blue" the morning of my wedding to Nathan, and it shamed me to think of how rarely I'd even looked at it since that day. All of us had come to the table with the air of those attending a very solemn occasion, and the only sound in the room was the click of the tiny latch when I opened the Bible's front cover.

"We're not going to read from *The Book of Mormon?*" Melissa asked, eyeing the Bible suspiciously.

"No," I said gently. "I told you I wanted to teach you what I learned when I was a little girl."

"New stories?" Lottie bounced in her seat.

"Some of them might be," I said. "To you, anyway. Now, where to begin?" I opened the Bible to a random page and allowed my eyes to skim the words. *Show me, Lord, where to begin*. Anxiousness bubbled within me. I'd never attempted to teach anyone about the Bible before, and soon my anticipation was consumed by my uncertainty. The words—tiny in their print—blurred in the lamplight, and I felt every bit as lost and confused as I did on those evenings long ago when I faced the intimidating tome that was our family's Bible. When I could bring a word into focus, I despaired of pronouncing it correctly or giving the isolated verses any meaning whatsoever. I stalled, flipping through the pages, murmuring about finding something perfect to begin our study. Occasionally I looked up around the table to Lottie's increasingly distracted expression, Kimana's indulgent focus, and Melissa's undisguised boredom. The three of them encompassed everything I felt as a young girl, forced by my parents to search for meaning within these complicated Scriptures.

Forgive me, too, Lord, for not feeling connected to you through your Word. And that's when I remembered. My journal.

"I'll be right back."

Lighting a candle from the lamp's flame, I went into our bedroom and to the wooden trunk in the corner. I lifted the lid and sifted through the first layer of treasures—baby things, mostly, dresses and caps and even a christening gown I'd made before realizing that my new faith called for no such garment. Underneath were some of my old dresses that hadn't fit since giving birth to Melissa, and at the bottom, packed away since the building of this home, the tattered notebook I'd brought with me all the way from Iowa. Holding the candle aloft, I let it fall open, my breath catching at the sight of my own unsteady script. Here, in these pages, the Word of God, faithfully copied from the text, word for word. Not a single letter altered. These pages were the place where my very self encountered God himself. Where I recorded whatever truth he had for me.

This was what I would share with my daughters.

I walked into the front room, where Melissa was spinning a small toy on the tabletop and Lottie was snuggled into Kimana's lap.

"When I was a little girl," I said, resuming my place, "my parents required me to read a chapter of the Bible every night and to record a verse from that chapter. I'd almost forgotten all about it."

Melissa was immediately intrigued. We'd just built a schoolhouse close enough for her to attend, and she was quite eager to go, as I'd done little more than practice the most rudimentary of reading and arithmetic with her up to now. She reached out. "May I see?"

"Of course." I slid the book across the table and allowed her to choose a page to open. She scanned it, scowling.

"I've never seen you write this much before."

"It's not an easy thing for me to do," I said. "I'm not very good at it. Sometimes it's much easier to tell stories than to read and write them."

"Is that why Papa always reads to us?"

"Partly." I allowed my eyes to linger on the journal page while I considered her question. The last thing I wanted to do was discourage my daughter from learning to read and write simply because it was difficult for me. "But since Papa is going to be gone for a while, I guess I'll have to get back into practice."

Interestingly enough, I'd begun my practice of copying verses when I was reading the book of Revelation, the last book in the Bible. I had argued with my mother, begging to wait and commence this practice when I started again with Genesis, but she refused. It was a summer evening—just like this very one—and she insisted this was the only way I'd have to practice my penmanship until school started again. In response, I'd chosen the shortest verse in the chapter, and there, living in what had been called the new Zion, the words fell over me like so many stones mined from the quarry. Years and miles away from the first time I touched a pencil to the page, I ran my hand over the words, cleared my throat, and drew up my courage.

"This is from the book of Revelation, chapter 2, verse 4." Another deep breath. "'Nevertheless I have somewhat against thee, because thou hast left thy first love.'" Tears filled my eyes, and I looked up, trying to blink them back, but to no avail.

"Why are you crying, Mama?" Lottie asked.

"That's it?" Melissa said, unmoved. "That doesn't even mean anything. Why would you write that down?"

I couldn't answer. I sat in my chair, eyes lifted to God, and wept. "How could you have known? All those years ago? I was just a child."

"Mama?" Lottie sounded concerned. "Why are you crying? Is it sad?"

"No," I said finally, wiping my eyes and nose on my sleeve—something I never allowed the girls to do. "And yes, a little. You see, it's like I've found something I thought I'd lost."

"Like a treasure?" Lottie asked.

"Very much like that." I longed to take my little girl into

my arms, but she seemed so content on Kimana's lap. In fact, Kimana's eyes looked hungry with more promise of life than I'd ever seen in them before. This, truly, was a moment orchestrated by God, and I would do nothing to disturb it.

"So what exactly does it mean?" My older daughter's voice held more than a hint of skepticism.

"I'm not exactly sure about the details," I answered honestly. "It's been so long. . . ." My words trailed as I reached for the Bible and turned to the last book, skimming the verses until I found the second chapter. Fearful of stumbling over the words, I read them to myself first before imparting them to Kimana and the girls. "This is the word of God going to a church in Eph—Ephesus. He tells them that they are good people, and that they have come through many hardships, but they have abandoned their first love. . . ."

"So who was their first love?"

"Their God." Kimana answered Melissa's question with quiet assurance.

"Yes," I said. "You see, it doesn't matter how good of a person you are or how much you overcome if you don't know Jesus."

"I love Jesus!" Lottie sang out.

"Of course you do, darling. We all do." My glance around the table included Kimana. "But it's important to love Jesus *and* know who he really is."

"He's our brother." The girls spoke in unison.

"No," I said with an authority that came from a power beyond myself. "He is more than that. He is our Lord. He is our Savior."

"But he was born to God just like we all were."

Something cold ran through my soul. My little girl, newly six years old, spoke with the same conviction in this teaching as I did in truth. I don't think I ever had such spiritual poise as a child; indeed, I never had, else I would never have been so easily led away. We'd been taught so differently—I from hours spent dozing in a pew or struggling alone with Scriptures at our table, and she adoring at the feet of her father. Nathan took such delight in teaching his children, and I knew they would never be able to fully separate the doctrine of Joseph Smith from the love they felt for their papa.

"Listen," I said, bringing my voice to a soft, warm place. "Just for now, for the summer while Papa's gone, let's try to learn some new things about Jesus. Things your papa hasn't taught you."

"Like what the Gentiles believe?" I could hear Nathan's disdain coming through Melissa's mouth.

O Lord, help me walk this bridge. "Like what followers of Christ believe. What Jesus himself said to be true."

"But God told Joseph Smith that all of the churches were wrong."

I felt myself rising to an argument when Kimana softly interjected. "Melissa, little one, your mother wants to share her heart with us. Not just words from a book."

Gratitude washed over me, and I reached out to touch the hand of this woman who, after so many silent years, was becoming my friend.

"That's enough for tonight," I said, closing both the Bible and my journal. "It's getting late, and we can talk more tomorrow."

Lottie, her mood largely unchanged, slid from Kimana's lap and came over to kiss me good night. "I'm sorry the story made you cry," she whispered.

"I'm not." I held her to me and breathed the scent of her—sweetgrass and milk. "It's good to cry sometimes. It gives our inside a good washing."

Melissa, however, would have no such sentiment; she barely tolerated my embrace.

"I love you, darling," I said, holding her stiff little body in my arms. "Say a prayer for Papa."

"I do every night."

Later, after supervising washups and tucking the girls in, I came back to the table, where Kimana—long past the time when she usually retired to her own little home—sat in the lamplight. She'd brought our *Book of Mormon* to the table, and it sat alongside the Bible and my old leather journal. Exhausted as I was, I joined her, and for the longest time we sat in silence. I stared at the ribbon of dancing girls painted on the lamp's globe; she stared at me.

"Are they so different, these books?"

I nodded.

"I never knew."

"Did nobody ever try to teach you?" The question burned because I certainly never had.

"When they first came here, into this valley, they tried to tell my people that your Jesus had been here before. Maybe walking this very ground and teaching our ancestors."

"Do you believe that?"

Her face was the softest I'd ever seen it. "Once," she said, "a long time ago, a little boy went to a stream to water his father's horse, and he saw the most beautiful girl on the other side, gathering water into a basket. Because he was a boy and did not know what to do with such beauty, he picked up a stone and threw it across the river. The stone hit the girl here—" she tapped her finger to her temple—"and the girl cried, dropped the basket, and ran away.

"Years later, when he was a man, he went back to the stream to water his own horse, and there she was again. But they did not know each other because they were very much changed. Being a man now, and knowing how to impress a woman, he picked up another stone, this one flat, and skipped it across the river. It bounced straight into her basket. Her laughter made him brave, and he rode his horse to the other side of the stream. When he was closer, he saw the tiny scar where he'd hit her with the stone so many years ago.

"He touched the scar and said, 'Could you ever love a boy who would do such a terrible thing?'

"'No,' she said, 'but I could love a man who will skip a stone into my basket.'

"That is why young men skip stones along the river—to make up for the mischief they might have done as boys."

I listened, puzzled at why she would tell such a story. My confusion must have been evident because she laughed.

"Do you wonder if that story is true, Mrs. Fox?"

"No, I'm just wondering why you chose to share it with me."

"That tale was told to me by my grandmother, who heard it from her grandmother, who heard it from her grandmother. It is a story that comes from our ancestors from as far back as there have been boys and stones and rivers. Don't you see? If our people will take such pleasure in handing down the story of a little boy and a stone, don't you think we would have preserved the story of this great Jesus coming to our land?"

Somehow, everything I'd been taught about this new religion came to the surface, and I found myself leaping to its defense. "But they teach about the wars—"

"You think our people have not known war? that we do not fight and kill one another, generation after generation? Yet we carry our past with us. What you know in your heart cannot be destroyed by war, Mrs. Fox. And tonight, you look like your heart has been broken."

"It has."

"But not destroyed. It cannot be destroyed while it beats inside of you. And I think, for you, it will heal."

"It will."

"And it will get stronger."

God help me. "Yes."

"And you will teach my heart to be as strong as yours?"

"We'll grow strong together." I reached for her hand. "Will you pray with me?"

"My prayer is different from yours," she said. "I pray to the God who created all—the sky, the earth, and everything that lives."

"That's all right. So do I."

"And I do not know exactly who Jesus is."

"He's one and the same," I said. "Let's start there."

What sweet summer evenings we had, the four of us. Without a man's schedule to consider, Kimana and I moved our evening meal up earlier and earlier, until we might have the dishes cleared and washed and put away before the hint of sunset. Kimana soaked up every word. I must say I envied her easy understanding, and one evening as we sat with the cabin door wide open to let in the cool breeze, I told her so.

She spoke, softly measuring her words. "Sometimes I think I hear these words with the very ears of God. I prayed to him and asked his Spirit to take the place of my own, so I could know who he truly is."

For the first time I noticed a spark of interest coming from Melissa. All summer she'd been enduring our Bible study with an air of unimpressed indulgence, but this caught her attention.

"I already know who God is," she said. "I learned in church."

"But you see, little one," Kimana said, "I have never been told. I know only what God himself says to me. You need to close your ears and let your heart open."

And, oh, how our hearts opened. It wasn't long before my journal served to open the door to the Bible, and though I intended to read only a chapter a night as I had in my youth, often we would lose ourselves in the verses. I would read until Kimana stopped me to ask a question, and we would talk together until we felt we had an answer. Through our readings, we—Kimana and I—came to truly know and love the person Jesus was. He became for us what God intended him to be—divine, yes, but a man, flesh and blood, living the harshness of life that we all know. As we read about his death, the cruelty of crucifixion, the suffering under the bloody whip, we both cried. Kimana's sweet, peaceful spirit could not abide details of such violence. My tears carried with them an almost unbearable mixture of guilt and gratitude.

"That's why Papa doesn't like to talk about it," Melissa said, her voice oddly void of emotion. "It's sad to think that Jesus went through all that and people still didn't believe. That's why he had to come again."

How to respond? I knew she spoke out of love not for her father's church, but for her father himself. I used to love the sight of her curled up in Nathan's lap, listening with rapt attention to Mormon teachings. Maybe that was the magic of it—the bond between the two of them, which she and I seemed destined never to share. A bond I'd never had with my own father. I couldn't remember a single time I'd ever curled up in his lap—or even at his feet. We'd only ever sat like this, at a kitchen table, Bible open and lifeless. I'd never wept over the death of Jesus with my mother; I'd never waited, breathless with anticipation for the moment when we would read those words: "Ye seek Jesus of Nazareth, which was crucified: he is risen; he is not here: behold the place where they laid him."

I'd never bounced in my seat like my precious little Lottie, who clapped her little hands and said, "He is alive! He is alive!"

I knew it was all true, I believed with all my heart the stories and the prophecies and the gospel, but none of it ever touched me until that summer. Finally one night, having finished the Gospel of Luke and wondering what book to begin next, I thumbed through the pages, asking the Holy Spirit to lead me, and I came across these words: *The True Christ Described.* That night, after a supper of white beans and corn bread, I opened the Bible to the book of Colossians.

"This is a very old letter," I said, "written by a man named Paul. He was an apostle."

"Our church has apostles," Melissa said.

"No, darling. Not really. A true apostle is one who witnessed the risen Christ. Nobody today can truly be called an apostle."

She pouted and sat back in her chair, but Kimana was intrigued. "Read the letter."

It began with Paul's greeting, how he gave thanks to God for the people he addressed. For just a moment my heart tightened, thinking of all the unanswered, unopened letters I'd written to my parents. If they could only know how grateful I felt for what they had given me. As I read further, though, all melancholy left, and the power of God's Word—in fact, that very power within me—came forth as the perfect words of one who truly knew Jesus Christ came out of my lips.

"'And he is before all things, and by him all things consist. And he is the head of the body, the church: who is the beginning, the firstborn from the dead; that in all things he might have the preeminence.'"

"What's *preeminence*?" Melissa asked.

I hesitated, thinking. Oh, my Missy was a bright girl. When I was her age, I never asked what words meant. If I didn't know, I didn't know, and I went on to the next one. But hers was such a seeking mind, if not an open heart, so I could not leave her unsatisfied. "Well," I began, "I think it means he should be first. He should be the first thought in our mind; we should consider him our first authority."

She seemed satisfied with my definition.

"Keep reading," Kimana said.

"'For it pleased the Father that in him should all fulness dwell; and, having made peace through the blood of his cross, by him to reconcile all things unto himself; by him, I say, whether they be things in earth, or things in heaven.'"

"Peace through blood," Kimana whispered. "Never have I seen peace come through blood, and I have seen—my people have seen—so much blood."

"What's *reconciled*?" Melissa asked.

"That means an end to a disagreement. When we don't believe in Jesus—the true Jesus—we are in a disagreement with God. And when we sin, we are in disagreement. But when Jesus died, his blood wiped away that disagreement. Listen: 'And you, that were sometime alienated and enemies in your mind by wicked works, yet now hath he reconciled in the body of his flesh through death, to present you holy and unblameable and unreproveable in his sight.'"

By the time I finished that first chapter, Lottie's good, quiet behavior was near an end, and Melissa was not nearly as enthralled as she had been with the stories of Jesus. So, earlier than most evenings, we joined our hands around the table and bowed our heads for prayer. That night, though, it was Kimana who lifted her voice, but my throat burned with tears as if the words were my own.

"Great Father in heaven," she prayed, "I did not know your Son, Jesus. But I know him now. I am clean. I am holy. I have peace through his blood. May you never be the enemy of my mind."

Never had I heard a petition more beautiful. From that night on, Kimana's prayer became my own—not only for my own soul, but for the souls of my daughters.

CHAPTER 17

Late in August, the news made its way out to our little village that the new immigrant party would be arriving in Salt Lake City within a week. It was always a cause for celebration—new souls won, new blood, new labor. In years past, I'd been a part of that celebration, finding all the bits and pieces of my own home to contribute to theirs. Food, clothing, whatever I could afford to part with would be bundled into a box and brought to the temple site to be displayed with everybody else's donation.

This year, however, I felt no such generosity of spirit. Instead, I packed my best dress and bonnet into a carpet satchel.

"You are sure you won't take the horse?" Kimana asked as she buttered bread and placed it in a milk bucket along with a few strips of dried beef and a sealed jar of water. "It is a long walk. Will take you all day."

"We don't have a saddle," I explained.

"Saddle," she said with disdain. "A good horse needs nothing more than a thick blanket and a firm hand."

"Well, of all of those, all we have is the blanket. I'll be fine. I walked across half the country to get here, didn't I?"

"But to go alone . . ."

"Perhaps some fine Saint will take pity on me and give me a ride." I picked up the satchel to test its weight, imagining how heavy it would feel that evening. "It's a busy-enough road."

"Please, Mama!" Melissa whined, still picking over her breakfast. "Please let me go. I want to meet Papa too."

"Me too!" Lottie chimed in, more concerned about accompanying her sister, I was sure.

"I've already said, it's too far for the two of you." And truly it was, though I knew Melissa would have been quite the trooper. My reason for leaving them home stemmed from a much more selfish root. I wanted to be alone when I finally had the chance to see their father again. Not alone, exactly, as I would have half the population of Salt Lake City plus the dozens of bedraggled new citizens fresh from the trail, but a nagging fear tugged at me, as I didn't feel in any way like the same woman he'd left in the spring.

So in those first minutes past sunrise, I kissed each of the girls good-bye and even subjected Kimana to a quick embrace.

"Take care of them," I said. "Remember us in your prayers."

"We will," she said. "Every night until you get home."

The road into Salt Lake City was well-worn, largely due to the constant pilgrimage of oxen and carts laden with the temple stones mined from the quarry. I passed no fewer than six such carts on my journey, half of them having a day's worth of travel separating them. Each would spend three days covering the same distance I would in less than one, and it gave me an odd feeling of strength and accomplishment to stride past, leaving them in the wake of my dusty skirts.

I could not remember when I'd last had so much time to be alone. I spoke to God throughout the entire journey—sometimes aloud, until my breath would give out, and then with a simple, constant prayer repeating itself in my head. *Lord, give me strength—for this journey today and the one ahead.* I couldn't articulate in any way what I thought that journey might be, but I knew I'd set myself on a new path, and I had no idea how Nathan and I would travel it together.

The temple stones and I weren't the only travelers on the road that day. Three wagons passed me by, driven by people I would have called friends and neighbors just a few months ago. Neighbors they remained, but I don't see how any true friend could crack a whip and speed the team past another. I'd grown used to having my greetings ignored at the trading post, and the basket of spice muffins I left at Sister Marguerite's door when she had taken ill was returned, untouched. Still, I was glad not to be wounded and waylaid by the side of the road because there didn't seem to be a Good Samaritan among them.

I gauged myself to be at a halfway mark when I spied a little grove of cottonwoods that seemed the perfect place for lunch. Walking in a little ways, I found myself hidden from the road, though I reckoned I would be able to hear a wagon passing by, in case some peril should befall me. My feet were tired—not accustomed to such arduous use—but I resisted the urge to unlace my boots. I knew from experience that I would have a hard time stretching the leather around their swollen mass; it would be relief enough to lean myself against a tree and prop them up on my satchel.

I opened the jar and drank down the cool water before spilling a dab on my handkerchief and wiping my face and neck. The shade felt cool and a breeze blew through. Given that I was all alone, I rolled up my sleeves and opened the first two buttons of my blouse, dabbing the damp cloth along the inside of my collar. The only intrusion on my comfort was the sharp pain of hunger, so I offered up a quick prayer of thanks before diving into the bucket and pulling out the slices of buttered bread. To my delight, Kimana had also coated each slice with honey, and I smiled at the sweet surprise.

"Thank you, Kimana," I said aloud, mindless of the fact that I could barely speak around the mouthful of food.

She had packed more than I could possibly eat at one sitting—no matter how sharp the hunger—and I debated as to whether I should continue on with the half-empty bucket or simply leave it tucked here in this grove to be retrieved when I journeyed home with Nathan. After a few minutes, though, the answer to that question lost its immediacy as it was replaced with whether or not I would continue on at all. Sated and comfortable, the idea of getting up and walking one more step seemed more like a foreign threat than a necessary action. I yawned and stretched and settled back against the surprisingly comfortable tree trunk.

"Just a few minutes," I told myself. "Until my eyes open up again." Thus settled, I closed them, shutting out all but the sound of a summer afternoon. So much buzzing and calling, the wind underscoring all as it rustled the leaves above.

And then, something else. Something so familiar, I had to

open my eyes fully to know I wasn't dreaming. The rumble of wagons. One simply cannot spend months walking alongside a train of wagons and ever mistake the noise of a dozen axles. Rising above even that, a sound that brought my heart to fully stop within me.

Nathan.

I scrambled to my feet, smoothing my skirt and my hair almost simultaneously. *How could it be? They weren't due to arrive for days. And why didn't they stop in Salt Lake City? And why . . . ?* I turned my eyes to heaven, staring straight up to the blue sky framed by the trees around me.

"Thank you, Lord." Although I wasn't exactly sure what I was thankful for. Nathan's safe return, of course, but I would have much preferred to meet him wearing my best dress and bonnet, not looking like something that just got dragged off the road. Still, he was *here*. He was *home*—or close to it. After a final tucking of loose hair behind my ears, I stepped out of the grove.

There he was, astride Honey, the horse that had spurred such bitter words between us. It looked none the worse for having journeyed across the known world and back. And he, from what I could tell, hadn't changed. I stood on the roadside, feeling every bit as though I were fifteen years old again, standing at the edge of the road to my father's property, wondering if I was going to see him that day, only now, I wondered if he would see me. At the moment, it seemed doubtful, given his attention was so fully focused on an engaging conversation with the older gentleman driving the wagon alongside him. I couldn't catch their topic, but there was no mistaking the animation on Nathan's part. He held the horse's reins with one hand, gesturing wildly with the other, his body turned in the saddle. That's when I realized why I felt so young—because the

Nathan I saw riding that horse wasn't the same man who rode into the dawn nearly three months ago. This was the man who had taken over my life the first day he walked me to school. It was like he had emerged renewed from the melancholy and frustration that had plagued him for the past year.

There was a woman on the wagon's seat too, her bonnet turned toward Nathan, showing nothing of her face. Suddenly she threw her head back in laughter, and I longed to know just what my husband had said to produce such a reaction. So enraptured were the three with each other, I doubted whether my presence would be noticed even if the gentleman ran over me with his wagon, so abandoning any pretense of what a refined lady would do under such circumstances, I flapped my arms as if scaring off a murder of crows and shouted my husband's name. Twice.

The woman heard me first, as she turned and looked straight at me. Though her face was mostly lost in the shadows of her bonnet, I could tell she was young. Much younger than the man driving the wagon. Her skin appeared pale and smooth, as did her hands, which I noticed when she brought them up to interrupt Nathan's speech and point straight at me.

"Camilla!" He couldn't have looked more surprised if I'd actually swung out of the tree's branches and landed on his saddle. He brought the horse to a halt and swung over the side, breaking into a run the moment his feet hit the ground and sweeping me off mine in the next minute. "Darling, what are you doing here?"

On closer inspection I could see that his skin was darker, both toughened by the sun and glazed with trail dust. New lines formed at the corners of his eyes, making him seem at once peaceful and wise. Nothing had aged in his embrace, though. His arms still felt like steel bands wrapped around me, and my hands spread across his muscular back, instantly loving the feel of him.

"I—I was planning to meet you in town." My words sounded so small in the midst of this moment. In fact, I didn't want to talk at all. It had been so long since we'd simply looked at each other or held each other. What I really wanted to do was kiss him, right there in the bright light of afternoon, and if it weren't for the couple sitting high on the wagon seat above us, I would have. Thankfully, Nathan felt no need for such decorum. In one motion he tore his hat from his head and drew me to him, his lips on mine briefly, but full of promise.

"There's so much to tell you." His face blurred before me as he touched his forehead to mine. "I don't know where to start."

I heard the squeaking of the springs beneath the wagon's seat and imagined the occupants squirming in light of our blatant display. This brought me to squirm a bit on my own. I pulled away, feeling suddenly shy, and suggested that Nathan introduce me to these fine people.

"Of course." He gave my arm a final squeeze before turning and tucking me to his side. "Camilla, this is Brother Kenneth Dunn, newly arrived from London by way of New Orleans."

The gentleman tipped his hat to me and, in that small gesture, revealed himself to be of an entirely different breed from anybody I'd ever met.

"And this," Nathan continued, "is his daughter. Miss—Sister—Amanda."

I don't think anybody else would have noticed the hitch in his voice, and if they had, it might have passed as a mere quirk of speech. But I knew my husband's voice as well as I knew my own. I heard it through my own ears, amplified and magnified. His speech was always flawless and smooth, every word seemingly rehearsed before given utterance. I glanced at Nathan, only to see his eyes steadfastly glued to Miss-Sister-Amanda Dunn. His lips tugged into a smile I knew too well; his throat bobbed as he swallowed, and my own burned at the thought of what he was holding back. Or not holding back, as the case was, for after a few seconds, that same stranger who failed to notice the hitch in his voice would have to be blind not to notice the way he looked at her.

A small, sweet voice laced with an accent that gave a soft, pinched quality to her words said, "How very nice to meet you."

I tore my gaze away from my husband and looked up to see Miss-Sister-Amanda having pushed her sunbonnet off her head, revealing a face prettier than I wanted to see. Her hair dark brown—almost black—and her skin contrastingly fair. How faithfully she must have shielded it from the sun for it to have that porcelain sheen at the end of summer after a journey of two thousand miles. Her eyes were bright blue, the kind people call cornflower, though I'd never actually seen the flower that inspired such a description. Her mouth was wide, but her lips narrow, and her nose could only be accurately described as pointy. The overall effect was one of a perfect English rose, though I'd never before considered what a perfect English rose would look like.

At my husband's nudging, I managed to offer a weak hello in response to her greeting. Then I turned to Nathan. "Are they not settling in Salt Lake City?"

"Brother Kenneth owned several businesses in London. He's been given the job of overseeing the work at the quarry."

"Oh, well . . . how nice." What else was there to say? Whatever had passed between Nathan and Amanda could not be discussed now, at this roadside, yet the same summer sounds that so recently had given such peace now grated in my ears, underscoring the awkwardness of the moment. "And do they have a home waiting for them?" I turned my attention back to the wagon. "Is there a house waiting for you two? Or will you be staying with some of our neighbors?"

"I was told there's a cabin," Brother Kenneth said.

"A small one," Nathan added. "Just one room built on the site. Not really suitable for a lady."

"Well—" I sent my brightest smile to Amanda—"we've all had to adjust to life on the frontier. It's a far cry from London, I'm sure, but you and your father will find the place to be a cozy little home in no time." Nearly exhausted from that last bit of false cheer, I dropped my weight against Nathan and said, "Speaking of home, shall we? I know the girls will be so surprised to see you."

"Oh," Amanda said, clapping her thin white hands, "I can't wait to meet them. Nathan has said such wonderful things about his daughters."

Our daughters. But I spoke no such correction.

Within the next few minutes I'd tossed my satchel into the back of the wagon with the rest of the Dunns' worldly possessions, which included great bits of furniture that would never find a home in the overseer's cabin at the quarry. I myself was handed up to the seat, where I squeezed between father and daughter Dunn. Following Amanda's example, my bonnet was again on my head, creating a world seen only through a tunnel of calico. This made it nearly impossible to communicate with Nathan, given I'd have to crane my neck around the figure of Brother Kenneth, so I simply sat back on the seat and listened to their easy conversation about the progress of the temple and the perils of the trail. Every now and then, Amanda made a little sound, something between a sigh and a laugh. After the third such noise I turned toward her, and she toward me—our bonnets connecting.

"I'm just so happy," she said.

"About being here?"

"About . . . everything."

Her words rang out like a woman who'd been given a promise.

At Brother Kenneth's request, we drove straight to the mouth of the quarry. It was, by now, late in the afternoon on a Saturday, and all of the workers had left to prepare for the Sabbath. There were a dozen places where I could have excused myself and hopped off the wagon to make my way to prepare for Nathan's homecoming, but I felt compelled to stay right by his side to ensure that such a homecoming would take place.

The accommodations left for Brother Kenneth were, by any definition, modest. I don't suppose anybody took into consideration that he might arrive with a fashionable young daughter—or any woman, for that matter. The quarry was overrun with bachelor quarters and crude bunkhouses meant to provide the minimal comforts of home for those men tithing their time in their labor for Heavenly Father.

Pulling up, it seemed the overseer's cabin was little more than that.

"Home sweet home," Nathan said, gesturing grandly. "I know it doesn't seem like much now, but wait. Soon you'll find yourself overwhelmed with blessings you could never imagine. Better a cabin in the land of Zion than a castle among the Gentiles, I always say."

In fact, I'd never heard him say any such thing, and now

he spoke with such forced energy that I doubted he believed his own words. I could only imagine what kind of house a man who owned several businesses in London lived in, though I had some idea after my peek at the furniture in the back of their wagon. My best guess was that none of it would fit through the door.

Brother Kenneth stepped down from the wagon and turned to offer me his hand. I would have preferred to wait, as Nathan was handing Sister Amanda down from the other side, but it seemed rude to refuse such an offer, so I accepted, giving myself over to his unusually steady grip. Like some odd little family, we walked inside—the door having been left open by the trusting previous tenant. All was neat and tidy in the large room. An enormous desk dominated the space, with a narrow sofa and two other chairs against the far wall; a small woodstove stood watch in one corner near a small shelf that held one pan and one pot.

"Bed's behind that curtain, I guess." Nathan appointed himself guide and walked across the room to poke his head behind the fabric hung over a rope. "Yep," he confirmed.

"Did they not think I would have a family?" Brother Kenneth asked.

"Guess not. But I don't know much of anything. I just offered to ride in with you."

"And we're so grateful that you did," Sister Amanda said, laying her hand on my husband's arm. "I think we might have been lost without you."

"There's a sign on the door," I said. Given another opportunity, I might have kept my mouth shut lest I appear ungracious, but I had no reason to regret my words, as it didn't seem anybody in the room heard me. Brother Kenneth was already steeped in whatever was written in the large ledgers on the desk, and Nathan and Sister Amanda seemed steeped in each other.

"I realize the house is less than ideal," Nathan said, not pulling his arm away, "but I'm sure you'll soon find our society will more than make up for what lacks in creature comforts."

There are no words to explain the sickness I felt—the utter lack of air in that room, as the atmosphere was so clogged with the two of them. It wasn't exactly a surprise. I suppose on some level I knew the day Nathan left that he would come back with another woman. After all, wasn't that how he'd found me? Our seven years' marriage hadn't changed so very much for him; he remained the man looking for an eternal family, while I was nothing the same. Looking at him now was like looking through some magical glass, seeing him as the man he was when we met. The honey in his voice, the promise in his eyes. Only now, I was seeing all of that being poured out on another woman. And she was falling, throwing herself straight into his path, uncaring that I, his wife, stood so close by, could touch the arm not claimed by her grip. I held my breath and held my tongue, determined not to judge the girl. She was young, after all. Older than I had been when I first met him, but somehow I knew that if, even then, he had told me that I would be one of a dozen wives, I would still have followed Nathan Fox. His hold on my heart was that strong.

As for that, little had changed. Still, it was not the fault of this young girl that she was so clearly in love with my husband.

"Perhaps . . ." I cleared my voice and repeated the word, louder. "Perhaps we can find someplace else for Sister Amanda to stay until this home can be made more suitable."

Nathan turned to me. "Oh, Mil, you don't know how happy I am to see you take such a kindness to her."

"I'll walk with her to Elder Justus's house," I said, easily avoiding what was sure to have been Nathan's suggestion. "They should have room to put her up. I've never known them to turn away a person in need." Though in her fine dress and bonnet—and whatever else might be in those trunks stacked in the wagon—she hardly qualified as a person in need.

"That sounds fine," Nathan said, doing a marvelous job masking his disappointment, something Sister Amanda failed to do.

"I don't think I like the idea of staying with strangers."

"None of us are strangers, Sister Amanda," Nathan said. "We are all brothers and sisters—children of Heavenly Father. Family, in every way."

"Don't you think her father should have some say in this?" I barely held back from physically placing myself between them.

"What?" Brother Kenneth said, preoccupied. He waved us off, never taking his eyes from the books. "Yes, yes. Whatever you think is best."

Dismissed, Nathan, Amanda, and I walked outside. The sun was beginning to set, and I thought of Kimana and the girls back home, sitting down to their evening meal, bowing their heads to pray for my safe passage and for God to bring Papa safely home. I wished I'd never left.

"You take the horse home." Nathan was speaking, putting the reins in my hand. "I'll drive Sister Amanda to Elder Justus's home. He has a barn and can put up the horses."

"We have a barn," I said, grasping at any logical argument that would bring Nathan home with me. Now. "She can take the horse—"

"She's not coming to our home, remember? And we can hardly expect her to find her way alone."

"I'm completely in your hands," Sister Amanda said. "A stranger in a strange land."

A strange land, indeed.

And so it was I found myself uncomfortably astride our newest horse while Nathan and Sister Amanda rode companionably in the wagon beside me until the time came for us to split off to our separate ways.

"You will hurry home?" I said before peeling off. "Our daughters will be quite eager to see their papa."

"Of course," Nathan said. "Just as soon as I help Amanda get settled in."

"And we'll see you in church tomorrow?" Sister Amanda asked. I sat, silent, trying to process exactly who she meant by *we*. She and her father? She and my husband? For months everybody in our ward had been asking me this same question, and for months the answer had been no. Before my eyes the vision of Nathan and Sister Amanda sitting on a wagon seat became one of the two of them sitting on the rough-hewn pew at church. In my mind's eye her arm looped through his, and my daughters—Melissa overjoyed to be in her house of worship—flanked the two of them.

"Yes." In the end Nathan, not I, supplied the answer.

Before I could say another word, he clicked to the team and off they went. I allowed Honey to pick her way slowly along the path home. Nathan's worn leather satchel topped the bundle behind the horse's saddle, and curiosity more than suspicion called me to lift it into my lap. I lifted the flap and saw it right on top—another bundle of papers wrapped in twine. With shaking hands I looked at my own handwriting. More letters, unopened.

Once the Dunns' wagon was well out of sight, I jumped down and dropped the reins. Every moment I'd lived since eating my little bucket lunch in the clearing roiled within me, and then it burst out of me as I gagged and threw up in the brush. The sour taste left in my mouth felt somehow fitting. I said her name, "Amanda," and got sick again. I longed for a swallow of water to wash away the taste of her, even if it could never take her away.

"Oh, Lord," I prayed, knowing only he and the horse would hear me, "you cannot ask me to do this. I love my husband and I will honor him, but this . . . you cannot."

And then, in the distance, I heard familiar laughter dancing across the rays of sunset. I'd know it anywhere. Melissa, Lottie. They and the Lord would be my strength. Wiping my mouth with my sleeve, I reached blindly behind me for the reins and, grabbing them, led the horse home.

CHAPTER 18

It is a strange thing for a wife to watch her husband court another woman, for *courting* was the only possible word to describe Nathan's behavior. A casual observer might consider his attentions those of a concerned villager striving to make a new resident feel welcome. Someone not privy to the ways of these people might overlook the way in which Nathan seemed always to be at Sister Amanda's side, his hand hovering too near her waist. The fact that their heads tipped toward each other more closely than propriety allowed might have been misconstrued as something as harmless as a bit of gossip-laden conversation.

But there were no casual observers in Cottonwood. Ours

was a ward dedicated to the scrutiny of each other. That first Sunday when Nathan and I walked up to the church house together, we were met with celebration dedicated to my return to worship as much as his return home. Why had I never before seen his need for such adoration? He grew a little taller with each hand extended and bowed indulgently to some of the older women who wished to greet him with an exuberant kiss on his clean-shaven cheek. I clung to him as I never had before, gripping his laundered shirt with all my strength, not sure if I relied on him to keep me in this place or to merely keep me standing. I doubt our welcome would have been as warm if everybody knew the prayers screaming inside my head.

Protect me, Lord, from the lies spoken here. I stand only at the side of the husband you sought to bring me. Forgive my silence in the midst of such distortion. I wait for the moment you will open my mouth.

Eventually we all moved inside and were given wide berth to the bench we had always occupied as a family. I must admit I had a twinge of bittersweet comfort being so wholly a part of Nathan again. The night before we'd been together in our bed as man and wife for the first time since that winter night so long ago, and I'd somehow been able to push the image of Sister Amanda far from my mind as I gave my body over fully to my husband. Her name was never spoken from the moment he walked through the door of our home to the moment we walked through the door of the church house. And here, with the memory of last night warming me from within and the heat of him pressed against my side, I began to think I'd imagined it all. Melissa sat on his other side; Lottie perched on his lap. We were surrounded by friendly conversation, and something close to contentment began to take root.

This could be enough, Lord. To have you in my heart and my family around me.

Then, like the gradual end of a rainstorm, the chatter in the church house trickled into silence. I didn't have to turn around. I knew. She'd walked through the door. Perhaps with her father; perhaps accompanying her hosts, Elder Justus and Sister June. I refused to join those slack-jawed, smiling Saints who cast such adoring glances to the apparition behind me. Whatever warm bubble of peace I'd had now burst, leaving me too empty to produce even the bile of yesterday. Nathan shifted beside me, and I felt myself becoming a shell, drained of everything I had to offer him as a wife. If I'd been standing, I might have collapsed. As it was, his weight moved away as he turned; I willed my back to remain straight, straighter.

It took all the strength I had not to claw at his sleeve to stop him from standing, to cling to him as he rose and beckoned for the woman to join us. To take her place on our family's bench. I remained rooted, no more inclined to make room for her here than to allow her into the bed my husband and I had shared just hours ago.

Now there were just as many eyes trained on me as had ever followed her journey up the aisle. My cheeks burned under the scrutiny. A tiny, cool hand touched my cheek as Lottie cupped her hand to my ear and whispered, "You need to move down, Mama. To make room."

I filled my arms with the warm bundle of my daughter, pulling her into my lap and drawing on her innocent strength to propel my body the mere inches I allowed to accommodate this intruder. Then Nathan was once again beside me with a protesting Melissa on his lap, and next to him Miss-Sister-Amanda Dunn.

I didn't allow myself even a glimpse of her until we stood

for the first hymn. All around me voices rose in song, and above them all floated a clear, controlled soprano. A new voice added to our Saints' choir and, by the appreciative glances thrown our way, a welcome one. More of a reason for me to silence my own, which I did, not even bothering to mouth the detestable words of heroism and persecution. I swayed backward and took in a sidelong glance of my new seatmate. She wore a beautifully cut suit of a burnt orange and gray plaid. Her hair cascaded in intricate curls from beneath a perfect gray velvet hat. I didn't need to see her face; it was burned in my memory from yesterday. I knew it held a perfect expression of reverence and poise; the inflections of her voice carried both.

Just before I tore my eyes away, I happened to glance down and see that Melissa was eyeing Miss-Sister-Amanda with every bit as much scrutiny as I was. With unabashed boldness, she moved her head up and down, taking in the entire vision before—without any prompting from me—turning to catch my eye.

I've often since thought of that moment as my first missed opportunity. So enthralled was this congregation with the words of their hymn and the newest voice among us, I could have grabbed the hands of my little girls and run out of that place. Surely our absence would have gone unnoticed until the beginning of the third verse, and we could have been halfway to Salt Lake City by the time they drew out the *amen.* The look in Melissa's eyes told me that I would have met very little protest from her. Never, not even the day she awoke to find that her papa had left before the dawn, had I ever seen such sadness.

In a move completely out of place with the reverent tone of the song, Melissa climbed up on the bench and walked behind her father's back and straight into my arms. We were of equal height now, and she laid her head on my shoulder. I wrapped my arms around her thin little body and wept into hers, and when we drew apart, she wiped my tears. We said nothing, but stood, our arms wrapped around each other.

When it was time to sit again, Lottie settled on my lap, and Melissa wedged herself between Nathan and me. Of course that meant that he was closer to Amanda, touching her, probably. The innocent touch of shoulders and sleeves. As much as I longed for that same touch, I knew I'd never truly have it again. Whatever had been innocent and sweet about the love we had for each other was destroyed in that moment. My longing had turned into a greed-fueled lust I detested.

I bowed my head. *Oh, Lord, but I love him.* Somehow, though, the prayer rang as false as any word spoken from the pulpit that morning.

I should not have been surprised when, after the service, Nathan invited the Dunns to Sunday dinner along with Elder Justus and Sister June. Standing at his side, I smiled and said, "Of course we'd love to have you." Still, I was grateful that Elder Justus's pastoral duties and the Dunns' introductions caused them to linger at the church house so Nathan and I could get a bit of a head start toward our home.

"I really don't know what we have to serve," I said, working to keep up with his stride. "Kimana was going to fry a chicken, but for eight people—"

"I told her we'd have guests. She's prepared."

"Oh. You didn't tell me."

"I didn't want to upset you any more than was necessary."

"A fine time to take my feelings into account." I hated

the small bitterness in my tone. The threat posed by Sister Amanda would never be thwarted by petulance.

"Girls," Nathan said over his shoulder to Melissa and Lottie, who trailed in dancing circles behind us, "run ahead home and see if Kimana needs any help with dinner. Tell her we'll have four guests joining us."

"Yes, Papa," they replied in chorus, thrilled to have him home to obey.

For a while we walked quietly, watching the kick of our girls' Sunday shoes behind their skirts. I spoke first, staring straight ahead. "How could you do that to me?"

"What have I done?"

"Your intentions couldn't be more obvious, Nathan. You intend to—" I choked on the word—"marry her."

"If you'll allow."

I can't explain the sound that escaped my mouth. Something between a laugh and a snarl, unfamiliar and out of character. "Allow? I've seen how you two look at each other. I wouldn't dare get in the middle."

"You sound like nothing more than a jealous wife."

"What do you expect?" My steps had accelerated, and I felt his hand on my arm, drawing me back. Planting my feet, I shrugged off his grip. "You leave us for months on end and come back with that woman."

"I told you I was leaving to search for God's will in my life."

"And I told you we could search for it together. Pray together. But of course that wouldn't do, not if we don't pray to the same God."

The grip returned. "What are you saying?"

"My God doesn't allow adultery."

"Don't be ignorant, Camilla. You know the prophet—"

"I don't care about the prophet, Nathan. Not anymore." I felt my strength growing, power from a source so far outside myself I barely heard my own words. "Brigham Young is not my Lord. Joseph Smith is not my savior. His words, his teachings, all of it. Both of us, I think, sought the will of God over the summer. But we both found very different answers."

"What did you expect? I know you haven't been to church. It's no wonder you're sounding so confused right now. It's not easy to understand the teachings of the Lord."

"I understand them, Nathan. Better than you know. And I don't think—"

"Listen to me." He bent low, the brim of his hat touching my bonnet. "The only thing you need to understand is that you are my wife, pledged to honor and obey me. For today, for this afternoon, for the meal we are about to share, that is the only thought you need to keep in your head. You will speak in agreement, or you will keep silent. I will not have Elder Justus think I am not in control of my household. Do you understand?"

I nodded, swallowing every word of argument.

He gathered my hands in his and kissed them. "I love you, Camilla. Every bit as much as I ever have. More, even, if that's possible."

"How can you say that?"

"How could I not? I made a vow to you and to God. We're a family, Mil. Anything we can do as a family will only make us stronger. Do you trust me?"

I shut my eyes, focusing only on the feeling of his fingers wrapped around mine, and chose my words carefully. "I have always trusted you, Nathan. More than that, I trust God. I know he will somehow make all of this work to my good."

"That's my girl." He gave my hands one last squeeze. "Now, we best hurry home or else our guests will beat us there."

Minutes later, I hardly recognized my own home. The table was set with the very best of our dishes—four complete settings. The other two places were set with simple pewter plates, but all six had bright red cloth napkins folded in the center, giving a festive air. A cut-glass goblet graced each place, and a quick, clandestine conversation with Kimana revealed their origin.

"Miss Rachel brought them last visit. I was told to hide them for a Christmas present."

There were no places set for her or the children; they would be eating a cold dinner in Kimana's small cabin. Part of me felt great relief, especially knowing that the girls always thought of such occasions as respite from strict table manners and good behavior.

I took off my bonnet and donned an apron, ready to help with the last-minute preparations. Kimana had spent the morning frying not one, but two of our chickens; she stirred the drippings into a gravy while I arranged the pieces on our largest platter. There was also a salad of pickled beets with turnip greens along with fresh biscuits and a plate of brown-butter cookies for dessert. A pitcher of cool ginger water sat in the middle of the table.

"Nathan arranged all of this?"

Kimana kept her eyes trained on the gravy in the pot, a convenient excuse to avoid my barely masked temper. "He said only that he want to come home to a feast. I give him a feast."

"You did, indeed."

I knew our guests had arrived when I heard Nathan's shout of welcome sing through the yard. As quickly as I'd donned it, I untied the apron and stashed it in the wood box. I smoothed my hair and had Kimana check my face for any stray mess before stepping through the front door to stand beside my husband.

What an imposing party they made: Elder Justus wearing his ominous black suit, his wife by his side in her equally black dress. Brother Kenneth looked positively dapper in dark green wool and a hat of brown straw. And Amanda, fairly bouncing on his arm, craning her neck to take in all of our property in one glance. I couldn't help but notice that the excitement drained from her face with each passing second, to be revived only when Nathan left my side and took her arm to usher her into our home.

Never, not even the day the entire village gathered to help me mourn the death of my newborn son, had our cabin seemed so small. I held my breath, fearing Elder Justus might scrape his knuckles while removing his hat, and I feared continually that Sister June would back into the stove and set her silks on fire. Brother Kenneth's face stayed set in a squint, scrutinizing every corner of the place. Measuring, no doubt, to see which of the great pieces of furniture he'd hauled could possibly fit. Sister Amanda's eyes darted nervously from Kimana to Nathan, demanding an introduction.

Determined to follow my husband's instructions as closely as possible, I remained silent, until Kimana herself, still unaccustomed to some of our social mores, extended her own grease-splattered, flour-covered hand.

"I am Kimana."

Sister Amanda took off her delicate lace gloves one finger at a time and pinched her fingers along the edges of Kimana's thick brown ones. "How very nice."

I heard the sound of crackling straw as Brother Kenneth

crushed his hat. "I didn't know you had *two* women, Brother Nathan."

"Kimana is not my . . . That is, she . . ."

Nathan looked to me for help, but I smiled in silent obedience.

"I was too weak to leave when my family was chased away." Kimana trained her narrowed eyes on Elder Justus. "Mr. and Mrs. Fox allowed me to stay."

"Her home was here first," Nathan said. He placed his arm across Kimana's soft shoulders. Only he could offer a gesture with such sincerity, and I was once again reminded of the warmth of his heart. "Jesus came to the Lamanites. He ministered to them. Why should we not show equal kindness?"

"We heard some were so wild they could not be tamed," Brother Kenneth said, holding his hat a little closer. "Heard about some terrible wars, and that we'd routed them."

"All true," Elder Justus said soberly. "But we have hope for this one's soul."

"Is she baptized, then?" Sister Amanda asked, leaning forward and studying Kimana as she would some token in a shop.

"Not yet," Nathan said, giving Kimana a little squeeze. "But someday."

Kimana's expression did not change. She simply excused herself to see to the children, leaving me to transfer the gravy from the pot to the pretty china boat—yet another Christmas present from Rachel.

At Nathan's command, our guests sat at the table, the places set with pewter at the head and the foot reserved for us. There was some brief conversation commenting on the beautiful, intricate carving on our chairs, none of it mentioning the fact that no two matched each other. Once the goblets were filled with fresh water and all the dinner had a place in the center of the table, Nathan held his hands out, inviting all of us to join for a blessing. I had Sister Amanda on one side and Sister June on the other, and as our hands rested together, I waited for the spirit of unity meant to accompany the gesture, but none came. Through the darkness of my closed eyes, I heard my husband's voice asking Heavenly Father to bless our food, our words, and the decisions we would make at this table. At that point, I felt a shifting in the clasps on either side of me. I couldn't wait to be free.

There was little more than small talk as our plates filled. The warm weather, speculation as to when it would turn. Crops. Gardens. Lumber and wool. Anybody who walked into the room would think we were nothing more than three friendly couples sharing a Sunday dinner, catching up after months spent apart. Such an observer might not notice the quiet woman at the end of the table. How she pulled the tiniest bits of meat from the chicken on her plate. How her eyes never left the pewter pitcher. How questions put to her were answered by the man at the other end, his joviality neither forced nor shared.

"Tell me, Brother Nathan," Elder Justus said through a mouth full of biscuit, "how did you find New Orleans?"

"Intolerable. Not just the heat and the swamps, but the people. So much need for the truth."

"And did you have a chance to share our gospel with them?"

Nobody but I could notice the shadow that flitted across his face. "I'm afraid I don't have the gift of evangelism, sir. I was sent only to be an escort."

"Oh, but you were a great deal more than that, weren't you?" Sister Amanda looked at him, her eyes hungrier than I could stomach. "I mean to say, you explained so much." She turned to me. "Your husband's a fine teacher. He read to us every night from *The Book of Mormon*, so much I'd never heard before. And with such fire! I don't know if he'd be better used as a missionary or an actor."

I alone refrained from the low, gentle laughter that rumbled around the table. I well remembered those evenings on my own journey to this place. The evenings in our home before he left. More than anyone here I knew the power of Nathan's words.

"We must be careful not to confuse the truth of Joseph Smith's revelations with the fictitious stories acted out on a stage," Sister June intoned softly.

"Oh no. What I mean to say is he just made the stories come alive. I had this sensation . . ." She set down her biscuit and laid her long, white fingers on her chest. "I can't explain it."

"Ah," Elder Justus said, looking satisfied, "what we call the 'burning in the bosom.'"

"Yes, that's it exactly. A burning. Like my heart was on fire. And I knew that everything he said was true."

I finally broke my silence, saying, "My husband has that effect on people."

I might just as well have dropped a temple block in the middle of the table for the shocked silence my simple sentence brought about.

"It is the testimony and confirmation of the Holy Spirit that brings about the burning," Elder Justus said, making my humble table his pulpit. "Nothing of man could bring it about."

"No ordinary man, maybe," Sister Amanda continued, her speech more breath than voice, "but you've got yourselves a real treasure here with Nathan—er, Brother Nathan. What a shame to waste him with woodwork when he could be spreading the gospel."

"Our Lord was a carpenter," Nathan said, amazing me with his humility. "I could not ask to be more than my brother."

"Besides—" I aimed my eyes straight at Nathan, though my sweet smile was for the benefit of all—"being a missionary takes him so far away from home. And for so long."

"Well, I for one am right grateful to have had 'im ride with us," Brother Kenneth chimed in, seeming oblivious to the preceding conversation. "Rides like one of your Indians, and able to fend 'em off like a soldier."

"Nathan, you didn't—"

"No, darling. I didn't shoot a soul. Heavenly Father gave us safe passage without bloodshed."

"A blessing, indeed," Sister June said.

"But you asked about New Orleans. . . ." Nathan managed to swoop the conversation into his net and spent the next several minutes regaling us with images I could hardly have imagined on my own. Stories full of music and women and color and wealth. He transformed himself with every new character, assuming accent and race to accommodate each tale. None of us had any reason to make the journey with him; he brought the city here to this little cabin in Cottonwood. I felt transported—rather, a longing to be transported. A burning desire, even though I felt I'd seen the city through his eyes.

That's what he'd done to Sister Amanda. That's what he'd done to me. While I wanted to hate him for bringing this woman into our lives, I could not. There at that table I was fifteen years old again, and he was a new creature to me. No doubt Sister Amanda and I had fallen under an identical spell. Pressed to speak truthfully, Sister June would have to admit to being similarly smitten.

"Then, of course," Nathan said in preface to bringing us all to a gentle, sloping stop, "I saw the fairest sight of all." I wondered if perhaps he'd forgotten that I still remained in the room, given the entirety of the table between us. His gaze lingered on Sister Amanda with such open admiration that there appeared to be a tunnel between them. "And I suppose," he continued, pulling himself from his own charm, "that it's time to address a very important question. As you all may or may not know, I have asked Sister Amanda to come alongside me as my wife, and she has consented."

Sometimes, in the midst of a winter storm, the wind will blow with such intensity, its howling blocks out every other sound. You shout above it until you realize your strength is better served trying to stay warm in the midst of the blistering cold it heralds. And then, all at once, it stops, and the silence that follows is equally deafening. Such a howling had been filling my head from the moment I saw Sister Amanda Dunn sitting atop her wagon seat, and it stopped the moment my husband announced his intentions to make her his wife. My sister wife. Any hope I had of stopping this storm died, and I felt the weight of a heavy, cold blanket covering every part of my body. I saw my smiling guests through a haze of white and heard muffled sounds of cheer attempting to make their way to my ears.

Finally one made it through. The dour, drooping voice of Elder Justus. "And what is your say, Sister Camilla? You know under the word of the prophet you have a right to refuse this marriage."

For the first time I had all eyes trained on me, and I felt my face and neck burn like flesh on snow. Looking back, I see this moment as yet another crossroad, like I was meeting a brash, young Nathan Fox for the first time. If I had thought for even a moment that my refusal would turn his heart fully to mine, that he would find contentment being a husband to me and me alone, that I would be able to share with him my rekindled faith in Jesus Christ and take him away from the false teachings of Joseph Smith, I surely would have refused.

But it would not. I'd witnessed Nathan's struggle for his eternity, and I knew this to be only one stone's skip in his quest for celestial glory. I would not share his struggle, nor would I prolong his suffering, for to do so prolonged mine.

Right there, in the presence of this company, I prayed for an answer—one that would satisfy my heart and Nathan's need. And it came to me, as clearly as if it were spoken aloud from the depth of my soul. This was not a burning in my bosom; no wave of emotion washed over me. Instead, I felt nothing but utterly calm, logical peace.

I picked my words as carefully as I'd picked at my meal. "Scripture tells us that all things work for good to those who love God and are called according to his purpose." Simply saying the Word of God aloud fought the battle for me. After all, I'd copied those same words into my journal years before I ever met Nathan Fox. Why should they be any less true given these circumstances? "I truly love the Lord. More, I think, than I did when Nathan married me."

Elder Justus stared me down. "Do I mistake your tone, Sister? For it sounds to me like you see this as an opportunity to test the goodness of the Lord, rather than an act of obedience to his command."

I stared straight back. "My Lord commands me to obey my husband. And he—" I shifted only my eyes to Nathan—"has been commanded to love me. As long as he is not in disobedience to his command, I see no reason to disobey mine."

Elder Justus planted his hands on the table, preparing to

rise from his seat. "I exhort you, Sister Camilla, to remember who it is that you address."

It was Nathan's honeyed voice that brought the man back to his seat. "I would remind you, sir, that you are speaking to my wife in my home." He stood up then and walked around the table to kneel at my side, squarely between his first and soon-to-be second wife. "I've never been prouder of you than I am in this moment. I do love you—every breath as much as I did the first day I saw you. And your beauty has only grown since that moment."

I sensed the women on either side of me had been moved to tears, but I shed none. I fought the heaving in my stomach, where the few bites I'd managed to swallow waged their own battle. Closing my eyes, I prayed for the peace of the Lord to come to me.

When it was clear that all were finished eating, Kimana and the girls were summoned in to help me clear the table and wash the dishes while Nathan led Sister Amanda and the rest of the company on a tour of our property. I would have liked to have been by his side when he walked them through the best of his work—the intricate, rejected chairs hanging on their hooks, the sketches for pieces commissioned by others. He would have a busy fall and winter ahead of him, and I looked forward to those evenings when he would come to supper smelling of sweet wood shavings. Then I remembered we would be sharing those evenings with Sister Amanda, and I refocused my thoughts on wiping the gravy bowl dry.

I fully expected to emerge from my restored home and wish my guests safe journey home, but to my surprise, only Sister June and Brother Kenneth took their leave.

"Sister Amanda must go through the Endowment ceremony if we are to be married in the temple," Nathan explained as we walked back inside. "Elder Justus has consented to conduct the interview here today."

"Of course. I guess I assumed—"

"She's been a convert only a year last July. The timing couldn't be more perfect."

"Indeed. Shall I take the girls down to the creek?"

"Why would you? I think Amanda would like to have you all here as support. You remember how nervous you were for your own interview?"

I did remember. At the time I feared giving a wrong answer would somehow make me ineligible to be Nathan's wife—a fear far greater than that of not being a Latter-day Saint. God alone knows what prompted Nathan to quiz me so thoroughly before, ensuring that I would answer each question perfectly.

"Did you give Sister Amanda the answers just as you gave them to me?"

He looked over his shoulder to see if Elder Justus heard my question, then leaned forward and said, "You know very well it is the Holy Spirit that prompts you to answer true." Still, he winked through his response, and I could imagine what he and Sister Amanda talked about during those long, long miles between Christian civilization and this place.

Elder Justus and Sister Amanda pulled two chairs so they could sit nearly knee to knee in front of our cold fireplace. Melissa and Lottie were finally convinced to go into their room, but they were allowed to sit in the open doorway with their dollies on their laps and listen as long as they remained perfectly silent. I sat at our table across from Nathan, both of us with our hands folded and still, prepared to be witnesses to the dialogue that would come. After a lengthy, impassioned prayer delivered by Elder Justus—during which I found myself nodding off several times—the older man cleared his throat loudly and began.

"Sister Amanda Dunn, do you believe in God, the Eternal Father, in his Son, Jesus Christ, and in the Holy Ghost? And do you have a firm testimony of the restored gospel?"

"Yes," she said, as I had.

"Do you sustain the president of the Church of Jesus Christ of Latter-day Saints as the prophet, seer, and revelator; and do you recognize him as the only person on the earth authorized to exercise all priesthood keys?"

"Yes." Once again she echoed my response from years ago, and I wanted to jump from my chair and shake her. That prophet was the man who brought her into our home, who made it acceptable to live in such flagrant disregard to the true teachings of Scripture. I could no more have answered yes now than I could have answered no when it was initially asked of me.

Holy Father, forgive me for sustaining any power other than you.

Despite my repentance, I remained silent.

"Do you live the law of chastity?"

"Oh yes." A bit of hesitation, enough to render me nauseous. When Nathan prepared me for that same question, he'd reassured me that the affection expressed between us had been good and pure, given that they were physical manifestations of the gift of love bestowed by Heavenly Father. Besides, we were already legally, if not spiritually, married.

What had he told her?

The questions went on, where she assured that she had no affiliations with anybody who opposed the church's teachings, that she paid her tithe faithfully, that she kept the Word of Wisdom.

"Has there been any sin or misdeed in your life that should have been resolved by the priesthood and has not?"

"No. Nothing."

Even my unseen smile was bitter. Apparently coveting her neighbor's husband did not apply.

"And finally, Sister Amanda, do you consider yourself worthy in every way to enter the temple and participate in temple ordinances?"

"I do, sir. In every way."

Looking up, I saw Nathan's face beaming with pride, and I believe we both exhaled for the first time. We all stood, and an unmistakable air of relief swirled around with the late afternoon breeze. Then, in a tone that matched the shadows creeping into the room, Elder Justus said, "Before we can proceed with the temple marriage plans, I think it best to discuss the matter of your particular temple recommend, Sister Camilla."

"Mine?" I thought about the slip of paper, tucked away in a drawer, that deemed me worthy to enter the temple, where the highest ordinances were practiced.

"I assure you my wife is a member in good standing." Nathan swiftly came to my side.

"There has been talk. And you may not realize that your wife did not attend Sabbath meetings during the months of your absence. Or, I might add, for several weeks prior."

"My wife was in mourning for the loss of our son."

"What better comfort could be had than the company of her fellow Saints?"

"She was quite inconsolable."

They might as well have been bargaining the price of a horse for all the say I had in my own spiritual condition. Yet I knew I had no answer that would satisfy either one, so I tucked in my chin and assumed a posture of meek acquiescence that would sate their need for control.

"You poor thing." Sister Amanda held a dainty lace kerchief to her mouth, and her bright blue eyes were wide with grief. "Nate—Brother Nathan said the boy died in your very arms. I would have wanted to die right along with the dear little thing."

"Part of me did," I said. The very part that made me worthy of witnessing a temple sacrament.

Nathan's hand on the small of my back stopped me from saying anything more.

Elder Justus took a step forward and loomed above me, his words dripping down like melting ice. "I will see to it that the bishop honors your current recommend. But I charge you, Nathan, that you bring your wife through a thorough examination before the baptism of your daughter."

"We will bring it before Heavenly Father."

I could tell by the control in his voice that he was not happy to have the matter brought forth in this manner, and his response brought an end to the discussion. Elder Justus and Sister Amanda offered their good-byes, and we wished them well on the walk back to the elder's home. I had only a moment to bask in the silence that came after I closed the door behind them, for as I turned around, I noticed the girls standing hand in hand in their bedroom doorway. Lottie rubbed sleepy eyes, but Melissa's were sharp and focused.

"You're getting married again, Papa?"

Time suspended as I waited to hear his response. Then again after the simple, spoken yes.

"To the lady that was here?"

"Yes. She's to be your aunt Amanda."

"She's pretty," Lottie said through a yawn.

"She is a good woman," Nathan said.

"Do you love her?" Melissa asked.

"Yes."

"As much as you love Mama?"

He put his arm around me and kissed me gently on my temple. "Nowhere near."

And I believed him.

CHAPTER 19

Nathan must have been confident that I would give my blessing to his proposal, because the next morning two men arrived at our home, each driving a wagon full of freshly cut lumber.

"We'll build a new room at the back of the house." He took my hand and led me through the plan, making me feel like an invited guest. "We don't have a place to cut a new door in the front room, so we'll get to it through the girls' room." Then we walked outside, where stakes and ropes marked the perimeters of the walls to come. "We'll build it all along the back. Twice the size of the other rooms. What do you think?"

"You keep saying 'we.' Whose room will it be?"

If he had an answer, he managed to hide it behind a sigh fueled with what seemed to be genuine confusion. "We'll decide that when the time comes."

"It seems cold. I'm thinking that, in the winter, so far away from the fire—"

He tapped his brow. "Already thought about that. We'll have a little fireplace right here." He walked away and tapped his foot on a hard clump of grass pierced by a wooden stake. "We could make part of it into a little sitting room. Like your own private parlor."

So it is to be mine. "It all sounds lovely, Nathan."

He came up behind me and placed his hands on my shoulders, gently turning me until my back was to the house and I looked out to where the sun had just fully risen over the mountains. "We'll put in two big windows—" he reached his hand out—"one at each end. Can you imagine seeing that sunrise every morning?"

"Certainly ensures that whoever's in here won't sleep past dawn."

Tears caught my voice, and strong arms pulled me close to the man behind me. Then breath on my neck, a soft kiss. "Promise you'll try, Camilla. You'll try to be happy."

"I am happy, Nathan." Oh, how grateful I was to have my face turned.

"You'll grow to love Amanda, I know. She'll be like a sister to you."

"I have *your* sister as my sister. And Evangeline." I turned in his arms and reached my hands to his face. "Couldn't you marry her? I already love her, and she so needs somebody . . ."

He smiled, a fitting expression for my petulant outburst. "The Holy Spirit did not bring me to love her as a wife."

"Because she isn't beautiful?"

He shrugged. "I cannot dictate what the Holy Spirit tells me. I can only respond."

"Well," I said with forced cheerful resolution, "if I am to

share my husband, perhaps Sister Amanda will be kind enough to share her furniture. We'll need something grand to fill this room."

Plans moved quickly after that. For a solid week my ears rang with the sounds of hammers and nails and saws. I'd seen Saints work together to build entire houses in one day, but the task of extending our home fell to Nathan alone. It was he who refused to accept the help, insisting that everybody had better uses for their time with winter coming on. I have to admit part of me thrilled at the progress. Our home had always been cozy and functional, but left to his own devices, my husband graced the new room with details of design and carpentry he would never have thought to include years ago. Most obvious of the improvements was the walls themselves—smooth planks rather than chinked logs. The windows were expertly framed, with boxes built out on either side of the wall for flowers to be planted outside and treasures displayed inside. The floor was smooth too, and when the space reached its point of empty completion, the girls had a marvelous time running its length, making a clatter of echoing footsteps.

I could tell Melissa quickly warmed to the idea of her father's taking in a new bride. She sparked off the fire in Nathan's eyes as he spoke of our celestial family and gazed at me with a triumph that made me ill. Regardless of my own temple worthiness, she would be baptized into the church when she turned eight, and I wanted nothing more than to grab her hand and run away.

Up to that point, I'd never considered such a thing. But right then, at our little family table, I realized I didn't need

Nathan's promise of a swift horse. He'd taken one away, and he'd come back. He'd never, never leave. He'd never take me away. He might not let me leave. The more he talked, though, about the prophet's plan for our family and the rewards we would receive from Heavenly Father for our obedience, the more I realized that I could have no part of this.

Still, I said nothing, voicing my resolve only to the Lord in my prayers. As far as anybody—my husband, my daughters, my neighbors, and my future sister wife—knew, I joined my husband in his joy, even if my expression was more reserved. Only Kimana sensed my unsettled spirit, and anytime we were alone, I sought her comfort. Her arms became my haven, as she would wrap them around me in a loving embrace I never remember getting from my own mother.

"It is not right," she'd say, patting my back, "all this business with another wife."

"Nathan is a good man," I reassured her. "As good as he's ever been. I know the Lord has a plan."

"I pray so."

I knew she did. She was the only other soul on the face of the earth who knew my true heart, and she was the only person in my life who shared my faith. We hadn't met together to study the Bible since Nathan's return; he kept the girls enthralled with tales of his summer's journey, and I'm sure I didn't imagine his watchful eye whenever Kimana and I did have a chance to whisper together in a corner. But well I remembered our early days as man and wife, and though I loathed the images I conjured, I knew Sister Amanda's arrival to the household would give him a new focus for his attentiveness.

The wedding was scheduled for the first Saturday in October. Sister Amanda would spend the intervening time as a guest in Rachel and Tillman's home, so as to be close to the temple to complete her Endowment. Melissa had asked once about what happened during the ceremony, but Nathan was quick to remind her—as she well knew—that the rites of the temple were secret, to be revealed only at a time ordained by Heavenly Father.

"People talk about things when they want to remember them," he explained gently. "But the time in the temple is sacred to the Lord, not something to be talked about like any other event. When we keep silent, we keep the sacredness of the sacrament in our hearts, and we remain holy."

My memories of the ceremony, however, were anything but holy. The humiliation of the ceremonial washing. I can still smell the oil touched to my head, neck, shoulders, stomach, and below. My legs. My feet.

"To cleanse you of the sins of this generation," the woman had said.

The sacred garments, the pure white dress and veil. The green apron. The faces of the actors performing the dramas. Why could Nathan hold me breathless and enthralled by firelight, when these dressed in costume proved so unsettling?

And my name. My whispered, secret, sacred name. The name that would buy my passage into heaven.

Mara. Bitterness.

I wondered what name Sister Amanda would be given. Would we have the same? Only Nathan would know, and he'd never tell. Moreover, I wouldn't ask. For the time being, Amanda was as absent from our life as she had been before her arrival.

How I cherished those final weeks. It's a rare thing in this life to know when your world is going to change. Every night Nathan came to our bed, exhausted from the day's construction labor, and every night I lay with him, hoping to prove myself a worthy offering. With every act of marriage, I prayed that God would give me another child, thinking that if I could bring us back to the joy we shared before our son died, I could shake him from this folly. Three days before the wedding, however, my time came and with it the end of that dream.

"Maybe you should stay home?" Kimana said when she noted my condition. "Do you feel up to making the trip?"

Of course I didn't feel like making the trip, but I still had three days. In the meantime, the Dunns' own wagon appeared in our yard, still laden with the furniture that had been precious enough to make the journey from England. Given that Sister Amanda was in Salt Lake City, I was given charge of what would come into our home and what would be left to some other fate. I'm ashamed to admit how much I relished even that little bit of power. Sister Amanda and I had spoken with each other only during the Sunday dinners she and her father shared with us, but I knew exactly what she envisioned. Somehow she thought our log walls would magically stretch to accommodate her mahogany breakfront and rolltop desk, just as our marriage would stretch to welcome her.

In my head I heard Rachel, deftly giving her sister wives instructions. I had that same authority. I'd never had authority over anyone or anything in my life. My children, yes, but that was a responsibility I shared with Nathan, and the balance of power was hardly equal. So that afternoon, as Nathan and Brother Kenneth stood, hats in hand, ready to do my bidding, my instructions were swift and sure. My voice dropped to a lower register, mimicking Rachel's confidence.

"Take the rolltop into the new room," I directed. "And both the upholstered chairs."

Nathan gave me one look askance. If he didn't approve my choices, he said nothing. Neither, surprisingly, did Brother

Kenneth, even though these were every bit as much his worldly goods as they were Sister Amanda's.

"Never cared about a bit o' this when her mother bought it," he said, hoisting the small table over his shoulder. "Nothin' but a load o' trouble since the day we landed. And a good bit before that, if you ask me."

"What about the breakfront?" Nathan asked, wiping his brow.

"They can bury it." I'd heard of such stories, emigrants burying pianos wrapped in canvas along the trail, marking the place so they could return later for it. "There's no room for it here."

Without any further discussion, Nathan and Brother Kenneth resumed their task. I watched, numb, as bits of Sister Amanda made their way into our home. Harmless pieces of furniture, yes, but also trunks that I knew held her dresses, her nightclothes, all the things that a woman hides away for the day she becomes a bride. I had none of those things. I became a bride with nothing but the dress on my back and a now-tattered journal.

The word *bed* jolted me from my reverie. I looked back to see the two men bringing an intricately carved headboard from the wagon. No need for discussion here. The bed Nathan and I had shared for all these years would be moved into the new room, while this one, infinitely more ornate, would preside in much humbler surroundings, accompanied by a six-drawer bureau and matching washstand.

That night, by the light of my blue glass lamp, I finished moving my things into the new room, hanging dresses on beautiful brass hooks attached to the wall and storing my other clothing in the trunk at the foot of the bed. A beautiful braided rug—woven by Kimana and presented to me as a gift after supper—warmed the exposed floor and softened my steps. On the other side of the wall, Melissa and Lottie were already in bed, early, due to the journey we would take the next day. The door between my room and the girls' was open, and I stepped as close as I dared, trying to listen to the prayers they said with their father, but I heard only soft, girlish, lilting voices, chorusing with Nathan in the final amen.

The next thing I knew he was in the doorway, then in my room, bathed in soft blue light. "It looks nice in here."

"Sister Amanda has some lovely things." I smoothed the doily on the small round table. "I crocheted this last winter and never had any place to display it properly."

"It's perfect."

"What do you know of doilies?" I cocked my head in near flirtation.

"I know they look good on tables."

Our warm, nervous laughter joined the shadows, and I felt more nervous than I had on our own wedding night. In fact, I could think of nothing else, given how closely my lamp produced a glow akin to that of the moon. Then he said it, my name, the way he had before our first kiss. Not my full name, just that first hard syllable dissolving into a sigh, and he stepped toward me, arms outstretched.

"No." Such a small sound, and I covered my mouth to hold back my sobs and to block his kiss.

Still he advanced, and I backed away until I felt the edge of my bed behind my knees. I sat upon it, burying my face in my hands and finally breaking down into body-wracking tears. A click of the closing door, and the room went dark. I felt his weight beside me. Not touching at all, we sat, side by side until, zapped of my own strength, I sought his. Just an inch or two and my cheek found his strong shoulder, then his chest.

My breath still ragged, I allowed him to maneuver my body until we were lying next to each other, my head cradled in the crook of his arm.

On the other side of the door, my daughters shuffled in their beds, and the sound of their little-girl voices echoed in my mind. I wanted to say my own prayer, but at that moment, my head was filled with such skull-splitting pain, trying to form words to lift up to God seemed too daunting a task. Instead, my spirit turned to the prayer I'd said as a little girl, and my lips moved against the warm cotton of my husband's shirt.

"Now I lay me down to sleep;
I pray the Lord my soul to keep.
If I should die before I wake,
I pray the Lord my soul to take."

For the first time since I had first uttered the verse under my mother's watchful eye, I felt no fear in the thought of the Lord claiming my soul that night. I could have died right there, warm in Nathan's embrace, and happily gone straight into the arms of my Savior. But then, just as I was drifting off to sleep, I heard a giggle on the other side of the door, and a rumbling beneath my ear as Nathan raised his voice.

"Girls. Settle down in there. We have a big day tomorrow."

And I knew I could not die. Not tonight. My soul might be kept by the Lord, but the souls of my daughters were at stake.

CHAPTER 20

"Are you happier today?" Lottie touched one little finger to the soft skin just below my eye.

Yesterday, when we'd piled into the wagon to make the drive into Salt Lake City, my eyes had been swollen nearly shut from sleep and tears. This morning, following a surprisingly long, deep sleep, I awoke feeling rested and at peace.

I hugged the girl tightly to me. She was snuggled between a still-sleeping Nathan and me in what I knew to be Rachel's bed; I looked across her head to where Melissa was sitting up in the pallet of blankets on the floor. "Every day is a reason to be happier than the day before. For we know the Lord has brought us through the night, and he has a plan for us to follow."

I cocked my ear and listened to the early morning sounds in the house. Just who had slept where, I could only imagine. Rachel and Tillman's home seemed ever-expanding. Amanda had been staying here for the past two weeks and had made herself quite at home in its luxury, as evidenced in her nearly possessive behavior the previous evening when we arrived just in time for supper.

"I'm glad she's marrying Nathan tomorrow," Rachel had whispered into my ear, pulling me aside from the livelier conversation. "Otherwise Tillman would snatch her up, and I'd be bunking with the children in the nursery."

In the gray light of morning, I stretched under the sheets, wondering if that wasn't where she'd slept last night.

A soft knock on the door, and Rachel's head appeared. "We're all due at the Endowment House at ten. Sister Amanda's already gone."

"What time is it?"

"Just after eight. You can imagine, she was quite excited."

"Oh, I can well imagine."

Rachel ducked out of the room and closed the door, leaving our little family alone together for the last time. I didn't see it as such at the moment, but looking back, it's clear. We fell immediately into the order Rachel established. The next hour we were out of bed and running to and fro, washing up, dressing. In the confusion of it all, I lost track of Nathan's whereabouts. I don't know what I expected—one last chance to plead with him, perhaps. Or even something as simple as a final moment together. Instead, I found myself securing a bow in Lottie's hair when I looked up and, out of the corner of my eye, saw him donning his hat, preparing to go. For the first time ever, I had no desire to follow.

The room was small and hot and dark. Windowless, lest any of the secrets leak through the glass to unworthy eyes. I could not but remember the day Nathan and I married. It was hot that day, too, but the heat came from the summer sun. The light bounced off the river, and I felt like our vows carried on the breeze, straight up to God. We had the entire wagon party as our witnesses, besides, but all I saw was Nathan, his face framed by cloudless blue sky, and I couldn't wait to start my life.

The marriage of Nathan and Sister Amanda held none of that magic, though the ceremony proceeded like the passage of some mystical rite. Bishop Johansson stood at the front of the room, looking as dour as he had the day he so gruffly dismissed Nathan's work last spring in the shadow of the new temple. Rachel and Tillman stood with me—all of us dressed in pure white. None of the sister wives had been invited. Sister Amanda would have no one. Without a recommend, her father could not witness the ceremony, and I admit to feeling a pang of companionship when I realized that this was something we would share, being married alone.

Then again, whom did we need but Nathan?

Bishop Johansson held his hands high, saying, "Let them enter!" and two doors on either side of the front of the room opened. So seamlessly did the doors blend into the wall, I hardly noticed they were there until that moment. Nathan and Amanda's entrance took my breath away.

Amanda's skin, pale and translucent, took on an iridescent glow, almost reflecting the white silk of the sacred dress. She'd been chewing on her lip—a nervous habit, I would soon learn—and her mouth stood out bold and nearly red in contrast, the crimson visible through the veil. Even though she knew her father would not be in attendance, she still took in the room, and I imagined a hopeful look in her blue eyes. For just that second, my feeling of companionship became one of temporary compassion. Her hair was left long and straight, simply parted down the middle and swept behind her shoulders to encase that perfect, porcelain face within wide, dark wings beneath the white veil.

This was an image that could never exist outside of this room. There was otherworldliness to her beauty, and for a moment I forgot about who she was and what she meant to my family. To my husband.

My husband.

I'd seen Nathan in temple clothing once before, at our own sealing ceremony the year after we were married, but our garments were made of coarse, homespun wool. Now, here he was, also in pure white, save for the green apron tied at his waist. Sister Amanda wore one, too, representing the garments worn by the first husband and wife—Adam and Eve. I knew that story, of course, enough to know that Adam and Eve only donned clothing to hide their nakedness. Their shame. Why was it, then, that neither Nathan nor Amanda felt shame in that moment? Why was I the one standing in this unholy place wishing I could hide from God?

Sweat broke out on my brow, calling me to instinctively lift my sleeve to wipe it. Rachel caught my eye and gave a quick, stern shake of her head, and I dropped my arm immediately. As Nathan and Amanda took their place at the altar, facing each other as they knelt on the padded benches on either side, I felt drops slide down my face, playing substitute for tears I dared not shed.

"Brother Nathan," the bishop intoned, "and Sister Amanda. Please join hands."

They did, as we had, their fifth fingers locked, hands overlapped with their first fingers pressed against the wrist of the other. I remember that grip, how Nathan had smiled and told me later that my pulse was racing like an Indian pony. I looked down and touched my own thumb to the tip of my first finger, felt rough ridges of my skin. In our years together he'd taken my hand to lift me when I'd fallen, to pull me through snowstorms, to bring me through the early pains of childbirth. Mostly, I loved the feel of his hand in mine—not in this symbolic intertwining, but when we were simply walking together, strolling without clear intent or direction. His hand would never feel the same again.

"Brother Nathan, do you take Sister Amanda by the right hand and receive her unto yourself to be your lawful and wedded wife for time and all eternity, with a covenant and promise that you will observe and keep all the laws, rites, and ordinances pertaining to this Holy Order of Matrimony in the New and Everlasting Covenant, and this you do in the presence of God, angels, and these witnesses of your own free will and choice?"

"Yes." No hesitation, and with just enough of a nod of his head that the tassel of his temple cap swayed like a pendulum below his ear.

Bishop Johansson repeated the vow, and Amanda gave the same answer, though I daresay with a good deal more enthusiasm than Nathan had displayed.

"By virtue of the Holy Priesthood and the authority vested in me, I pronounce you, Nathan and Amanda, legally and lawfully husband and wife for time and all eternity . . ."

Sweat now gathered at the nape of my neck, pouring down my back in rivulets, yet I felt cold—chilled in this stifling, airless room. I do not know how I remained standing, feeling neither my feet nor the floor throughout the rest of Bishop Johansson's pronouncement.

"... and I seal upon you the blessings of the holy resurrection with power to come forth in the morning of the first resurrection clothed in glory, immortality, and eternal lives ..."

Those words ushered in a new level of mourning. Not only was I losing my husband as I knew him for the rest of my life here on earth, but he would be no part of my eternity. Not if he believed that this man, this awful, little unkind man, had the power to bestow his salvation.

"... and I seal upon you the blessings of kingdoms, thrones, principalities, powers, dominions, and exaltations, with all the blessings of Abraham, Isaac, and Jacob ..."

I listened to the words as I never had before. I saw Nathan as I never had before. My humble, pleasing, loving husband, driven by spiritual greed. Those words, eerily familiar, the temptation offered to Christ by none other than Satan himself. What dominion did he need beyond our little home and his workshop? What exaltations besides the excited shouts of our little girls every time he entered a room? He made love to me telling me I was his blessing, that if Heavenly Father never gave him another thing, I would be enough. But for me, he would spend eternity alone. And now ...

"... and I say unto you: be fruitful and multiply and replenish the earth that you may have joy and rejoicing in the day of our Lord Jesus Christ. All these blessings, together with all the blessings appertaining unto the New and Everlasting Covenant, I seal upon you by virtue of the Holy Priesthood, through your faithfulness, in the name of the Father, and of the Son, and of the Holy Ghost. Amen."

The room echoed, "Amen," but I chose to breathe instead.

If my voice was missed, no one seemed to notice. Nathan and Amanda stood, and she shakily lifted the veil from her face.

"And now," Bishop Johansson said, "Sister Amanda Fox, you were given a new name at the time of your Endowment, the name that will be written in the Lamb's Book of Life, the name that you will answer to throughout eternity. You must whisper your name into the ear of your husband, that he may call you to him at the time of resurrection, when you will continue to keep your vows unto each other in celestial marriage."

Amanda moved toward Nathan and placed her right hand on his shoulder. Then, cupping her hand around his ear, she leaned in to whisper. It was the most intimate moment between them I'd ever witnessed, and I loathed the instinct that brought his hand to her waist to steady her.

When she pulled away, they stood, motionless, staring into each other's eyes. In a tone completely indifferent to the moment, Bishop Johansson said, "You may kiss her if you like."

Sometimes I think if I'd only looked away at that moment, I might have been able to bear a life sentence of plural marriage. It was, after all, only for this lifetime, and there was no reason to think the Lord could not bring me comfort in the midst of this pain. But the sight of his lips touched to hers—sweet and chaste as the kiss might have been—brought my heart around a corner to a new, dark place. I wanted to believe this was their first kiss, that my husband had respected the boundaries of our marriage to that extent. And if it were, I well knew just how Amanda felt at that moment. That first kiss. The tantalizing combination of joy and fear fluttering between her stomach and her spine. I'd felt it just the same. Not only in our first kiss, but with nearly every embrace. Brief as this moment was, my mind raced through it, seeing every kiss, feeling every touch. I brought every moment of our love to the surface, wishing I could somehow take them in my hands, wad them up, and hurl them at his feet.

But then, they were my treasures, because I loved him. From the moment he met me at the crossroad until the moment he kissed his new wife, I loved him. In truth, I love him still, that being the one burden the Lord has refused to lift from me. As I watched them draw apart from each other, her lips newly christened by his, I realized they did not vow to love each other. They were lawful and wedded, for time and eternity, according to the ordinances of Joseph Smith's church, and I was not so naive as to think that they did not, but I knew Nathan *could* not love her as he did me. He might someday, but for now, no. Amanda did not rescue him. She was not his salvation, as he had once claimed I was.

There I was in borrowed robes, deep in the center of a pagan temple, witness to words spoken by an unholy priest, and yet clearly the Lord was speaking to me.

Listen. Think.

When I married Nathan, I'd vowed to join my life to his under a mantle of false teachings, binding me to this church as much as to him. It wasn't until I heard my husband bind himself to another that I could finally be set free.

O *Lord . . .* He drew me in, even in that place, even at that moment.

I longed to get away, be alone, find a quiet place to devote my spirit to the Lord and listen for his voice, but I was swept away by the hand of Rachel, back to the room where we stepped out of our temple dresses. I turned my face from the sourness of mine, folded it, and laid it on a bench for some sister Saint to retrieve and, I hoped, launder.

"It will get easier." Rachel turned so I could button up the back of her dress. "Pretty soon, she'll just be like a part of you."

"She'll never be a part of me." I slipped the last little piece of round, painted wood through its hole and smoothed the back of Rachel's dress. "She is his wife."

"And your sister wife."

"No." I stepped into my skirt and slipped my arms through the sleeves of the bodice. "She is nothing to me."

And neither is he. Though I dared not speak such a sentiment aloud. I wasn't sure myself what it meant. I only knew that, over the course of this ceremony, Nathan had once and for all been displaced as the center of my life. His home would not forever be my home. His god would never be my god. I was bound to him by the law, and I still loved him, but that love was swiftly becoming something akin to nostalgia—a passion relegated to the girl I was long ago. I would live my life as a bride of Christ alone.

Rachel and Tillman hosted a wedding luncheon in their home, and I could only imagine the amount of barking Rachel must have done before we left in order to have everything laid out by the time we returned. Nonetheless, we returned from the Endowment House to find the Cranes' house transformed. Guests—strangers to me—milled about the front parlor and sitting room. Conspicuously absent was Evangeline.

"I invited her," Rachel told me in the midst of the guests' arrivals, "but she wouldn't come. Weddings make her a little sad, I guess."

Thin white paper, cut into strips and looped into chains (probably by the hands of the children), hung about the room. Vases of flowers sat atop every available space, including a prominent arrangement on the mantel. Just where Rachel found flowers in October in Utah remained a mystery that bore testimony to the power that came with being in favor with the prophet.

Being somewhat an honored guest, I was not allowed into the kitchen, but Melissa and Lottie snuck in and came back reporting trays upon trays of food: platters of shaved meat, tiny sandwiches, cookies, cakes, and all manner of treats.

"And a wonderful red punch in a big glass bowl," Melissa concluded, her eyes as big as the dipper, I supposed.

"Your aunt Rachel certainly knows how to host a celebration."

I blended into the crowd—or out of the crowd—as much as possible. Nobody seemed to notice; they weren't here to see me. Most were friends of Tillman's, but there were quite a few men whom Nathan had met on his forays into Salt Lake City when he delivered temple blocks. Elder Justus and his wife were the only guests who made the drive in from Cottonwood, but I overheard Sister June tell Amanda that she had organized a small reception to follow the next day's church meeting.

"Oh, how lovely!" Amanda's enthusiasm heralded a much larger affair than would be offered. I'd attended dozens of our ward's receptions. We were not, by nature, a festive people. Their mood would be much better suited to my state of mind, but this was one reception I would not attend. I could tolerate humiliation among strangers I would never see again, but not among those with whom I had to share my day-to-day life.

I sought Rachel out in the kitchen, where she supervised the carving of an enormous turkey. "Smaller slices, Marion. See if we can't set back enough for our own supper tonight." She caught my eye and crossed the room to wrap her arms around me. "This'll be over soon. And then you'll just go home and see that it's not nearly as awful as you think it's going to be."

Marion huffed at the statement. "Not easy being the one coming in, either."

"Well, that's one reason to hold out and wait to be somebody's first wife, isn't it?" Rachel's words sliced as sharp as the knife Marion wielded.

"Why do you think Brother Nathan locked her down the minute she stepped off the boat? If she'd come into this place an unclaimed woman, she could have had her pick."

"Stop being such a gossip, Marion," Rachel said, placing herself between the two of us. "Have a little bit of respect."

"It's all right," I said. "I'm fine. But I did want to talk to you."

Rachel shot one more scathing look at Marion before looping her arm through mine and leading me out the kitchen door and into the backyard. I filled myself with the blast of cool, crisp air and smiled at the myriad of children who had escaped the stuffiness of adults to build and destroy mountains of leaves. Melissa and Lottie were among them, playing with an enviable sense of abandon.

I folded my arms close against me. "What is she like?"

"Sister Amanda?"

"I've barely had a chance to meet her. She's been here for the past few weeks; you know her so much better than I do. What do you know?"

There was a wood-slat bench on the back porch. Rachel backed her way to it, sat down, and patted the seat next to her. I followed.

"She's nice."

"That much I hoped."

"She's a strong believer. Much more so than her father, according to her. I think he's immune to all that fire that comes with a new convert."

"Nathan's never lost that fire."

"No, no, he hasn't. I guess in that way . . ."

"She's a perfect mate?"

She gave me a sidelong glance and a smile to match. "Well, aren't you singing a different tune?"

"Somewhat." Though I wasn't sure exactly what that tune was, nor how I could ever explain my heart to her. I picked at my skirt, focusing on the deep blues and grays of its fabric, keeping my eyes engaged there so she couldn't see the depth of my request. "I was wondering, Rachel, if I—if the girls and I, actually—could stay here with you for a little while."

"You mean, while Nathan and Amanda settle in?"

"Something like that."

"Well, I'd have to talk with Tillman, but I'm sure it would be all right. Was this Nathan's idea?"

I shook my head. "He doesn't even know I'm asking you."

The pause before her next question took on greater meaning when I heard the tinge of suspicion in her voice. "For how long? A week? two?"

"Maybe longer." I dared not look at her. Words came to my tongue as they came to my head, announcing the very formation of ideas. "Maybe until the spring."

She made a small sound, like "*Hm.*" I looked straight ahead, watching the children as they filled their arms with leaves and, laughing, tossed them into the air, creating great crispy showers of brown, red, and orange. Lottie tried valiantly to start a game of tag, but the older children refused to chase her, leaving her to simply run from one to another proclaiming, "You're it! You're it!"

"What happens in the spring, Camilla?"

"I don't know."

"Are you going to leave him?"

"I don't know."

Her voice dropped to a whisper—unnecessary, seeing as the children were so involved in their play. "Are you thinking you'll *divorce* him?"

I turned to find her placid face looking straight at me. "No. I would never seek a divorce. I married him in good faith. I think, in some way, we will always be married in God's eyes—"

"In *some* way?"

"—and in the eyes of the law, of course. But, Rachel, I just can't—"

"I've warned you about this, Sister. This is our life. This is Heavenly Father's plan." She held a hand up to stop my protest. "You cannot let your jealousy interfere with what your husband, what the prophet, what God *himself* bids you to do." She leaned closer. "And even if you did, do you honestly think I would shelter an apostate in my home? an apostate who betrayed my brother?"

"Didn't he betray me?"

"No. He complied with the teachings of his church. Your church too, I might add. Say what you will now, but I was there at your baptism. And your wedding. And your sealing." Her voice softened. "I know it's hard, and maybe it is best that you stay here for a couple of weeks. But then you need to go home, Camilla. I'll drive you there myself. You'll see." Smiling now, she reached over and squeezed my knee. "She's a sweet girl, really. Simple, but sweet. You'll enjoy having another woman to talk to during those long winter days. Let her tell you all about London. Make it a history lesson for the girls."

Though hardly convinced, she did manage to coax a weak smile from me.

Just then the back door burst open, and Marion flew out.

"He's here!"

Rachel twisted in her seat. "Who?"

"Brother Brigham." Marion clasped her hands in glee. "The prophet himself!"

"Relax, girl," Rachel said, standing. "This isn't the first time the man has been to the house."

"I know, but it's always so exciting." She pointed at me. "And he says he wants to see you."

"Me?" I couldn't imagine.

"Brother Nathan said his first wife was every bit as lovely as his new bride, and Brother Brigham said, 'Now, *that* I'd like to see.'"

She laughed, and I gave her the benefit of my doubt that she knew just how malicious she sounded, but Rachel extended no such grace.

"You know, Marion, you really are an idiot sometimes. I'd call you cruel, but I don't know that you're bright enough to deserve it." She added, behind her hand, "Prophet he may be, but the man loves a free lunch."

By now the children had caught on about our special visitor, and they rushed past us into the house. Our efforts to get them to move quietly and slowly went unheeded. Whatever else I might think of him, however, he was known to be a kind man who loved children, and by the time I found my way to the front parlor, he was surrounded by them. He sat in the leather wingback chair by the window, welcoming them with extended arms. Only my Lottie hung back, looking on with her wide, green eyes, thumb firmly planted in her mouth.

He was a large man by any standards, Brigham Young, and imposing in his own way. Were he just an ordinary man in a room full of other ordinary people, he might have gone unnoticed. But even I have to admit that he was no ordinary man. The moment he stood, a hush fell over the room as his followers waited for a new pearl of wisdom to drop from his thin, dry lips.

"Mrs. Fox?"

It was the first time I ever heard his voice, this man whose words dictated the circumstances of my very life. I stood in stunned silence in front of him until I finally noticed the large extended hand and placed my own in his.

"I commend you, Brother Nathan," he said, speaking just over my shoulder. "Two lovely wives indeed. How pleased Heavenly Father must be with you."

I tried to take my hand away, but the strength of his grip intensified and I found his steel gray eyes staring into mine.

"It is a great, unselfish act you have committed today, Sister . . ." He searched for the word.

"Camilla," I supplied.

"A great, unselfish act, Sister Camilla. You have done a great thing not only for your family, but for our church." He let go of my hand and held his own high, turning our little gathering into a congregation. "We are under siege, you know. Our church and our ways. Our government, the government of the very nation founded on religious freedom, seems intent on denying us our constitutional rights. And you women, like our Sister Camilla here, are soldiers in our fight. You may never pick up a gun, but when you embrace the role of womanhood revealed by God himself to our prophet, you stand shoulder to shoulder with us."

There was a collective sense of hearts beating faster as he spoke, united in a single, rhythmic pulse. I felt like David facing Goliath, but I remained small, powerless. Whatever stones I might have thrown stayed lodged in their sling. I didn't speak. I didn't move. Nathan stepped up to put a comforting, protective arm around me, and Amanda followed, close at his side. Lottie backed into my skirts while Melissa broke away from the group of admiring children and came to stand between her father and me. There we were, our family on display, a living example of the prophet's vision. That's when I knew.

They'll never let me go.

CHAPTER 21

The first night was the worst, or at least I imagine it would have been. Late in the evening, still full from the bounty of Aunt Rachel's buffet and exhausted from arguing about not being able to stay there for one more night, Melissa and Lottie fell asleep in the back of the wagon on the ride home. Amanda sat between Nathan and me, her own head bobbing for the last mile or so, not that there had been much talk to keep her awake.

When we pulled up in front of our house, Kimana came out to meet us, wrapping her bright, nubby shawl around her shoulders. A more welcome sight I couldn't imagine, and I leaped down from the wagon almost before Nathan brought the team to a complete stop. I stayed in her embrace, listening to Nathan help Amanda down from the wagon's seat.

"Come help me with the girls," he told her.

"No," I said, pulling away from Kimana's warmth. "I'm sure she has other things to put away. I'll help you."

Most of Amanda's clothes had actually arrived before we left for the wedding, and they consumed every available bureau drawer, hook, and empty trunk in what used to be my bedroom. But she did have one small bag, which Nathan handed to her.

"Good evening," she said shyly to Kimana, who appeared at her side, taking both my satchel and the girls' from the wagon.

"Good evening," Kimana returned, marking the end of their conversation.

Nathan climbed into the wagon's bed and lifted a sleeping Melissa as if she were a feather, a fact remarkable considering how I staggered a bit under her weight when he handed her down. I couldn't remember the last time I carried my older daughter, and as I adjusted my grip under her weight, it occurred to me that I wouldn't be able to do so for much longer. She was becoming a big girl—six years old. Next year seven. She'd be baptized when she turned eight, and then I'd never get her away. . . .

"Are you all right?" he asked. "Is she too heavy?"

"Not yet," I said, holding her close, trapping her doll between us.

Nathan managed to jump down from the wagon while holding Lottie, jostling her no more than did the bumpy ride. Together we walked into our home, passing Kimana, who left us a plate of corn bread and a pitcher of milk in the light of a warm, glowing lamp. I could hear Amanda in the next room, humming to herself. I didn't allow myself even the smallest glimpse into the room. Melissa made a contented sound against my neck, and I took step after stoic step until I stooped to lay her on the bed she shared with her sister. Nathan deposited Lottie on the opposite side.

"Nightgowns?"

"No." I moved to the foot of the bed. "Let's just take off their shoes and dresses."

Working together, we prepared our girls for bed as if they were the dolls that rested in their listless arms. We tucked the blanket up around their chins and leaned down to kiss warm, soft cheeks. It was a familiar routine. I leaned across Melissa to kiss Lottie's cheek, and Nathan to kiss Melissa. Any other night we would have exchanged a quick kiss with each other above the both of them, but not tonight.

"I saw Kimana left out a snack." The words caught in his throat. "Are you hungry?"

I tried to imagine sitting in the lamplight with him and his wife knowing full well . . .

"No. I'm tired. I'm going to bed."

"Mil . . ."

Luckily there was a bed with two sleeping girls between us, and I'll never know exactly what he intended to say to me in that moment. I took two brisk steps into my new room and closed the door between us. It was dark, and I wasn't familiar enough with the room's setup to immediately find my way around, but before long my eyes adjusted to the moonlight streaming through the window, revealing the familiar form of my bed. I sat upon it—perched on the edge, my hands nervous in my lap. Somewhere outside, Nathan was unhitching the team, tending to the rest of the stock. And if I were Amanda, I'd be undressing, quickly shedding my clothes, and donning my nightgown lest Nathan find me in a moment of immodesty.

Were it just he and I, we would meet at the table, enjoy a late-night meal, talking in whispers, concerned less about waking the girls than having a few cherished moments alone.

I don't know how long I sat on the edge of my bed. Long enough to hear Nathan come inside. Long enough to hear the two of them talking at the table. This was what prisoners must feel as they await their execution. The darkness in my room drew closer like a hood, my breath constricted like the rope. My muscles grew stiff, and I began to think I might never move again. That I might be sitting right there come the dawn, watching the sunrise through my new windows.

Then I heard the scraping of two chairs across the front room floor. After that, the unmistakable sound of a closing bedroom door.

Quickly, I grabbed the quilt from my bed and folded it over my arm. I tiptoed silently through the girls' room, lest I wake them, and through the front room, lest I attract Nathan and Amanda's attention. The front door latch lifted noiselessly, and I wedged my toe underneath to lift the door so there'd be no scraping sound as it opened. And closed.

A crystal-clear night sky greeted me, lit by a three-quarter moon. Kimana's small cabin was well within sight, and I knew she'd surely still be awake. But I longed to be alone. After living one day and night amid the chaos of Rachel's household, not to mention a stifling afternoon among her sainted friends, I drank in the still, calm coolness of this night. I looked up and could well imagine Jesus in heaven, more infinite than the sky, looking down on his creation. More than that, I knew God himself dwelt within me, no less vast.

"My God." Breath streamed from me, a mist of prayer. "Watch over me while I wait."

I made my way across the yard and used my shoulder to

open the heavy barn door. I picked my way through gingerly, in case Nathan had left a pitchfork or spade out of place. One of the horses gave an indignant snort as I passed its stall, but the cow gave no complaint. We'd all grown quite used to each other during the time that Nathan was away, though I admit to being relieved that he was back to take over the barn chores.

Soon I found what I sought—the pile of sweet-smelling hay in the back of the barn. He'd brought in a fresh supply since his arrival home, and I knew it stacked up nearly to the ceiling. There was, however, enough of it tapered along the floor to serve my purpose. With one snapping motion, my quilt was spread upon it. I lay down, grabbed one corner of the quilt, and wrapped myself cocoonlike within.

And God granted me sleep.

Of course Nathan knew I'd spent the first night out in the barn—and the nine that followed—but he had the good grace not to remark upon it. Each morning I awoke nearly an hour before dawn and would creep back into our house, back into my bed, where I fell immediately into a deep slumber until sunlight woke me again. A splash of water on my face, a fresh dress, and a quick pat of my hair nearly readied me for the day, but some days, as I busied myself with the breakfast dishes, he would sidle up behind me and silently present a piece of straw I'd somehow missed. He'd say not a word, merely raise one quizzical brow, and I offered no explanation. We entered a new season of silence.

My night lodging did not escape the watchful eye of Kimana, either, but unlike Nathan, she did not spare me her disdain.

"It is not right for the woman of the family to live like an animal," she said. It was a Monday morning, and we knelt beside the creek, our hands numb from the cold water as we did the washing. "Mr. Fox should not allow it."

"I've not consulted Mr. Fox."

"Why do you not come sleep in my home?"

I couldn't tell by her voice if she found my choice illogical or hurtful, so I strove for the same neutrality in my reply. "I'm just not sure where my place is right now. And if I were to sleep in your cabin, it would be too easy to stay there. With this, I know some night it's going to be too cold, or—" I sat up from my washing and rubbed my back—"I'll wake up too sore to face another night out there. But until then, I need to be alone. I need to search my heart and pray."

"You cannot do that in your room?" She took one of the girls' dresses and plunged it into the water.

"Not yet."

"You know they will be man and wife after it turns cold."

"I know. That's why every night I pray that God will show me what to do."

"And what has he told you so far?"

I laughed. "To keep sleeping in the barn."

Kimana offered the rare hint of a smile. "I think, maybe, you are confusing his voice with your fear. What good is an answer if it can change at any time?"

I took the dress from her and began to wring it out while she washed another. The fabric, cold and wet in my hands, chafed my skin and chilled me to the point of pain. Still, it served as a welcome relief from the numbness I'd felt since the wedding.

"It's not that easy to discern God's will, Kimana."

"Maybe not, if you are looking for new answers. Maybe you should look for old answers."

"Old answers?"

"In the book. The Bible. I remember last summer you teaching that it is the words of God himself. Answers are made of words. And true answers never change." She looked up. "What color is the sky?"

I indulged her. "Blue."

"Aha. And if I ask you that question tomorrow or a year from now. Or if I asked it last summer. Or the day Lottie was born. Would the answer not be the same?"

"No," I said triumphantly. "Sometimes the sky is gray. Or even black."

"It may seem so, when it is covered by clouds. But behind the clouds, the sky is the same. And it may seem so when the world turns away for the night and the sun is hidden. But the answer is the same, always, just waiting for the dawn."

I sighed. "Kimana, when did you get to be so wise?"

She took the dress from me and wrung additional water drops out of it. "My people are wise because we speak little so we can listen to the voice of creation. Now I have the Creator inside of me. My eyes cannot hear him from the pages in your book, but my heart can listen."

"But I *have* been listening."

For the first time in my memory, Kimana's voice was stern. "You have been listening to yourself out there alone in the dark. God has given you a home; sleep in it. He has written you a Word; read it. I have not seen you open it since Mr. Fox came home."

"You know he wouldn't approve."

"Maybe not in his home, but you have your own home now."

She handed the little dress back to me. Silently, I untwisted the wet mass, folded it, and laid it atop the other newly clean garments. When I looked at her again, she was looking quizzically at a pale green blouse dotted with tiny purple flowers.

"It's hers," I said, wondering what she was doing right now back in my warm, dry home.

"It is pretty," Kimana said before plunging it into the creek to wash.

That night we gathered together for supper, plagued by the usual awkward silence that had marked every meal taken at this table. Melissa shared a story about a scuffle two boys got into in the school yard, and Nathan described in detail a new shelving system he would be building in our trading post.

"Clear to the ceiling." He waved his fork in demonstration. "And a new service counter with shelves underneath. Place is going to shut down for two solid weeks while I work. Going to look just like the city stores."

His beaming pride was contagious, and we echoed Lottie's enthusiastic "Hooray, Papa!"

It was an unguarded moment of joy, and within it came an answer I would never have heard surrounded by nothing but darkness, self-pity, and a quilt out in our barn. I loved my husband, still, and I loved my daughters. In the midst of that laughter I realized I had to love Amanda, too. For reasons I would later understand, God allowed her to come into our lives, and I tried to see her through the eyes of my Savior. Grudgingly, I had to agree with what Rachel had told me. She was a sweet girl. I found it hard to imagine her having a single thought or saying a single word outside the confines of our home. Those she'd said inside our home were confined to the most polite of conversation. So when our laughter died down and we were once again engrossed in our food, I looked across the table.

"Amanda, why don't you tell us a little something about your life in England?"

Nathan caught my eye and smiled at the gift I'd extended. Amanda nearly choked on whatever morsel she'd just taken off her fork. "What'd you say?"

"Yes! Tell us!" Lottie and Melissa begged in chorus.

"Well, to start," she said, her accent stronger than I ever remember hearing it, "we don't have great, vast plains to drive our wagons across like you do here. And we don't have Indians, and we don't have great big mountains. . . ."

She launched into tales of dark cobbled streets with a castle and a river right in the middle of them.

"Bigger than Salt Lake City?" Lottie asked.

"Oh, much," Amanda said. "And many, many more people."

"Is there a temple?" Melissa asked.

"No," Nathan said. "That is why so many converts come here to live and worship."

"Thank God," Amanda said, "or I would never have met your father."

I believe, even in the midst of that sentence, she wished she could have stopped, but too late, she snapped her pretty mouth shut and stared down into her plate. I summoned up all my strength and reached across the table, resting my hand on hers.

"He always has a plan," I said. "I believe that now more than ever."

Later, after the table had been cleared and the dishes done, after Nathan read to us from *The Book of Mormon* and we had our first time of family prayer, I took the girls by their hands, saying, "I'll get them ready for bed." In fact, I brought them into my room and let them wash their faces in the pretty washbowl, and I let them look at themselves in the mirror above it as I brushed and plaited their hair.

"I wish I was as pretty as Aunt Amanda," Melissa said, catching my eye in the glass.

"You're as pretty as you."

"But don't you think she's pretty?"

"I do, indeed."

"I think *you're* pretty, Mama."

"Well, thank you, Lottie." I turned around and, in light of the compliment, chose not to chastise her for bouncing on the bed.

"Yes," Melissa said, "but you're older."

As she will be someday.

"Does it bother you that Papa married Aunt Amanda?"

I had to be honest. "It did at first, but I know God has a reason."

"It's his plan for our eternal family." She winced a bit as I worked out a knot in her hair.

Nothing but the sound of bristles against my palm. How to explain? More importantly, how to explain in a way that would not send her to her father in protest. So I brushed and I prayed, *Father, forgive my silence*, before forcing a cheerful tone to my voice.

"You know, Kimana reminded me earlier that we haven't been having our Bible time since your father came home. And since I have this whole room to myself now, maybe we can have a special time together, just the three of us, like it was last summer. Wouldn't that be nice?"

"More stories!" Lottie still bounced.

Melissa was less convinced. "Papa already read to us."

I moved to sit on the edge of my bed and gently pulled Lottie into my lap, beckoning Melissa to my side. "I grew up reading the Bible. And it's very important to me that you girls read it, too. Your father wants you to know what Joseph Smith said, but I want you to know what *God* says. Do you understand?"

"But I heard Brother Brigham telling somebody that some parts of the Bible are wrong."

I clenched my fist and sweetened my voice. "Brother Brigham may say what he likes. Nothing in the Bible is *wrong*, but some parts are hard to understand. I know when I was a little girl, it seemed very difficult. So hop up." I patted the mattress beside me.

While the girls settled in, I turned up the flame in my blue lamp and opened to the first book of Samuel.

"The very last days that I lived at home, this is the book I was reading. It begins with the story of a woman who very badly wants to have a child."

"And does she?" Melissa asked, immediately intrigued.

"We'll have to read and find out." I climbed in between the girls and leaned against the headboard, thrilling at the feel of them snuggling against me. When we got to the end of the chapter, I felt as if God had worked a miracle. Maybe it was because I was older, maybe because I'd read so much over the summer, but I hardly stammered over any words—not even the names. Somehow they seemed larger, clearer, more familiar, and it warmed my heart to hear my daughters begging me to read just a little more.

I kissed the top of each head. "Not tonight, but tomorrow. And only if we keep this our secret."

"From Papa?" Lottie asked.

"From everyone."

CHAPTER 22

Oddly enough, I count the next months as some of the sweetest in my life. Just a year ago I'd been pregnant with my little son, and as much as I knew I would never hold him in my arms again, I knew that I might not have this time with my daughters forever. They would grow up; they would leave home just as I had. Every night, before I sent them off to bed, I put my arms around them and prayed, "Heavenly Father, thank you for leaving us such wonderful stories so we can know just how great and powerful you are."

I thought back to my days with Rachel and allowed myself to exert some of the privileges of being a first wife. I asked Nathan to shoot as many of the migrating geese as he could, and while our neighbors enjoyed the plucked birds we shared with them, Melissa and Lottie and I enjoyed new, soft down pillows plumped up behind us as we read. In an effort to establish some friendship with Amanda, I asked her to show me some of the treasures she'd brought with her from England, one of which was a large, leather-bound Bible.

"May I take this?" I asked. "I like to read from the Scriptures in the evening."

"Go on." She put it right in my lap. "I don't think Nathan will mind."

"It can be our little secret. Wait here." I took the Bible to my room, set it on my bedside table, and returned with the tiny blue book we'd been using. "Take this one. It was a wedding gift to me from Sister Ellen."

"Well now," she said, entranced, "isn't that charming."

"You'll do better with it than I do. Your eyes are younger."

"Oh, I'm not much for reading, I'm afraid."

"Someday you might feel different. And when you do, it'll be here."

Apparently reading was just one of the things that Amanda wasn't "much for." As we prepared our home for winter, it was apparent that she also lacked skills in gardening, canning, cooking, and preserving. While she could charm every woman in our quilting circle with her stories of living in fashionable London, she herself was hopeless with a needle. When Nathan took her to the first wool carding party of the season, she came home with red, bloody fingertips from continuously misunderstanding the direction of the cards.

"My people would have thrown her out to the wolves," Kimana muttered under her breath after taking the latest flat, rock-hard loaf of bread out of the oven. "And the wolves would have thrown her back."

Gifted with an unseasonably warm day that made me think we were nearing the end of summer rather than fall, Nathan took us out for a picnic on the shores of the Great Salt Lake. On the drive, I sat in the wagon's seat with Nathan while the girls kept Amanda and Kimana entertained in the bed acting out stories with their dolls, Lilly and Rose. Gradually, the land grew flat—no hint of a hill—and a vast expanse of gray water appeared on the horizon.

"There it is!" Melissa called out, prompting a clattering of activity as the girls stood to look over the side.

"Careful," I cautioned. "It's still a way off."

Amanda was no less impressed than the little girls. "It's like being at the edge of the world now, isn't it?"

It was. We were the only family to venture out this day, giving an eerie feeling that we might just be the only family in existence. I pictured what we must look like to God—just six tiny dots on the face of his creation.

"That's why it's so important to have God inside our hearts," I said, voicing my thoughts. "Otherwise, we'd be lost."

My words themselves, however, were lost on my traveling companions as they commented on the color of the sky—violet—the expanse of the valley—vast—and smell of the air—vile.

"It's sulfur," Nathan explained. "You'll get used to it."

We drove on, bringing the wagon to a stop next to a shock of tall grasses. I asked Kimana to help the little ones take off their shoes and socks, assuming Amanda could fend for herself, and when all were down to their bare feet, the girls and Amanda jumped from the wagon. Kimana took a little more time. Nathan and I remained perched in our seat, watching them diminish before our eyes.

"Come on, Papa! Come on, Mama!" Lottie's voice trailed behind her.

"In a minute!" Nathan called, but he made no sign of moving. Instead, he set the brake and sat back, lolling his head in my direction. "When's the last time we were out here?"

"Right before Lottie turned three." Right before I discovered I was pregnant.

Seconds passed.

"Do you remember the first time?"

"Of course." I remembered nearly every moment we'd spent together. "I felt like Amanda did today. It was like looking out to the edge of the world."

"I ran and ran and ran for the water. Felt like I was running for miles. Then I looked back, and you were—"

"Right there." We spoke in unison and laughed.

"Like one of those dreams," he continued, the reins loose in his hands. "Where you run and run and get nowhere."

"Ugh. I couldn't run anywhere, it was so hot."

"You were fine once you took your shoes off." He leaned over, bumping his shoulder against mine, and stayed there.

"Yes." I felt my face growing as warm as it had that day.

"And your stockings, remember?"

The children were well out of earshot, but still, there was no mistaking the slight lascivious tone of his voice. Plus, I knew how the story ended. "Stop it."

"And you lifted up your skirt to keep it from getting wet, then decided that was too much trouble."

I put my hands to my face, both to hide from him

my longing to return to that time, and to seal the memory within.

"Like we had the whole world to ourselves. Adam and Eve at creation." I know I did not imagine the wistfulness in his voice. He was transported too.

"That was a long time ago, Nathan."

"Not so long." He touched my knee, and I'd loved him long enough to know what feelings lived behind that touch. It was the first gesture of its kind since before his marriage to Amanda. "I miss you, Mil."

The back of my throat felt like I'd swallowed the salty water of the lake.

"Well," I said, "you remember what happened to Adam and Eve?"

"Oh yes." He squeezed. "They were exceedingly fruitful and multiplied."

"No." I pulled myself away from him and hopped down from the wagon, forcing as much of a teasing lilt into my voice as possible. "They sinned. And they were cast out of the garden."

Later, our family sat spread out atop two moth-eaten blankets on the hard-packed, wet sand. Part of our lunch included two loaves of bread that we spread with honeyed butter, and we tossed bits of the crusty ends to the half-dozen gulls that hopped nearby.

"We could have saved the bread Amanda made," Nathan said as a pair fought over the final piece.

"Then they might never fly again," Kimana said, and we all laughed.

"It's so vast out here," Amanda said. "You'd think our voices would echo. But it seems like all the sound is swallowed up."

"The mountains are too far away to echo," Nathan

explained. We all craned our heads, seeing the mountains rising up in the distance. Miles and miles away, they jutted from the ground, turning us into scraps in the middle of a great shallow dish.

"The old woman bids us to be quiet," Kimana said.

"What old woman?" Melissa sat up, ever ready for a story.

"Long ago, before the white men came to the valley, there was no salt in the lake. An old woman was traveling with her grandson—they were very poor—and they came upon the people of the pueblos to beg for food.

"The people of the pueblos were very busy preparing for a feast, and nobody would bother to feed her. So she told her grandson, 'Go out to the edge of the village and laugh and play.'

"He did, and soon the children of the pueblo, curious, followed the sound of his voice. When all the children had gathered, she took a magic stone out of her pouch—a solid white rock, white as snow—and blew across its surface."

Kimana held such an imaginary stone in the palm of her hand and blew, causing Lottie to jump in fright.

"Her magic turned all the children into jabbering jaybirds, including her grandson. But her heart was so hard, she showed no mercy.

"She continued her journey alone until she came to this valley, where the people—my people—took pity on her and gave her food. But her heart was too heavy to eat.

"'Just a taste,' they begged her, 'or you will die, and your spirit will be on our hands.'

"The old woman took her white stone, sharpened it to a blade, and shaved off a piece of her flesh to drop into the cooking pot."

This, too, Kimana demonstrated, and we all shuddered with Lottie.

"Her flesh was full of the salt of her tears, and it flavored the stew, making it very delicious to everyone. When my people asked her how they could ever hope to have such delicious stew in the future, she said, 'I will take myself to your water and die there in it. I will salt the water for your food, as payment for the kindness you have shown me.'

"When my people asked how they could ever pay her for such an eternal gift, she thought back to the rash decision she made when she turned the children into jaybirds and said, 'I ask only this: that when you bring the children to play at the edge of the waters, you bid them be quiet, that I might rest in peace.'"

We all sat in silence following her story, until, in a small voice, Lottie asked, "Is that true?"

Kimana shrugged. "It is a legend; that is all."

"Well, I don't think it's very nice," Amanda said, "filling the children's heads with a lot of pagan nonsense."

I felt compelled to leap to Kimana's defense, though her face remained placid. "There are stories far more dangerous than an old Indian legend."

"But such a tale flies in the face of God." Amanda's voice remained sweet, but her narrow eyes took on a glint I'd never seen before.

"And the tales of Joseph Smith fly in the face of Scripture, but you don't have any problem filling my children's heads with those."

Amanda looked from me to Nathan, and he did not disappoint her silent cry for support. "Yes, the stories of our heroes of the time when Jesus walked among them were not preserved in the usual way, but there is a difference, Camilla, between the inspired word given from Heavenly Father and a story passed down from fireside to fireside."

"I like Bible stories," Lottie piped up.

My heart seized. "Amanda does have a point," I said, more to divert conversation away from our secret studies than to support putting faith in Mormon lore. "We must be very careful what we choose to believe. Some stories are just for fun—"

"Those are called myths," Nathan said, indulging in the moment.

"They are for our children," Kimana said, sounding far more dignified than any of the rest of us adults. "When I was a little girl, I did not have the stories of Jesus. My people did not know of him. You are lucky to hear stories of truth from your mother. And truth from your father when he tells you about the mountains."

Neither Nathan nor Amanda realized the gravity of what Kimana just said, and if they did, then it was a miracle of God that their tongues remained still rather than leap to offer up what Kimana so graciously ignored. Melissa had been twisting her neck, bouncing from speaker to speaker throughout the argument, but now her eyes looked past us all, out to the far-off place where the water touched the sky. Oh, what I would have given to know her thoughts. To answer her questions. But God held me silent like he did the others as he worked upon her spirit.

Just then Lottie let out an enormous yawn. "I want to go home."

Sobered by our conversation, all agreed, and we packed up what few dishes we had and loaded the wagon. I climbed into the back, followed by Kimana; Nathan handed both sleepy girls to us. Melissa settled in the crook of my arm; Lottie curled up in Kimana's ample lap. The sun was beginning to set, bringing the chill of evening with it, so he beat as much of the sand out of the blankets as he could, and we snuggled underneath them.

The lake was still in sight when Lottie's eyes closed in sleep, but I felt Melissa shift her weight against me.

"Mama?" She spoke in a whisper, her finger beckoning me closer; then she lifted the blanket and I slipped my head beneath it. A two-inch hole let in an odd square of light, but other than that we were bathed in green darkness. Our little makeshift tent smelled of wet sand and my sweet daughter's breath. "Does Kimana believe in God?"

"Yes, dear. Very much so."

"Has she been baptized?"

"No. But she did ask God to live in her heart. And he does."

"Why doesn't she go to church?"

"The church here doesn't teach about God the way she believes."

"You mean, she doesn't believe the prophet?"

"That's right."

"Sometimes it seems like you don't believe him either."

It wasn't a question, so I offered no answer.

"Why do we have to keep our Bible time a secret from Papa? Does he think the Bible is a myth?"

"No, darling. He knows that the stories in the Bible are true."

"Are the stories in our *Book of Mormon* true?"

I pulled her to me and closed my eyes against the small square of light, praying for God to give me the right words—those that would allow me to preserve the love she had for her father. I considered one phrasing after another, but in the end there was only one answer. Slowly I opened my eyes and shook my head. "No, Melissa. They are not."

"But Papa thinks they are." She sounded afraid. "We all do. If Papa can believe in both, why can't you?"

"I did for a while. For a long time. And then I asked Jesus to come into my heart. And when he did, there just wasn't room for both."

She didn't say anything, but I could imagine the serious, contemplative expression on her little face.

"You are a very smart little girl. Keep listening for God's voice, and he will tell you what you should believe. Ask him every night before you go to sleep. Ask him to show you the truth, and he will."

"All right," she said, then cuddled closer.

I pulled the blanket down and breathed in the fresh, cool air. *Oh, Jesus, please make yourself plain.*

Nights grew cold, but it wasn't until the first week of December that we had our first snowfall. No matter that it heralded such a dangerous season, there is always something magical about that first dense, white blanket. Amanda transformed into a child right before our eyes. She tilted her head up and opened her mouth wide to catch falling flakes on her tongue. "Oh, isn't it marvelous!" I watched from the front door, happy to experience the fun vicariously while behind me, Kimana stirred a pot of soup to warm everybody up when they came inside.

"You do not want to play, Mrs. Fox?"

I pulled my shawl closer about me. "No." A strange, passive peace had invaded my spirit. "It's just as much fun to watch, and your fingers don't get numb."

"You know, I always have a vision before the first snow."

"Careful, Kimana." I walked over to the stove and sipped a dipper of soup, then added a pinch of salt. "Such talk of visions will get you in trouble with Sister Amanda."

"I talk about a dream I have at night, as the snow is falling for the first time. I think God knows how much I am going to miss seeing the flowers and hearing the birds, so he gives me a look into the future so I can be comforted that spring will return."

"Well, then. What did you see?"

"I cannot tell you now. But I will someday, and when I do, remember that I told you on this day I had a vision from God. Will you remember?"

I nodded. "When will you tell me?"

"When it is time."

A thick blanket of snow surrounded our little cabin as January's bitter cold tried to creep through every crack, but Lottie and Melissa remained undaunted. Amanda romped with them, red-nosed, steamy puffs of laughter floating around her face, flinging herself down to make snow angels and pelting Nathan and the girls with snowballs.

I turned from the window and tended the fire, knowing my girls would need a warm hearth to come home to, but I was soon distracted by a new sound coming from outside. Silence. Curious, I went to take a quick peek outside and was surprised to see Elder Justus in what looked like deep, serious conversation outside. Amanda was on her way inside, ushering the girls.

"Over by the fire," I said, setting in to unwrap Lottie's muffler as she pulled off her mittens. Clumps of snow clung to the wool, hissing when they fell to the hearth.

"There's to be a special-called meeting tonight," Amanda said, obviously pleased to have some inside information. "Brother Brigham was to be here, but for the snow."

"Well, well." I held Lottie's coat as she walked out of it,

then took Amanda's and looped it over my arm. "I suppose that means an early supper." I grabbed Melissa's coat and hung each one on its peg before poking my head out the door and calling an invitation to Elder Justus to join us.

"No thank you, Sister Camilla." He tipped his hat. "Many more neighbors to inform."

It was obvious from the way they looked at me that I was now free to go back inside.

It would be an hour before Nathan came in. Little chores around the house brought me to the window again and again to see that they talked for another ten minutes at least, after which Nathan took himself to the barn to settle the stock in early for the night. What possible bit of business would call for all of us to trudge through deep snow for a gathering?

If Nathan knew the nature of the meeting, he said nothing. In fact, he was unusually quiet throughout our meal, the kind of silence that didn't invite any questions. I directed my conversation instead toward Amanda.

"You can wear my coat, if you like, in case yours isn't dry."

Nathan's spoon clattered to the table. "What does that mean?"

The force behind his comment surprised all of us.

"I—I just thought that she would want to go with you."

"We're all going."

"Surely not the girls. Not out in the snow. All their things are wet."

He considered that for a moment. "Fine. The girls can stay home."

"And I—"

"Kimana can stay with the girls."

"But—"

"I'll get her." Without taking another bite, he was gone.

CHAPTER 23

Amanda and I followed in Nathan's footsteps, creating a fresh path between our home and the meetinghouse. Nathan had continued being vague—not giving any clue as to why we were meeting or how long the meeting would last or even what time it was supposed to begin. So rushed were we to get out the door, I worried we might be the first ones there, burdened with laying a fire in the stove in preparation for the others. I should have felt a twinge of relief when I saw light coming from the windows and smoke spiraling into the silver sky, but something in me wanted to plant my feet in Nathan's steps and stay there until the spring.

Once inside, gathered with the others, it seemed very

clear who knew the purpose of our gathering and who didn't. Faces varied from dour, to curious, to frightened, with few other representations. Amanda and Nathan and I took our normal bench, squeezing in to share it with an older gentleman and his wife. Few people spoke, and those who did kept their voices to a whisper.

My back was to the door, but I sensed Elder Justus's arrival with the wave of silence that swept across the room. I heard two sets of heavy footsteps making their way to the front of the room, and when I looked up, I saw another man, one I'd never seen before. Unimpressive—average height, average age, and average fringe of hair framing a bald dome. Elder Justus introduced him as Elvin Childress, a bishop from a prominent Salt Lake City ward. After opening our meeting with a brief prayer, he turned us over to the bishop.

"Brothers and sisters of Cottonwood." The words sounded like they were scraped from the depths of an iron kettle. "I see by your hale and hearty faces that you fared well despite our season of drought. I only pray that you spent a fair amount of time weeping for your brothers and sisters who live in hunger, while you feast upon the blessings Heavenly Father has bestowed upon you. Amen?"

"Amen," they chorused. I longed to be home.

"You lead your comfortable lives here, self-appointed guardians of the temple quarry, for which the church thanks you, but which also grants you shelter from the hardships of our people. You did not see your harvest disappear beneath the relentless beating of the locusts' wings. You do not lie in bed at night, fearful of the gunfire from the soldiers sent by the ungodly president to which we are bound by law. You do not see the pain in our prophet's eyes as he hands over his governorship—the very office afforded to him by the powers of heaven—to a Gentile appointed from Washington. I ask you again. Do you weep?"

"Yes." In sincere chorus.

"Do you weep?"

"Yes!" With greater conviction.

"Our brothers and sisters have armed themselves against the advancing army. Men study the Word of Wisdom, then go to sleep with a rifle in their hands. Women kiss their children good night, then take on the task of melting down the very silver they brought from the homes they were chased away from to make bullets to defend their home in Zion. Are you prepared to follow?"

"We are!" Beside me, Nathan's voice seemed to rise above all others.

Bishop Childress tapped his very ordinary-looking fingertips together and allowed the room to become silent once again. "Dare I ask you, are you worthy?"

To this, nobody seemed eager to reply.

"This war we fight will not be won with bullets. There is no militia strong enough to defeat the forces of the United States Army." He stepped out from behind the pulpit and strode up and down the center aisle. All around me people twisted and craned their necks to keep him in their sight. In front of me, Brother Thomas wore a buffalo-skin coat, and I kept my eyes focused on one solid square of fur.

"We are farmers, craftsmen, and shopkeepers," Bishop Childress continued. "If we win, it will be through the mighty power of God, who will set up his kingdom here in Zion as we build our temple to his eternal worship. We will win through our solidarity, our commitment to the one true church, the only people who live the truth of the final words of Jesus Christ. The Lord protects his own. Your strength is in your baptism. I ask you—" he was back at the front—"is there any among you who has not been baptized?"

Shuffling then, and muttering. Oh, how glad I was that the girls were home with Kimana, safe in their warm bed.

"Any at all? For it takes only one weak link in the chain of God's glory to give Satan victory over all. Will you let your ungodliness bring about the ruin of Zion? I ask again, is there one among you who is not baptized?"

Slowly—and so slowly at first I thought she must simply have been preparing herself to look about the room for an unbaptized neighbor—Amanda stood beside me. Nathan looked to be just as surprised as I, but I'm sure he did not harbor the fear I did, that my sister wife was about to expose me as a rogue apostate in the midst of this fledgling ward.

"My . . . my father," she said, her voice so small even I, right next to her, barely heard. "My father has not been baptized. Not for this—nor any other—church."

A gasp went up through the crowd; Bishop Childress silenced it with one raised finger.

"And your father is a part of this community?"

"Yes."

Nathan took Amanda's hand, bidding her to sit down, but she would have none of it.

"You are her husband? Stand." Nathan complied. "And were you aware of the spiritual state of your wife's father?"

"I was not," Nathan said. Not even I knew if he was speaking the truth.

"And where is he tonight?" Bishop Childress directed his question to Elder Justus. "Were not all members of the community told to come to this assembly?"

"He doesn't come to meetings," Amanda offered, her voice choked with tears. "When I went to the meetings back home, and converted, and told him I wanted to come here—to Zion. And I showed him all the . . . the pamphlets and writings and whatnot, he said he'd bring me. Sold our businesses, we did, because he said this was a . . . a *gold mine* he called it. And, no—no other reason . . ."

She broke down, sobbing into her hands. Nathan, to his credit, looked visibly shocked at her confession, though no amount of prodding on his part could interrupt her.

I stood now and put my arm around her shoulder, more to support my own shaking self than to lend her support. "You'll have to forgive her. She's still such a new convert, and it can be difficult when your loved ones don't share your zeal." I leaned over and hissed in her ear, "Hush, now, and sit down."

By now Elder Justus stood beside Bishop Childress, and everybody else in the room seemed to disappear. "I recall, Sister Camilla, a time when you yourself lacked a true dedication to your faith. I believe it was three or four months that you did not go to meeting?"

"She was in mourning," Nathan said before helping Amanda to sit, leaving me standing alone.

"Ah, yes," Elder Justus said, tapping his chin. "For the child that died in your arms." His voice held such a tone of accusation, I could feel the change in the way each person in the room perceived me. "But I recall a span of time this summer, when your husband was away, that you were less than faithful to the assembling of your brothers and sisters. Were you in mourning then, too?"

"Of a sort," I said. "It was difficult without my husband."

"And I recall, the night I came to question your sister wife, a distinct uncooperative spirit about you."

"It is difficult, sir, to see your husband take another wife. But I've not missed a single meeting since then."

"If I may . . ." Bishop Childress dismissed Elder Justus, escorting him to his seat before taking the pulpit once again. I moved to sit down, but he bade me remain standing. I looked at Nathan, silently pleading with him to stand with me, and to my relief, he did. "You there are an example of the reinvigoration of the Holy Spirit within you. You, Sister, having found yourself in complete compliance with the teaching of our prophet were once again drawn to worship with his people. You and your husband and your sister wife represent all that we are striving to keep sacred and safe from a Gentile government who would rob us of both our religious freedoms and our ability to live in obedience to the commands of Heavenly Father. Tell me, Sister, how long is it since you've been baptized?"

I swallowed, thinking. "Seven years."

"And you, Brother?"

"Twelve years." No hesitation. "In Nauvoo."

"Ah, yes." Bishop Childress lifted his eyes in reverence to the name of their holy city. "Perhaps, as a show of your rededication, you will be rebaptized? I'll have you know that, in the great city of Salt Lake, scores of brothers and sisters are coming to the waters again, as testament to their faith. Tell me, will you? Even she—" he waggled his fingers at Amanda, bidding her to stand with us; Nathan grabbed her elbow and pulled her to her feet—"newly converted as she is, could be rebaptized, symbolizing your place as an eternal family. What say you?"

His final question was not directed at us, but to all assembled, who thought it a fine idea, as expressed in their enthusiastic cheers. When they died down, Bishop Childress looked once again to us and, with a piercing gaze that gave him an appearance far less harmless than was his ordinary countenance, said, "State here, before your fellow Saints. Will you be rebaptized?"

"We will," Nathan said, clearly intending to speak for all of us. Amanda nodded enthusiastically at his shoulder.

My head filled with prayer. *Lord, I would never . . .* But I said not a word. There would be time enough to protest. Time enough to escape such a display. We might have quietly taken our seats if Elder Justus hadn't risen from his, like a specter rising from its tomb, and pointed a finger so long and bony, I imagined the feel of his hard, white nail on the tip of my nose.

"Sister Camilla, I sense again an uncooperative spirit."

Strength like I'd never experienced before infused me. Even as I felt my mouth open, I had no idea what words would follow, only that they would be true and right. "My spirit is with the Lord," I answered. "Perhaps he is uncooperative."

Again, a collective gasp. Bishop Childress looked like I'd hit him in the face with a snowball. Amanda trembled beside me, and I dared not look at Nathan.

"Do you speak such blasphemy against our Lord?"

"I do not seek to blaspheme my Lord."

"I ask you plain and simple. Will you consent, with your family, to be rebaptized?"

"I will not."

As vociferous as they were to Nathan's reply, the congregation was doubly so to mine, though with an opposite fervor. Amanda collapsed to the bench again with rejuvenated tears, and the couple who had been sharing the seat with us stood and walked to the back of the room. Voices amplified to the volume of a mob twice the size of that gathered here. Both Bishop Childress and Elder Justus pounded their fists on the pulpit, shouting for order. Only Nathan and I remained silent in the midst of it, our eyes fixed on each other.

Once the commands for "*Quiet!*" gained compliance,

Elder Justus came to us, standing in the aisle, seeking privacy to his commission. "Mr. Fox, it seems you do not have all of your house in order." Nathan said nothing, but I noticed his clenched fist and clenched jaw and considered Elder Justus very lucky that my husband chose not to unleash either one. "Go home now, and make it so. I will visit you in the morning."

Without another word we left, finding our trail intact, despite the light falling of snow. The walk home was equally silent as the walk to the meeting, without even the slightest attempt at conversation. We arrived home to find the room full of soft lamplight. Kimana sat at the table, her hands folded and her head bowed. I knew then what had given me the strength to speak. The minute we were all inside, she rose and wished us good night, wrapping her shawl around her as she stepped out.

"Go to your room, Amanda," Nathan said with the authority of one directing a child. She, like a child, pouted, then took the lamp from the table and went into the room she shared with my husband and shut the door.

"Good night," I said to Nathan and attempted to walk to my room, but he caught my elbow. Rather than struggle, I stopped.

"This is my fault." He drew me back, and the warmth of his body seeped through the heaviness of my coat. "I haven't been the husband I should have been. I've neglected you, Mil."

His words were so perfect, I felt I was imagining them there on the spot. But his breath on my neck was real and warm; I softened my weight against him and lifted my hand to touch his face.

"I forget sometimes—" his lips brushed my ear as he spoke—"how fragile you are."

I turned in his embrace. Even this close to him, I could barely make out his features in the darkness of the room. But I didn't need to, so perfectly were they etched in my memory. I didn't need to see him; feeling him was enough. I ran my fingers along his features, and to my thrill, he returned the touch, softly outlining the planes of my face. I knew I was not as beautiful as Amanda, but here in the darkness, I knew his hands touched the girl I once was. He drew me close and kissed me.

Oh, the Lord knows how I prayed to take away the feelings that stirred within me. Ever since I first set eyes on Amanda, I'd been laying stones to build up the wall that would shield my heart from the intense physical desire I'd felt for Nathan Fox from the moment I saw him. I'd barely begun to find peace alone in my bed, without mourning the emptiness beside me. That night, though, his kiss knocked one stone away. Then another and another, until all scattered between us, and I prepared to give myself to him without boundary.

How fitting it seemed to walk past our sleeping children on our way to share my bed. We paused long enough to stand, arm in arm, and gaze at them in the soft light coming from my room. Kimana had thought to leave a small fire burning in my fireplace, though it was down to little more than embers. Nathan tossed in one log, then another, as I took off my coat. We both jumped at the sparks that shot out.

"Come here." He held his hand out for me and I took it. "Will you ever forgive me?"

I smiled. "I did a long time ago."

He looked puzzled for a moment, but it passed. "Tonight—all that ugliness—would not have happened if I'd been the husband I was supposed to be."

Hope flickered within me like the vigilant little flames nearby. "You've only done what you think God has directed you to do."

"But, somehow, along the way, I forgot my first priority."

"Oh, Nathan." I brought his hand to my lips. If God can grant grace to the adulterer, why couldn't I? Especially as he stood before me, begging for forgiveness.

"I failed you. Failed to remember just how fragile—"

"You keep saying that, darling. But I'm strong. Stronger than you know."

"Your soul—it's as much my responsibility as it is yours. I'm your husband, your spiritual leader. And for me to be so blind to your lack of faith. But together, I know we can restore—"

"No." I dropped his hand and stepped away. "You can't. Not only will I not be rebaptized, but tonight was my last meeting. I want no part of it anymore, Nathan. I was deceived—you were; they all were. The only gospel I believe is that of Jesus Christ. My salvation, my eternity, is because of his sacrifice, not anything that you or anyone else can bestow on me."

He stepped closer as I spoke, not quite menacing, but almost. "I won't have an apostate for a wife, Camilla."

"Then I will not be your wife."

"You are sealed to me."

Every time I felt myself falling victim to tears of weakness, a new strength surged. "Not anymore. Not since the day you married Amanda. It is not God's will that I remain bound to an unrepentant adulterer."

"She is my wife, every bit as much as you are."

"In your eyes—and in the eyes of your false prophet. But not in God's. And not in mine."

"You," he said, now gripping my arm, "do not have the authority to decide whether or not you are my wife."

"Maybe not." His grip should have made me feel pain, but instead I found little more than pity. "But I can decide whether or not you are my husband. And you are not." I managed a weak smile, still wanting to please him. "We'll go to Brother

Brigham and plead our case. Charge me with adultery if you want. Say I have chosen Jesus Christ over you. He'll grant us a divorce."

"Never!" He released me then, and I staggered. "Don't you see what a failure I'll be in the eyes of God?"

"Are you worried about what God will think? or your fellow *Saints*?" I could not contain my sarcasm. "Marry somebody else, Nathan. They'll forget about me. You nearly did, and I've been living under the same roof."

"And just how, my wife, would we forget about you?"

I took a deep breath, preparing to voice for the first time what had been lingering in the back of my mind for so long. "We'll leave."

"We?"

"The girls and I. We'll go back to Iowa. Back home."

"To your loving father?" His words dripped bitterness. "To the man who stood on the bank of a river and let you go? To the man who would have killed me if he'd had a decent shot?"

"When he sees his grandchildren—"

"He doesn't know he *has* grandchildren because he won't even open your letters. What makes you think he'd take you back? And for that, what plan do you have to get there?"

"You promised you'd—"

"Oh no." He paced the room, went to the window, and pulled the curtain aside to look at the snow that was now a solid blanket of white on the other side. "Why should I keep my promises if you won't keep yours?"

I stood beside him, laying my palm on the cool glass next to his. "Because you haven't changed. I have."

"I can change you back."

"You can't, Nathan. I'll never be the woman you need me to be."

Now tears slid unbidden down my face. I knew I wept for him, for he would never understand his own powerlessness. Suddenly he took me in his arms and kissed me with what can only be described as violence, his mouth bruising against mine, his grip agonizing, yet I did not fight. How could I, when we both waged such different battles? Knowing I had but one weapon to strike the final blow, I surrendered, and his advances took on a hunger as if he'd been denied a woman just as I'd been denied a husband. His hands roamed my body with all the purpose of the man he'd been when he touched it for the first time, his breath haggard.

"Still so beautiful." His words stopped against my throat. His hands tore clumsily at the row of buttons down the front of my dress. Gently, I took over the task, unfastening them one after another. With each button he stepped back, until he could take in the whole image of me.

Perhaps I should have felt shame, not being prone to immodesty, but I sensed nothing but power as I pulled my arms out of my sleeves, baring them to him for the first time since before our son was born. I stepped away from the fire and let my dress fall to the floor, and when I did so, Nathan reached for me again, but I granted him only the smallest kiss and gently nudged him toward our bed. He backed away, never taking his eyes off me, and sat on its edge.

I sat on the chair next to the fire and unlaced one boot, then another, setting them carefully by the fire to dry. I rolled down my stockings, leaving them as wet balls of wool on the floor, and when I stood again, my petticoats were piled on top of them. There was a touch of self-conscious laughter when I stood before him in my wool union suit, but it disappeared as I nimbly unfastened its hooks and dropped it to the floor. Nothing remained but my chemise, which I lifted over my head, and my corset, which I untied, breathing deeply at its release.

I wore nothing now save the garments given to me when I'd gone through my Endowment ceremony. Sacred garments, as they were claimed to be, infused with God's protection. Woe to me, I'd been told, should I die without their protection. They would follow me in death. Identify me as one set apart. Nathan had never seen my body without them since that first visit to the lake. I'd been a new convert, a new wife, ignorant and bold. How was it that the same boldness came to me this night in my room, once again facing my husband? Naked in his eyes, but clothed in chains in mine.

"Come here." He held out his arms.

"Not yet."

The garment had two parts—a shirt and short pants. In a swift gesture, I untied the drawstring to the pants and stepped out of them as I lifted the shirt over my head. This would be the last time I would wear their pagan symbols upon my breast, and I felt more freedom here than even the moment I unlaced my corset.

"Camilla, don't—"

He must have somehow preconceived my intentions, for Nathan leaped from the bed. But too late. Holding the shirt, I scooped the pants from the floor and, in an instant, tossed them on the flames.

I think he would have pulled the garments from the fire, laid them burning against my flesh had he been given the chance. But even as he reached in, a flame rose up, and a single burst of power consumed them. As Nathan knelt, staring in disbelief at such sacred destruction, I stood behind him, slowly pulling the pins from my hair, then running my fingers through its braids, until it fell loose about my shoulders.

"Look at me."

"I can't."

"Then know this. I have no shame. You cannot judge or condemn me, nor can any of your faith. I am a child of God."

He grabbed the quilt off my bed and, keeping his eyes averted, said, "Cover yourself."

I clutched the blanket to me. "I am covered by his grace. Do you understand? My soul washed clean by his blood."

"How can you speak of our Lord when you are standing there, like a—a whore?"

"That," I said, pointing to the fire, "is what made me a whore. And you—the minute you took another woman—you turned every minute we ever had together into something illegitimate. Now, look at me." He did, slowly taking in every exposed inch. "This is what I am, Nathan. What you've brought me to. You and your prophet."

Everything broke. I could see it in his face—his hope, his love, his desire gone. I needed him to know that he could not save me, that I would never return to his fold.

His shoulders dropped, hands listless at his sides, and he turned to leave, then stopped. I heard it too. Relentless pounding on our front door.

I looked at the clock on my mantel. Half past ten. "What in the world . . . ?"

Nathan was gone in an instant and back just as I finished buttoning my dress.

"Get out here," he said, no softness to his voice. "They've come to talk to you."

CHAPTER 24

"We did not feel it was right to let the sun set on this matter," Elder Justus said, warming his hands at the newly built fire.

"The sun set on our walk home," I said, fearless. I'd spent the last hour destroying the life I'd built with the man I love. What harm could these men do?

Bishop Childress pulled a small black notebook from a pocket within his suit jacket. "Mr. Fox, I suggest you explain to your wife the gravity of the situation."

Nathan placed himself between them and me and leaned close. "This is my home, and these men are guests in it. Show them respect." He pulled out a chair and I sat down in it, pulling my shawl more tightly around me.

Amanda had poked her head out the bedroom door just moments before only to be dismissed brusquely by Nathan.

"Gentlemen," Nathan said, assuming the air of a negotiator, "I hope you will overlook my wife's behavior. It's late, and it's been a stressful evening for all of us. You're sure this can't wait until morning?"

The two older men looked at each other, then at Nathan. "It was a grievous display at the meeting earlier," Elder Justus said. "Our strength is in our unity. Sister Camilla, will you consent to an interview?"

"That depends on its purpose."

"Let *us* be mindful of the purpose," Bishop Childress said. "Now, will you answer our questions?"

"She will," Nathan said, and he sat in the chair beside me.

Elder Justus stayed near the fireplace, staring into the flames, but Bishop Childress sat across from us at the table, thumbing through the pages of his notebook. "Mrs. Fox, do you believe in God, the Eternal Father, in his Son, Jesus Christ, and in the Holy Ghost; and do you have a firm testimony of the restored gospel?"

"I am already in possession of a temple recommend, Bishop Childress."

Elder Justus spun on his heel. "Answer his question!"

"Mind how you speak to my wife," Nathan cautioned.

Elder Justus relaxed his posture, and Nathan inclined his head toward me.

I locked eyes with Bishop Childress. "I do believe in God and his Son, Jesus Christ, and the Holy Ghost. I believe they are a holy Trinity. I believe the Gospels of Matthew, Mark, Luke, and John to be true and complete and in no need of restoration."

Elder Justus paced in short, tight steps, and Nathan ran his hand over his face, but Bishop Childress merely jotted a few notes into his notebook, unfazed.

"Do you sustain the president of the Church of Jesus Christ of Latter-day Saints as the prophet, seer, and revelator; and do you recognize him as the only person on the earth authorized to exercise all priesthood keys?"

"He is no prophet."

Elder Justus slammed a fist against the wall. "Bishop! Will you allow this?"

The bishop ignored him. "Do you sustain the other general authorities and the local authorities of the church?"

"I do not."

"Do you live the law of chastity?"

My gaze never wavered. "I do."

"Is there anything in your conduct relating to members of your family that is not in harmony with the teachings of the church?"

Everything. But I swallowed, looked to Nathan, who sat, elbows on the table, head buried in his hands.

"Yes," I said.

For the first time since we began our interview, Bishop Childress looked up. "Would you care to explain?"

"I—I would seek a divorce from my husband."

Again, the calm notation. "Because your husband took a second wife?"

"Yes."

"The woman consented." Elder Justus planted his hands on the table between us. "I sat in this very room, at this very table, and heard her give her consent."

Bishop Childress raised an eyebrow. "Is this true?"

"Yes."

"Yet you still seek a divorce?"

"For my husband's sake as much as my own. I know I could never be the wife he needs me to be."

"You realize, Mrs. Fox, that what you have stated here tonight brands you as an apostate, in complete rebellion with the teachings of our faith?"

"Yes, Bishop Childress. I do."

Nathan drew a sharp breath, and I instinctively put my hand to his shoulder, offering what comfort I could. How ashamed he must feel, shame for both himself as a failed husband and me as a failed Saint.

"And you do realize, *Sister* Camilla, that you will forever bear the mark of your sin? that your skin will turn as dark as that Indian woman you keep?"

It took all the strength I had not to respond to his question with laughter, but a change had taken place in our last few exchanges, and suddenly the mood seemed very dark.

"You realize of course, Mrs. Fox, that were you to be granted a divorce, you would be asked to leave the community."

"With nothing but the clothes on her back!" Elder Justus contributed. "Tell me, Brother Nathan, what more did she bring into the marriage?"

"Nothing," Nathan said, lifting his head at last.

"And," the almost-soothing calm of Bishop Childress prevailed, "are you prepared to leave your children behind?"

"Of course not."

"You will not take our daughters."

"You have another wife. You can have other children."

"Have the children reached the age of accountability?" Bishop Childress was once again in his notebook.

"The oldest is only six," Nathan said with a proud smile, "but if she had her way, she'd be baptized tomorrow."

"No." I spoke softly, garnering no response.

"Tell me, Mrs. Fox, if our president were to grant you your divorce, how do you plan to support yourself?"

"I—"

"Don't tell me you expect to find support from your brothers and sisters—excuse me, your *former* brothers and sisters. Do you think they will feel inclined to offer you shelter or employment?"

I thought back to my conversation with Rachel. My sister in the truest sense. "No."

"And do you think it's best to take your daughters out of their warm, comfortable home, to face an uncertain and dangerous future simply because you have chosen to abandon your faith?"

I swallowed my retort and sat silently next to the man to whom I had pledged my life. Both of us had been crushed under the scrutiny of my interrogator.

"No," Nathan answered for me. "She will not." He turned to me, twisting his body and leaning in to block my view of Bishop Childress. "I am your husband. I am your authority—in this house and in the eyes of God. You will not bring this into my home, and you will not interfere with the instruction of my children."

"Our children."

"My children. They will be sealed to me in the temple—"

"No."

He stood, looming over me. Whatever power Bishop Childress represented disappeared in that moment. In fact, everything disappeared as I felt myself being lifted from my seat, held up by Nathan's powerful grip. His face—twisted into something new, something I created—filled my vision.

"Will you be rebaptized?"

"No."

"Then you must leave. I won't have it, Camilla." His voice broke, and I knew he'd taken the final step from anger into pain, because he took me with him.

"But where will I go?"

"That, Sister Camilla, is something you should have thought about before you gave yourself over to this evil spirit of doubt."

Nathan had the grace to ignore Elder Justus's outburst, and I felt his grip soften to something close to an embrace.

"Go to Rachel."

I shook my head. "She won't have me." I didn't explain more.

"Go to Evangeline." And as he said it, the picture formed in my mind. The two of us, nattering around her cold, gray home. Sitting in her kitchen with cups of tepid water, her reading her *Book of Mormon*, me my Bible, until we grew old and withered from the lost love of Nathan Fox.

"And the girls?"

"I'm afraid you forfeit the right to your children if you abandon your husband," Bishop Childress said from somewhere behind Nathan's elbow. "And I speak there from a legal standpoint, not just a spiritual one."

"What will we tell them?"

"*I* will tell them the truth," Nathan said. "It's only a matter of time before they would hear it from somebody else."

"And what a powerful lesson to teach them: the lonely road of those who choose to live outside of God's kingdom."

"Justus, please," Nathan said, finally losing his composure. "This is a private matter."

"It is not a private matter when it affects the spiritual health of the church," Bishop Childress said. "And this is a matter of grave importance to this community. The seed of apostasy must not take root. As our Lord said, 'Beware the leaven of Herod.'"

"I will escort you myself," Elder Justus said, sounding less than inviting. "I'll be here to collect you tomorrow."

"Tomorrow?" Nathan sounded on the verge of protest.

"That doesn't give me any time to collect my things or explain to the girls." My words failed as Nathan held me against him.

"You have no *things* to collect," Elder Justus said. "Mark me, young man. She is to leave with nothing that she did not bring to you."

I spoke against Nathan's shirt. "May I take my coat? After all, we were married in the summer and I didn't have one then."

"Hold your tongue, Sister Camilla. You have asked to be released from your marriage, and against the ordinances of the faith and the will of God, your request will be entertained. You will not be given leave to determine the particulars."

"Take her to my sister's." Nathan spoke over my head, then stepped back from me. "Tell her everything; she'll take care of you."

I didn't argue further.

Bishop Childress snapped his little notebook closed and dropped it back into his pocket. Our late-night visitors put on their coats and hats as Nathan pulled on gloves and lifted a stick of kindling from the fire to light their lantern.

"Until tomorrow." Elder Justus had the nerve to tip his hat. And then they were gone.

It was like the aftermath of some great battle. We stood as two survivors, unsure whether we were blessed with life or cursed at having to look upon so much death.

"I'm so sorry," I said, not sure if I was apologizing for the past few moments or the years he'd wasted on me.

"Take all that you need. I don't have much money in the house."

"I don't need—"

"You will."

"Nathan, you realize this isn't just another visit to your sister's."

"You'll be back."

"Not as your wife." I paused. "Not as a first wife. You have to believe that."

"Then you won't see the girls, Camilla. You have to believe *that*."

Oddly enough, he smiled, and he'd gone back to the place where I couldn't reach him. This was the Nathan who wouldn't leave me on the riverbank. This was the Nathan who came close to tears with the rejection of his handiwork. This was the Nathan determined to leave his wife and daughters to escort a wagon train.

"Oh, darling," I said, my heart infinitely softer than his, "I wish you could see. You don't have to work so hard. Love God, love me. Accept that Jesus Christ is exactly who the Bible says he is. And then just trust him."

His laugh was sharp. "Is that what you plan to do, Camilla?"

"What choice do I have?"

"None. You trust him your way, and I'll obey him mine. And we'll see whom he favors."

"It's not a competition, Nathan."

"Of course it is. And I have the nation of Zion on my side. You came with nothing; you'll leave with nothing, in this life and the next."

But he was wrong. I had my salvation. I had peace, somehow. And in that moment, that was enough because I also had faith that God would show me mercy. I gave him my heart; he would give me my life.

CHAPTER 25

The rest of the night was little more than a dreading of the dawn. I spent most of it on my knees before the fire, pouring myself out in prayer.

"Lord, forgive my rash decisions. Keep me strong for Melissa and Lottie. I know you can restore our family to reflect your design. Father, I will follow in the steps you plan for me."

In the depths of my being I wanted to go home. Without voicing it as prayer, my mind lingered on a vision of walking through the gateway of my father's stone fence with Melissa and Lottie in tow. Nathan stood on the other side, watching, until my father ran from his barn, my mother close behind, and the five of us fell into each other's arms, weeping.

But that could only happen with the grace of God. With a grateful heart, I claimed that grace, and I pleaded with the Lord to share that grace with my girls.

As the fire died down, I sought the warmth of my bed, but I willed myself to stay awake. I thought of the story of the disciples with Jesus in the garden of Gethsemane. I longed to be worthy of my Savior's praise, able to stay awake and struggle with the Holy Spirit, hoping to find some way to follow his prompting that would allow me to stay with my children.

Bring me back to them, Father. Or better yet, bring them to me.

I eventually slept in the final hours of darkness and awoke to a whimsical answer with the warmth of my girls crawling into my bed, thrusting icy feet against me.

"Papa and Aunt Amanda are already gone," Lottie said once I'd kissed her good morning.

"Really?"

"They went to visit Uncle Kenneth," Melissa said. "Papa seemed upset and Auntie Amanda sounded worried."

As well they should be. If I were held in such contempt for refusing to be rebaptized, what hope did the unbaptized have in the church's new fervor?

"We had a bowl of hot porridge to warm us up on the inside," Lottie said. "Then Auntie Kimana told us we could get in bed with you to warm us up on the outside."

"Well I'm very glad she did."

"She let us have snow and molasses while you were at the meeting last night," Melissa said.

"My goodness, how spoiled you are."

Melissa pulled the quilt up to her chin. "I heard people talking last night. They sounded angry."

I relived every word of the conversation before asking if she remembered what they were talking about.

"No, not all of it. Only Elder Justus yelling something about your clothes."

"Nothing but the clothes on her back!"

I could not, in that wonderful moment, tell them all that had befallen our family the night before, but I knew my oldest daughter would not rest until she had some explanation.

"Your father and some others—they aren't very happy with me right now."

"Because you don't believe the prophet?"

"Yes." Such truth in simple answers. "And I'm leaving today, to go visit with Aunt Rachel for a little while."

"Until they aren't angry anymore?"

Oh, Father, wrap yourself around her heart. "Something like that, yes."

Lottie tugged at my sleeve. "Can we come too? I love Aunt Rachel's."

"It's too cold for you to travel such a distance," I said, thankful for the handy truth. "But promise you'll pray for me every night while I'm gone?"

They nodded, creating crackling static with their hair.

Sometimes I think if I could have any moments to relive, I would choose that morning. The girls smelling of sleep, the pocket of warmth on a frigid winter morning, and the innocent belief that we would have these days forever.

"Tell me," I said, "what else did you and Kimana do last night? Did she say prayers with you?"

"Yes," Melissa said. "And she told us a story about a mama fox and a bear."

"You're a mama fox, Mama!" Lottie brought her little hand out from under the warm blanket and touched my nose. "Only you're not red and you don't have a tail."

"That's right," I said, playing like I was about to snap her finger between my teeth. "But you never know . . . I can be tricky."

Melissa did not appreciate our silliness. "It was a story about a mama fox who leaves to find food for her kits because it's cold and snowy and they have none. And when she didn't come back, they cried and cried until a mama bear heard them."

I conjured Kimana's soothing, flat voice, hearing every word through the sweet retelling from my daughter. My own was scratchy and dry, more so now as the Indian woman's myth took on new meaning. "What did the mama bear do?"

"She went to their den—"

"But she couldn't fit all the way because her bottom was too big!" Lottie exploded into giggles, quite pleased with being able to deliver her favorite line of the story. Melissa had no patience for such foolishness.

"Well, of course she couldn't. She was a bear."

"So—" I strained for a casual lilt—"what finally happened?"

Lottie took a deep breath, but it was Melissa who charged in. "The mama bear just stuck her head inside because that's all that would fit. She used her breath to keep them warm and her body to block out the cold. So when the mama fox came back, they were safe."

My eyes filled with tears, but I whisked them away before the girls could see them. "Well, wasn't that a lovely story for a snowy night?"

"You're going away, just like the mama fox in the story," Lottie said.

"And Kimana's the mama bear who's going to take care of us," Melissa added sagely.

"Because she has a big bottom too," Lottie giggled, and despite the cloak of trepidation hovering over that day, I joined in. That Kimana could have known what story to tell that night made God's plan and path so clear. She would care for my children, not only keeping them warm and safe but covering them in prayer breathed by the Holy Spirit.

I gathered them close to me and kissed each cheek before playfully pushing them out of my bed. "Now, go see if Kimana has a big fire in the front room. You can take your clothes and get dressed in there."

"Yes, Mama," they chorused as they climbed out.

How I wished for such a fire, as my cold-stiffened fingers worked the same buttons that gave so little resistance the night before. Was it only the night before? How was it that one night could drain away everything that had sustained me for so long? I worked my hairbrush through the matted mess of tangles, just enough that I could create three sections to plait into a loose braid, which I left hanging straight. If nothing else, I could keep the back of my neck warm.

In the front room, my half-naked girls glowed pink in the light of the fire. Kimana was at her familiar place by the stove, and I walked right to her, wrapping my arms around her ample waist, and laid my head on her shoulder.

"Good morning, *mama bear*," I whispered.

"They told you the story."

"How did you know? Even I didn't . . ." But that wasn't true. On some level I think I'd known since the day Nathan came home.

"I told you. The night before the first snow. God sends me a vision."

"But I'm not leaving in the spring. I'm leaving today."

"I think my vision is not about you going away. God gives me a vision for the spring. My vision is the fox returning to her nest. In the spring, you come home."

I glanced at the girls, relieved to see their backs to me as Melissa buttoned Lottie's dress, because I was on the very verge of collapse, my chin quivering, my words something between a choke and a whisper. "I don't want to go. I don't want Elder Justus to drive me away like some *criminal*."

"This is the path God has left for you. Follow his steps." She reached for her ladle, filled a bowl with porridge, and handed it to me. I held it, more grateful for the warmth in my hands than the promise of food. Kimana kept her bright brown eyes focused on me.

"You are going to the great city?"

"For now, yes." To throw myself on Rachel's mercy.

"You do not need a swift horse to go to the great city. You need only your two legs."

"I can't walk to Salt Lake City in the snow."

Kimana shrugged. "So take a horse. One that Mr. Nathan will want to bring back home."

I felt it as she spoke. Freedom. I did not need to be carried back in the arms of the one who betrayed me; I did not need to be driven by my oppressor. I'd been set free from all that bound me to this place. I could take myself away. And I could bring myself back to gather my children, leading an army if I had to.

But then . . . "What if he won't let me go?" I don't know if I meant Nathan or Elder Justus.

Kimana shrugged. "Leave before you can ask."

I chose carefully—every stocking and petticoat I owned, two dresses. No room for my shawl, but Rachel had a plethora, and I wouldn't be above asking one of the other wives if it meant being warm. I moved swiftly, telling myself I was not running away. I was not abandoning my daughters.

"It's an expedition."

Still, Elder Justus's voice echoed in my head. *"Nothing but the clothes on her back."* I held Amanda's Bible and remembered what Nathan said I had brought into the marriage.

"Nothing."

Not nothing. I'd brought my heart and my faith and my trust that he worshiped the true God. That and my journal. I leafed through the pages, one verse standing out:

> *When I was a child, I spake as a child, I understood as a child, I thought as a child: but when I became a man, I put away childish things.*

In truth, though, it was the belief of my childhood that drew me back, although this day, I felt I'd almost become a man, for only a man could so easily get on a horse and ride away. And I knew God would direct my path.

I'd brought the notebook with me, but I would not take it now. I would leave it for my daughters—a part of me until I could read the Word of God with them again. Nor would I take Amanda's Bible. I did, however, venture into the room she shared with Nathan and, after a little bit of foraging, managed to find the small, blue, latched book that had been a gift to me on the day of my wedding.

"Forgive me if I take this one thing." I spoke to the empty bed.

When I emerged, bag in hand, Melissa and Lottie were seated at the table with a pile of rabbit skins.

"Auntie Kimana says we can make winter coats for Lilly and Rose," Melissa said.

"She's going to help with the stitching," Lottie said, swaddling Lilly in a pelt.

"And hats, too. If there's time."

"It will be a good way to pass the time today," Kimana said. "Time goes fast when hands move most."

"How wonderful!" I nearly shouted in my attempt at cheer. "I can't wait to see them."

"If Papa lets us come to Aunt Rachel's, we'll bring them. She'll think they're so pretty."

"She will. And that will keep them warm for the ride."

I felt guilty, almost, for tearing them away from their project to say good-bye. Each girl dutifully got up to give me a hug, and it took every ounce of control I had not to sweep them up with me to carry out the door.

I can still feel the way my arms doubled up as I wrapped them around their little bodies. They smelled of brown sugar and snow, and there's a particular place on my cheek where the coldness of Lottie's nose pierced when she kissed me.

"How long until we see you, Mama?"

"Only the Lord knows that, my Missy. If you'll pray with your auntie Kimana every night, he'll tell you."

"Can I pray with Papa, too?"

"Of course you can. He needs you to."

I glanced outside to see Honey already saddled. Her breath puffed from her nose in great bits of steam, and it relieved me to see that the snow barely reached her forelocks. We might come across some deeper drifts, but I was small, and she was a strong, prancing thing. We were matched in spirit.

Kimana held my coat out, and I backed into it. Like a child, I stood very still as she fastened the buttons, wrapped a woolen scarf up past my mouth, and tugged a tight woolen cap over my hair. My gloves were leather, lined with fur, and once they were on, I felt completely disguised. I knew Kimana could see only my eyes, and I hoped they conveyed the depth of my heart when my words got lost within the folds of the muffler.

"I love you."

"I love you, too."

We'd never spoken such words to each other, and yet in that moment, I could not have felt them more strongly for any person other than my own children.

She closed her eyes and lifted her hand. Her palm hovered an inch from my face, and she began to chant what sounded like one long, extended syllable, her lips never closing against each other until she came to the end.

"It is a blessing of my people, that the path you follow will rise up to bring you home. God be with you, my daughter."

God be with me, indeed.

The first sting of cold morning air brought tears to my eyes, and I held a gloved hand up to shield them from the sun. I fastened my bag and swung myself up in the saddle. I'd ridden her only a few times, and from her reaction, Honey was not immediately happy to have me astride. I clicked to her gently as I'd heard Nathan do, and by the time we reached the first white, swelling hill, we'd grown used to each other. I kept a keen eye out for Nathan and Amanda, knowing my initial direction would take me past the route to the overseer's cabin at the mouth of the quarry, but I saw not a soul. I don't know if God was hiding me from the Saints or if he was hiding them from me. Honey and I picked our way across the snow; I used familiar landmarks to identify the buried road to Salt Lake City. This clump of trees. That rock. As long as the sun was in the sky, I would be able to gauge my direction—north. Our pace was slower than I'd hoped, though, and by the time the sun reached full noon, I began to worry that we might not arrive before dark.

"Good girl, Honey," I said, leaning forward in the saddle to pat her neck.

My eyes burned with the glare of the snow, and my breath began to crystallize on the muffler wrapped up to my nose. I began to ride with one hand holding the reins and the other tucked inside my armpit, alternating at the count of one hundred. I wore three pairs of socks, but at some point I pulled Honey to a halt, hopped off, and pulled a petticoat out of my satchel. I ripped it into thick strips and wrapped the material over the top of my boots, creating another layer of warmth. It meant my feet fit poorly in the stirrups, but we were moving at a slow, easy gait.

I fought drowsiness by stopping to scoop handfuls of snow into my mouth—shocked into alertness until long after it melted. I spoke to Honey, quoting all the Bible verses I could remember and paraphrasing those I couldn't. I kept the image of my daughters forever in front of me, planning our future. I would arrive at Rachel's door, half-frozen and deserving of her pity, if not her approval. I would stay the winter in Salt Lake City, finding work where I could. Laundress, perhaps, or cook. Certainly an apostate could be worthy of such manual labor.

It was in the midst of such a vision that I realized my eyes no longer stung. I panicked, thinking evening had fallen, and I was nowhere near Salt Lake City. Nowhere near anything. Not a cabin, not a puff of smoke. But the sky did not have the hue of sunset; it had turned gray. Where before I could look out on the horizon and see a clear line where the white of snow met the blue of sky, now all merged into this one colorless shade.

"But it's blue behind the gray," I said out loud to Honey. "Remember that."

Then I heard it. A hum at first, and I remembered what it felt like to lay my head upon my husband's chest and listen to his laughter. The humming grew, and what had been a harmless, soft, distant gray wall took on life and speed and sound.

Lord, no!

If Honey and I were on course, the storm was coming from the north. Northwest, actually—off the lake. Sensing danger, Honey came to a stop, waiting for my command. My heart went out to this poor creature, caught up in my rash decision. But for my pride she would be safe in her barn, and I would be safe at home.

Or I'd be facing this storm in the cutter with Elder Justus.

Either way, God was throwing a wall between me and Salt Lake City, and I knew enough of grace to know he would forgive my impetuousness and guide me to another path.

I tugged on Honey's rein and turned her around. To my delight, there was our home, Lottie and Melissa playing run-ribbons on the fresh green grass.

"No!" I shook my head and welcomed the sight of solid gray.

Honey pranced, venturing a few steps on her own. I saw a clearing dotted with a dozen cold fire pits. A gust of wind slammed against us, scattering the ashes.

"Zion." I gave a decisive yank to the reins and dug my padded boots into Honey's side. She reared up and broke into the fastest run she could manage. The sting of snow pelted my face, even though she carried me through a dark forest as I ran, ran to warn Nathan. To tell him my father was going to kill him. Kill them all.

"Nathan, go!" But my warning was swallowed up in the snow, the force of the storm nearly knocking me out of the saddle.

I heard nothing but the roar of the wind, punctuated by the laughter of my daughters. Pure white enveloped me, and I thought about the white stones of the temple. How envious they would be, those Saints, to know that I was a spire in the midst of God's creation.

Honey struggled beneath me, her muscles straining to keep us upright. My legs gripped her, I'd long since dropped the reins. Then, in the next gust, she was gone. For just a few seconds, I swirled with the snow—free. When I fell, I knew only that the earth was beneath me now, though I had no idea if I'd landed with my face buried in snow or raised to the sky. I might have stayed there, if not for Honey's gentle nudging. I somehow found her bridle, then grasped her mane and pulled myself to my feet.

"Even in this," I said, fancying myself whispering into her ear, "God is in control. Behind all of this is blue sky. Behind that blue sky is his power."

Then we walked. Together for a while, I think; then I was wrapped in snow. Alone. I bent to the wind, lifting my worthless arms as useless shields against the onslaught. After a while, I didn't know if I was walking or if I was just being buffeted to and fro with the whim of the wind. Finally, I surrendered, falling to my knees and lifting my hands to what I thought was the sky.

"Holy Father." I spoke, though my lips would not be torn away from the ice wrapped around them. "Take me home."

To open my eyes and to close my eyes meant little more than seeing white or seeing black. At that moment, black seemed so much warmer. So I closed them, knowing full well that they would open again. Until then, I called back every moment that brought me to this place, beginning with that evening I looked out the window and heard them, the Mormons, singing in the darkness.

Turn the page for an exciting preview from
ALLISON PITTMAN'S
next book,

FORSAKING *All* OTHERS

Available Summer 2011 at a bookstore near you.

TYNDALE FICTION

CHAPTER 1

Smoke. And darkness. And warmth.

"I think she's wakin'. Go fetch the captain." A man's voice, one I didn't know. A momentary blast of cold air, and I remembered the storm, the roaring wind and swirling snow that carried me here.

"Ma'am?" Closer now. I felt a warm hand against my cheek. "You're going to be just fine."

I wanted to smile, but my lips felt dry, tight. When I tried to speak, they peeled apart, grating against each other like thin, dry bark.

"Don't you try to speak none. Just show me, can you open your eyes?"

I wanted to, if only to see where the Lord had brought me, but already the voice was falling away, like words being dropped down a well. Sight seemed too heavy a burden, so I contented myself with what senses I could muster—the soft sound of the crackling fire, the sweet smell of the wood burning within it, and the warmth, blessed warmth, covering my body from my toes to my chin. The weight of it pinned me down.

Time passed. How much, I couldn't know, but enough for me to develop a powerful thirst. I pried my lips apart, worked my tongue between them. Just that little movement brought a presence to my side again. A new touch to my temple, a new voice in my ear. Deeper, stronger.

"Ma'am?"

Of their own accord, my eyes opened. I saw nothing at first, but then he moved into my sight. Long hair brushed behind his ears, a full mustache covering his top lip. His eyes, at first, were closed, and the mustache bobbed as he said, "Thank you, Lord." Then they opened, and in the firelight they shone warm and brown.

"Where—?"

"Shh." He held a finger to his lips. "Time enough for that later. I'm Captain Charles Brandon of the United States Army. Outside of Jesus himself, you couldn't be in better hands. Now, how about some water?"

I gave no response, but I didn't need to. I tracked him with my eyes as he reached behind and produced a blue tin cup. He took a sip.

"Just testing. Don't want it too hot."

Then my head was cradled in his hand and he placed the cup against my mouth. The first sip burned, then soothed as I swallowed.

"Little more?"

I opened my lips wider in response, and I heard him whisper, "That's a girl," as he gauged when to take the cup away. He must be a father, too.

"Now," he said, taking the cup away and laying my head back, "if you'll consent." He reached into his coat pocket and took out a thin silver flask. "I'm in no way a drinking man myself, and I don't want to lead you down the path of evil, but if you'll permit me to mix just a few drops of whiskey in that water, it'll toast your blood right up."

My first instinct should have been to say no, but speaking was still beyond my strength, and truthfully, my thoughts were still cloudy enough that his words had no impact. He took my silence as permission and twisted the lid off the flask. With caution and precision, he drizzled a bit of the amber liquid into the water remaining in the blue cup and swirled it.

"For this, you'll need to sit up a little straighter."

He moved behind me and this time put his arm beneath my shoulders. I could feel the brass of his cuff-buttons against my skin, hitting me with the realization that I was fully naked beneath a pile of wool blankets and bearskin. I twisted my head, panicked, and he instantly interpreted my terror.

"I know and I'm sorry. But we couldn't have you wearing twenty pounds of wet clothes. Now I wish we'd had some old Indian woman to help us out, but we're just a bunch of soldiers. If it helps, I held a gun on 'em and kept 'em blindfolded."

I didn't believe him, but I cared a little less.

"When you're ready, drink this down."

Just the smell of the whiskey in the water brought new life to my senses. Sharpened them, somehow, opened me up to the thought of drinking it down.

"All one drink," he said behind me. "If you sip it by half, you won't drink the rest."

I nodded, braced myself, and closed my eyes. I don't know what I was expecting, but I felt only warmth. Heat followed by clarity, and when Captain Brandon lowered me once again to what I now recognized as a buffalo skin–covered cot, I was fully ready to speak.

"Thank you." My voice was hoarse, and then I remembered screaming into the storm.

He cocked his head. "Doesn't sound to me like you're quite up for telling your story."

He was right. I couldn't. But it had nothing to do with my throat.

"If it's all right, though, I'd like to ask you just a couple of questions." He set the cup on the ground next to him and took a small piece of yellow paper out of the same pocket where he kept the flask. "Can you tell me who Missy is?"

The name shot through my heart. "My daughter. And Lottie."

He checked his paper, and the pleasant expression he'd worn since my eyes opened to him disappeared, replaced with a furrowed, worried brow. "Are they—were they traveling with you?"

I shook my head as tears gathered in my eyes.

"They're safe at home?"

"Yes."

"Well, thank God for that."

And I did, as my head filled with visions of them, cozily tucked into their bed or sitting on the braided rug in front of the stove happily playing with their dolls at the feet of—

"Nathan? Is he your husband?"

"Yes." I tried to sit up. "Is he here? Did he come for me?"

"Shh . . ." Again his warm hand soothed my brow; exhausted, I lay back. "No, ma'am. Nobody's come for you."

"Then how do you know?"

He showed me the paper. Three words—*Missy*, *Lottie*, *Nathan*—and one letter: *K*.

"Kimana."

He smiled. "Private Lambert wasn't sure of the spelling."

"She's taking care of my daughters."

"I see." I could tell he wanted to know more, but I hadn't the strength. It wasn't the time. "You've been sleeping on and off for close to thirty hours now, and that's just since we found you. Now, for me you've been nice and quiet, but I guess when Private Lambert pulled his shift, you decided to talk a little bit. He picked out a few names."

"Oh."

"And he said you seemed to do a lot of praying."

"Yes."

"The way I figure, those prayers brought my scouts out to find you. Nothing but unbroken snow, they said; then there you were, hanging on to that horse. Why, that animal herself is a miracle."

"You have to send her back. To my husband. I stole her."

"Time enough for that. We'll get you feeling better, and then we'll get both of you safely home."

More tears, and now they fell, sliding straight down into my ears. "I don't have a home."

He leaned forward, elbows on his knees. "Now, don't be silly. Everybody's got a home."

"Not me. I had one, and I left it. I had to."

His voice dropped to a whisper even though, as far as I could tell, the two of us were quite alone. "Are you one of them, then? a Mormon?"

"Yes." Then quickly, "No. I mean I was, for a time. But not really, not in my heart. And now . . . God, forgive me . . ."

Whatever else I meant to say disappeared in the drought of my throat. I mustered what strength I could and turned on my side, my back to Captain Brandon, to curl up with my regret.

Taking a liberty I could have never imagined, he put his hand on my shoulder, tugging me to face him. As I complied, he smoothed my hair from my brow and brought his face so close to mine I could feel his breath.

"Now you listen to me. I don't want you to be frightened for one more minute. Not for yourself and not for your girls. I'm here for you. The United States Army is here for you. And as I've sworn my life as a sacrifice for freedom, I will make it my promise that you'll have a home."

"How?" I'd brought the blanket up to my face, and it muffled my question. Still, he heard.

"You leave that up to me. Another drink?"

As an answer, I sat myself up on my elbows, holding the covers nearly to my chin.

Silently, he filled the cup with water from a pot sitting on a grate by the fire and then a little from a clay pitcher. Then he lifted the flask, holding it like a question. Remembering the pleasant warmth, I nodded, and as before, he measured in a tiny stream and swirled the cup. I continued to hold the covers as he tipped the cup against my mouth, and this time I took the drink in several satisfying gulps.

"That's the last of that for you."

"That's fine," I said, lying down.

"Now sleep. And don't worry. When you wake up, I'll be here."

"And then?"

"And then, it sounds like we might have a bit of a battle on our hands."

ABOUT THE AUTHOR

In 2005, Allison Pittman left a seventeen-year teaching career to follow the Lord's calling into the world of Christian fiction, and God continues to bless her step of faith. She heads up a successful, thriving writers' group in San Antonio, Texas, where she lives with her husband, Mike, their three sons, and the canine star of the family—Stella.

READING GROUP GUIDE

A CONVERSATION WITH THE AUTHOR

How did the idea for this book come to you?

I knew I wanted to write a love story, but not a romance. The character of Nathan came to me fully formed—this deeply passionate, wounded, charismatic, charming man. Then, having grown up in Utah, I knew that Christianity played almost no role in the early history of the state, so I needed Camilla to be a woman seduced away from not only her family but also her Lord. In fact, I saw the understanding and worship of God as being almost a third element in a love triangle. I wanted Nathan and Camilla to love each other as much as they loved God.

You seem to know a lot about the Mormon faith and community. How did you research this story?

I lived in Utah as a child, and my husband is an excommunicated Mormon who came to know Jesus as his Savior when he was in high school, so I had a lot of anecdotal experiences to pull from. But to get a real feel for the history, I spent some time in Salt Lake City. The pioneer women's museum there is a treasure trove of artifacts, all the little household trinkets that made up a woman's life. The blue lamp is just one of the artifacts I fell in love with—that and the crazy jug that will appear in the next book.

I think what really struck me—and this is something I've shared and confirmed with other Christians—is the spirit of Temple Square in Salt Lake City. The city is beautiful and meticulously maintained, but there is an oppressive air. It's quiet, but not serene. Something about that huge, white temple topped with a golden angel is unsettling.

I also spent a lot of time browsing Web sites and discussion boards reading posts by ex-Mormons. They gave me a clearer understanding not so much about why people join the church, but why they stay and why they leave. It's heartbreaking, the stories of bitterness and betrayal, even more so seeing how so many leave the Mormon faith with a mistrust of God and religion in general. I wanted to capture that sense of a desperate need for love and acceptance in Nathan's character. There are many anonymous people out there who were so helpful in my efforts to capture both Nathan's fervor and Rachel's just-beneath-the-surface disdain.

Why did you choose a historical setting?

It's a fascinating time in our nation's history, something that doesn't get a lot of attention, especially looking into the next book, which will touch on the so-called Mormon War and the conflict between the church and the United States government. However, even though this story takes place with the first generation of the LDS church, their method of amassing converts has changed very little. Today, in these times of fractured families, the Mormon message of family values has so much appeal. In fact, that's what drew my husband's family into the church back in the mid-1970s. I took that idea and molded it to fuel Nathan's devotion to the church.

I also wanted to address the idea of polygamy outside the realm of modern controversy. Plural marriage as Mormon doctrine is a historical fact—interestingly ignored in the Church History Museum but openly addressed in the Pioneer Women's Museum. I was intrigued by the idea of looking at the practice through the eyes of a first wife—not with the wide scope of examining the sociopolitical implications, but a snapshot of the powerlessness of the time.

Camilla's father is often harsh and unloving toward her. What was your inspiration for their relationship?
First of all, he's nothing like my own sweet, loving father! I wanted Arlen Deardon to interact with the story on two levels. First, as Camilla's father, he can appear harsh and unloving, but then his protective actions, no matter how misguided, are absolutely motivated by love. We cannot overestimate how important the father-daughter relationship is in terms of the kinds of decisions a girl will make when it's time to choose a mate. I know Camilla's choice when she stood on that dock would have been different if she'd had a history of affection and acceptance with her father. It's not enough that he loved her if he never demonstrated that love.

Deardon also, though, is a representative of what I truly believe is behind much of the early growth and success of the Mormon church. Bear in mind, early converts (like converts today) were people seeking a meaningful relationship with God. Christians felt the need—and rightly so—to protect the truth of the gospel in the face of such heretical teachings. But like Camilla's father, they too often expressed that desire through acts of violence.

I am in no way saying that the "Mormon problem" was ill-treated at the hands of the church functioning as a unified body. But think about it: if you're searching for truth, and one group is telling you that God loves you and you can be just like Jesus, and the other group is shooting and burning the first group, who are you going to choose? The Mormons have a right to see themselves as victims in those early days, and there's nothing like a common sense of persecution to strengthen faith. After all, look at the first-century Christians.

How much of Camilla did you draw from yourself?

Very, very little that is remotely admirable. I am not spontaneous or strong, and in my younger years I was pretty susceptible to whatever line a good-looking guy might give me. I think I come out the most in the part of the story after Amanda comes along, when we see a few snarky, sarcastic remarks coming from Camilla's otherwise long-suffering, noble lips.

In the story, Rachel tells Camilla that she has to let Nathan take another wife. "You have to. You're his salvation. Joseph Smith was his savior in life, giving him direction. Your job is to save him in the next one." What does it mean that she's his salvation?

This touches on the Mormon concept of celestial rewards. According to their teaching, if Nathan is ever to achieve the highest, godlike, eternal status, he needs to have at least one eternal wife to bear his spiritual children. She is not so much his "salvation" in terms of his eternity, but in terms of the quality of that eternity. I think it's important to note here that the Mormons believe that women must be "called" into eternity by their husbands, which explains Evangeline's plight.

In the end, Camilla is forced to leave her children behind, and we see her lost in a snowstorm. What motivated you to end the book in such a way?

I've said all along with this project that I didn't want to take on the entire Mormon faith; I wanted to tell the story of one woman's journey back to Christ. The decision Camilla makes is a direct result of realizing her need to completely break away from the church, to live out her faith in Jesus Christ and trust him. Even Jesus told his followers to leave their families and possessions and not look back.

Camilla's story is far from over, but I wanted to end it the same way I started it. In the first scene, she is essentially alone, struggling to understand God's teachings. In the end, she is alone physically but so strengthened spiritually, she knows where to put her trust.

As for her children—I urge readers to understand that Camilla's story takes place in a time far removed from ours. There are elements of society and history that make her choice acceptable for that time and place. The physical safety of her children is her top priority, something any mother can understand. She does not have the options and support that women who are trapped in bad marriages have today. What hasn't changed, though, is the fact that she has the Lord. Because she is spiritually healed, she can trust his prodding, even if it seems to fly in the face of what might seem logical.

Today Mormons are intentionally aligning themselves with evangelical Christians. What similarities in their beliefs enable them to do this? In what crucial ways are their beliefs different from biblical Christianity?

Mormons believe Jesus Christ is the Son of God and that he died on the cross for our sins and rose again after three days. They love and admire Jesus. They pray in his name. They identify Jesus as a redeemer and savior. But they do not acknowledge that Jesus' death and resurrection constitute the full completion of our reconciliation and salvation. To the Mormons, this act is incomplete, and true salvation depends not only upon one's belief in the death and resurrection of Jesus Christ as depicted in the Gospels, but also on acceptance and belief in the prophetic writings of Joseph Smith and the practices of the Mormon church.

In the story we see fear and mistrust between the Mormon church and the Christian community. Do you think that mistrust still exists today, or have we become more tolerant of each other?

Sadly, I think we've become more tolerant of each other. It may seem odd to say *sadly*, but God does not call us to be tolerant of false teachings. From the beginning of their church, Mormons capitalized on the hostility demonstrated by their Christian neighbors, using it to reinforce their presumed chosen status. By cultivating a strong "us" and "them" mentality, Mormons could maintain the undivided attention of their members.

I think there's been a subtle shift in the past thirty to forty years with the political recognition of Christian evangelicals. The media tends to lump Mormons and Christians together, and for practical reasons, Mormons have publicly aligned themselves with Christianity. When I was driving through Utah and searching through radio stations in the rental car, I stopped when I heard a Casting Crowns song. Right after it came a song about God giving us the gift of eternal family. Mormons use—and have always used—much of the same vocabulary, but in this world of sound bites and small print, the cavernous differences in theology can hide. Political correctness hates to look at a church filled with good, loving, earnest people and call it a cult, but remember: Satan introduced himself to humanity by twisting God's word into a lie.

What was the biggest challenge you faced in researching or writing this novel? the greatest reward?

More so than any other book, I had to give this over to God.

I knew this had to go beyond the average spiritual content found in most Christian fiction. I tried very hard to represent the truth of the gospel of Jesus Christ in contrast with the lies of the Mormon faith without making the book sound like a 350-page tract. It was quite challenging to craft theology into dialogue, to make the deepest questions about salvation relevant to the characters' relationships. So I hope I pulled it off!

The greatest reward? Honestly, I came away with such a deeper understanding and appreciation for my own salvation. As I wrote about Nathan's struggle to be "good enough" for God, I felt so loved by my Savior. I realized how wonderful it is to worship a God I cannot fully understand with my finite little mind.

What do you hope readers will take away from this novel?

First, I'd love readers to recognize that, despite any outward appearances, many Mormons are empty, wounded people. As I tried to get inside the head of a Mormon, I spent a lot of time online reading through forums devoted to those who had left the church, and there was so much sadness and bitterness there. I think most Christians approach Mormons in one of two ways: we either avoid any opportunity to witness because doing so is usually fruitless, or we relish the idea of arguing with them. We need to simply love them.

Second, we need to be so rooted in Truth that we can recognize any aberration of the gospel, no matter how subtle. Mormonism and Christianity use largely the same vocabulary; the differences in theological text can seem little more than spin and semantics. We must be wary of works and messages that openly claim to be a "new" way of understanding Scripture.

DISCUSSION QUESTIONS

1. The community, the church, and Camilla's father are all afraid of the Mormons who are camping in their town. Where does that fear come from? If they had acted toward the Mormon people in another way, do you think Camilla might have chosen differently? What might Camilla's parents have done differently to prevent her running away with Nathan? How much responsibility do they share for her choices as a young teen?

2. Camilla's parents have a grasp on true Christianity, yet they fail to convey the reality of it to their daughter. How is this experience reflected in the church today? How have you experienced it in your own family or circle of friends? What do you make of the difference between the way Camilla's father provided spiritual instruction to his daughter and the way Nathan taught his daughters?

3. As a Mormon, Nathan believes that his salvation depends on successfully converting Camilla to the Mormon faith and on taking a wife and starting a family. Yet he promises Camilla that on her first unhappy day, he'll take her home. Do you think he ever meant to keep that promise? Why or why not? If he did mean to keep it, when and why did he change his mind?

4. What causes Camilla to doubt the Mormon faith after the birth of her son? When she questions the Mormon faith, she sees fear in Nathan's eyes. What is he afraid of?

5. When Nathan finally convinces Camilla to go back to church, the elder preaches that there are those among them who need to confess their sins. He singles out Nathan and Camilla's loss of a child. Nathan suggests that Camilla needs to seek forgiveness. What does he think she needs to confess?

6. It was part of God's plan all along that Camilla write Scripture in her journal so that she would have it as a resource in teaching his Word to her children. Can you think of anything in your past that didn't seem to have a purpose at the time but made sense later, in light of what you were going through?

7. When Camilla senses the Lord calling her to take a stand for the truth about him, she tries to convince herself that what she has "could be enough." Has there been a time in your life that you've sensed God calling you out of your comfort zone in order to grow closer to him or to become more like him? How did you respond? How would you like to have responded?

8. When the elder is questioning her, Camilla says, "My Lord commands me to obey my husband. And he has been commanded to love me. As long as he is not in disobedience to his command, I see no reason to disobey mine." Is Camilla right to use God's command to justify obeying her husband even in his unbiblical desire to take a second wife?

Under what circumstances today do wives need to heed this command? When might it be appropriate to disobey one's husband?

9. After Camilla refuses to be baptized again in the Mormon church, she returns home and discovers that Kimana has been praying for her. Have you ever been forced to defend what you believe even if it isn't popular? And have you ever felt strong facing a difficult situation and realized later that someone had been praying for you?

10. Discuss Camilla's decision to leave her children. Why does she feel she must do so? What would you have done in her place? What comfort does Camilla have as she leaves her home? Have you ever had to sacrifice something for your faith?

11. What do you think will become of these characters? If you were writing the second part of the story, what would happen to Camilla? Nathan? Amanda? Kimana? the children?